ADVENTURES OF UNFAILING LOVE

AWARDS

D1593703

Gold Medal Winner: *Huntress*

2018 Illumination Awards

First Place Winner: *Huntress*

2012 Women of Faith Writing Contest

Best Debut Author: *Julie Hall*

2017 Ozarks Indie Book Festival

USA TODAY Bestselling Author: *Shattered Worlds*

August 17, 2017

Best Inspirational Novel: *Huntress*

2017 Ozarks Indie Book Festival

Second Place Winner: *Huntress*

2017 ReadFree.ly 50 Best Indie Books of Year

PRAISE FOR THE
LIFE AFTER SERIES

"**Dominion is the perfect ending to a beautiful story.** While Audrey questions her own existence, she remains fiercely loyal to the ones she loves, especially Logan. Gripping and emotional, it's filled with hope and unconditional love."

Cameo Renae, USA Today Bestselling author of the *Hidden Wings* series

"**The romance is sweet, mysterious, frustrating, and perfect.** With fantastic world-building, Julie Hall has created an interesting and desirable afterlife. I love the unique take on angels, demons, and the life after death. Characters are likeable: Audrey, flawed and confused, but also filled with untapped strength; Logan, strong and swoon-worthy. Enough action and mystery to keep me flipping the pages."

Jaymin Eve, USA Today Bestselling author of *The Hive Trilogy, A Walker Saga* and *Supernatural Prison* series

"**The *Life After* series is wildly creative** and packed with heart pounding adventure, plot twists that leave you reeling! You will not be disappointed."

Leia Stone, USA Today Bestselling author of the *Matefinder* series

"**Julie Hall is destined to be one of the great fiction writers of our time.** Not since Frank Peretti has an author had the writing genius to weave together spiritual and physical worlds into a believable epic journey. Her first work will keep young adults riveted, expanding their sense of wonder and challenging them to think about forces and powers beyond what they can see."

Rebecca Hagelin, Bestselling author and columnist with *The Washington Times*

"**You will be holding your breath and falling in love.** Beautifully creative! Julie Hall expertly weaves an action-packed plot and swoon-worthy romance with powerful, heartfelt themes of love, family, forgiveness, and redemption."

Kelly Oram, author of *The Supernaturals* series and the *Jamie Baker Trilogy*

"**Julie has created a world so imaginative and exciting that I can't help but want to be there.** In Audrey, Julie Hall has given readers a heroine who is strong, vulnerable, and relatable. She creates a safe place to ask questions, but also shows us we will not always get the answers we want. The adventure is in moving ahead, in faith, even without them."

Catherine Parks, author of *A Christ-Centered Wedding*

DOMINION

LIFE AFTER BOOK 3

Julie Hall

Dominion (Life After Book 3)
Copyright © 2018 by Julie Hall

Julie Hall
www.JulieHallAuthor.com

ISBN-13: 978-0-9989867-3-9

ISBN-10: 0-9989867-3-9

Cover Design by Nathália Suellen
Formatting by Lucas Hall

CONTENTS

1

HELL

I coughed for the hundredth time. Hell was . . . well, hot as Hell. As clichés went, this one was turning out to be extremely accurate.

We'd only been here for an hour, tops, and I was already dying to leave.

Oh look, I made a funny!

My quiet laugh turned into another round of nasty coughs. Once they subsided, I half expected to find a lung lying on the ground.

If the incessant hacking didn't get me, the stench was going to kill me.

I'm on a roll.

The atmosphere was filled with a nasty cocktail of rotten eggs, rotten meat, and rotten souls. That last one was just a guess—but if souls could rot, I'm pretty sure the mystery scent in the air was what they would smell like.

Our small group—my fellow friends and hunters—baked in the funk as we trudged through the barren and rocky terrain on our top-secret mission. We'd been transported from our realm to this barren one only an hour before. The conditions were just shy of unbearable, despite the protection provided by Joe. I mean Jesus. I mean the Creator's Son. Oh geez, I was still struggling to wrap my brain around Joe's identity.

He'd been the first person I met when I woke up in the afterlife. He'd introduced himself as Joe, so that was how I thought of him—even after he'd recently revealed himself to be the Son of God. I could swallow the news that he was the Savior of mankind, but actually processing the implications of that information was a little too much for me right now. My finite brain could only handle so much at a time.

In the last twenty-four hours alone, I had discovered my beloved quirky mentor, Hugo, was actually the Holy Spirit; defended my family on Earth against a horde of demons, including Satan; and contracted the heavenly equivalent of a fiancé. And yes, I say contracted as if the engagement were a virus, not the romantic proposal every girl dreams of. It happened much like one would get mono. One kiss and bam I was stuck with him forever. Technically we'd shared a couple of kisses, but who was counting?

As I trekked along behind my friends, my face reddened at my thoughts.

Oh gosh, I really hope no one was counting.

The slight tug on my brand-new internal Logan-GPS—the sense I had of his whereabouts and well-being, activated upon the fateful kiss—was physical proof of the bond between us, as certain and permanent as the Epstein-Barr virus. So here I was, sneaking around a realm I had no business entering and sucking down sulfuric fumes on a quest to rescue my viral love.

Another round of rib-cracking coughs racked my frame. I pressed a hand to my burning throat. Every breath seared my windpipe.

Gosh, he's lucky he's so good looking because rescue missions in Hell are totally overrated.

Something slimy rolled in my gut. I tried hard to ignore the sensation.

Jokes and grumbling could only cover up so much of my concern for Logan's welfare. A throbbing awareness in both my wrists accompanied the pull of my Logan-GPS. I suspected the pain was an echo of what he was experiencing. Phantom twinges had sliced my body since we entered Hell.

I tripped on what looked to be a black lava rock, and Jonathon shot his arm out to steady me. I started to offer thanks, but he was already walking past. The rapier hanging from his waist slapped his thigh with every step. Covered from head to toe in hunter's armor, Jonathon blended well with our trained band of warriors. He looked the part, even if he was a skilled healer rather than a proven fighter.

"Watch where you're going." His words carried a frosty bite that contrasted with the suffocating heat bearing down on us.

Sigh. There was another unneeded complication to this mission. My ex-boyfriend was along for the ride as our group's medical support—the "ex" was for sure . . . the "boyfriend" part debatable.

Why he'd even bothered to stop me from face planting into the craggy red ground was a mystery. He'd made it clear he wanted nothing more to do with me when I told him there could never be anything more than friendship between us. He threw that suggestion back in my face like I'd offered him a bite of a moldy sandwich.

A peace offering he wasn't interested in—and actually offended by.

My chest tightened as sadness blanketed my heart. I lost his friendship, but whatever attraction had existed between us was never going to be strong enough to go the distance. Maybe when he realized that, he'd forgive me.

Of course, he thought I'd cheated on him, so maybe that day would never come.

Another round of coughs compressed my chest and burned my throat. I sucked in the putrid air like it was laced with honey rather than whatever dark pollution caused the stench, but I couldn't catch my breath.

"Hey, you all right?" Romona's chocolate eyes were round as she patted me on the back until my coughing fit subsided.

"Yeah," I croaked.

Great. Apparently a frog had crawled down in my throat and taken up residence.

I did a quick sweep of my traveling companions. All five of them: Kaitlin, Kevin, Jonathon, Romona, and Joe. They all struggled to varying degrees in our new environment. Kaitlin covered her nose with her hand. Romona's eyes watered, whether from the smell or emotions, I wasn't sure.

My throat screamed for some moisture-filled air.

Whoever said dry heat wasn't as bad as humidity didn't know what they were talking about.

Kevin wasn't doing anything to ward off the stench, but sweat dripped down his face. He lifted an arm to wipe the moisture away every few minutes. Guilt washed over me when I realized I was mollified that someone else was suffering from the heat.

Jonathon strode forward as if completely unaffected by our environment, but I suspected his bravado was out of pride and sheer determination to appear strong.

As for Joe, the only sign of distress he revealed was the expression on his face. A sadness had invaded his eyes the moment we reached this realm. The emotion showed itself in the creases around his eyes and the tightness of his features as he surveyed the landscape.

Stumbling and hacking, I was having the worst time of it.

Romona grasped my elbow to help me stand upright, and she kept her hand loosely on my arm to steady me as we continued. We'd fallen a little behind the rest of the group and hurried to catch up.

A stabbing pain in my gut caused me to lose my footing again and cry out. If not for Romona, I would have been on my hands and knees on the scorched ground. The agony was enough to double me over and stop my forward progression.

I took deep breaths with my arms around my middle, protecting myself from the phantom pain.

My Lamaze-like breathing probably made me sound like I was about to give birth. I'd laugh about that if the truth weren't so horrific. I half expected to look down and see blood leaking from my gut. But this wasn't my pain. This was a whisper of whatever Logan was enduring. Panic churned in my stomach, but I stuffed the dread down.

Horrible as that was, the knowledge kept me going. If I didn't know to the very fiber of my being that he was here somewhere and in a tremendous amount of danger, I wouldn't subject myself to this misery any longer.

First train back to the heavenly realm? Yes please. Sign me up.

But I wasn't physically capable of leaving him here, thanks to our bond. And even if I were, I'd never abandon Logan in this horrid place.

"Guys, hold up," Romona shouted.

One breath in. One breath out. One breath in. One breath out.

A cool hand touched my forehead, and the pain subsided. I looked up into Joe's sad, kind eyes.

"Better?" he asked.

"Yeah, thanks." The frog had vacated my throat, and I could speak again. I straightened my frame.

He nodded once. "I know. I can feel it too."

"You can?" Could have fooled me. Besides the hidden sadness in his gaze, he appeared fresh as a daisy.

He rolled his eyes. "Appearances can be deceiving."

Right. He probably knew every thought flitting through my mind. Awkward.

Turning his head, he addressed the small group, "Let's stop for a bit."

No one talked as we all pulled out our canteens to gulp down some water. I took a seat on a spiky rock. That had to be a better alternative than the ground. Wrong. My backside had become a pincushion.

I chugged my drink too quickly, and some of it dribbled down my neck and fell to the dusty soil where the liquid sizzled before evaporating. The desire to drink it all rode me hard, but I'd need it later.

I capped my water and secured it to my belt. Waiting for the go-ahead, I looked around.

Red ground littered with small mounds of black stones stretched as far as the eye could see. When I looked up, there was no blue sky but rather a rocky surface that could have been a mile above our heads.

We were truly entombed in the Earth.

I had no idea what dim luminescence lit this place, but whatever the artificial light was, rather than enhance color, it drained it. The faces of my companions were chalky. Even the dirt beneath our feet seemed leached of color. Devoid of vegetation, the barren wasteland laid out in all directions.

Hell was bleak.

Looking at the grey faces and dull eyes of my friends was a bit like looking at reanimated corpses. Waves of trepidation rolled down my spine, wracking my frame with full body shudders as my thoughts, steeped in the macabre, worked their way through me.

"Is it all like this?" Kaitlin swept her arm in an arc as her eyes scanned the vicinity.

"No." Joe was the only one of us still standing. His gaze remained outward even as he addressed Kaitlin's question. "This part hasn't been filled yet."

Filled? What did that mean?

The look of disgust marring his face was unmistakable. "I wanted to make sure we weren't detected, but entering an empty part of this realm calls for a lengthy walk. You all are holding up well." His eyes found mine. "Considering the circumstances."

He turned to face the whole group. "Listen. There are a few things you all need to know before we go any farther. This realm was created for the Betrayer and his followers, but there are others here as well. It isn't Our desire that a single soul should end up in this vile place, but . . ."

He paused and scrubbed a hand down his face before going on. His expression was tormented, his mouth was pressed into a hard line, and veins pulsed at his temples. "You're not going to like what you see. You need to prepare yourself. We're here for one reason alone, and that is to bring Logan home. You are going to have to come to terms with the fact that you can't do anything for anyone else here. They are not your responsibility."

Then whose responsibility were they?

I snuck a glance at my companions. Mouths pressed in hard lines and scrunched brows were a common theme.

"What else can you tell us?" Romona asked.

Joe motioned for us all to come forward. With his sword, he drew a circle in the red volcanic cinder at his feet.

"This realm is composed of rings." He drew several more circles within the first, each one inside another until there were nine circles. The center one was no bigger than a quarter.

"We're currently in the outermost ring." He indicated the space between the largest circle and the next one with the tip of his sword. "As we travel farther, each ring is more inhabited, and the discomfort you're all feeling will intensify."

I blinked back at him. *Intensify?* I wasn't going to make it.

Squirming, sharp pains of discomfort stabbed my backside. This rock made a horrible seat.

"Audrey."

My attention snapped back to Joe.

"A lot of what you are feeling is leaked to you from Logan, so you're already experiencing what it's like to be in a deeper ring. I'm not saying it won't get worse for you, but not by much."

Dread sunk my heart to my belly. *Logan.*

Multiple pairs of concerned-filled eyes swung my way. Jonathon didn't look at me. He was staring at the circles Joe had drawn in the ground as if they held the meaning of life. Jonathon's features were hard. I couldn't help the tendril of compassion that spun around inside when I looked at him. Knowingly or not, I'd played a part in the stone-like façade he now wore.

"Do you know where he is?" I asked, turning my attention back to our leader.

Joe nodded and made an X in the space between the fourth

and fifth circles, four rings away from where we currently resided. "Logan's there, and we're here. This is an oversimplification of the realm, but it's basic information you should have."

"Why didn't we just drop into his exact location, grab him, and get out of here?" Cocking my head toward Kevin, I silently admitted he had a point.

"Your bodies need some time to adjust to the atmosphere down here. The demons are extremely active where Logan is. If we'd gone straight there, you'd be forced to defend yourselves against upper-level demons while you struggled to breathe."

We nodded, our faces broadcasting a range of emotions.

"Your bodies weren't meant for this realm, but by going through the circles slowly, you'll be able to handle its intensity better. We're going to skirt around as much of the demonic activity as possible, but at some point, you will all have to fight to defend yourselves. The creatures residing in this realm have been here many millennia and have adapted to its climate. This is their home turf, and it's important you remember that. Our primary objective is to get Logan and get home. You need to readjust your thinking." He took a moment to look each of us in the eye. "You are no longer the hunters, but rather the hunted."

2

ZOMBIES

Despite the heat, chills raced up and down my spine. Joe sheathed his sword and turned to continue our journey. We wordlessly followed, each one of us likely processing the information he'd just given.

We walked and walked, and the scenery never changed. This journey felt like an exercise in futility—like a nightmare where we were running from something without actually getting anywhere.

I struggled against the feeling of despair as much as I fought to remain upright. Romona stayed suspiciously close, with her gaze on me as often as our surroundings. As my best-friend-slash-grandmother turned kick-butt huntress in the afterlife, her concern for me was expected—if not slightly overbearing at times.

Kevin was up ahead with Joe and peppering him with questions like an inquisitive child trying to make sense of the world around him. For his part, Joe was playing the patient parent well. Kevin wanted to know how big the realm was—

Big. How many different demons resided here—*A lot.* Why was the ground red—*It was, in fact, made up of volcanic cinder.* When would we run into another being—*Hopefully not for a while.*

"So where is the light coming from in this place? It looks like we're in a giant cave." Kevin tilted his head up to survey the stone-like sky above.

"It comes from the lake of fire that makes up the innermost ring. The flames shoot up from the lake like a pillar."

Kevin jerked his head toward Joe, mouth hanging open.

"But we won't be going anywhere near there." Joe's steps halted. "Okay, everyone, we're here."

Here?

I looked around. We stood in the same barren wasteland we'd been trudging through for hours.

"Wow. Yep. This is . . . something?" Kaitlin's confusion was mirrored on the faces of my other companions.

The corner of Joe's mouth twitched as if he were struggling to hold back a smile. "This is the beginning of the next ring."

"But how can you tell?" I asked. Scanning our surroundings, the landscape was still a flat plane of red sprinkled with black rocks.

"I can feel it," Joe answered with a frown. The strain around his eyes told me there was more he wasn't saying. "Join hands."

I bit my lip and grasped Romona's left hand with my right. I was at the end of the chain. Joe held Kevin's hand and walked forward. On the second step, our leader disappeared.

I gasped as Kevin said, "What the—" before he disappeared too.

I started to pull back on Romona's hand, trying to slow my steps as Jonathon was swallowed by the nothing, but the momentum of the group propelled me forward.

"This is trippy," Kaitlin said a moment before she vanished.

"Romona, are we sure—" Romona turned her head toward me, and I watched her fade out of sight. I squeezed my eyes shut. I was next.

A flash of heat washed over me—like when passing a finger through the flame of a candle without lingering long enough to actually get burned.

My eyes popped open when the feeling passed.

The world had transformed. The ground was still red, but that was where the similarities ended. The terrain was dotted with the skeletal remains of trees. Gnarled and bone-white branches protruded from twisted trunks at awkward angles, a distorted mass of intertwined appendages that appeared to have grown with the intent of hiding from the life-giving light rather than reaching for it.

Beyond the blanched dead forest was a blackened mountain range that cut a jagged line across the horizon.

Not comparing the frightening sight with the peaceful landscape of our own realm was impossible. They were opposites in every way. But just as the mountain range had been the first site to captivate me in the heavenly realm, the hellacious mountains were what drew my attention now. Rather than standing in awe of its majesty, my attention was captured by its grotesqueness. Lined up like rows of shark teeth, multiple peaks were completely black except for occasional pustules that oozed red magma down the sharpened slopes like never-ending streams of tears.

"This is seriously disturbing," Kevin said, and I couldn't have agreed with him more.

Bile churned in my stomach with the wrongness of this place.

"Why do the trees grow like that?" Jonathon asked.

Several heartbeats passed before he received an answer. "They are the pathetic attempt of a creature trying to create life in its own image. But even in this desolate place, there is only one Creator." There was a hollowness to Joe's voice, and his face was stoically masked, hiding whatever emotions might lie beneath. "Let's go, everyone. We have several more rings to go through until we reach Logan."

That I could have forgotten about Logan even for a moment caused guilt to settle into my gut.

"Yeah, let's get going." I started forward without waiting for direction.

"Yo! Audrey!"

I stopped walking and turned in the direction of Kevin's bellow. He—along with the rest of the group—was about thirty feet behind me.

"It's this way." He hitched his thumb in the opposite direction.

"Oh." I grimaced. "Sorry." I scurried to join back up and this time waited for Joe to lead.

After five minutes of traveling in the eighth ring, the sensation of being watched washed over me like a surge of static electricity.

The fine hairs on the back of my neck prickled. I swiveled my head, searching for the source of my discomfort.

Was that movement in my peripheral vision? I snapped my attention to the left. The only thing there was one of those creepy dead trees.

My gaze stayed glued to the tree as we passed. Nothing there. Just as I turned my attention forward, a cracking noise like brittle twigs being snapped in half echoed in the gloom. I cast a glance over my shoulder to see one of the bleached branches of the tree I'd just passed stretching in my direction—reaching out to me.

I yelped and tripped over some rocks—okay, my own feet—in my haste to get away. Landing with a thud on my right hip, I threw my arm out to catch my upper body.

Without bothering to stand, I scurried on my hands and knees to put distance between the tree and me. Thank goodness for the body armor. I would have been a scraped-up mess without it. Nothing about this realm was soft.

"What are you doing?" Jonathon's voice held only disgust.

Jarred out of my fright, I assessed him. Where was the compassionate guy I knew? Had he never been that person to begin with, or had I somehow broken him?

A gentle hand tugged on my arm and helped me to my feet. If I didn't know any better, I'd say Joe was trying hard not to laugh at me.

My companions stared at me, waiting for an explanation. "Dude, I think those things are alive. And I don't mean like they're-sucking-nutrients-in-from-the-ground alive, but rather they're-moving-their-branches-at-will alive."

"They're not alive," Joe assured me. "They're reanimated."

"What? Reanimated? Like . . . like zombies?"

Joe just blinked once but didn't expound.

"You're telling me we're walking through a forest of zombie trees?" I let out a yap when I accidentally brushed up against one of the boney branches, almost flattening Kaitlin in my haste to get away. "Oh my gosh! Are they going to try to eat us?"

Finally my point was getting through. The others shifted on their feet and started looking around with wary eyes. Jonathon even pulled out his sword, although what he expected to be able to do with the thin blade he carried against a hardened tree limb, I had no idea. We needed a machete . . . STAT!

Oh wait, I had a sword that caught fire. That was, if it worked down here. If so, I could char these things in no time. As dry as they were, they'd probably ash as quickly as kindling.

I followed Jonathon's lead and pulled my sword from its sheath on my back. With a sigh of relief, I watched the blade catch fire like usual. It looked like the holy fire was ready to torch some petrified zombie bark.

A deep belly laugh had us all looking in Joe's direction. *Seriously?*

"Are you messing with me right now?" I asked. I wasn't willing to put my sword down until I knew we were safe. A quick look around the group said that despite Joe's blasé attitude, they all agreed with me.

A long few minutes passed before Joe composed himself enough to speak.

"I'm serious. These things aren't alive. Reanimated is the best way to describe them, but they aren't going to try to eat your brains." The last few words were spoken with a chuckle.

"Well, what do they want then? Because they are definitely interested in something." Over the time we'd been standing still, a few more branches had slowly stretched my way.

"They're attracted to what you have that they don't."

"Which is?" I prompted.

"Life."

I wasn't willing to lower my sword just yet. "But I'm dead."

Joe shrugged a shoulder.

I swung my sword at a branch that was a little too close for comfort. My blade cut through it as easily as warm butter. In response, the tree let out an ear-piercing shriek—from where exactly I wasn't sure, because it's not as if it had a mouth—and I stumbled back a step. The remainder of the limb retracted, burying itself within the tangle of branches closest to the trunk.

Hands down the creepiest thing I'd ever seen. No lie. And I'd seen a lot of creepy things since becoming a hunter.

"What. Just. Happened? That was a very lifelike reaction for something that's not supposed to be alive!" I held my weapon out in front of me like a flamethrower rather than a sword and turned in a circle to make sure no other limbs entered my personal space.

"This place is seriously messed up," Kevin muttered, and I nodded my agreement. We were so in sync at the moment.

"Okay, my vote is we get through this forest of horrors as fast as—" My words were cut short as my body convulsed violently and I dropped my sword.

I fell to my knees hard, and my back bowed in pain. A scream caught in my throat. One I desperately wished I could expel.

My vision flickered to another scene.

A smirk appeared on the sadistic face in front of me. "I told you the fun had only just begun."

The pain at my side was beyond what I thought I had the capacity to feel. My instinct was to fold over and protect myself from the worst of it, but with my arms restrained, I could do nothing but bear it.

I blinked. Romona's face blocked out part of the rock-like sky overhead.

"Audrey!" someone screamed and reached for me.

I sucked in a lungful of air, and with my next blink, I was gone.

3

LOGAN

"That's enough playtime for now, Adramelech." The dark being cocked his head to the side. "He looks properly tenderized for the moment."

If I weren't in so much pain, I might have laughed. Through my non-swollen eye, I could see bits of my flesh. Whatever wasn't torn was covered in layer upon layer of blood. These short reprieves from the torture would give the blood just enough time to dry before the next round began and the sticky wetness started flowing again. I was like a bloodsicle now—nothing more than a battered hunk of flesh.

My human body would have failed long ago, and at this moment I wasn't sure whether to be glad for or curse the new one the afterlife provided me.

The creature who had just been dismissed bowed and scampered out the room on all fours.

The creature left standing in front of me was less vile in form but infinitely more so beneath his façade. His attractive illusion was only that: an illusion. "Ah, Logan, this all feels so familiar to *me.*"

I lifted my chin and stared him straight in the face—right where his eyes should have been. He was right. We'd been in this position before. And just like the last time, I would endure.

"I believe I recognize that look in your eyes. Excuse me, I mean your eye. One is out of commission at the moment. The look I'm seeing is"—the sockets narrowed around where his eyes should be—"ah yes, I'm right. It's defiance."

He leaned in closer and put a hand on my bruised shoulder. I flinched involuntarily but refused to look away from the face of pure evil.

Satan.

The sharpened tips of his fingers grew into claws that slowly cut into my skin, sending trickles of hot blood weeping down my shoulder and onto my exposed chest. The liquid was almost cooling in the oppressive heat of this place.

He ripped his hand from my shoulder, increasing the blood flow from the wounds he'd inflicted, and took two leisurely steps back.

"That look is fine by me." The cruel twist of his lips said that the shredding of my flesh pleased him.

"Whada you wa?" Like honey clinging to a jar, my words stuck in my throat.

Blood started to ooze from a crack on my lip.

I didn't bother trying to spit the coppery substance from my mouth. It would have only dribbled down the front of me anyway.

He heaved a breath as if this was all a giant bore. "Haven't we already been over this? From you? I want nothing more than exactly what you are already doing. And might I say you are doing it beautifully. Even the weakest bond would be pulsating in agony right now. You're acting as a beacon, drawing in *exactly what I want."*

Audrey.

Fear sliced through my heart. Not for myself but for her. Oh God, *I sent up a desperate prayer,* Please don't let her anywhere near this horrific place.

A pull deep inside me said it might already be too late. I'd been trying hard to ignore the feeling. The torture drowned it out, but during my few short respites, I'd sensed she was close.

I hoped I was simply delusional, that the sense of her being near was a fabrication of my psyche that wanted her close even as my rational mind wished her as far away from this place as possible.

"Hmm. I wonder if He'll answer whatever pathetic plea you just lifted up to His name."

The sound of footsteps echoing off the walls outside my cell halted our conversation.

"Ah, a visitor." Satan clapped his hands together as a figure *entered the chamber.*

The air punched out of my gut even as my brain scrambled to put together the pieces.

Alrik. My friend. My closer-than-a-brother friend.

Yes, a deeply buried part of me had considered this as a possibility ever since I'd woken up in this God-forsaken place, but seeing reality was more painful than any of the wounds that had been inflicted in this realm. I had been betrayed.

Again.

Something inside me began to boil.

"You were right." Alrik's voice was steady. "They've been spotted in the eighth ring. They'll cross over to the seventh shortly."

A flicker of annoyance crossed Satan's face before the emotion was wiped clean. "Perfect. It's like they heard the dinner *bell and have come running, not realizing they're on the menu. Let me know when—"*

"You!" a shredded voice bellowed. A moment passed before I recognized the shout as my own. What I lacked in clarity, I made up for in volume. "How could you?"

Pure rage punctured my skin like rusty nails. With energy I shouldn't have possessed, like a rabid animal I struggled against the manacles that kept me tethered to the stone wall.

Alrik had led me to Earth and directly into an ambush. We'd been attacked the moment we'd materialized. I'd lost track of him when I was taken down and feared he'd been captured as well. To think, this whole time I'd been hanging here I'd also been concerned for his safety. The snake.

"History does seem to be repeating itself, doesn't it?" Satan mocked.

"Betrayer!" I spat at Alrik. My gaze fixated on my ex-friend even as staring at him made me sick.

Deadened eyes stared back at me. I'd seen that look from him on the battlefield, but I'd never been the recipient of that expression before.

I breathed like a raging bull. Before I even realized what I was doing, electricity crackled to life inside me, building in my heart and then exploding outward. White-and-blue zigzags of energy shot from my hands, harmlessly scorching the walls of my cell rather than the two beings at whom my fury was directed.

I'd revealed my hidden power.

Big mistake.

Yet the dread that should have settled in my chest was snuffed out by my righteous anger.

I strained against my chains with an otherworldly power. They groaned, and for a moment I thought I might be able to free myself. That was until Satan flicked his wrist and a second set of binds clamped down on my forearms, further securing me to the jagged rocks at my back.

"Interesting. You might be worth more than I thought." Satan tilted his head in a birdlike manner, examining me like an alien specimen. "That little trick of yours betrays your alliance. Interesting that you've been able to hide it from me for so long." A grin spread across his face. "My arms are always open to welcome another solider as fodder for the battlefield."

He turned from me and addressed an uncharacteristically stoic Alrik. "I think it's time we thin the herd a bit, don't you agree?"

Alrik merely shifted his weight and gave a quick nod of agreement.

They both turned to leave, but before stepping out of sight, Satan turned his head my way.

"It appears that prayer of yours has gone unanswered after all."

Logan!

I jerked upright with a silent scream lodged in my throat and my face wet with tears. Turning to the side, I retched not once but twice onto the ground. The measly amount of food and water in my stomach was expelled the first round, and yellow bile came up the second.

A face filled my watery view, and hands came down on my shoulders, straightening my hunched form.

"It's okay." Joe's voice soothed me. "It's going to be all right."

I whipped my head back and forth, still unable to find my

voice.

Joe pulled me forward and squished my face against his chest as sobs wracked my frame. Rubbing soothing circles on my back, he let me cry.

I didn't have the luxury to fall apart. Every moment we wasted was extra torture for Logan. And that vision confirmed my deepest fear—Satan was using Logan to lure me closer, but I still had no idea what the evil being wanted with me.

Terror pressed on my bladder. I beat the fear back as best I could; my welfare wasn't my primary concern right now.

"N-no," I stuttered. "You don't understand." Still seated, I pushed away from Joe's chest so I could look him in the eye.

"I do." His eyes bore into mine, a fire burning deep within them. He nodded, his gaze never wavering from mine. "I promise, I do."

My pulse started to calm.

"And when the time comes, you'll do what you think you need to do. Just know that you've already been forgiven."

My heartbeat kicked right back into high gear with Joe's bizarre statement.

"Huh?"

He placed his hand over mine, and sadness overtook the righteous fire burning in his eyes.

"You'll know soon enough." He squeezed my hand before standing. "We should keep moving now that you're back with us."

I hadn't considered the rest of the group or even my surroundings for that matter, until Romona stepped into view.

We appeared to be in a cave. A fire burned several feet away, giving light to the cramped space as well as adding to the already unbearable heat.

I turned my head and located Kevin, Kaitlin, and Jonathon

standing close by.

They all stared in silence. Seeing me jolt awake and then proceed to have a complete meltdown must have been unnerving. Did they have any idea what had happened while I was out?

They watched me with wide eyes and faces leeched of color despite the orange glow of the fire's flames. They were spooked. Even Jonathon's expression matched the rest.

"Audrey"—Romona drew my attention—"your hair . . . it's white."

I swallowed a gasp and brought a chunk forward to inspect. Color usually streaked my hair, but this time the white completely swallowed any trace of pigmentation. I shivered despite the heat then took a moment to change it back. It had never turned that shade before, but considering what I'd just witnessed, the color change shouldn't have been a surprise.

I set my hand on the ground, intending to push myself to my feet, but snatched it back when I connected with something warm and sticky. My gaze tracked down, and with a yelp, I rolled-crawled off the makeshift bed I'd been sitting on.

Oh no they didn't!

"Please tell me you didn't drag me through Hell on a bunch of dismembered zombie tree limbs?"

Romona's eyes twinkled. "Okay, I won't tell you that."

I spared a glance at my hand, smeared with—something warm and sticky.

"Is that blood?" My voice was shrill even to my own ears.

I glared at the pallet I'd been resting on. A dozen or so skinny branches had been secured together to make a semi-flat surface just wide and long enough to fit my frame. With caution, I leaned forward. The dim lighting made it difficult to see, but sure enough, something red was leaking from the broken tree limbs.

"Oh my gosh! Did they suck my blood while I was unconscious?" I frantically searched my body armor for rips or tears. "How could you put me at risk like that?"

"Vampires suck blood. Zombies eat brains," Kevin piped up.

"Well then, why the heck are those things leaking blood?"

"It's not blood," Jonathon snapped, clearly over any concern he had for me. "It's sap."

"Sap?"

"Yeah sap. You know, like maple syrup." Jonathon's tone and eye roll made it clear he thought I was an idiot.

My stomach churned at the thought of pouring the blood-like substance on my pancakes. I slapped a hand over my mouth as if the action would somehow ward off my macabre thoughts, unintentionally spreading the substance over my lips and chin.

"That's nasty." I furiously scrubbed my face with the back of my clean hand, the bile in my stomach churning once again. "I can't believe you guys dragged me around on that thing."

"Well, technically we didn't drag you; we carried you." Kaitlin shrugged at the glare I shot her. "What? It helped disperse your weight and allowed us to move faster. You were all floppy and stuff."

"This is by far the most bizarre thing that's happened to me since I woke up dead." A day jammed with firsts.

"That's saying something," Kaitlin noted.

"Truth." I bobbed my head in agreement.

"So what happened?" Romona laid a gentle hand on my arm. Leave it to her to recognize my very real need for comfort.

"Yeah." I swallowed in a vain attempt to wet my suddenly parched throat. "I saw Logan." Correcting myself, I shook my head. "No, that's not entirely true. I didn't see Logan. I *was* Logan."

Kaitlin gasped.

"Trippy," Kevin whispered.

"He's . . ." I closed my eyes and rubbed them with my clean fist before going on. "He's in real bad shape right now. They're doing . . . things to him that are beyond horrible." Letting my hands drop to my sides, I speared each of them with my gaze. "If we don't get to him soon, I'm not sure how much of him there will be left to save."

"What's that supposed to mean?" Jonathon demanded.

How could I explain the horror Logan was experiencing right now? "It means he's on the verge of breaking."

"Was Alrik there?" Kaitlin asked in a small voice. Her eyes were wide and glassy.

Just the mention of his name spiked my anger. With gritted teeth, I nodded curtly. When I got my hands on that traitor, he was going to suffer.

"Audrey." Joe's soft but assertive voice broke through my haze of fury. "Alrik's ultimate fate is one you wouldn't wish on anyone."

"Do you . . . feel *sorry* for him?" Every word came out with a bite. I wanted to expose my teeth like an angry dog and snap at him.

The skin was literally being peeled from Logan's body while Alrik stood and watched. After witnessing his betrayal firsthand, I'd never have anything but hatred in my heart for him. He'd led Logan to a fate worse than death.

Willingly. Knowingly. For personal gain.

My muscles tensed, fingers curled inward, and knees bent as I readied myself for a fight. I was acting like a provoked animal—ready to fight dirty to protect what was mine.

"It is not Our desire that We would lose even one. If you truly understood what awaited him, you'd have a measure of compassion as well."

I growled. Literally growled at Joe. He only shook his head and turned from me.

A moment of shame settled on my heart before I shoved the disgrace aside. I didn't have anything to be ashamed of. I got that Joe's ability to forgive was larger than mine, but no one responsible for the atrocities being done to Logan should be forgiven. There was no room for that kind of forgiveness. Their actions were unforgivable.

Alrik deserved the punishment coming to him, and nothing Joe said could make me feel otherwise.

I turned my back on him and walked away from the fire. "You're right," I threw over my shoulder, "we should get going."

4

RINGS

"You carried me through the rest of the eighth ring?" I asked in a whisper as we trudged along behind Joe. Sometime while I'd been unconscious, we'd left the zombie forest behind and entered a completely new terrain.

"Yep." Kaitlin nodded.

"I don't know whether to be impressed or embarrassed."

"Definitely embarrassed."

I half-heartedly shoved Kaitlin, lacking the energy to do much more. She took a step to the side and righted herself, not even bothering to try and hide her smile.

Brat.

If Romona was my best friend, then Kaitlin was the annoying—and somewhat immature—older sister I hadn't asked for. Rolling my eyes at my friend, my mind wandered elsewhere.

The ground crunched beneath my feet with every step. I'd been told the volcanic stones and cinder had disappeared when we crossed through the last ring. If I tried hard enough, I could pretend we were walking on bleached seashells, but the shape and general appearance didn't quite line up with that theory.

But, whatever, I preferred it to the zombie trees. Shivers wracked my body when my mind even brushed against the thought.

The seventh ring had similarities to the eighth. The same jagged mountain range cut a crooked path along the horizon. When we'd emerged from the cave, I learned we'd actually been taking shelter within the black monstrosities to hide from any roaming demons. Joe explained that the creatures inhabited the rings closer to the center, but occasionally one would appear in this section. The height of our hidden shelter had also given us the advantage of being able to scout great distances.

How they hauled me up the sharp terrain to find the cavern was a mystery. Dragging my unconscious body straight up that hunk of rock must have been near impossible, but I was thankful.

Even without carrying my dead weight, it took the better part of a half hour to descend. From our perch, I had assumed the area was covered in desert sand.

I was so wrong.

The particles were larger than granules of sand, ranging from the size of a dime to a quarter in a variety of distorted shapes. A sickening snap and crack sounded with each heavy footfall.

No, this wasn't sand at all. I knew these were bleached bone fragments.

I shoved all thoughts of the ground we traversed into a tightly sealed box and stored it in the far recesses of my mind. We were one ring closer to Logan, that's all that should matter—even if I had to fight the urge to wince with every crunchy step.

As we'd been warned, the heat increased, but after experiencing what Logan was going through, I hardly registered the uptick in temperature. If anything, I was actually doing better than I was before. Perhaps I was just that much more motivated. Seeing the person I lo—

I caught my thoughts. Whoa, wait a minute. I almost just let the "L" bomb drop. Did I actually lo—lov . . . Oh. My. Gosh. I couldn't even spit the word out mentally. There was a time I had thought my feelings ran that deep for Logan, but was it even possible I felt that way when I couldn't even force my conscious mind to say it?

Our relationship had gone through so many ups and downs. Just when I thought I knew where we stood, he kissed me, and we were bonded. Then he was kidnapped and gone. My head and my heart ran into each other like colliding freight trains. I'd been acting mostly on instinct, but when I stopped to really think about us, my head throbbed.

I took a casual look around to make sure no one was paying attention to me and my existential crisis. Kaitlin morbidly kicked bone fragments as she strolled forward—blessedly ignoring me. Kevin and Jonathon trudged on in front of us, their attention firmly forward.

Up ahead of them, Joe and Romona led the way. I squinted and tilted my head just a bit as I stared at Joe's back. His shoulders were hunched in a way that had my suspicion meter spiking. Was he . . . laughing?

He put a hand up to his face and shook his head. A moment later, he glanced over his shoulder and shot me a quick look before turning back again. The smile on his face said it all.

That booger was laughing. At me.

"Yeah, live it up!" I yelled.

His shoulders just shook harder, and he brought a hand up to wipe something from his eyes. Were no thoughts sacred?

Kevin and Jonathon looked my way, both set of brows furrowed.

"What's going on?" Kevin asked.

"Nothing," I grumbled and pushed forward, leaving our footprints as well as my thoughts about love behind.

"Sooo. This is it, huh?" I stared ahead at nothing. And by nothing, I mean the exact same thing we'd looked at for the last few hours: a sea of white with the angry dark mountain range to our right.

We'd followed the mountains until Joe called a halt and let us know we were about to enter the next ring. I cocked my eyebrow and pursed my lips, ready for another optical illusion of some kind that hid the entrance of the next ring.

"Do we need to hold hands again?" Kailtin asked. "Because if so, I think this time we should sing Kumbaya."

"Did you have to do that when you passed between the eighth and seventh ring?" I asked.

"Sing songs?"

I rolled my eyes. Smart-mouthed blonde.

"Hold hands."

She grinned back. "Yep." She popped her p as usual. "It was tricky, since we were lugging around your dead weight. We all had to keep one hand on your zombie stretcher and another on you so we could all get through together."

"Do not call it a zombie stretcher." I cringed even saying the words.

Her smile grew.

"Join hands. No singing. I'm expecting company this time," was all Joe said before he clasped Jonathon's hand and walked through the invisible veil.

Company?

Wait, maybe we should discuss this "company" before going through an invisible wall.

Before I could voice my concerns, Jonathon grabbed Kevin's hand and disappeared. Kevin grasped Romona's, Romona snatched Kaitlin's, and then Kaitlin grabbed mine and everyone was steadily moving forward.

"Seriously, peeps, I'm thinking that maybe we should . . . Oh shoot."

Kaitlin vanished. This was happening whether I wanted it to or not.

Rotten eggs. I choked on the stench. Great, we were back to the stinky part of Hell. When I crossed over to the sixth ring, my eyes started to water from the intensity of the smell. The nasty odor had been absent from the last two rings but was back with a vengeance.

I waved my hand in front of my face to clear the air of not only the stench of rot but of some sort of smoke or mist as well. This ring was a little like stepping into a smelly, dense cloud. Foul-smelling and horrible visibility.

Someone to my right retched. Jonathon bent at the waist, dry heaving into the skeletal remains of a bush. The leafless twigs did little to hide the sight. A gag worked its way up my throat, but I managed to choke the bile down.

Everyone else's complexions were tinged green, but the others fared far better than Jonathon. Most covered their mouths with their hands.

Pfft—like that's going to do much. Not even a gas mask could clean this air.

Despite the distracting assault on my senses, something familiar rolled in my gut and punched awareness to the surface. And it wasn't my Logan-GPS . . . this sensation was something altogether different.

Turning in a quick circle, I scanned our murky surroundings. We were no longer alone.

They're everywhere.

"Huh?" Kevin asked.

I must have spoken that last part out loud.

"Demons," I answered without allowing my eyes to rest on any of my friends. I was too busy searching for unseen enemies. In this crazy fog, they could be upon us before we spotted them.

"You know, my built-in demon-detector thing. It's going berserk right now." That indescribable feeling that wasn't a feeling. The smell that wasn't a smell. I'd never been able to properly articulate the freak power that had sprung to life on Earth that no one but me seemed to have. Right now my gut churned, and awareness poked at my senses.

I grabbed the sword from my back, and when the blade blazed to life, a fresh wave of heat flared along my arms.

"Where are they?" asked a straightening Jonathon. "I don't see anything."

I spared him a glance. He wiped his mouth with the back of his glove and scanned the hidden terrain with a squint.

Had Jonathon ever actually seen a demon before? It's not like he would have had opportunity to do so from the safety of our realm. This might very well be the first time he would come face-to-face with the reality of our enemy.

I hope he's up to the task.

Something shimmered around us, and I recognized Joe's dampening effect on the environment. The smell became somewhat bearable again, and the heat lessened.

"The Fallen do inhabit this and the remaining rings of Hell. We'll have to be more vigilant than before."

"Is that the company you mentioned before pulling us into this ring?" I was still wary, ready for an attack at any moment. Why hadn't they already charged?

Joe nodded. He was the only one of us whose focus was on the group rather than our surroundings. "You're feeling their presence because there are so many of them here. It's overwhelming your senses. It doesn't mean any are as close as you think. You're feeling them like I do."

My gaze snapped to Joe. His stare remained locked on mine . . . steady and unflinching.

"Yes, Audrey. That part of you comes from me." He answered my unspoken question.

My muscles locked. So. Many. Questions.

"Whoa." Kevin's murmur reached my ears.

I didn't disagree.

Joe shook his head. "Not now. We'll have to discuss this later. Just know that you can't trust your instincts down here. Not like you do on the surface. You're going to feel suffocated by their presence sometimes, but that doesn't mean you have one breathing down your back."

"Are you seriously going to drop that bomb on me and just leave it hanging there? I mean . . . what? I'm not supposed to ask any more questions? All I've ever had regarding this . . . this ability of mine . . . has been questions."

"We'll talk later." His eyes told me that was a promise. "Let's find shelter and a place to rest first."

I wanted to argue, but it would be fruitless. Joe's answers would come when he was ready and not a moment sooner. I released an unintelligible grumble and let it go. Maybe this meant I was maturing?

Pfft. Yeah right. It simply meant I was starting to recognize battles I wasn't going to win.

"You guys." Something about the tone of Romona's voice caught me off guard. "Maybe we should start looking for that shelter sooner rather than later."

The mountain range that had been our steadfast landmark was still with us, but in this ring, it wasn't simply ugly . . . it was angry. The pustules that had leaked molten lava in the previous rings were spewing it freely here. They were also spontaneously erupting on the mountainside like exploding zits.

One of which had just appeared several hundred feet above our heads. Its contents were headed straight for us.

"Move!" Joe commanded.

As a unit, we ran forward into the hazy mess. We weren't going to luck out and find shelter in the mountain this time.

5

SHELTER

Hours later, we were still traveling on high alert. We grouped close together because if one of us strayed too far, there was danger of being swallowed by the dense fog. The shrieks that occasionally emanated from it were far from comforting. Kaitlin jumped more than once at the sounds.

My blade was out and on a near-constant swivel. The whoosh of the fire as I swung the weapon back and forth to ward off the inevitable attack grated on my already frayed nerves.

The sense of demons—everywhere—never dissipated.

Sweat dripped down my back and between my shoulder blades. My arms shook with fatigue. The strain I'd felt ever since the ninth ring was now evident on all my companions' faces, save Joe's. I didn't take any satisfaction from the fact that my friends were finally experiencing my level of discomfort.

To my left, Romona stumbled. She took several shaky steps before losing the battle against gravity and landing on her hands and knees.

I sheathed my blade and helped her to her feet. She teetered a bit before finding her footing then sent me a weary smile and nod of thanks. Sweat dotted her brow and upper lip, and her breathing was labored despite our slow pace. Lines of exhaustion ringed her eyes, and she weaved as if drunk.

"Joe," I whisper-yelled to our leader. When he turned toward me, I jerked my chin in Romona's direction.

His lips thinned to a grim line.

"Almost there," he called back.

I cringed at the volume. Despite Joe's assurance that no demons were close enough to attack us, the creepy feeling in my gut said otherwise.

A few long minutes later, Joe held up his hand, signaling us to stop.

Romona sank to her knees. I watched her with concern. The others in the group were bent over, hands on knees and sucking in air as if they'd just run a marathon.

Phantom pain still zinged throughout my body, causing me to jerk from time to time with the intensity. Fatigue weighted my limbs, but at least I could remain upright. Perhaps my earlier exposure to this discomfort had conditioned my body for the hardships of the sixth ring? Or maybe the little "nap" I'd taken allowed me to rest when the others hadn't gotten that luxury? Referring to the experience of Logan's torture as a luxury seemed beyond wrong, but I couldn't ignore the fact my body had the chance to refresh while my friends had hauled my unconscious form through an entire ring.

Joe was hunched over a spot on the ground, doing who knew what. His lips and hands were moving, reminding me of the first time we'd met—back in a time outside of time—when he'd literally created the heavenly realm in front of my eyes. There was a strain to his face that hadn't been there before.

A moment later, the ground shook beneath our feet. The

other hunters jumped and pulled out their weapons, searching with wild eyes for the perceived threat. I was too busy watching the hole growing at Joe's feet to join them.

What the what? Are those stairs?

When the shaking stopped, Joe stood and called us forward.

Kevin's eyes grew when he spotted the hole that had appeared while he was scanning for threats. The rest of my friends simply shifted their weight back and forth with unsmiling faces. I'd wager a guess none of us were wild about going down there. We stood in a circle, looking into the darkness.

"Abandon all hope, ye who enter here."

Had Jonathon not been standing right next to me, I might not have heard his whispered words.

"Huh?"

Jonathon didn't spare me a look; he only rolled his eyes.

"Is that from Dante's *Inferno?*" I pressed. "Weren't you already dead by the time that was written?"

"No. I'm not that old," he sneered. "Did you remember that from a 'quote-a-day' calendar?"

Ouch . . . and he wasn't wrong.

I held up my hands in defense. "Geez, sorry. I didn't mean anything by it."

Okay, new strategy when dealing with Jonathon: Ignore his presence entirely. He seemed to prefer it that way.

A set of stairs led into a black abyss. Joe took the first step into the dark hole.

"Come on," he said. "We'll rest here for a while. You all need it."

"You want us to follow you into a black hole in the ground. Deeper into Hell?" There was a wild glint in Kevin's eyes when he spoke. He took a step away from the rest of us.

I got it. This was unnerving but hardly the scariest thing we'd encountered so far. I mean, come on, zombie trees for the win. At least Joe was offering us a break. My weary body screamed for rest even as my mind rioted against anything that would slow our mission, but if we were going to be in any shape to rescue Logan, we all needed a breather.

Joe motioned the rest of us down before him as he went to Kevin, laying a hand on his shoulder and quietly speaking to him.

I strained my ears to hear their conversation even as I took my first step into the hole, but I couldn't catch a single word. Disappointed, I focused on following Kaitlin into the darkness. On the tenth stair, I lost sight of her completely. Only the sound of her feet crunching on the steps assured me she was still there. I settled my gloved hand on the grooved wall to steady myself and continued my descent.

"I'm at the bottom," Romona called up. "Careful walking. The ground is uneven down here."

Figures.

"Ouch!" Kaitlin yelped. "A little heads-up about the ceiling height would have been nice, Romona. Anyone have something to light this place up?"

"Oops, sorry. Anyone taller than Audrey and me needs to watch their head." Romona yelled up.

The belated warning echoed off the walls of the darkened chamber.

I reached the bottom without realizing and took a stumble-step forward, knocking into what I assumed was Kaitlin's back. We both staggered several uneven steps before righting ourselves.

"Yikes! Sorry."

"That's okay. It's impossible to see down here."

"What in the world are you girls doing?" Jonathon's perturbed voice was close enough that I knew he was about to walk right into me.

I spun around and put my hands up. They connected with overheated body armor a milli-second later. "Whoa there."

"Don't touch me," Jonathon spat, and he swatted my hands away.

I heaved a frustrated sigh. *Geez, it's not like I was trying to cop a feel.* Would he rather have run into my back? I wanted to march farther ahead of him, but in the total black that engulfed us, I wasn't sure what I'd run into. Scooting as close to Kaitlin as possible, I kept my mouth shut.

"We're coming," Joe called down to us. "I'll start a fire in a moment so you all can see."

I heard, rather than saw, Joe and Kevin shuffle into the space with us. After several long moments, a spark ignited off to my right. By the time I'd fully turned my head in that direction, a small flame danced on Joe's palm. I cocked my head and blinked.

Joe transferred the light to a fire pit in the far corner of a small enclosure. The flame grew in size until a full-fledged fire, large enough to light the entire space, blazed. I had no idea what material was actually burning. The already oppressive heat ratcheted up, the space becoming almost too hot to breathe in, but I preferred the heat to the darkness.

"Holy fire," Kaitlin whispered in my ear. "It burns clean so we don't need a vent."

Right. Had I been thinking clearly, I could have pulled my sword out a minute ago to act as a torch.

Joe put his hands flat on the soil beneath our feet, and the ground shook again. Loose dirt fell around us in dusty waves. Coughing, I glanced toward the stairs and found they were gone. I shivered.

We were literally encased in earth and stone. Kaitlin, Romona, and Jonathon looked around our surroundings with eyes filled with unease, but at least they were holding it together. Kevin was hunched over; his unblinking gaze darted from the floor to ceiling, and his breaths came out in snorts. He was one second away from hyperventilating.

Joe motioned for us to sit as he went back over to Kevin, murmuring something in soothing tones. Kevin squeezed his eyes shut and nodded. A violent tremor shook his body before he sank to the ground with the rest of us.

Someone was not comfortable in enclosed spaces. But who could blame him? I felt both oppressed and oddly safe in our mini-sanctuary.

Just don't think about it, I chanted to myself.

There was enough space for all of us to lie down if we wanted, but that was about it. Sleeping on the uneven, rocky ground was going to be challenging. I looked around at my companions, some of whom were practically sleeping sitting up. Exhaustion would make up for the lack of comfort in this refuge.

"We'll stay here for a few hours," Joe announced. "You all need the rest. I expect to reach Logan tomorrow, so use this time to recharge."

The statement was met with nodded heads and softly spoken thanks as my friends all shuffled into as much of a comfortable position as possible. Joe waved his hand in the direction of the fire, and the light dimmed.

I tried to settle, but as much as I squirmed, I couldn't find a position where something sharp wasn't poking me. It was distracting. And annoying.

I flipped over again . . . and swallowed a scream. Joe was

hunched down in front of me, with his knees bent and his weight resting on the balls of his feet. I pressed a hand to my chest and felt my heart pumping furiously.

"I thought we could talk now." Joe spoke softly, probably so he wouldn't disturb the group.

"Okay, yeah." I nodded and pushed myself up on my elbows. Quiet snores rose from behind me. My money was on Kevin.

Joe sank down into a seated position while I carefully wiggled up into one as well, careful not to disturb Kaitlin to my left. I bumped her once and turned to apologize, only to find her out cold, her even breaths in tune with the rest of the sleeping forms in the dirt bunker.

No worries about being overheard, I suppose.

"You have questions," Joe started.

"When don't I?"

He chuckled. "An inquisitive heart was stitched into the very fibers of your being. It's part of what makes you, you." He held his hands out as if that explained everything.

"O-kay. So, my demon radar?" I left the question open ended.

Joe's lips pressed together, but the corners of his mouth tipped up. I waited for several moments before he spoke. As if he needed that time to compose himself. "Audrey, as I'm sure you've noticed, you have certain . . . abilities and skills, that most hunters or others who have passed on to our realm do not possess."

"Yep. Flaming sword was the first thing that tipped me off."

Again with the pressed-together lips. I got the impression he was finding something I was saying amusing. He reminded me of Hugo.

"Right, well, the flaming sword isn't the only thing that has set you apart. Being able to sense the presence of demons is another."

I nodded at him to continue.

"Just as the power from your sword comes from Hugo, sensing demons comes from me."

He leaned back a bit, as if that was explanation enough. My mouth dropped.

Ah, no. "Let's back up," I whispered. "The flames from my sword are actually Hugo's power. Check. I got that one. But sensing demons? That's not an external thing; that's an internal one. I don't get it. And more importantly, why am I the only one who has that ability?"

"Audrey, I am part of you. I am part of your very soul. You were made in Our image."

"But wasn't everyone else as well?" I gestured to the sleeping forms around us.

"Yes, of course."

"But I'm the only one with demon-dar."

"Demon-dar, huh?"

"It seems like a fitting description."

He laughed under his breath.

"You're not wrong about that. There is no short answer for your question. Nor should every question be answered. But to *attempt* a short answer anyway—you've been equipped with everything you need. And so your . . . demon-dar . . . is just another talent you've been given to fulfill your purpose. If you didn't need it, you wouldn't have it." He smiled at me, knowing full well I wouldn't be satisfied with that response.

"But—"

"Get some sleep, Audrey. And learn to trust that the Creator not only has a plan but your best interests in mind as well."

I scrunched my nose and bit my tongue to keep from peppering him with questions. When Joe was done talking, that was that. Didn't mean I had to like it though.

I awoke to the ground trembling beneath me, coughing and choking on dry dirt that swirled in the air. The rest of our group was in various states of waking up as well. All except Joe, who stood with his eyes fixed on the low ceiling above.

"What's going on?" Jonathon asked after a coughing fit subsided.

I already knew what Joe's answer would be, thanks to the familiar rolling in my gut.

"It's a horde of demons passing right above us," he answered.

"Dude, that's not cool." Kevin's knees were pressed against his chest with his arms squeezing them tight. An impressive feat for such a tall guy. The whites of his eyes practically glowed in the low lighting. He rocked back and forth gently with his head immobile, staring at nothing but the wall of rock across from him.

If we stayed down here much longer, he was going to either lose it or turn so introspective who knew when we'd be able to snap him out of it?

"Once they pass, we're going to head out. We're almost to the end of this ring; then we'll be able to cross into the fifth. The one where Logan is being held."

Joe lowered his gaze. His eyes passed over each of us briefly. "I won't lie to you. We will come into contact with opposition before we reach him. The most important thing from here on out is to make sure we get Audrey to Logan."

"Me?" I squeaked.

Five sets of eyes blinked back at me. I mean, yeah, I wanted to be there when we set Logan free, but why was it so important that I be the one to make it there? Was it something to do with our bond?

"This is your mission, Audrey," Joe said, answering my unasked question. Knowing he could get into my head that easily was freaky. "I can send the rest of them back at any time if I need to, but you're the one who's going to have to free Logan. It's the way it was meant to be."

The way it was meant to be? Cryptic much?

Wouldn't that play exactly into Satan's plans? In my vision, he'd been clear that Logan was the bait to lure me to him. I still didn't know why.

Terror punched my gut like I'd been run through with a rusty blade. I rammed my reaction down, hiding my fear.

Joe's gaze lingered on me a moment longer before he scanned the faces of my friends. "So that means it's all of your jobs to ensure she makes it there. Got it?"

There were nods all around. While he'd been speaking, the rumbling from above stopped, and it left an eerie sort of quiet in its wake.

Joe placed his hand on the wall. Another mini-earthquake revealed the set of stairs we'd used to descend into this pit.

We scrambled to our feet. A world of horrors might be waiting above, but I was ready to leave this tight enclosure. The feeling of being buried alive was a little too strong within its walls.

Joe motioned for us to follow him. We shuffled in his wake; somehow I found myself at the rear of our little train. The moment I placed my foot on the bottom step, the fire that had lit the cave extinguished, pitching me in almost complete blackness.

A chill skated up my spine despite the oppressive heat. I used the wall as my guide as I ascended until some of the unnatural light from above filtered down.

When I reached the surface, my companions had already formed a semi-circle around me, all facing out with weapons drawn. Whatever might or might not be out there was shrouded in a thick layer of fog.

How had I forgotten about the fog? Or the smell?

Barf.

The assault on my nose was worse than I remembered.

"Let's move," Joe said.

We fell in step together and progressed as if we were a single being—yet this time I found myself surrounded on all sides.

I rolled my eyes.

Was this really necessary? I was the one with the sword loaded with holy fire. Shouldn't I be given a prime defensive position?

I elbowed my way to the front between Kevin and Joe. Kevin tried to push me back into place, but I pulled out my sword, looked pointedly at the flames, and then back at him with lifted brows. He shook his head but didn't try to reposition me again.

No attack came. The farther we marched, the less I remembered to be on my guard and the more my mind wandered. Between my Logan-GPS and my overactive demon-dar, my insides were a mess.

Everything was going fine . . . until Romona's pain-filled scream pierced the silence.

6

DEMONS

I swung around. Kaitlin and Jonathon were spinning in circles, looking for Romona, who up until a moment before had been right between them.

"Where is she?" I yelled, no longer caring about detection.

Kaitlin's frightened gaze snapped up. "I don't know. Sh-she was just here."

Joe barreled through the lot of us and took off in the direction we'd just come from. No one questioned his decision; we all just ran after him. He moved so quickly the thick fog swallowed him, making it challenging to keep up.

We heard nothing more from Romona after that first scream.

My heart beat fast and erratically. Exertion wasn't the only culprit. I didn't allow my mind go down the rabbit hole of what could have happened to her. I completely focused my attention on staying with Joe.

I looked down to search for footprints. Big mistake.

Was that blood?

Dark, narrow lines appeared and disappeared on the dry

ground as we flew over it. They might have been left by her fingers as she was dragged away from us.

Joe disappeared and reappeared in the fog time and time again. Were we running in circles? There was no way to tell. The only consistent was the bloody trail we followed and the glimpses of Joe.

I yelled Romona's name time and time again, careless of the repercussions. But she never answered. And then Joe appeared, crouched over Romona's motionless body.

In my haste to reach her, I almost tripped over him but managed to stop myself just in time. Kaitlin, Jonathon, and Kevin skidded to a stop as well. I leaned over Joe to get a better look and immediately clamped both hands over my mouth, holding in a scream.

Romona lay on the ground in front of him. Pieces of her armor had been shredded at her thigh and abdomen. Thick, gooey blood spread in a circle around her, and the ground slurped up the scarlet liquid almost as fast as it left her body.

A low groan left her lips. With horror, I realized she was still conscious.

"Fan out," Joe barked. "Protect us. We've been discovered."

We obeyed without argument.

I felt them. Demons.

Now that I was paying attention, their presence practically slithered under my skin. But I couldn't pinpoint exactly where the threat was coming from, leaving us blind to their location.

"Jonathon, switch places with me. Try to stanch the flow."

Joe didn't wait for Jonathon to comply before joining the circle around Romona. I heard clothes ripping and Jonathon's murmured words behind me, and I knew he was tending to Romona the best he could.

"They're here!" Joe shouted, and then the rest of the world

fell away as I found myself in a battle with abominations that were hidden and half-invisible in the fog.

Sharp, blackened appendages came at me from multiple directions. I couldn't see the creatures attached to them to anticipate their moves. They were using the dense fog to their advantage. Their strikes were precise and powerful; the fog clearly wasn't affecting them negatively.

My sword cut through every attack aimed my way, and soon I was cringing under the onslaught of demon shrieks. My eardrums throbbed, but I did what I could to ignore the pain in my head and continued to hack away at anything that appeared out of the mist.

Abruptly, the attacks on me stopped.

I scanned the area, but it seemed I no longer interested the demons. In contrast, my friends' struggles echoed around me. The sound of metal meeting hardened flesh rebounded off the blanket of vapor. Without the ability to slice off limbs, they were only able to defend themselves against the demons. A demon's vulnerable points were concealed in the trunk of its body, but no creature came out of the fog far enough to be seen. I made a split second decision I hoped I wouldn't regret.

"Kaitlin," I yelled in her direction, somewhere to my right. "Close the gap between us. I'm going in."

"Wait, what?" she yelled back. "Are you crazy?"

"Probably."

I ran head-on into the fog, blind to the creatures I stalked. My hope was the demons would be so distracted trying to injure everyone else that I could ambush them from behind. That is, if I could even find them.

My eyes failing me, I strained my hearing to its limits. To the right were sounds of battle and the distinctive piercing chirp of a demon. It must be the one fighting Kaitlin. Oh gosh,

I really hoped I was right.

Here goes nothing.

I ran toward where I *thought* the demon was with my sword held out in front of me, the blade blazing like an inferno. I'm sure I looked like a complete idiot, but if I was going to accidentally run into something demonic, I wanted the pointy end of my sword to hit first.

I skidded to a stop when the mist cleared enough to reveal the backside of the Goliath battling Kaitlin. My gamble paid off—the giant creature was too distracted fighting my friend to notice me—but its sheer size gave me pause.

Thank goodness Kaitlin couldn't see this thing, or she'd probably pee herself. Heck, I was close to losing bodily control, and that beast wasn't even facing off with me.

One cut was not going to do it, holy fire or no. The thing was easily the size of a small house. Even if I plunged my blade right into the creature, it would most likely swat me away like a fly before I got the chance for a second blow.

An idea formed in my head. Not one I liked, but the only one I could come up with. If I could take care of the tentacle-like appendages attacking Kaitlin first, there was a chance I could then climb up its back and sink my sword into something that would put the creature down.

This was insane.

Once I started cutting off appendages, this massive demon was going to start attacking me right away.

Shoot, I'd better be fast. This was going to get messy.

I bounced on the balls of my feet for a quick second before jumping into the fight.

I managed to cut through two of the barbed tentacles in one swing. They flopped to the ground and wiggled as if still attached. *Nasty.* The stumps that remained squirted black blood. That was new. Usually my sword left only charred flesh in its wake. And the things I cut off weren't turning to ash either. It had to have something to do with the realm we were in.

Lost in thought, I ducked a moment too late, and one of the creature's wiggly arm-like things clipped me on the shoulder. I slammed into the ground, hard. With a shake of my head I bounced back to my feet and charged.

Now that I could see clearly, I zeroed in on the demon's remaining limbs. They flailed through the air like knives aimed at my head.

Time disappeared as I fought. Any blow I landed cut through its shell-like flesh without difficulty. Shrieks of pain and outrage rent the air.

One more wiggly limb to go, and I would be on to phase two of my plan. The crazy part where I somehow managed to get high enough on the demon's body to take off its head, or at least plunge my sword into its skull . . . repeatedly.

With a satisfying swipe, I lopped off the last limb. I was covered in the demon's slimy black ichor. I preferred it when the creatures charred and ashed. So this was what the other hunters went through when they fought with the enemy.

Didn't like it one bit.

In a surprise move, the demon suddenly threw its body in my direction. I dove to the side to get out of its way. My sword flew from my hand and landed somewhere unseen.

Did that fat demon just try to squish me?

Dazed, I shook my head and looked up in time to see the creature lumber to its feet and come at me again.

Scrambling for purchase on the parched ground, I only just managed to evade getting flattened a second time. The demon's razor sharp jaws were only feet from where I lay, and it twisted and snapped at my feet.

Holy cow, it's trying to eat me!

It would almost be funny if this weren't so dangerous.

The demon twisted to its feet once again. Shoot! My sword. It had landed somewhere to the left. I dashed into the mist with my eyes down, searching the ground for a glint of metal and praying I didn't get crushed before I found my weapon.

Tripping over something, I fell to my knees. Looking back, my sword lay at my feet. My own weapon had thwarted me. So stupid.

I grabbed it, and it blazed to life. The ground shook around me as the demon took another kamikaze dive at my body.

Thank goodness this thing's aim was so off. But it had also unknowingly done me a favor. With its body sprawled on the ground, scaling its side was a breeze.

As the creature rose, I jumped and threw myself as high up on its body as I could get.

Needle-like spikes penetrated my armor, and I screamed out in pain. The demon's flesh was covered with thin barbs, some as long as four inches. No wonder the fatty had been trying to get me under itself. The spikes alone would have shredded me. They had already pierced several spots in my left hand and thigh.

I was close enough to its head that I could do some damage—no need to chance climbing higher. Not exactly where I wanted to be, but it would have to do.

With a loud cry, I brought my arm down and sliced through the demon, roughly where the neck would be. When it tried to let out its own scream, black blood spurted out of the hole I'd created instead.

I choked down the bile rising in my throat and took another swing.

The creature began to tip. I gritted my teeth and held on tight to the spikes that had impaled my hand, readying myself for the fall. The impact almost dislodged me, but I managed to keep from being flung through the air.

The blood that had been gushing out of the demon slowed to a gurgling river. I wasn't taking any chances and took another swipe at its flesh. Its head was halfway off its body, and the demon finally stilled.

Pushing the savage battle out of my mind, I jumped off my perch and landed in a roll before popping to my feet. My shoulder throbbed, as did the hand and thigh that had been on the receiving end of the nasty demon's barbs.

Hardly giving my body a thought, I turned in a circle to locate my group.

The land was unnervingly quiet.

I cupped my hands and shouted for Kaitlin. Her answering cry came from my left. I took off running, heart pounding with relief. I stumbled onto the group in no time. We were a mess, but we'd been victorious. Or as victorious as we could be in Hell.

No more demons attacking meant we'd won, right?

As I stepped closer, I got a better view of the scene. Kaitlin stood with her sword still out. Her wild gaze locked behind me, like she expected the creature to come back through the fog at any moment.

"What happened?" she asked.

"I took out the demon you were fighting. Big ugly thing. Lots of tentacle-like appendages and spikes all over its body." I shuddered. "And it bled a lot."

"I can tell."

"Yeah."

Behind her, the rest of the group was on the ground.

Jonathon held his post over Romona. A tourniquet had been tied around her upper thigh to slow the bleeding. He was applying pressure to her stomach area with a white piece of cloth that was quickly turning red. He'd stripped the top part of his body armor off, revealing a torso drenched in sweat, and used his shirt to slow down the flow of blood. To her side, there were two other clumps of cloth that were already soaked through.

"I can't stanch the flow," Jonathon called to Joe, who was bent over an obviously injured Kevin.

Ignoring Jonathon, Joe looked into Kevin's eyes and said, "On the count of three, okay?" Joe held Kevin's arm at an awkward angle—his shoulder was out of joint. At his nod, Joe yanked up on his arm without giving the count. Kevin screamed out in pain.

"Sorry. I thought surprising you would be kinder than the anticipation of the pain."

Kevin panted and nodded. Sweat streamed down his face. I was sure he'd sustained more injuries than were evident.

"I said I can't stop her bleeding!" Jonathon shouted this time. Joe leaned over and put a hand on the medic's shoulder.

"I heard you." Joe's voice was clear and calm and free of censure.

Jonathon's shoulders sagged, and a vein in his forehead stopped pulsing as some of the tension left his body.

"What do we do now?" he asked.

"You're going back with Romona and Kevin," Joe told him.

Jonathon started to argue, but Joe silenced him with a look. "Romona and Kevin are in no shape to continue on. I need you to take care of them. Make sure they arrive safely and are cared for." His eyes shifted to Romona's prone form. "Especially her. If only Kevin was injured, I'd send him up alone, but she needs your attention."

Jonathon's shoulders sagged, but he nodded his agreement.

Joe shifted his gaze to Kaitlin and me. "The three of us will continue on."

"Yeah, okay, can I just . . ." I gestured to my grandmother's still form. Joe nodded, stood, and walked a few paces back.

I rushed to Romona's side. The shirt Jonathon held against her was almost completely drenched now. The ground around her body was oddly dry, although stained red. My earlier impression had been right—the ground was actually drinking up her blood.

My stomach turned.

I pulled off a glove and pressed my hand to Romona's face. Her skin was clammy, and she didn't stir. Bending over, I pressed a kiss to her forehead before looking up at Jonathon.

"Please take care of her." My eyes welled with tears.

He returned my look with compassion. "I will. She'll be fine."

I nodded and stood.

"Thank you for being here," I told him sincerely.

He nodded back.

I turned toward Kevin, who was watching me with hooded eyes. He was barely conscious. "You heal up fast."

"You get him back," Kevin croaked.

"I will," I promised.

"Kaitlin and Audrey, step back," Joe instructed. He urged Kevin to scoot closer to Jonathon then laid hands on them both and closed his eyes. Within moments, the four of them were encased in a light so bright I was forced to turn away. It faded quickly, and only Joe remained.

Where we had been six, now we were only three.

Joe stood and brushed his hands against his legs. "Let's go.

7

HIDDEN

The rest of our trek through the mist-filled ring was somber and tense. No one spoke until Joe signaled for us to stop and explained we were about to cross into the fifth ring. I was anxious to leave the sixth, regardless of what new horrors we'd face.

The first thing I noticed when we crossed into the next ring was that I could breathe again. Yes, the ever-present smell of rot and sulfur still lingered in the air, but I was able to suck in a lungful without wanting to retch.

The second was the light. Where we had just traveled through a land of fog-induced blindness, this new ring was overexposed and washed in brightness.

My eyes watered, and I blinked several times before adjusting to the change. I swiped at a tear that leaked out the corner of an eye and ran down my cheek. Finally acclimated enough to take a good look around, I choked on a gasp that escaped my lungs.

My legs gave out, and my knees hit the packed ground. Hard.

There were people. Everywhere.

They wore manacles around their wrists, feet, and even sometimes necks, connected to glowing lava-red chains that were anchored into the earth.

Each one of the poor souls was tethered to the ground by at least one point of contact, sometimes several. Their bodies were fully corporeal. Their flesh torn and scarred, though no blood leaked from their wounds as if they'd already been drained and there was nothing left. Their anguished faces cried out in pain, yet barely a whisper of sound could be heard.

These were the ones Joe had warned us about. The ones who couldn't be helped.

I turned my head to beseech Joe to give us some kind of instruction. Surely there was *something* we could do. But the Savior of Man was on his knees as well. His hands were fisted in his hair, and water rolled from his eyes, raining tears to the ground.

The souls closest to us stretched as far as they could in their chains, even tearing at the flesh that kept them captive in a desperate attempt to get to Joe—to reach the water flowing from his eyes.

His face crumpled. I had never seen a look of such anguish on a person before. It was as if he himself was one of the bodies surrounding us, yet their despair and torment was piled upon him a hundredfold.

With wide eyes, I looked to Kaitlin, who watched Joe with a worry-filled gaze as well.

"Who are they?" she asked him in a whisper.

"They are the lost ones." His hands slid from his hair to clench at his sides, his gaze falling on the person closest to him—a woman, or what had once been a woman. He squeezed his eyes closed as if he could shut out the world around him.

When they opened again, renewed suffering washed over his features. Sweat trickled down his temples and mixed with the tears still dripping from his cheeks.

The . . . thing—for she barely resembled a human anymore, with only patches of hair and flesh sagging off her bones—reached out as far as her tethers would allow. A single word was desperately trying to escape her cracked and split lips, but the only sound that emerged was a scratchy whisper too quiet to hear.

Pleading arms stretched forward—even her bent and broken fingers strained to their limit. I stared at her mouth as she repeated the same thing over and over again.

Water.

The rest of the bodies around us appeared to be asking for the same thing. Some of them drew out their soundless plea in one long word, while others hysterically repeated it in a rapid loop.

If water was all they needed to find a moment of peace, that was something I could offer—at least to some of them. I reached for the canteen attached to my belt, my hands shaking, but Joe placed his hand on mine and stilled my movements.

He stood tall beside me, with dried tear tracks on his cheeks. "That's not what they need."

"What do you mean?" I swept my hand across the macabre crowd. "They're obviously asking for water. I still have some in my canteen. I can help some of them."

"No. That water will never quench their thirst."

I yanked my hands away from Joe. There must be something we could do. Something *he* could do. He was the Creator's Son after all. With a word, he could probably flood this place if he wanted.

I glared at him. Accusing him with my eyes if not with my

words. Yet Joe heard my unspoken words as clearly as those
that passed my lips.

"I cannot ease their suffering." His voice was hollow.

"But if you would just—"

"I can't!" he yelled back. "They have already rejected me, so
there is nothing I can do for them. I did not pick this fate for
them. My gift was freely given, yet they didn't claim it.
Whether from pride, fear, or disbelief, they didn't take it. We
did not want this fate for even one of them. Not one." He
punctuated his words with a slash of his arm.

"But if they had understood . . . "

Something in Joe's eyes made my words falter.

"Yes," he said, "if they had only understood."

He turned his back to me and swiftly set off through the sea
of bodies, not once looking back.

Kaitlin and I silently followed Joe through the sea of bodies for
what must have been hours. Occasionally one of the poor souls
would get ahold of our legs or ankles and we'd have to tug
ourselves free. The sensation of their stiff fingers grasping at
my body stayed with me long after I untangled myself from
their hold.

Joe moved forward at a relentless pace, seemingly
unaware—or uncaring—if Kaitlin and I still followed. If I
hadn't seen his initial reaction when entering this ring, I'd
consider him cold and compassionless. But the remembrance
of the agony etched on his face, his hands pulling at his hair as
he fell to his knees, was forever burned into my memory.

Out of all the horrors we'd witnessed in this realm, this was by far the worst. Forward progression was like walking through a mass grave of desiccated corpses that were not yet dead but were dying forever.

I tried to numb myself, but hopelessness for these people, or souls, or whatever they were, hung heavy in the air and saturated everything it touched. It seeped into my pores and settled unnervingly in my gut. Much more of this torture and I wasn't sure I'd be able to keep my sanity. I was already half mad. My brain wasn't built to process these monstrosities.

Yet to reach Logan, I was forced to press on. There was no going back. Joe had warned us this realm would challenge us physically and mentally, but I still hadn't been prepared.

Joe's raised hand was the only warning we received before he halted.

Kaitlin and I skidded to a stop, almost barreling right into him. Kaitlin's weary glance skated to me before landing back on Joe. Neither of us knew what was going on. Joe remained silent.

I forced my gaze to remain on our leader, not wanting to get another look at the scene around us.

"There's an illusion in front of us."

I jumped at Joe's unexpected voice. Even though I couldn't see his face, emotion clogged his words, making them slightly hard to understand. He cleared his throat before continuing. "Once I dispel it, we are going to be at the base of a mountain. Logan is hidden away in a cell deep within these caves."

Logan!

My heartbeat sped at the mere mention of his name. When was the last time I felt one of his phantom pains? It had been hours.

The absence of the discomfort should have been reassuring, but it alarmed me instead.

Why couldn't I feel anything from him? What did that mean? Had our connection somehow been severed?

"I can't feel him anymore! Why can't I feel him?" My frantic thoughts fed my hysterics. "Is he still all right? That was stupid, of course he's not all right. But what I mean is—"

"Audrey"—Joe turned and took my face between his hands and pinned me with his gaze—"he's passed out. That's the reason you aren't feeling his pain anymore."

I inhaled a breath of relief.

"It's a small mercy Satan hadn't intended to grant him, but it will help you keep your head for the moment."

I nodded and opened my mouth to ask what was ahead. I had no idea what we were going to see beyond this illusion he spoke of, but to have a fighting chance, we needed as much information as he was willing to give us.

Kaitlin stole the words right from my mouth. "So what should we be prepared for? I doubt we're going to be able to walk right in, find Logan, and then strut back out the front door with him. What's the plan?"

"Finding Logan might be easier than you expect. After all, he's only the bait." His gaze flicked to me and lingered. "It's getting him and ourselves out unscathed that's going to be the tricky part. Follow my lead, but stay on guard."

"What aren't you telling us? What is it Satan wants with me?" I crossed my arms over my chest. I was pretty sure Joe was being purposefully vague. Satan had attacked my family and then, when that failed, stolen Logan practically straight from my arms. Whatever the game was, there was a part scripted specifically for me. I just needed to figure out what it was. What could I possibly have that Satan wanted badly enough to go through all of this trouble?

Joe stared at me a moment longer before turning forward,

effectively evading my questions. "Let's get going."

Before I could press him further, he swiped his hand at the air in front of him, and the illusion dissolved.

There was no longer a never-ending sea of bodies in front of us. The face of a blackened mountain range jutted up high into the sky. Stealing a look behind me, the bodies had disappeared there as well. A cracked and barren desert landscape replaced that horrid nightmare.

"Did we just cross through another ring?"

"No. They're still there, just covered by the same illusion that blocked these mountains from sight. The land itself is poisoned with lies and deceit. You can't take everything you see at face value." Joe pointed toward the base of the mountains. "We'll enter there. The caves under this range form a labyrinth you'd never be able to navigate alone. Don't stray from me once we enter."

A chill skated up my spine even as sweat trickled down it.

This didn't feel right.

"Why aren't there demons at least guarding the entrance? They obviously know we're here. We fought them in the last ring."

"Like I said before, finding Logan is going to be the easy part. Satan wants us to find him. Logan was brought here for a reason. There's something he wants."

Yeah, me. "Then why even bother attacking us in the last ring? Why not just let us stroll right up to where he's been leading us this whole time?"

"Thinning the herd." Kaitlin's words were as hollow as her gaze.

Joe's stare shifted to her blank face, and he nodded. She was right. We'd lost half our group in that one attack.

"What's he truly after?" I asked Joe . . . again.

I thought Joe's gaze flicked over to me, but it happened so fast I couldn't be sure. When I blinked, he was staring back at the opening to the cave. "I'm sure it will be revealed soon enough."

There was something Joe knew that he wasn't sharing with me. I just didn't know what or why. Why wasn't he keeping me informed? Making wise snap judgments wasn't really my thing. I had an embarrassing history of rash decision making that if put to the test could very well bite us all in the butt.

I bit my tongue to keep from voicing my annoyance.

For probably the millionth time, I wished I just knew how everything was going to play out in advance.

Waiting stank worse than Hell.

I trudged along beside Joe and Kaitlin, just short of dragging my feet. Half of me wanted to break out in a run—we were closer to Logan than ever—but the other half was filled with trepidation. Joe's cryptic comments and pointed looks, losing half our team, and knowing that at some point in the near future there was more than a good chance I'd be facing off against Satan again had my anxiety—and adrenaline—levels spiked higher than ever before.

Best-case scenario, we find Logan quickly and are magically able to slip out of this demonic realm with him right under Satan's nose.

Worst-case scenario . . . well, I didn't even know what that could be. Was it possible to end up like those living corpses we'd just picked our way through? I wasn't sure. Maybe there was an even worse fate?

Heck, I already knew there was. I'd been privy to some of what Satan had inflicted on Logan. Even the echoes of his pain were debilitating at times. Kaitlin and I could end up in adjoining torture cells for all I knew. And Joe . . . I didn't know the rules of the game when it came to him. Was there anything Satan could do to harm him? If so, this would be the realm where Joe would be at his weakest. But as the Son of God, wasn't he untouchable?

We were completely off script now. There were things I didn't even know I didn't know.

My internal demon-radar was blaring as well, but not one of the disgusting creatures was in sight as we reached the cave's entrance and descended into darkness.

8

DESCENT

The moment we stepped foot into the cave, we were pitched into complete darkness. Considering the blinding desert terrain at our backs, there was no logic in the sudden change of light. Some of that brightness should have bled into the cave—eventually being swallowed by the darkness—but instead it was as if we walked into a windowless room with the lights off.

Did anything make sense here?

I pulled my sword from the sheath strapped to my back, and we used the blade's light to illuminate our path. Joe's strides were even, and he seemed to know exactly where he was going without the assistance of the blaze to direct him. Kaitlin and I, however, stumbled along the uneven and rocky ground like toddlers. Our shared struggle was my only consolation. There was something satisfying in not being the only bumbling one in our shrunken group.

I pressed a hand to my temple as we trekked forward and forced my eyes to remain open even as I ordered myself to ignore the crushing sense of being surrounded by demons. I trusted Joe to let us know if we were in any immediate danger, but there were definite lurkers nearby.

Besides the sickening sensations on a constant roll in my stomach, the heat was even more intense in the caves, furthering my discomfort. The hot breath puffing from my lungs was actually cooling to my skin. I imagined that with every step we descended closer to the Earth's molten lava core. Sweat didn't simply dot my skin but poured down it. At some point, I was going to run out of moisture to sacrifice to this forsaken realm. I itched to strip out of my body armor, but doing so would be the height of stupidity—and I was working on lowering my stupidity batting average.

A ghostly wail echoed from the tunnel in front of us, and Kaitlin and I lurched to a stop.

"Wh-what was that?" I managed to stammer through my dry lips.

"You don't want to know," Joe answered.

He was right. I didn't.

"So . . . are we there yet?"

Joe shot me a droll look over his shoulder. "Did you seriously just ask that?"

"What? It's a legit question. It's hot as you-know-what down here. We've got ghost noises added to the mix, demons are practically breathing down our necks—and quite frankly, I'm hangry and would like to get my . . . my Logan back."

Apparently a bad case of cranky pants, sweating worse than a sumo wrestler, and going a couple rounds in Hell made me extra salty.

I glanced at Kaitlin for some back-up, but she just gaped at me.

"What?"

She cupped her hand to the side of her face and whisper-yelled at me, "Did you really just talk to him like that?"

Crap. That was a teensy bit disrespectful . . . I mean, he was the Son of God. Wincing, I offered Joe an apologetic grimace. He swiped a hand down his face before rolling his eyes and gesturing for us to keep moving.

"Well, I'm still hangry," I whisper-yelled back to Kaitlin.

"I can hear you," Joe called back.

Whoops!

"I'll just pretend to get over that then."

"Good luck with that," Kaitlin piped in.

"Alrighty."

"In the meantime, give this a try." Joe pitched a small drawstring bag over his shoulder at me. I snatched the sack out of the air one handed without dropping my sword-turned-temporary-torch.

Score one for improved reflexes!

The bag was no larger than my fist. Tugging open the sides, I couldn't see anything, so I reached in and pulled out a loaf of bread.

What the what? How did that fit in there?

There was still some weight in the small pouch, so I awkwardly shoved my hand in and drew out some sort of dried piece of meat. Bringing it to my nose, I sniffed then used the very tip of my tongue to lick the supposed food. Its briny tang assaulted my taste buds.

Is this a dried piece of fish?

"Hey, what's in there?" Kaitlin asked.

"See for yourself." I handed her the bag.

A few minutes later, she chuckled before starting to munch on her own loaf and fish.

"Classic," she murmured.

"If it's not broke . . ." Joe mumbled in response.

As Kaitlin and I filled our empty stomachs, we continued through the winding tunnels. Whenever we'd hit a section where the tunnel branched, Joe always continued forward without breaking stride, as if he was as familiar with these underground pathways as the back of his hand.

Just as I finished my fifth piece of fish jerky—it sounded grosser than it actually was—Joe held up his hand, signaling us to stop.

Kaitlin lifted her eyebrows and shoulders to confirm she didn't know what the holdup was either.

"Quickly, this way." Joe tore off down the tunnel then banked to the left, disappearing from view.

Kaitlin and I scurried to keep up. I didn't even realize there was a small opening off to the side until we had almost passed it.

We ducked through and followed the sound of Joe's feet smacking against the stone.

He was suddenly standing in front of us, facing what appeared to be a wall. He'd stopped so fast I almost stabbed him with my sword.

"Whoa!" My feet slid forward on the gravelly floor as I came to a stop. My hand shaking at the close call, I sheathed my weapon. Joe had created another blue-and-red fireball that lit the area around us.

"In here," he ordered.

What? In where? He wants us to walk into the cave wall? Last time I checked, this wasn't Harry Potter.

Joe stepped forward, and the stone that had been there a moment before dissolved and revealed a crude doorway.

Didn't see that one coming.

An agony-filled groan struck my ears and my heart in the same moment. In the next instant, I was pushing my way past

Joe and Kaitlin without even realizing it.

Logan!

A lone figure sagged against the far wall. But something was wrong with the hair. Logan's wasn't black. He had a gorgeous blend of blond and honey browns.

Even matted and dirty, that hair was not attached to the person I was expecting. This wasn't Logan.

The prisoner's head slumped forward, effectively obscuring his face. He was trussed to the stone wall in exactly the same manner Logan had been in my visions. Logan or not, we couldn't just leave this poor soul here. He was obviously being tortured.

Rivets of dried blood ran from his shackled wrists down the arm suspended above his head. His chest was covered in so much blood that whatever color his shirt might have been before, it was now dyed completely red. There were gashes along his left rib cage, deep enough to see muscle and bone.

I swallowed back a gag.

He was wearing pants, which obscured any damage to his legs, but his bare feet looked like they'd been dipped in blood before they'd been rolled in black volcanic cinders.

Like a soft-serve ice cream cone dipped in chocolate and rolled in sprinkles.

Why did I have to think that?

Vomit rose in my throat, but I choked the chunks down before they made an uninvited entry into my mouth.

As if the world ran in slow motion, I took stock of the man and our surroundings in a matter of heartbeats. Even so, these were moments we didn't have.

"What do—"

Before I could finish asking what to do, Joe pushed past me. He tenderly took the man's head in his hands and tilted his battered face.

The gasp that echoed throughout the chamber was not mine, although it might as well have been.

The young man's face was covered in bruises and lacerations, and only one eye was partially opened, but there was no mistaking who he was: Morgan.

Kaitlin's eyes were wide and glassy. Her hands covered her mouth. I didn't know the history between the two of them—if there even was one—except that Morgan had fought off demons to make sure she was safe when we were outnumbered on Earth.

Perhaps just seeing a person so broken affected her?

Perhaps it was something more.

My insides swirled with confusion. Morgan was the enemy. A traitor. He'd threatened my family and betrayed not only Logan but the Creator as well. Yet the traitor in front of me also risked much to save Kaitlin and was obviously being horribly abused in this place.

I just . . . I just didn't know.

In the back of my mind, there was a clock tick-tick-ticking down every moment we didn't reach Logan. I both wanted to leave Morgan to the fate he'd chosen and stay to help. If I hadn't been staring at Morgan's beaten body with my own two eyes, the choice to bolt would have been easy. But seeing the devastation in front of me, I froze.

As I watched with one foot in the room and the other in the hall, ready to run in either direction at a moment's notice, Joe spoke quietly to Morgan. His one good eye opened to a slit, and he groaned. A trail of blood leaked out of his mouth when he tried to talk.

Joe laid a hand on Morgan's neck and supported his head. I was unable to see the look on Joe's face as he continued to speak quietly. Despite Morgan's ravished face, his expression crumpled at Joe's words as he weakly shook his head back and forth.

Not in defiance but as a broken person would.

"It's true." I heard a note of steel in Joe's voice as he forced Morgan's attention. "Not too late."

Tears leaked from Morgan's functioning eye.

Joe pressed a kiss to the crown of Morgan's head, not unlike a father would his son. He then placed a hand over each shackle holding Morgan upright, and they broke one at a time. His body slumped into Joe, and he took a step back to support the weight. Although conscious, Morgan couldn't stand unassisted.

Shoot, what are we going to do? We can't drag around his dead weight and search for Logan.

"Kaitlin"—Joe's voice was quiet yet strong—"come here."

Kaitlin rushed to Morgan's other side. He mustered enough strength to tilt his head in her direction.

"Extreme measures to get me in your arms, luv," he mumbled.

Oh my.

Was I more shocked by what he'd said or that he'd managed to speak at all?

Joe rolled his eyes and shook his head with a soft smile on his face.

As for Kaitlin . . . whoa. Her face puckered as if she tasted something particularly disgusting. For a moment, I thought she might take a swing at him. That was certainly a one-eighty mood flip.

"Kaitlin."

Her attention snapped back to Joe, ending the murderous stare directed at a partially conscious Morgan. "You're going to take him back, and Audrey and I are going to go ahead."

"What?" Kaitlin was already shaking her head. "No! I can't leave you guys down here alone. We already lost the rest of the group."

"Yes, you can, and you will. Audrey."

I jumped at my name.

"I want you to go ahead and continue checking these cells room by room. Logan is here somewhere. Go find him."

"Alone? But I can't even see the rooms."

"Don't use your sword to light your way. You won't need to, and it might attract attention. I'll catch up to you."

My feet might as well have been superglued to the floor.

"You can do this. Keep one hand on the right side of the wall. When your fingers touch an opening, the illusion will shatter. This was something you were always going to have to do. I'll be there soon. You can't get back without me, remember."

I nodded, half-numb. The fire in his eyes was telling me something I wasn't picking up.

"Audrey, I'm so sorry." Kaitlin was practically in tears now. "Please, find him. If he's anything like this . . ." Her voice caught. She didn't need to spell it out for me. Seeing Morgan in this shape she could now imagine what Logan was like.

Why was I still here?

"Right." I nodded. Resolute. "I'll see you soon."

"Soon," she repeated.

With a final glance at Kaitlin and Joe, I bolted into the darkness.

9

BROKEN

He was close. I suspected he was still unconscious because the phantom pain was missing, but every step I took brought me closer to Logan.

His nearness wasn't just something I hoped for. It was something I knew to be true.

His soul cried out to mine, latched on, and dragged me forward. I didn't even bother putting my hand against the wall as I blindly ran forward. His presence was like a lighthouse beckoning me home.

I was so close . . .

And then I was there.

I pitched my body against the stone, expecting resistance where there was none, and fell to the ground, sliding forward on my hip and shoulder. A single torch lit the room I'd busted in on. The light was secured to the stone wall to the left of the shackled man.

Logan's head hung forward much in the same way Morgan's had. His body was . . . I could hardly finish the thought. As if a wild beast had attacked, Logan's flesh was shredded in spots.

His once silky hair was no longer blond, now red-stained, matted clumps. His whole body sagged forward, suspended by the shackles on his wrists. One of his shoulders hung at an odd angle. It was dislocated.

My heart shattered.

His body jerked as if in reaction to my broken heart. Broken for his pain. Broken because I hadn't been there for him when he needed me. Broken because even now that I was present, I didn't know what to do.

His eyelids fluttered before his gaze locked onto mine. A garbled sound came out of his mouth.

With a cry, I scrambled to my feet and ran to where Logan hung from the wall. My hands fluttered around the air in front of him before I fisted them and brought them back to my sides. I couldn't chance touching him anywhere for fear I'd cause more pain.

A muffled noise came from his mouth again. His words were so faint and distorted I couldn't make them out.

"What can I do? How can I help?" I asked as I stared into Logan's pain-laced eyes while my body throbbed with the aftershocks of his agony.

His throat worked as if he were trying to swallow, but lack of moisture made it impossible. Chains scraped against the uneven stone wall as he tried to move one of his hands closer to me but failed.

"Don't cry." His weak words finally made sense.

I reached a hand and wiped at the tears I hadn't even realized were free flowing down my face.

Don't cry? I didn't know if I would ever stop.

This picture of him hanging here, beaten beyond what a normal person could endure, would forever remain burned into my psyche.

"I'm going to get you out of here. *We're* going to get you out. Joe is with me. Oh, or rather Jesus, but I know him as Joe too. Never mind, not important." Apparently I still rambled when I was nervous.

I brushed a clump of red-stained hair off his face so I could see his eyes and know that he understood what I was saying. His beautiful blue eyes, so filled with pain yet also with longing and tenderness for me.

This man was truly amazing. He was the injured one, yet he was desperate to offer me comfort in any way he could.

Forget my insecurities and hang-ups. I loved him. We were getting out of here, and I was going to shout that word at him as soon as we were safe.

I threw a glance over my shoulder. Where was Joe? We needed to leave this awful place, like five minutes ago.

No sounds of pounding feet on the stone floor of the hallway reached my ears, which made me both relieved and nervous.

Focus, girl. One thing at a time. Get Logan out of those shackles. Then worry about the next step in this super messed up rescue attempt.

Focusing on the chains that held Logan suspended, and the manacles secured around his wrists and ankles, I quickly realized I wasn't going to be able to use strength to pull him free. If that were possible, he would have already freed himself. His dislocated shoulder said as much. The echoes of his injury shoot down my arm.

Reaching behind me, I pulled my sword from its sheath. The warmth from its flames was different than the oppressive heat of Hell. This fire wasn't stifling; this blaze was filled with life.

"Time to see what damage some holy flames can do to these chains," I muttered to myself.

Logan had slumped forward once again. He'd either passed out or was close to it. I didn't want him to fall on me while his feet were still bound, so I started on the restraints down there first. "Here goes nothing."

I swung my blade like a golf club, aiming so the sharp edge would break the chain from his ankle. We could worry about getting the actual manacles off later. Right now I just needed to get him off the wall.

At the point of contact, the chain shattered, freeing his left leg. I really wanted to do a victory dance, but there wasn't time for that.

This was going to work.

I took a swing at the chain attached to his other leg, and that fell away with ease too.

Almost there. Almost free.

Chewing my lip in indecision, I took a precious moment to consider my next step. When I broke the chains holding him up, he was going to fall forward, so I needed to be careful. Whatever way I sliced, it wasn't going to be a pleasant experience for Logan. But if I could somehow keep him from crashing to the ground, that would have to help a little.

Just as I brought my sword up to hack at the first chain attached to his wrists, a sharp sound caused me to whirl around toward the entrance of the cell.

Alrik stood in the entrance, leaning against the wall. He clapped—slowly, mockingly.

I clenched my sword hilt, itching to lash out.

"You," I spat at him.

His eyebrow arched, and his hands finally stopped moving.

"This is touching." A cocky smile rode his lips. "I see you

finally came to your senses and noticed what was right before you the whole time. He makes a pretty damsel in distress, doesn't he? Well, at least he did before Satan turned him into a bloody pulp."

The bones in my hand cracked as I gripped my sword even tighter.

"I gotta be honest, little Aud, I didn't think you'd make it this far. I may even be a bit impressed."

"Do not call me that," I growled. "You are the worst kind of scum this universe ever spit up."

He tsked. "Sticks and stones, little Aud, sticks and stones."

If it didn't mean leaving Logan exposed, I would have attacked Alrik. Human or not, I was confident my sword would inflict damage on his blackened soul.

"He was your friend," I said.

"Was he?"

"It couldn't have all been a lie."

He lifted a shoulder. "Some of us are just more convincing than others. You, my dear, have a horrible poker face." He tilted his head, his smile widening. "Oh, I am getting you worked up, aren't I? A whole head full of black-and-red hair doesn't lie."

I couldn't care less what color my hair was right now let alone what it broadcasted to him. I had a super good reason to be angry and wasn't trying in the least to hide it.

"When I get Logan to safety, I'm going to make sure you suffer in every way he did . . . tenfold."

Alrik laughed at me—laughed until tears streamed down his face. He ran a hand across his eyes to clear them before responding. "Hon, when this is all over, you're going to be rocking in a corner, a drooling puddle of nothing."

His attitude and words stoked the coals of anger in my soul.

How long had he been spying on all of us, reporting back to his real master? How long had he been our true betrayer?

I asked. "How long?"

He didn't pretend to misunderstand me. "From the very beginning, of course. I have a few neat tricks up my sleeves that none of you knew about."

He lifted a hand in front of his face, and before my eyes, it transformed into a familiar ominous mist before solidifying back into a hand.

I only just kept myself from gasping. That was the same mist that had chased me through the forest when I'd tried to follow Logan. Even then, I'd known something about that fog was off, but I'd been the only one to see it. Alrik had been spying on us for ages.

"That's right. I see the hamster finally turning the wheels in your head. This handy skill let me slip in and out of lots of interesting places."

I understood where he'd come by the ability. When souls chose darkness, they developed a new power—one given to them not by the Creator but by Satan. Morgan had been able to manipulate shadows. Logan thought his electricity came from the same place, but I had my doubts. Alrik's ability reminded me of the grotesque substance that had poured out of the demons' mouths during the battle at my family's home. That fight was only days ago but felt like years for all that had happened since.

"Why?" My cool had long ago been lost, but the volume of my voice finally matched the boiling magma churning in my gut. That one word echoed off the chamber walls. "Why would you do this? Why would you turn yourself into this . . . this monster?"

And for what?

What could possibly be worth not only betraying the people who cared about Alrik but also risking the fate of his soul? What could be so important that he'd knowingly ban himself from our realm, let alone the Creator's love?

Alrik had to know that once he'd crossed that line and lured Logan into a position to be captured and taken to Hell, he'd be exposed for the traitor he was.

The betrayer's face hardened, and his joking demeanor disappeared. "That," he said, "is none of your business."

He shoved off the side of the wall and straightened to his full impressive height. I had to tilt my chin up to keep holding his gaze, and that annoyed me.

The sense of another presence nearby slid over my skin like the scales of a snake, forcing an involuntary shudder.

"Time's up, little Aud, the boss is here. A bit of advice: Play nice and just agree to his terms. It will be easier on everyone that way." He looked pointedly at Logan before stepping to the side.

I swallowed hard as Satan himself walked right into the cell, wearing his fraudulent angelic skin. A pretty covering to conceal the twisted form of the evil being inside.

At his arrival, I wanted to both scream in frustration and cower in fear. I should have just stabbed Alrik and figured out a way to haul Logan out of here when I had a chance.

Where is Joe?

I was in no way prepared to face Satan with an unconscious hunter pinned to the wall behind me. An unconscious hunter I loved. Joe was the powerhouse. I was simply the semi-hysterical human trying to get her man back, and more than a little scared to admit the lengths to which I would go to protect Logan. Breaking some of the Hugo-approved rules was a definite possibility.

I needed backup, STAT.

"Sorry I missed the reunion." A smirk curved Satan's lips. "It would have been entertaining to watch." He examined one of his hands, turning it this way and that at an unhurried pace. Where a human's nails should have been, sharpened claws gleamed and dripped red fluid to the ground. "But as you can see, I was busy elsewhere. I'm looking forward to picking up where I left off."

No doubt he was trying to intimidate me. I'm not too proud to admit that it was working. My only hope was that my face didn't betray my fears.

I lifted my sword higher so the flames danced blue between us, the blade's holy fire my only comfort.

The last time we'd had a physical showdown, I ended up feeling like a squeezed tube of toothpaste, but I was ready this time. If I had to hack through him and every other forsaken creature in this grotesque realm to get Logan to safety, then that's what I would do. I braced myself for the hardest fight of my life.

"Don't point that at me like you intend to use it." Satan flicked his wrist, and an unseen force tried to bat my weapon away.

I held firm. His eye sockets narrowed, and his jaw worked back and forth.

"Well, it must be time to have some fun with your boy-toy. Wakey-wakey, sleeping beauty."

Satan lifted a clawed hand and raked it through the air in front of him. Logan's pain-filled yell threw me off. I cast a glance over my shoulder to see a very conscious Logan with a fresh set of tears on his chest, blood running freely from the injury. How?

I almost dropped my weapon as I swung around to face

him. With tears running down my face, I tried to use the remaining rags hanging off his body to staunch the flow of blood, but I only managed to coat my glove-covered hands in it instead.

Logan grunted, and I looked up to see a fresh slice appear on his cheek. He sealed his jaw and gritted his teeth as he fought to keep from shouting in pain.

I snapped like a rubber band. With a banshee cry, I used my sword to break the remaining chains holding him captive. A moan slipped past Logan's lips as his battered body slammed into mine, forcing me to take a step back. I lowered him to the floor then tensed to deal with the threat behind me. Satan and Alrik first. Then I'd drag Logan out of this place, fighting off demons with one arm if I had to.

Bring it.

The righteous anger building inside me was a breath away from shooting forth like steam from a teapot. But before I could spin around to face my foes, a warm, wet hand landed softly on my cheek. I halted.

"Shouldn't . . . have . . . come." Logan's voice was weak but clear. His eyelids were heavy and he blinked slowly, battling to remain conscious.

"I will always fight for you." I stared intently into his eyes, willing him to absorb my words. "Always. Just like you would for me."

A strange wheezing sound started in his chest. With a gasp I leaned forward. Was he having trouble breathing?

No.

He was laughing.

"Took you . . . long enough," he got out between breaths.

"Are you kidding me right now? You're going to give me crap at a time like this?"

"Always." His eyes slipped shut as he succumbed to his body's demands.

Our audience had been suspiciously quiet.

"I hear that was a long time coming," Satan said conversationally to Alrik.

I jerked my gaze over my shoulder.

Alrik dipped his head. "Indeed."

With one look at the smirk on Satan's face, my frustration and anger increased and my fear diminished. I was sick of this twisted being messing with my life . . . or rather my afterlife . . . and the people I cared about.

I lifted my chin as well as my sword. The blaze turned entirely blue. The openings where Satan's eyes should have been narrowed slightly.

"You're not hurting him anymore," I said.

His head cocked in that creepy bird-like manner of his and sent a slimy shiver down my spine. Alrik stayed a silent statue behind him, acting as a sentry for the door.

"It's so . . . interesting, that you think you have control over that."

I lifted my sword higher to act as an unspoken reminder. This sword held the power of the Holy Spirit. This sword he was afraid of, even if his pride would never allow him to admit it. This sword—wait, what?

He stepped closer to it without a lick of apprehension in his movements. This shouldn't happen.

His odd behavior threw me off my game. He came within inches of the flames and stopped to inspect the blade. His head tilted one way and then another as though appraising the weapon rather than fearing it.

I watched, transfixed, as he reached a claw-tipped finger out and ran it through the blue blaze. The flesh on his finger bubbled, but he simply considered it with a tilt of his head and a slight narrowing of his eye sockets.

"Hey." I pulled the sword back and took a fighting stance, my voice shrill. "Don't touch that."

"That sword, my ugly sheep"—he pointed the same clawed finger at my weapon—"is the whole reason you and your bonded are even in my realm. The whole reason I sent my demons to attack your family. The whole reason for all your pain"—he ticked his chin toward Logan—"and a good deal of his pain as well. Had you been willing to listen the last time we stood face to face, you could have prevented your boyfriend from being turned into a bloody hunk of flesh."

Guilt nipped at my gut, but I pushed the shame away. This was the Father of Lies; I couldn't take anything he said as truth.

"You want my sword?"

"In a way."

"But it won't work for you," I blurted. "Didn't Knuckle-Head behind you report on that?"

A bubble of near hysterics threatened to burst free from my chest. If all of this pain and suffering was due to a misconception, I was seriously going to lose it.

"I won't be using the sword . . . You will." Satan's lip curled.

I blinked. Twice.

"You *want* me to stab you?"

Satan blew out a breath of air and turned slightly to Alrik. "She is exceedingly stupid, isn't she?"

Alrik simply tipped his head in agreement. He'd never been so quiet before. It gave me the creeps.

"That insult might have bothered me if it came from anyone other than you."

Satan lifted an eyebrow above those creepy empty eye sockets.

"And *you're* stupid." I couldn't believe the word vomit coming out of my mouth.

Gosh, what was I, five?

If Satan had eyes, I think he might have rolled them at me. Can't say I blamed him for that last comment. "You won't be stabbing me, you idiot sheep. You'll be using that blade to cut through this." He reached behind him and roughly jerked something forward. He pulled it with such violence that sparks shot from the rough ground where it grated.

It took a moment for my eyes to adjust to what I was seeing. Clenched in his fist was a semi-transparent chain. Each link at least the size of my fist. Rather than metal, it appeared to be made of black smoke encased in a transparent glass-like material—though clearly much stronger than glass. How long had he been dragging that thing behind him?

My eyes widened. What exactly was I looking at?

"What is that?" I stammered.

"That, Daughter of Eve, is the chain that binds me to this and the earthly realm. And you are going to be the one to break it. Then I will be free, and you will be one of mine."

10

CURSED

The tip of my sword shook, but not from fatigue. "Yours?"

"Yes, my little lamb. The one who frees me, willingly or not, from these chains will be cursed to become one of my children, bound to me for eternity. The rules were established by the Creator Himself. But your beloved Logan will be free."

He tilted his head toward the still form behind me. "Well, what's left of him at least. I'll even grant you some time with him before I come to collect what is rightfully mine."

The dam keeping my hysterics on lock-down burst. I didn't scream or cry—I laughed. It sounded maniacal even to my own ears, wild and uncontrollable.

The creature in front of me was beyond insane. He was delusional. I wasn't going to help him. I would never help him.

An unearthly growl burst from Satan and vibrated throughout the small chamber where we stood, causing dirt and small stones to rain down on us. His outburst snapped me out of my hysteria and reminded me exactly where I was. Standing in a cell, deep within the earth, with Satan, a traitor, and the man I loved.

Satan grabbed the smoke-wrapped, transparent chain and chucked it toward me. It landed dangerously close to my feet. I had no idea where it attached to him, and I wasn't going to ask. I flicked my gaze down to what, according to him, was the only thing keeping him out of the heavenly realm, and then back to his face.

"Break it!" he roared.

For all Satan had done to me, this was the first time he raised his voice in my presence. Something inside begged me to search for cover. Evil-soaked power permeated the very air we breathed in the aftermath of his furious bellow.

I held my ground, standing firm and tall in front of Logan as if my fragile flesh and bone could protect his broken body.

"No." My voice was quiet but firm.

"My patience has run its course. You will do this, or I will end him." Satan brought a taloned hand up in front of his face and slowly closed each digit into a fist.

At first I was confused . . . until I heard Logan in agony behind me. His cries of pain echoed off the walls like the sounds of a dying animal, and fresh second-hand pain sliced across my chest.

I dropped my sword, the flame instantly extinguishing, and fell to my knees at Logan's side. He thrashed on the blood-soaked ground. I moved my hands frantically over his body, trying to find an uninjured spot to touch to lessen his convulsions.

Suddenly Logan's back arched, and all the muscles in his body contracted. His fingers contorted and bent like claws. The arch in his back was so severe that only his shoulders and part of his legs touched the ground. His eyes were squeezed shut and his mouth open in a silent scream—as if the horrors being done to his body were so atrocious that they couldn't be verbalized.

And then a gurgling noise started deep in his chest. The cough that worked its way up his throat was wet and splattered blood on my face when it finally escaped.

My entire being vibrated with the watered-down version of his agony. With black-dotted vision, I battled my body's defense mechanism to shut down in the face of the painful onslaught. Gritting my teeth, I forced myself through the invasion and willed my body to obey my commands.

"Stop it!" I screamed over my shoulder. "What are you doing?"

"Ending him." Satan's cold demeanor was once again in place.

"You can't do that!" I yelled, but Satan's depthless gaze was trained on Logan and not on me. A steady flow of blood bubbled out of Logan's mouth and dribbled down his cheek.

I spotted Alrik behind the evil being. There was a horror in his eyes that was surely reflected in my own.

"Do something!" I yelled to him, but when the words left my mouth, a mask of fake detachment slid over Alrik's features. I'd find no help there.

"You can't do this," I reiterated. "He is a Child of God! He's not yours to end!" The shriek in my voice shredded my vocal cords. I was coming undone in a way I never had before.

But as quickly as it started, it ended. Satan opened his fist, and Logan's body unclenched and fell unconscious in a pool of his own blood. Relief flooded my limbs as well, and I was able to unclench my muscles.

My tears fell unfettered onto Logan's prone form. I didn't even try to stop them. The shock of seeing him so destroyed caused my hands to tremble.

I didn't know what to do.

I didn't know how to comfort him.

I didn't know how to fix him.

Why hadn't I tried to stop this? Instead I just threw insults at Satan and made it worse.

"Oh God, what have I done?" The whispered words of desperation slipped unknowingly out my mouth.

The deep chuckle behind me was chilling. "You think He hears you? You think He actually cares?"

I must have verbalized my plea.

"Yes," I whispered, not bothering to turn to the monster behind me.

"He doesn't. If He did, He would have stopped me. But look what I've done to your beloved."

"You can't take him. He's not yours." My whispered words were barely a breath leaving my mouth.

"I know this game better than you do. I can, and I will." Satan's voice was so close his hot breath washed over my neck. He brought his clawed hand in front of my face, taunting me. My vision blurred through a veil of tears.

Ever so slowly, he closed his hand again.

I watched in horror as Logan's battered body responded as if the evil being was squeezing his heart of flesh. A spasm and crushing pain pierced me deep inside.

With a crazed scream I spun, whipping my sword off the ground. My hands gripped the pommel tight enough to hurt as I brought the holy weapon behind my head and used all my strength to arch it downward.

The flames flashed blue before my face as the fiery blur headed toward its target—Satan's head.

But with a clang that echoed throughout the chamber, the blade connected with the chain that bound Satan instead.

The force of the impact threw me back into the stone wall. My head smacked against the hardness, and my vision winked in and out before clearing.

I shook my head to clear the fuzziness. Big mistake. My brain felt like a giant bruise rolling around in my skull. Every movement hurt.

Logan? My sword?

I pushed through the pain and realized my legs were sprawled over Logan's injured body. I let out a noise of distress and as gently and quickly as possible pulled myself off him.

Next I noticed my sword lying in the dirt to my left, the blade broken in two.

I grabbed the handle and gasped when nothing happened. No fire sprang to life.

Had the sword itself rejected me?

What had I done?

The edge of my sword had been intended for Satan's skull, not his chains. Striking his bonds had been an accident.

"No!" His angry roar shook the chamber.

I put a hand against the wall to keep my balance. What was happening?

Satan stood in the middle of the room, his back to me, the leathery shadow of his wings blocking my view of whatever he was holding in front of him.

I blinked, and he was in my face. His contorted in rage as his angelic mask melted away. Bits of charred flesh peeked out from holes in the porcelain skin he hid behind.

"Strike it again," he ordered with a growl. Red dots lit the middle of his eye sockets—the beast inside peeking out.

Several heartbeats passed before I even understood what he was trying to command me do.

He held the chain that I had struck.

Held it *intact.*

The blow hadn't worked. But my sword no longer wielded holy fire. Was my soul condemned, or had I somehow been saved?

Logan lay on the ground between us. Satan's hate-consumed face filled my vision. Without breaking eye contact, I brought my sword up between us.

"I can't. The flame is gone."

Satan didn't utter a word, but the very ground beneath us began to shake.

And it didn't stop.

A fissure appeared in the ground by Logan's head. I gasped and took a step back as the crack climbed up the wall to my right. Large rocks began to fall from the ceiling. I released my broken sword and threw my body over Logan's, grunting when chunks of debris pounded my back.

"Stop!" I screamed.

And suddenly, it did.

I looked up. Through the debris still floating in the air, Satan stood in the middle of the room, looking at the chain in his hands and muttering to himself. I heard only snatches of his nonsensical ramblings—"Must be," "blood," and "key."

Where was Joe? We needed our ride out of here, like yesterday. I didn't know what the ramifications of my rash act would be, but I was supremely glad Satan's trick hadn't worked. Even if it had cost me my weapon. The real question was what else had it cost me?

That was a concern for another time. Now was my opportunity to get Logan out of the room while Satan was lost in his own insanity. I inched my fingers under Logan's arms— ignoring his dislocated shoulder—prepared to drag him out.

"Blood." The melodically vile voice broke the silence.

"What?" I crouched in a protective stance over Logan's head.

"You need to coat the blade with The Lamb's blood."

I didn't even try to pretend I misunderstood what he was saying. The thought was so horrific, words thoughtlessly tumbled from my mouth. "Are you insane?"

"That question is idiotic . . . even coming from you." Satan's calm demeanor was back, but the melted patches on his face revealed his true nature.

"It was rhetorical," I spat back. "Of course you're insane. Only an insane being would expect me to stab the Son of God."

"The fire didn't work. So the key must be in the blood instead."

I didn't answer. I shook my head so violently that my hair slapped my face.

"It's the only way. And when you do this, you will be one of mine. Your soul will forever be covered in blackness. You will become the betrayer."

"I'm not doing anything you want me to do."

"Oh, yes you are." The calm confidence in the smile that split his grotesque face made my stomach churn as if snakes were wiggling inside and wanted out.

"I already said . . ."

He brought his hand up, fingers spread wide and itching to curve inward.

Threat received, I cut off my words.

"You find him and run him through with that blade of yours. You come back here and cut the chain, and I'll send you and what's left of him"—he indicated Logan with a jerk of the chin—"back. You will have time to say your goodbyes before I claim you. It's more than fair."

My mouth opened and closed. I didn't even know how to

answer. Of course I wasn't going to stab Joe. That wasn't an option. Apparently I took too long to respond because Satan's fingers started bending inward.

"No!" I held a hand out in a pathetic attempt to stop him. "No. Take me instead. Let Logan go, and keep me down here."

"Our bargaining period is long over. You passed that up when we conversed on Earth. You either do what I want, or you both—"

I let out another banshee scream and rushed Satan with what was left of my weapon. He easily sidestepped, and I crashed into another rough wall.

I spun. "I. Will. Gut. You." *Was that my voice?*

"Oh, I highly doubt that."

I saw red as I ran at him again, focusing on the exposed parts of his face. The real beast behind the façade. With a soul-shredding scream, I was just about to impale the monster when I was jolted to a stop. My arms were forced to my sides and caught in a bone-crushing grip.

I struggled like a wild beast against the hold. Kicking, grunting, and even trying to bite whoever, or whatever, was holding me back.

A voice at my ear stopped me. "I'd do what he says, Little Aud. It's the best deal you're going to get today."

Alrik. Liar. Coward. Betrayer.

I'd forgotten about him. A fresh ball of rage consumed me, and I thrust my elbows back into his gut, forcing the air from his lungs. A hot whoosh of breath coated my exposed neck and accompanied a surprised grunt of pain.

He was the one I would end.

I spun and blindly lunged forward with the jagged end of my sword, right into the space where Alrik's blackened heart should have been. Before I could enjoy the satisfying feeling of shoving my weapon into his body, he dissolved into a poof of mist.

My forward momentum continued, and my sword struck something else. I came to an abrupt stop. I pulled my weapon back through the dissipating cloud of mist—to the sickening sound of suction.

My hand shook when I saw the red liquid that coated the entirety of the jagged blade.

I snapped my head up and stared into the eyes of my friend.

11

BETRAYER

NO! No, no, no! This couldn't be happening.

Joe squinted in pain, and he brought his hand to the wound in his chest. His blood flowed over his fingers and down his front to drip onto the dry dirt. The ground sizzled wherever his blood touched, slurping up the life-giving substance and bubbling its thanks.

The sword slipped from my fingers. My pounding heart was so loud it drowned out the rest of the world.

Tha-thump, tha-thump, tha-thump.

Joe's mouth moved. The words didn't register. They were buried under layers of shock and the crazy erratic beating of my heart.

What have I done?

I fell to my knees, overcome with emotion as I watched Joe struggle for breath in front of me. Because of what I had done to him.

Satan hadn't driven that blade into his chest. Alrik hadn't done it. I had.

I stabbed the one being who loved me unconditionally.

Who had traveled through a realm filled with fire and brimstone and horrors—things I was never going to forget—all to save the other half of my heart.

He'd been with me every step of the way, and in repayment, I made him bleed.

I had become the betrayer.

My eyes were glued to his bloody wound.

And then, by some miracle, his words penetrated the fog that weighed down my senses.

"Audrey, look at me." His words carried such love my heart broke all over again.

I blinked and shook my head. My vision blurred and filled with crimson. I didn't need to touch my cheek to know my face was coated with tears.

"You have already been—"

A blast of power from behind thrust me forward onto the unforgiving ground. My mouth filled with dirt and grit. Stones pelted my body as a shockwave of energy washed over me. I covered my head with my arms. The pressure was unrelenting and seemingly unending. Despite my efforts, I remained flattened against the earth.

I spotted Joe through the maelstrom of debris whirling around the cell. His eyes were focused on something beyond me. They held a mixture of sadness and disgust. He was propped against the craggy wall; the only part of him affected by the blast was the hair whipping around his head.

And then the chaos stopped.

Pushing to my feet in one fluid motion, I whirled around, steeling myself to face the source of the pandemonium. Bending an arm behind me, I reached for a blade that was no longer there.

I didn't immediately recognize the beast as Satan. He stood

tall, his body in some half-transformed state. Flesh-like skin only splattered his body now. Spikes jutted out from the joints in his arms and hands, some as long as six inches.

He rolled his shoulders, and his leather-and-smoke wings stretched as far as possible in the confined space.

In his right hand, he held what was left of my weapon and its blood-drenched blade; at his feet, lay the shattered pieces of the glass-like chain.

He was free.

I pressed a hand to my stomach to stop its revolt and only just managed to keep myself from falling to my knees.

Satan's head swiveled in my direction in a very inhuman manner. Fluid and fast. Not a single part of his body had moved except his head. It reminded me of an owl, and in my overwhelmed state, I vaguely wondered if he could perform a 360-degree turn. Would he vomit green bile next?

"Perfect, my child," he said, and his voice bounced painfully in my head. "You did well holding up your end of our bargain."

No, there had been no bargain. I hadn't agreed to any of this.

I shook my head. "No—"

"Oh yes. This"—a claw-like hand gestured to the broken binding on the ground—"couldn't have happened without you. No need to be modest, my dear."

He distorted the truth. It was an accident. Not a premeditated action.

But in the end, Joe had bled and Satan was free, so did it even matter? Willingly or unwillingly, I had been the instrument used to release Evil Incarnate—and according to what he said before, I now belonged to him.

The snakes in my gut writhed and snapped their jaws. I was

going to be sick.

Then Satan swept his wing out of the way, revealing Logan's motionless body.

A fresh wave of panic washed over me. Logan's features, at least what wasn't covered in blood and gore, were pasty white. The rise and fall of his chest was imperceptible.

Since we were already dead, I didn't know what his death-like vitals meant, but they frightened me nonetheless.

"I believe per the conditions of our deal this now belongs to you; at least, what's left of it."

Without thought, I rushed to Logan's side. Practically sliding into his body, I fell to my knees to be closer to him.

Was he breathing? His skin was that of a chalky vampire. Dirt and grime from the floor was mixed into every wound. Some seeped blood, and others were crusted over.

He was bleeding. That meant his heart was still pumping . . . right? I held tight to that unverified hope. He couldn't truly be gone.

"And you," Satan spat.

I jerked my head up, but he wasn't speaking to me. He was angled toward Joe, who was still bleeding freely from the wound I'd inflicted. "In your supreme arrogance, you never thought I'd figure out how to free myself from your chains?"

Joe took a weary step forward. His gaze was locked on Logan and me, and Satan's taunts went unanswered. The enemy did nothing to stop Joe's advance. His eyes lightened when he reached us, and he lifted a hand to wipe the wetness from my face, but the warmth of Joe's freshly spilled blood coated my cheeks in his hand's wake.

Satan continued to mock Joe, throwing words at him like stones. But whatever was said garbled and bounced off me as I looked into the eyes of my truest friend.

Blood leaked from the corner of his mouth. Accidental or not, I'd done a horrible thing. But Joe had to be all right. There wasn't a force in any realm that could take him out. He was literally the Creator of all, right?

Satan's verbal jabs continued . . . until Joe roared, "Enough!"

I jolted. Joe spared a glance over his shoulder at the dark being. "Go do what you have been waiting to do."

Satan's eye sockets narrowed, and his eyebrows pinched. His gloating had been interrupted and ignored. Served him right.

His attention snapped to me.

"I'll be seeing you soon," he promised. His body coiled before he sprang straight up, punching through the layers of stone that trapped us. Rocks rained down on our bodies in the wake of his departure. I once again threw myself over Logan's defenseless form. We'd be buried in no time.

Where was Joe? I searched for him—and breathed a sigh of relief. He was right beside me.

"Fear not. You'll both be returned to your realm shortly."

"Joe," I coughed, knowing our time here was short. "I didn't mean—or rather I didn't know—"

He laid a gentle hand on my cheek. "I know. Let's go home."

Home.

I couldn't help thinking that the heavenly realm might not be my home for much longer if Satan made good on his threat. How much time did I have before I was dragged back to this pit of death and decay?

I nodded, but mid-bob, something struck my head, and my vision swam. I blinked, and my vision was filled with Joe's light-brown eyes before I was swallowed by black nothingness.

I sat up with a gasp and a sob. I was blind, drowning in blackness.

Wait, no, I was just in an unlit room. The muted outline of objects started to appear as my eyes adjusted to the darkness.

Breathing was like trying to take in air through a straw. There wasn't enough.

My heart pounded so hard I could feel it without laying a hand on my chest.

Where am I? Where are the lights?

As soon as the thought flitted through my mind, brightness flooded the room. My eyelids fluttered at the sudden change.

The Healing Center.

That's where I had to be. I recognized the chairs against the white walls as well as the small bed I was lying in. I brought a hand to my face and pushed my grimy hair behind my ear.

Everything came back with crashing clarity.

Logan's and Alrik's disappearance.

Our journey through Hell.

Romona, Kevin . . . fighting with me and injured.

Discovering Morgan.

Then Logan. Finding his broken and bleeding body chained to the wall.

My sword shattering when I tried to attack Satan.

And then the unthinkable. The blood I'd spilled that freed Satan from his chains and cursed my soul in the process. I didn't want to believe Satan, but how could I spill holy blood and not be cursed?

I put my face in my hands, but my tears had all been spent.

How long did I have with my friends before I'd be dragged to Hell for my sins? I'd sold my soul to Satan the moment I'd unknowingly plunged that sword into Joe's chest.

A wail lodged itself in my throat. If only I'd kept my head and hadn't gone after Alrik.

Regret was a bitter pill. Regret for the things I wish I'd done differently, and regret for the things I'd never get to experience.

Logan.

I'd done what I set out to do. I'd returned him to our realm. He would be safe here. That was a small consolation considering what I'd done to bring him back.

I'd been the tool that broke Satan free from the leash that had held him captive for eons. And to do so, I'd drawn holy blood.

My soul was now surely a shriveled black pit.

Would I end up like those poor souls tethered to the ground, begging for a drop of moisture? Or worse, would I somehow be forced to work against my loved ones?

No. I'd never do that.

There was nothing Satan could do to make me fight against the living, or against heavenly powers. I'd rather end up a wasted shell of a person in Hell for eternity.

Which was a real possibility at the moment.

I sucked in a deep breath. At least my lungs finally worked properly.

How much did people know? Did they realize Satan was free? Had Joe returned? Was it possible that he'd sent Logan and me back and not had enough strength to return as well?

Questions swam and looped in my head like darting fish. Every time my mind reached out to catch one, it zipped out of reach while I was distracted by another.

I drew my knees up and rocked back and forth in an unconscious effort to soothe myself. Too much had happened in the last few days—heck the last few hours—for me to process.

But one thing I knew with absolute certainty: What I'd done was too horrific to ever ask for forgiveness, let alone receive it.

If Satan didn't haul me back to the pit, the Creator would eventually cast me there Himself. I couldn't even turn to Him for help—which was what my soul was crying to do—because He was the one I'd betrayed.

Captivity to Satan was what I deserved for my actions. Actions that had ramifications not only for myself but for all mankind—both dead and alive.

Now freed from his tethers, it would only be a matter of time before Satan stormed this realm. Why else would he have fought and schemed to be free from his bondage? This had to be the one place his chains had forbidden him from entering.

He was right: I didn't know, didn't understand the rules. Was he now an unleashed beast with the freedom to roam where he pleased?

And should I out myself as a betrayer or hide what I'd done?

"Oh thank goodness you're back. We've all been so worried."

I snapped my head up and stopped my crazed rocking. Kaitlin rushed to my bed and pulled me into a fierce hug. All things considered, I was in pretty good physical health.

It was almost annoying. The Healing Center and I had a tumultuous relationship at best.

"How is—" I choked on my words, my face muffled against Kaitlin's shoulder. So many of my friends had been hurt, and I couldn't even find the inner strength to ask about them.

Kaitlin pulled away and looked into my watery eyes. "Everyone is fine. They're all going to be all right, Audrey. They are all safe. And it's because of you."

No, I thought, *no one will be safe. And that is all because of me.*

12

KINDRED

Kaitlin left to find a change of clothes and grab me some water, but I slipped out of the room before she returned.

Once again, I stared at the wrong mop of hair. Black hair that should have been sun-streaked blond. Why my feet had taken me to this particular room, I wasn't quite sure. But here I was, standing at the foot of Morgan's bed, watching his sleeping form like a creeper, and I couldn't puzzle out why.

Or maybe I just didn't want to.

"Should I be flattered?" Guess he wasn't asleep. His usually smooth accented voice was full of gravel and grit. Raw as if his vocal cords had been stripped bare. Maybe they had been.

Old me would have startled at his voice, but new me felt dead inside. New me no longer felt whole.

When I didn't immediately rise to the bait, Morgan cracked an eye open. The other was still swollen shut but looked considerably better than the last time we met. The swelling had gone down, and the blood, both dried and fresh, had been washed from his skin. With all the stitches patching his face back together, he looked like Frankenstein's monster—but given time, the evidence of what had been done to him would fade to nothing. That was if he could work through the emotional damage that had been inflicted. If not, he might carry those scars for the entire realm to see.

Through my numbness, I wasn't sure if I even cared. Maybe this was what it felt like to be soulless?

With effort, Morgan shifted on his bed, and the smirk that was flirting with the corners of his mouth dropped suddenly as his good eye took me in. Did I have a scarlet letter pinned to my chest only other betrayers could see? The change in his demeanor told me he'd picked up on something Kaitlin hadn't. I didn't have to wait long to find out what.

"I know that look." His voice might have been soft if his throat wasn't so damaged. I resented that.

"What look?" I went for neutral but heard the accent of defense in my tone.

"What did you do?"

"I got my friends back."

"How?"

"By doing what was necessary."

Morgan let out a sharp burst of air. "Yeah, that's what it looked like to me."

"What's that supposed to mean?"

"That you have the look of a girl who just made a deal with the devil and is going to live to regret it."

The hiss of air I sucked in was the only confirmation Morgan needed. I suspected he knew something, but not that he'd cut to the truth so quickly.

"What's worse, luv, is that I know enough about the monster to know he wouldn't have been satisfied to just bring you down. The taste of your soul was likely only his appetizer.

What's to be his dinner and dessert?"

Probably the destruction of the world and this realm as we know it.

"What do you mean?" Why was I asking questions I already knew the answers to? I was perfectly and painfully aware of what Morgan was asking. And he wasn't wrong. If all I'd done was damn my soul . . . well that would have been bad, but what I'd done was so much worse than that. I couldn't even fully wrap my brain around the repercussions.

Not now. I didn't want to understand. Not now or ever.

"What I mean is—"

"Stop!" I held a shaky hand up in front of me. "Stop. I can't. I won't. I just . . . Everyone is back. That's all I can focus on for the moment."

Morgan was silent. For once.

His lips pressed into a grim line. We stared at each other for several moments before he gave me a sharp nod. A silent acquiescence to my request.

The air slowly leaked from my lungs. Whatever conscious or subconscious reason I'd sought Morgan out had been a mistake. There were some hard truths I was going to have to deal with in the upcoming days, but my heart of flesh was bleeding freely. My deeds were too fresh to face today.

I turned to leave but missed my window of escape when Kaitlin popped her head in the room.

"There you are! You were gone when I got back to your room with some water"—she waved a bottle in the air—"been looking for you everywhere. Logan's awake." Kaitlin's eyes were expectant and her smile radiant.

"Oh."

Her smile dropped.

My wooden demeanor was going to get the wrong person

asking the right questions sooner or later.

"Oh? Ah, don't you want to see him?" Even the trickle of confused doubt in her voice wasn't enough to snap me out of the tortured haze that blanketed my mind.

Morgan saved me the trouble of a response by addressing Kaitlin himself. "It's nice to see you too, beautiful. I was just about to call for someone to give me a sponge bath, but now that you're here, it seems you'll be able to save me the trouble."

Kaitlin's eyes narrowed, buying me a few extra moments to pull myself together.

"You wish," she shot back.

"Oh, I do. I do very much."

She scoffed at him.

"Is that any way to treat someone who endured unspeakable torture on your behalf?" Morgan infused just the right amount of pout into his damaged voice. The man was skilled. I'd be worried for Kaitlin if I thought for a moment she might fall for his antics.

"Whatever you had to endure rests solely on your own pathetic shoulders."

"Well, I suppose that's true. It was my decision to rescue you from those demons." A flicker of something akin to sympathy rested on Kaitlin's face, but the emotion was erased by Morgan's next words. "I can't blame you for falling prey to them. You are only a girl after all."

"Ah, whatever." Kaitlin rolled her eyes and fixed her attention back on me.

I dug deep to find the shadow of an appropriate emotion. It was go time.

"Yeah, Kaitlin, you're totally right. Let's go see Logan. I'm so . . . happy he's awake."

Face palm. That was some seriously bad acting. And the

look on Kaitlin's face confirmed it. But I was terrified of seeing Logan. Fear rode me hard, warring with relief that he was safe. I was worried he would take one look at me and see all my secrets, all the ugly deeds I'd done.

And that when he saw them, he'd reject me.

"Audrey? Are you okay? Do you maybe want to—"

"No, I'm good! Promise!" Internal cringe. That was way too loud.

"Smooth move." Morgan coughed.

Without sparing him a glance, I spun Kaitlin toward the exit.

"Yikes." The turn was so sudden she lost her footing before righting herself.

"Let's get going." I continued with false cheeriness in my voice, nudging her toward the doorway.

Kaitlin peeked over her shoulder at me as she moved forward. "Yeah, all right I guess."

I followed her while willing myself to hold it together.

"Some things can't be undone, luv. But others can." Morgan's final words were softly spoken, and they threatened to undo me.

The straightening of my spine was the only indication I gave that I'd heard him before striding from the room.

13

REUNION

Logan was awake . . . just as Kaitlin said, but even so, part of me wasn't expecting him to be conscious considering the severity of his injuries. After ushering her out of Morgan's room, I sent her on some other meaningless errand I'd already forgotten. I wasn't ready to face Logan with an audience, but he apparently already had a visitor.

One of the voices that floated down the hall as I approached was most definitely Logan's deep timbre. It was scratchier than normal—making it sound as if he was recovering from a cold or had just woken up—but I still recognized it. The other voice was . . .

Jonathon?

I slowed my steps as I neared the open doorway, padding forward carefully. Was I planning on eavesdropping on their conversation?

Absolutely.

These two didn't have a cozy relationship. And considering my history with each of them, I wasn't about to pass up this juicy opportunity. Perhaps Jonathon's visit was only medical . .

. but then again, perhaps not. Thank goodness I'd sent Kaitlin off on another errand, or she never would have let me do this.

Stopping a few feet from the doorway, I strained to catch their words.

"Thanks, man," Logan said.

There was a pause before Jonathon heaved a sigh. "I didn't do it for you."

"Yeah," Logan chuckled. "I'm well aware of that. It doesn't mean you don't deserve my gratitude."

"Maybe that's exactly what it means."

"Naw, your heart was still in a good place. That's all that really matters. Just because you were doing it for her instead of me doesn't matter. In fact, that makes me even more grateful."

I bit back a groan. Did they really have to talk about me? I really shouldn't be listening to this.

"You know what she means to me." Logan's words were quieter, forcing me to take a step closer even as I chastised myself for listening to their private conversation. But if I was damned anyway, what was one more sin to add to the ever-growing pile? Besides, new Audrey's emotions were still somewhat on lock down.

The room was silent after that.

What I wouldn't give to be a fly on the wall in there. But not an actual fly, because, eww. Maybe have the power of invisibility? Yeah, that would be sweet.

I fidgeted as I waited for one of them to say something . . . anything.

Eavesdropping was overrated.

Why was no one talking?

Forever seemed to pass before Jonathon responded.

"Yeah, I do know. But I think more importantly, I finally know what you mean to her."

"Would it have made you choose differently if you'd known that before?"

Wait, was Logan Doctor Phil'ing Jonathon?

"No." Jonathon's answer came out gruff. He was agitated. "But maybe it should have."

"You're a good man, Jonathon. The right one is out there somewhere; it's just not her. You can't force these things." There was a bit of warning to Logan's words I wondered if Jonathon picked up.

A self-deprecating laugh shot from Jonathon. "Learned that lesson the hard way."

Another few beats of silence. What was happening in there? Were they staring into each other's eyes and having a bro moment or something?

"It's been . . ." Jonathon started and then stopped. Another deep sigh before he continued. "Lonely. I've been here for a long time."

Perhaps Logan nodded or something because I didn't hear a response. Since when did guys open up to each other like this? Were they having some sort of post-traumatic bonding moment, or did this happen all the time under our female radar?

"There's something special about her. If there wasn't, I wouldn't have held on so long."

Me? Special?

I slapped a hand to my face to cover my snort of disbelief— old Audrey stirring a little inside. A part of my heart that had hardened against Jonathon during our mission melted a bit.

He was lonely, and he had acted out of his hurt. I found it hard to stay upset at someone when they were in pain. Emotional or physical.

"Yeah, I know it, man. I've known it since the beginning."

Wait, what? He's known since the beginning? That didn't make sense with how he first treated me.

"Well, maybe if you'd done something about it right away, you would have saved us all a bit of trouble." Jonathon's words were just short of biting. The guys were civil to each other, but there was still more than a touch of animosity hanging in the air. Mind you, if I'd been in the room, I would have been nodding in agreement. *Took bonehead in there long enough to get with the program.*

Maybe that was a touch hypocritical. Whatever.

Logan ignored the not-so-veiled jab. "Thank you for keeping an eye on her for me."

The laugh that burst from Jonathon was humor-filled. "Yeah, right. No. It didn't go down that way. She's a true warrior, Logan. She singlehandedly took down a demon the size of a small building. It was pretty disgusting, but you would have been proud of her."

A sharp pain lanced my heart. Old Audrey was fully awake now and trying to shove new, cold, unfeeling Audrey out of the way. But if that happened, I'd fall apart.

No one should be proud of me after what I'd done. I existed in this realm on borrowed time. For all I knew, a portal to Hell could open any minute and suck me back down to that kingdom of despair.

I deserved nothing less.

I rubbed my eyes with my fists as an overbearing weariness permeated my body and soul.

"Except for perhaps if you'd seen her reaction to the hell-trees." Jonathon chuckled, and I cocked my head. What was he about now? "She squealed like a girl whenever one got too close to her."

Hey, I am a girl, you doofus!

My throat itched to spit the words at him. Too bad I was playing spy at the moment. I pulverized the warm fuzzies that had started to grow for Jonathon. Wonder if he thought a throat punch would be girlie?

Anger issues? Yeah, maybe. So what?

Wait, was Logan laughing too? Not cool.

Those blood-sap-leaking zombie trees were nasty.

Oh, shoot!

I'd missed the last few exchanges, but I heard the slapping of hands in some weird dude bonding handshake, and then Jonathon was saying his goodbyes.

And I was just standing outside the door . . . like a creeper.

Abort mission.

Where to go? Where to go?

I performed a ridiculous foot shuffle followed by a spin as I searched for a hidey-hole, but it was too late. There was nowhere to hide.

Jonathon strode out of Logan's room—and spotted me.

We both froze.

I grimaced, braced for a well-deserved tongue lashing, but after several moments Jonathon just rolled his eyes, shook his head, and then continued on his way down the hall without a single word.

Wait, what happened? Had I pulled that spy junk off without getting in trouble?

Old Audrey—the one untainted by Hell's nightmares—demanded a happy dance.

"You can come in now, Audrey."

Oh. So busted.

I reached up and patted my matted hair. I hadn't given it much of a thought until now. The mess was sure to be a kaleidoscope of colors. Looking down, I also took in my rather filthy body armor. The material was intact but caked with dirt and blood. Not even the dark color of the suit could hide the grime. My face was probably just as nasty.

Even though I'd woken up in The Healing Center, I obviously hadn't been tended to—probably because I hadn't sustained any serious injuries. I should have taken care of my disheveled appearance sooner. I had not thought this through.

Typical.

"After taking a trip to Hell to spring me free, you're gonna leave me waiting now?" There was a teasing note in Logan's voice I wasn't used to hearing.

I wiped a hand down my dirty face. How was I going to do this?

Pain-filled grunting noises reached my ears. "Okay, if you're not gonna come in, I'll come out there to you."

Wait, what? "No! Don't move!" I barreled through the doorway . . . to find Logan sitting in bed with an amused smile on his face. "Huh? I thought you'd gotten out of bed."

"I figured that's what it would take to get you in here." He laughed and pointed at my head. "Not amused I see."

"Let me guess. Red?"

"Yep." He didn't look the least bit remorseful.

I rolled my eyes and stepped farther into the room. He'd caught me lurking outside his door after all. I supposed that gave him license to mess with me.

I took a long moment to check him out. That is, check out his physical condition. Not check *him* out.

Yeah, keep telling yourself that.

I cleared my throat and chewed on my lower lip.

Logan appeared . . . fine . . . especially considering the condition I'd found him in outside this realm.

He was wearing a clean white t-shirt. There were some

bandages on various parts of his exposed arms but no bruising. His face had a few small scratches, and a little discoloration, but no swelling at all.

He was certainly cleaner than I was. Another reminder that someone forgot my sponge bath. Did the guys get all the special attention in here now?

But the real question was how had he healed so quickly?

"Why don't you look worse?"

Logan choked on a laugh. "I'm going to take that as a compliment, even though I know you didn't intend it as one."

"I just meant . . ." How did I delicately explain that he'd looked like ground beef only a short while ago? Delicate didn't seem to be part of my skill set.

"You were in bad shape, Logan." A swell of emotion clogged my throat as I remembered what it felt like to find him in that underground cell. Old-weak-emotional Audrey was really fighting tooth and nail to take over new-cold-unfeeling Audrey. She took advantage of the cracks in my heart and slipped though. Before I could lock my feelings down, my eyes filled.

I turned and stared out his window before going on. I couldn't face him at the moment.

"You . . . I've never seen someone beaten so badly." A shudder wracked my body, and a tear slid down my cheek.

"Hey."

The gentleness in Logan's voice lulled my senses. I turned, and my gaze traveled up his body until my eyes connected with his. He wasn't smiling anymore.

"Can I hold you?"

His request was simple. And perfect. And exactly what I needed.

And rather than fight what we both wanted, I did what I should have done long ago—I surrendered.

14

REUNITED

I stayed in Logan's arms until I couldn't stand my funk anymore. There was only so long a girl could live in crusty clothes.

After slipping into the small bathroom in Logan's room, I peeled the bloody form-fitting armor from my body. The protective garb was extra crunchy from dried demon blood and stuck to my skin in places.

My gloves were coated in a different type of blood. Red flakes of it fell to the ground. My hands shook as I yanked the gloves off and stuffed them in the bottom of the garbage can. I stood for a moment, staring at nothing as I wrestled my thoughts into submission—but the questions slipped through anyway.

Joe, what had happened to him? Was he okay?

A fresh wave of guilt slammed into me over the result of my anger-filled actions. If only I'd not lost it, I wouldn't have lashed out at Alrik and accidentally struck Joe instead.

The feeling of my blade sinking into soft flesh was too close to the surface. Squeezing my eyes shut, I fisted my hands and wished those horror-filled moments away. But they were branded to the forefront of my consciousness.

"Audrey, you all right in there?"

Logan's voice and soft knock on the door jarred me back to the present.

"Yeah, sorry. It's just taking a bit to get this nasty armor off. I'll only be another minute." That sounded normal, right?

I set about ridding myself of the rest of my gear and chucked it all in the corner. That left me standing in days old workout clothes, but that was better than the alternative . . . still being in the blood-saturated armor.

My next step was to attempt to clean up. Although free from bloodied and dirty outerwear, I had sweated buckets in these clothes.

I seriously missed waking up in the Healing Center fresh and washed.

Surveying the small space, I found some washcloths. A sponge bath was the best I could do.

After soaking and lathering the soft terry cloth with soap, I pulled my tank with a built in bra over my head and set to work scrubbing off as much funk as possible.

Reaching my back was a challenge, and I twisted and contorted my upper body to scrub the hard to reach places. In the middle of a twist, I caught my reflection in the mirror over the sink.

I froze, limbs at awkward angles, and then half turned.

What was that on my back?

The soggy towel dropped from my hands and landed on the tile floor with a splat.

There, beneath my left shoulder blade, a black spot about the size of a quarter marred my otherwise flawless skin. I backpedaled closer to the sink for a better look. The mark wasn't perfectly round, nor was it all black. Thin black-and dark-green spider veins reached out in all directions from the central mark.

What is that? That's definitely new. Did I . . . catch something in Hell?

A more sinister explanation occurred and sent shockwaves of fear through my body. Was this part of the curse Satan spoke of?

A small part of me still believed Satan's words were a lie, that I wasn't actually cursed to spend an eternity in torment. But this . . . this hideous mark wasn't a lie. It wasn't made up. It was sketched on my skin like a tattoo. My own personal scarlet letter—a reminder of what I'd done and the consequences to come.

The door shook with the force of Logan's knocking, and I yelped. "Audrey, not to invade your privacy, but I'm a little worried about you out here. Are you sure everything's all right?"

I searched the floor and found my tank, quickly sliding it over my head and concealing my shame. No one could know of this.

"Gimme a sec." That was all I could push through my suddenly dry throat.

The last bit of hope that I could be redeemed slipped through my fingers.

This was real. This was happening. And there was nothing I could do to stop it.

Shortly after Logan banged on the bathroom door, I emerged

from the small space to find him resting. I crawled onto the narrow bed next to him. I was still pretty nasty with my ratty hair and days old clothes, but I was too exhausted and soul crushed to care.

He stirred when I slipped in next to him and pulled me into his arms. Without the self-constructed barrier of self-doubt or suspicion I'd built for months to protect my heart, the feel of his strength encasing me was heaven.

My silent tears streamed down my face, but rather than snap into his usual fix-it mode, he just let me be. Softly stroking my back with one hand and holding me tight with the other.

If only he knew that my tears were not only shed for the horrors I'd seen in Hell, but also for the tomorrows we'd never have together. I wanted to tell him, but I couldn't. If he knew the full truth, the spell would be broken. And I was selfish enough to want whatever time I had left with him to be beautiful. We'd already wasted so much of it.

In that moment, I decided he wasn't to know. Not until the separation came. We'd enjoy the limited time we had together, and I would cherish the memory throughout the torturous days that I would endure for the rest of eternity.

We sat on his bed, tucked up against the headboard, Logan sitting with one knee bent and an outstretched leg, and me curled into a ball against his chest, practically cuddled on his lap.

When my tears were spent, I let out a shaky breath of air.

"Audrey, I can't—" Logan's voice caught on something. His head rested on top of mine. When he continued, his voice dropped an octave, thickened with emotion. "I can't imagine what you went through down there. I'm so very sorry. I should never have bonded with you."

I savored the warm thud of his heartbeat on my cheek for several seconds before what he'd said sunk in. The leakage from my eyes along with a bad case of the feels must have dulled my reactions.

I jerked to a sitting position to stare at him in disbelief—and anger. My face was crusted with the salt of dried tears. There was no doubt I was a hot mess and a half. But that was nothing compared to the mess he'd just spewed.

He reached for me again, but I put a hand up to ward off his movements and curled my upper lip.

Where to even start?

"What *I* went through? Are you insane?" His gaze jumped around my face as if he couldn't decide on a safe place to land. "Logan, I actually felt an echo of what you went through. I even experienced some of it in a dream or a weird out of body experience where I *was* you. What I went through was nothing."

He opened his mouth to speak, but I slashed a hand through the air to stop him. "*Nothing* compared to what had been done to you. You were torn to shreds. Literally, in some spots."

His face paled. I shouldn't have gone there and instantly regretted bringing it up—but I couldn't handle his concern for me when *he* had been tortured. We'd get to the "should never have bonded with you" comment next.

"You experienced some of . . . of what I went through?" he asked.

Shoot, I gave him another reason to beat himself up. Rookie mistake. "Never mind about that. And what's this business about regretting bonding with me? Frankly, that's kind of—hey!"

He grabbed my upper arms and held me still as I tried to

push away even farther. His blue eyes flashed, and his face was hard as stone. "If bonding with you caused you to feel even a second of what I endured in that place, then yes, it's something I deeply regret and would do anything to take back."

Buried under the caveman response was something sweet, but I wasn't feeling it.

"Argh. You . . ." I pointed a finger at his face. "You just . . ."

As I sputtered to find the right words, the corners of Logan's lips just barely tipped up. I stopped talking when I spotted his involuntary reaction. Of course I'd find a guy who thought I was cute when riled up. Actually, that was probably pretty lucky considering I did tend to have a short fuse.

I pressed my lips together and narrowed my eyelids before performing another visual sweep of his body.

Yep, he looked to be relatively healthy.

I launched myself at him and grabbed the sides of his face, and then I planted my lips right over his. Just like the first time I'd surprised him with a kiss, he was momentarily stunned.

I gently but firmly bit down on his full bottom lip in a silent demand for him to get with the program. Then I pulled back a fraction, just far enough that my lips grazed his when I spoke.

"Less talking, more kissing," I ordered.

I'd gone to Hell and back for this guy. I wanted to collect my reward . . . with interest.

A lazy smile spread over his mouth, and his lids dropped to half-mast. "Yes, ma'am."

I pulled back and lifted my eyebrows. "Ma'am? What am I, a zillion years ol—"

Oh.

A warm pair of lips cut off my rant, and I wasn't upset about it in the least. *Mmm, yes.*

My body flooded with warmth. Every nip of his lips and

change of position spiked my heart rate until an electric current zipped under my skin, energizing my molecules and enhancing my senses.

I needed this. I needed to get lost in this moment and forget this world or any other realm existed.

I curled into Logan's embrace and slid a hand into his gloriously thick and soft hair. With my other hand, I grasped his bicep as if to hold him in place.

He growled low in the back of his throat, and with a grasp on my waist, he pressed me even closer. I liked that. His other hand made a slow trek from the hair beside my ear—probably the only non-crusty strand—down the side of my face, to rest in a light embrace at my neck. His thumb played lazy circles with my pulse point.

But I wanted more.

Despite the gentle touches, the soft press of his lips, and the light nips at mine, the fear that this—or any other time—could be our last time together stirred a frantic sort of panic in my gut.

If this was all I was going to get with Logan, I wanted as much as he would give me.

I made a sound of protest at one of Logan's toe-curling yet tender kisses. Moving even closer, I scooted to my knees and pressed my lips more firmly against his. A silent demand.

Logan tried to slow things down again, but I wasn't having it. Now both my hands were buried in his hair, and I was kissing him like there was no tomorrow . . . because I wasn't sure there would be.

There was only a slight hesitation before desire overcame Logan's sense of propriety, and he hauled me against his chest in a savage move.

Yes, the beast inside me whispered even as a soft voice

cautioned me to slow things down.

I pushed the voice away. Desperation released the beast from its cage. There'd be no hesitation from me.

What had started out sweet and innocent was quickly moving toward unrestrained passion. I didn't care. Scratch that, I did care. I wanted it.

I dragged a hand from his hair down his neck to settle on his arm, unconsciously searching for warm skin. When my other hand reached the bottom of his shirt, I slipped it underneath. A shudder ran through his body, and the next thing I knew I was on my back. But not in the way I had anticipated.

Logan had broken our kiss and pushed me back onto the mattress. He held both my hands in his against the sheets but away from his body. With his arms straightened and his body to the side, he'd moved as far from me as possible while still holding my wrists immobile. His breathing was as hard and erratic as mine. A cobalt ocean churned in his eyes.

We just stared at each other. Me wondering why he had stopped. And him . . . Well, I had no idea what he was thinking. His gaze searched my face erratically, and his features were drawn and pinched, almost as if in pain.

"Wh-what?" I asked. "Why did you stop?" I didn't miss the breathy tone in my voice.

Logan squeezed his eyes shut and then pushed away from me, sitting back against the head of the bed. He shoved a hand in his hair and then fisted it for a moment before letting it go.

When he opened his eyes, they didn't meet mine right away. I propped myself up on my elbows to watch him. Cocking my head, I scooted back to a sitting position. The sharp pain of rejection pierced my chest. He was a guy. Why the heck had he just stopped us?

Logan finally looked back at me, and I licked my lips, tasting his familiar peppermint sweetness.

He slammed his eyelids shut again with a groan and shoved another hand roughly into his hair.

"Can you please not do that right now?" he asked. Just the deep sound of his post-kiss voice made my heartbeat spike again.

"Do what?"

His growl was followed by a reverse head-butt to the wall. "You're killing me. You know that, right?"

I grinned like the Cheshire cat. I found getting under his skin very satisfying. I made a move toward him again, but he put up a hand to ward me off. Did he really not know me by now? Like a hand gesture was going to deter me. *Ha!*

I grabbed his arm and used it to pull myself closer to him. His eyes and chin snapped down so he was facing me.

"I wasn't done with you yet," I said as I pulled him in closer, my eyes already shutting. Any second now, I'd get a second taste of heaven. But then the world tilted, and pain shot through my butt as it hit an unforgiving surface.

What the what?

My eyes snapped open, and I blinked several times.

I was on the ground.

With one very sore backside.

I looked up. Logan peered over the bed with an expression that was simultaneously angry and sheepish—an emotional mix that had to be hard to pull off.

"What was that?" I shouted at him. "And *ow*, by the way."

Getting to my feet, I rubbed the sting out of my tush. I think I bruised my tailbone.

I eyed one of the chairs, but sitting might hurt, so I jutted out a hip, crossed my arms over my chest, and glared at Logan instead.

The big jerk.

He rubbed his eyes with his fingers and then covered his face with his hand. I spotted a smile he couldn't quite cover.

"That was rude." I landed a fist on my hip as I pointed an accusatory finger at him.

He opened his fingers to peek at me and bit his lip to keep the smile from getting too far out of control.

"You better not be laughing at me right now." I crossed my arms back over my chest and attempted to stare him down.

A full belly laugh escaped his mouth I widened my eyes in disbelief.

I. Am. Out.

I spun on a heel and marched to the door.

"Good luck saving yourself the next time you end up in a super stinky realm. I'm probably going to smell like rotten eggs for a week because of you," I grumbled on my way out—too quietly for him to hear the full sentence, but I was confident he'd picked up the gist.

A strong hand caught my arm and spun me back around, sending me tumbling into a warm chest.

This is more like it, the beast inside rumbled. I told it to shut up.

"Now, Audrey, come on, be reasonable." There was still a healthy dose of mirth in Logan's gaze and words.

I struggled against his hold, but the defiance was halfhearted at best.

He brought his other arm around and locked me in place. The urge to nestle into his warmth rode me hard. The man *had* just dumped me . . . literally.

"When have you ever known me to be reasonable?" I muttered. Wait a minute, I'd just insulted myself. Logan one.

Audrey zero. "I mean, don't try to be cute with me now. It's not going to work."

His brows lifted. "It's not?"

"No." I shook my head and caught a glimpse of red-and-pink streaks. Argh, this hair.

"Are you sure?"

"Yes." But I refused to meet his gaze.

"Well, that's good. Because that means you won't be affected if I do this." He placed a gentle kiss on my temple.

"No, not at all."

"Or this." He brought his face down and nuzzled the spot behind my ear before placing another soft kiss on my skin.

Not responding to that one took a herculean effort. My throat dried up, and so I just shook my head while a quiet chuckle vibrated through Logan's chest.

"Perfect. That means I can do this as well." He slid a hand up and cupped the back of my neck.

I was caught in his spell without even knowing it had been cast. Obediently, I tilted my head back with only the slightest pressure from his hand. His lips grazed my neck before nibbling on the sensitive skin and finally placing a scorching kiss below my ear.

The shudder that wracked my body was completely involuntary. I'd closed my eyes without even realizing it.

Logan's breath touched the shell of my ear as he whispered, "You can't kiss a guy like you did before and not expect him to lose control. We don't have to rush. We have eternity together now."

His words doused all the warmth and passion coursing through my body. My eyes popped open, and without thought I wrenched from his hold.

We didn't have eternity anymore. I didn't even know if we

had another full day.

Logan's brow pinched, but he let me go. The confusion on his face was clear, but he was a smart guy. He knew I was hiding something. His gaze roamed my face as he tried to pick apart the enigma. Like I was a puzzle that needed to be solved.

"Audrey, what's wrong?"

I opened my mouth to speak, but nothing came out.

"If you're worried I don't want you, that couldn't be further from the truth. But I don't think it's wise to get too . . . close until we've officially and therefore permanently bonded. We can have a short engagement period if you want; it doesn't really—"

"Engagement? Wait, what are you talking about?" I stumbled a step, and the back of my knees hit one of the chairs. I wobbled for a moment before regaining balance.

He reached out to me again, far more agilely than before, which made me think he'd been playing me in the beginning. I sidestepped his advances.

My head started to pound under the pressure of the secrets stuffed inside.

"You know our bond can only lead to one of two places"—Logan held his hands up in front of him as if to show me he was keeping his distance—or else he was treating me like a spooked animal—"and I think it's safe to agree we're on the same page with how we feel about each other." His gaze pierced me. "This bond is not going to dissolve, Audrey. We both know that. I just thought, considering"—he gestured to the crumpled bedding with his hand—"considering that, you wouldn't want to wait."

A hysterical laugh bubbled up my chest and burst from my mouth. A crazy sound I tried to shove back down my throat but failed. *Oh gosh, is it getting hot in here?*

"You expect us to get married because we made out?" My eyes were wide, and I started sucking in too much air. "That's nuts."

My emotions were bouncing around like a pinball, and I wasn't even sure if my reaction was because the idea of being bonded permanently freaked me out or because now it could never happen.

Hot mess . . . inside and out.

I glanced at the door. I'm not sure why. Maybe I was subconsciously looking to make a quick escape.

"Now, Audrey." My head jerked up. Logan had moved several feet closer to me, his voice annoyingly calm. "You know people don't get married here."

"Married, mated, soul-bound for eternity"—I waved a hand in the air—"who cares what you call it; it's all the same thing." Except marriage was 'till death do you part.' This was a way bigger commitment. Like I was going to let some overzealous hormones make that decision for me.

Oh gosh, did it even matter? I'd be gone soon anyway. Separated from Logan . . . permanently. I didn't even have a choice anymore. We'd never be whatever we were meant to be.

I started sucking in air like I was drowning. And in a way I was. Drowning in the folly of my foolish actions.

I held a hand out to ward off Logan's slow and steady advance. If the bond was doing the same thing to him as it was to me, he was probably itching to have me back in his arms. This bonding thing was seriously whack.

My breathing accelerated. I gulped air between phrases, panting like a dog in the desert. "I just need . . . a minute . . . to process."

Logan's face hardened, and he advanced on me anyway. I backed up until my rump bumped something. I glanced over my shoulder and spotted the bed. I yelped and jumped away from it, stumbling into the side table and smacking my shin in the process.

I bent over to rub the bruised limb while still sucking air as if I could inhale all the oxygen in the room. I started to see black spots around my vision and lost track of Logan.

Warm but firm hands took hold of my shoulders and forced me to sit in a padded chair. Right now what I needed was a padded room.

Logan's face appeared before mine as I tried to blink away the black spots. He'd crouched in front of me and filled my hazy vision.

"Audrey, love, I want you to take one deep breath and hold it for the count of two before releasing it."

Did he just call me 'love?' Something went a little melty and gooey inside. *Did he say something else? Oh shoot, black spots are blocking out his perfectly formed face. Man, he has perfect bone structure.*

I pitched forward. My stomach leaped to my throat, but with a grunt, Logan caught me before my face became acquainted with the floor. I held on to consciousness with both hands but felt it slipping through my fingers.

My back rested against something soft, and I was pretty sure I was horizontal. I blinked rapidly at my diminishing vision. Cobalt orbs were all I could see clearly.

"You know if you'd listened to me, you wouldn't be passing out." Logan's words, full of soft vibes, were missing his usual sarcastic bite. "But I appreciate the effort to make me feel like your rescuer again."

A gentle pair of lips kissed my forehead before my vision winked out completely.

15

AWKWARD

Naps were amazing. I loved naps. They were so magically awesome I wanted to marry them and have a nice long relationship with them.

My body buzzed with energy even as I snuggled into the soft bedding. Something warm and solid was at my back. Some sort of heated pillow?

Mmm, I like.

With eyes still closed, I shifted closer to it and nuzzled a second heated pillow beneath my head.

"Finally. She's alive," a campy male voice announced.

"Oh, don't wake her just yet. They look so cute together. I feel like I need to capture this with a camera."

Wait. What?

"You know how mad she's going to be when she wakes up and finds out you've all been staring at her sleeping. Especially with her hair all crazy-like."

That male voice rumbled along my back and shifted my warm pillow. I cracked an eyelid.

That's not a pillow; that's an arm! Which means . . .

I grabbed the top blanket and hauled it over my head. Jerking myself away from Logan's arm and the side of his body, I armadilloed into a ball beneath the covers.

"I hate you all."

"What was that?" Kaitlin asked. "You love us the most and think we are the best? Oh, so sweet! We love you too." She blew loud kisses at me from the other side of my makeshift blanket shield. She was the worst.

Tremors from Logan's direction started to shake the bed, reminding me that I was very much still lying next to him ... in front of our friends.

Letting my legs lead, I slipped out of bed and then army-crawled beneath it. The room was silent for several heartbeats.

"Did I just see my granddaughter slide out of your bed and sneak under it?"

I slapped a hand over my mouth to hold back the groan. When did Romona arrive? I thought only Kevin and Kaitlin were in the room with us.

"Yes, yes you did," Kaitlin supplied helpfully.

"Um," Logan cleared his throat. "Romona, I'm so glad to see you're up and moving around already."

"Yeah, sure you are." Romona's voice dripped with sarcasm. "Care to explain to me what Audrey was doing in your bed ... and now hiding underneath it?"

I covered my eyes with my hand as if that would transport me out of this situation.

Silence blanketed the room.

Logan cleared his throat. "It's not what you're thinking. Audrey was just—"

"Oh, it's exactly what you're thinking," Kaitlin cut in.

"Kaitlin." Logan's voice was a sharp censure.

Only their feet were visible to me, so I couldn't read their body language. But I knew Logan was both uncomfortable and annoyed.

I think I'll stay here for a while longer.

I snickered.

"I heard that, young lady."

I pressed my lips together and covered my head with my arms. *Stay very still and quiet, and they'll forget I'm here.*

"Logan, I'm waiting." Romona's foot tapped a quick staccato against the glossy floor.

"Well, Audrey got a little upset about something and started to hyperventilate. I couldn't calm her down, and she passed out, so I put her somewhere more comfortable."

Way to make yourself look like a hero, buddy. I rolled my eyes.

"Why was she hyperventilating?" Romona asked. There was a note of genuine confusion in her voice.

"I'm not sure. One second she was fine, and then she just freaked out."

"Are you kidding me?" I shouted from my hiding spot.

"You've got something to add down there?" Logan thumped on the bed, and a spring knocked my head.

I shot the offending mattress the evil eye and rubbed my head.

"You said we were going to get married."

Logan let out an exaggerated sigh. "Audrey, be reasonable. And I already told you people don't get married here."

I flipped on my back and punched the mattress as hard as I could in the limited space I had, hoping I'd managed to hit part of his body.

"You still don't spring a commitment of that magnitude on someone. You take your time and work up to it."

"Where's the popcorn? This is getting good."

"Shut it, Kaitlin," Logan and I said in unison.

"Oh cute, they're synchronizing now."

"Kaitlin," we both yelled.

"I think there's some popcorn in a vending machine down the hall," Kevin piped in, "but no way am I leaving now. This is like watching a movie in 4-D."

"Logan," Romona went on completely ignoring Tweedledee and Tweedledum. "You asked to spend eternity with my granddaughter without talking to me first, and in that brutish manner? Is she not worth more to you than that?"

I fist pumped in my confined space. *Way to go, Grams!*

"Audrey, will you please get out from under the bed now?" Romona's voice was authoritative.

"No thank you. I'm good."

"Audrey—"

"I'm too young to get married," I moaned, cutting off Romona's censure.

"That's right. You're obviously too immature to make a commitment like that."

"Yep, not even offended by that comment. You're totally right. One hundred percent too immature."

Logan huffed out a frustrated breath. "Romona, you're right, I should have handled the situation with a little more finesse. But in all honesty, Audrey was all over me, so it was kinda hard to think straight."

"What?" I squawked, nailing my head on a metal beam. I flipped over again and kicked the mattress where I thought his butt might be. "You did not just say that out loud."

The bed squeaked, and Logan's upside-down head appeared. The tips of his golden hair brushed the ground.

"I'm just keepin' it real, babe. You know that's how it went down." His eyes twinkled, and a grin lit his face.

"Ouch." I twisted an arm to rub my back, feigning pain. "Oh my gosh, can you see them?"

Logan's eyebrows pulled together, and the smile slid from his face.

"What happened? Are you hurt?" His hands landed on the floor by his head while I twisted my face to a mask of agony.

I blinked, and Logan was off the bed and on his belly on the floor, his head right-side-up and peeking under the bed at me.

"It really hurts," I whined.

"Did the mattress squish you?" He assessed the amount of space between the bed frame and me.

"No, no, it's just . . . the tire marks on my back from the bus you just chucked me under!" I screamed at him.

At my outburst, Logan's head jerked up and he nailed it on the bed frame. He gave me a side-eye while he rubbed the sore spot.

Kaitlin lost it. Her hysterical laugh was broken up by the occasional snort.

Logan army-crawled under the bed after me, which was quite a feat considering his size. The dude was a lot bigger than me.

"Wait, stop," I protested.

Ignoring me, he wrapped an arm around my waist and hauled me out from under the bed with him. We ended up grappling on the ground for a few minutes before a loud throat clearing reminded me of our audience.

Straddling Logan's hips with my hands planted on his chest, I froze. A quick check over my shoulder revealed Romona staring me down. Logan wore a smug smile, the back of his head rested on his crossed arms. He looked as if he enjoyed this spot on the floor immensely.

"You see what I mean?" he asked Romona without taking

his eyes off me.

I was about to throat punch him when I noticed red blossoming on his white t-shirt.

"Oh my gosh, Logan, you're bleeding." Twisting, I scrambled off him and tried to tug his shirt over his head. I needed a better look at where that blood was coming from. How stupid was I? He was still injured, and I was wrestling with him.

A belly laugh rocked his body as he swatted my hands away. "Audrey, stop trying to undress me. This is exactly why I suggested a short engagement."

Did he not have one iota of self-preservation? He was so close to a throat punch right now. All it would take was one quick jab. But another look at the blood blooming on his stomach had me pushing aside my annoyance and renewing my search for the source.

"Stop fighting me. I'm trying to check out your wound."

"You're definitely trying to check something out," Kaitlin added.

Logan grabbed my hands and captured my gaze. "Audrey, I'm all right, I promise. How about you let me up and I'll go take a look?"

I chewed my lip in indecision but nodded, the concern for him threatening to overwhelm me.

We both stood. Logan let out a quiet grunt. "Hey"—he placed a hand on the side of my face—"I promise, I'm fine. There are just a few places still healing. You're here, you're safe. That means I'm all right too."

Oh. That was sweet.

He bent forward to kiss the corner of my mouth, and even that chaste contact sent my heart rate into overdrive. When Logan pulled back, his eyes broadcasted he'd been affected as well. Black pupils nearly swallowed the blue.

Someone cleared their throat, and he headed to the bathroom in the corner. I caught a glimpse of his smooth back as he tugged his shirt off and tossed it to the ground. Stepping into the bathroom, he turned and grasped the door. A bandage taped to the left side of his . . . I tilted my head—was that an eight pack?

One, two, three, four, five six, sev—

"Hey, Audrey. My face is up here."

Words tumbled from my mouth in a guilty rush. "I was checking out your bandage. Obviously. What else did you think I was doing?" The bandage was almost completely soaked through. His eyes danced with laughter as he closed the door, blocking his body from view.

Holy smokes. As in—Holy. Smoking. Hot!

I fought the urge to fan myself.

"Hey, Audrey," Kaitlin called to me, breaking my hormone-induced daze.

I spun to face her.

"Yeah? Huh? What?" My voice was fast and breathy.

"You have a little something-something right here." She indicated the corner of her mouth.

"What?" I scrubbed a hand over my mouth, but there was nothing there. "What are you talking about?"

"Don't worry. You got the drool wiped off."

"Funny."

"I thought so." She giggled.

I shot her a look that said you can shut up now, but she just laughed harder. *Brat.*

"How's Morgan, Kaitlin?" Her laughter turned into a choking sound.

Kevin started slapping her on the back.

"Pfft, I don't know." She shrugged and looked at the empty wall.

"Sure you don't," I said with a smirk.

She stuck her tongue out at me.

"What, Morgan's here?"

Shoot, how had I forgotten Romona hadn't been there? She'd been taken out of the fight before we'd found Morgan. Kevin, too, for that matter, but he must have been filled in because his face reflected a look of resignation rather than surprise. But she was my best friend, and here I was ignoring her.

"Romona." I rushed over and squeezed her.

"Ow."

I pulled back and scanned her from head to toe. She was in a tank and loose-fitting pants that reminded me of scrubs. "I'm so sorry. Are you still hurt?"

"Just a bit sore."

I cringed and looked at the floor, toeing a spot that didn't exist. I was the worst.

"Audrey." Romona's soft voice brought my gaze up. She gently placed both hands on my cheeks. "You did it, baby girl." Were those tears gathering in her eyes? "I'm so proud of you."

Guilt slammed into my gut like a Mack truck, knocking the wind from my lungs. I was incapable of speaking for several seconds. New unfeeling and blessedly numb Audrey wanted to take back the reins.

"You shouldn't be," I whispered back. Yeah, we'd brought Logan and Morgan back, but at what cost exactly? Besides my soul that is.

"Of course she should be," Kaitlin interjected from across the room. "She was amazing, Romona."

I craned my neck in Kaitlin's direction. "How do you even

know? You were sent back with Morgan."

Kaitlin gaped like a fish. "You're joking, right? You single-handedly took down a demon the size of a yacht. You marched through that desert of—whatever those things were—with determination. You were fierce, girl. Tiger on steroids fierce."

"You weren't there at the end," I argued. "And if you had been connected to Logan and experiencing what he was, you'd have been laser focused on getting him out of there too. If you had seen what that . . . that abomination was doing to him, then . . ."

Logan wiped away the wetness on my cheeks with his thumb, and he rubbed my back. I hadn't even realized I was crying—or that he'd re-entered the room, where I could bring up all his horrific memories for him to relive.

Stupid old Audrey and her stupid emotions.

The fact that Logan wasn't rocking in the corner somewhere, but was comforting me instead, was a miracle. In fact, why didn't he have any scars? I saw his smooth back in my mind's eye. His old scars were completely gone.

I sucked in a sharp breath of air. He was standing in front of me now, gently cradling my face.

"Would you mind giving Audrey and me a few minutes?" He glanced over my shoulder, and the smallest of smiles ghosted across his face. "I promise, no more bed cuddling."

While Logan spoke, I caught the fast-paced clicking of heels in the hallway. As my friends started to get up, I cocked my head—the clipping grew louder and then abruptly stopped.

"Just a minute, everyone. I have some news." Shannon's voice made my blood run cold and struck fear in my heart, because deep inside, I knew what her announcement would be. And it wasn't going to be good.

16

HALF-TRUTHS

I twisted to stare at the formidable angel. Shannon stood in the doorway, barring retreat. I'm sure she wasn't actually trying to restrain anyone from leaving the room, but considering I had a fairly good idea what this announcement would be, unease twisted in my gut and crawled up my throat. Were the walls closing in on us?

Logan wrapped his arms around my waist. I itched to pull away—unworthy of his silent support.

Shannon glanced our way, the frown on her face deepening for a moment before her lips straightened. She surveyed the rest of my friends and then jumped right in. "I'm glad you're all back safe, but there's been a development. Satan's broken free of his chains."

There was a beat of silence, and then the room erupted in shouting.

I stayed quiet as everyone bombarded Shannon with questions. Eventually my transgressions would come to light . . . time was my enemy. My friends' voices turned into a steady buzz in my ears.

Shannon held up a hand, silencing everyone. Logan tightened his arms around me.

"You'll be briefed more thoroughly. But as you can imagine, this means all hands on deck until we neutralize the threat." Shannon's gaze landed on Logan and me. "That is except you two. You're both benched for the time being."

I shrank back into Logan's embrace. Shame filled my being.

Logan wasn't as compliant as I was. "Wait a minute. You need all able-bodied hunters. Forcing Audrey and me to sit this one out doesn't make sense."

"There will be no debate about this decision, Logan."

I didn't have to view Logan's face to know his eyes were narrowed in determination and that there was no way he'd let this go. But for the moment, he held his tongue.

"How do we know about this?" Romona asked.

Did Shannon's eyes linger on me a moment before turning to Romona to answer? "The Son himself confirmed the news."

I sagged in Logan's arms. The injury I'd inflicted on him hadn't prevented Joe's return.

"Shh, everything will be all right," Logan whispered in my ear, wrongly interpreting my body language as fear, when in reality relief pumped through my veins. Joe was back, which meant one less stain on my soul. Goodness knows it didn't clean my slate, but a weight lifted none-the-less.

"What does this even mean?" Kaitlin asked.

Shannon's gaze shifted to Kaitlin. "It means we need to prepare for the possibility of an attack."

Kaitlin's gasp filled the silence in the wake of Shannon's words.

"How is that even possible?" Logan asked. "Satan can't enter this realm."

"His chains kept him bound to Hell and Earth. He's now

free of those restraints. We have to assume he's set his sights on us. We aren't sure of anything yet, so I ask you all to be very discreet about this information. We'll be disseminating emergency protocol methods throughout the realm, but without further information, we're not looking to insight panic."

"So, you're not telling everyone about this?" Romona asked.

"No." Shannon scanned the room once again. "You are all hunters. As such, it's your job to defend people against evil—and that extends to our home as well. Along with the warrior angels, you'll be our defense."

"But that means you need—"

"As I mentioned, there will be a full briefing." She didn't let Logan finish his sentence. "We're currently collecting data. Those of you who can, get cleaned up and meet at the training center in an hour. Strategy planning for all scenarios starts immediately." Without allowing further discussion, Shannon turned on her heel and left.

"How does she deliver news like that so calmly?" Kevin wondered out loud.

"I'm pretty sure she's stripped of regular emotions," Kaitlin answered. "My gosh, how did this happen?"

"I expect we'll find out soon enough. Come on."—Romona motioned to Kaitlin and Kevin—"let's get going."

They nodded, and chairs scraped the floor as they left. Before shutting the door behind her, Romona said she'd update us on as much as she could.

Logan nodded. "Thanks."

When the door clicked shut, he gently turned me in his arms. I knew he wanted to talk, probably to reassure me everything would be okay. But I didn't want to think about Satan any longer. In an hour's time, there was a solid chance my ugly secret would be exposed to everyone.

Joe was safe, but I wasn't.

I slipped my hands up the back of Logan's t-shirt.

"Whoa, Audrey—" He moved to extract my hands.

"No, wait. Just give me a second."

He froze, and we stared at each other. His blue depths connected to my brown gaze. I whispered my fingers over his back, starting at his waist and then moving both hands up toward his shoulder blades. When I reached his shoulders, I lightly brushed down the center of his back. I didn't miss the tremble that passed through his body. But he held my gaze and stayed still, allowing me my innocent exploration.

Okay, mostly innocent. I didn't have to linger quite so long on his skin to verify he wasn't scarred anymore—but he felt so good. The muscles and contours of his back were like warmed steel.

I dragged my hands off his flesh and brought them up to rest lightly on his shoulders. This time on top of his t-shirt.

"You're not scarred anymore." This was as good of a distraction as any.

He bit his bottom lip and then smoothed it with his tongue before shaking his head.

"Why not?"

He transferred his gaze to my lips. I unconsciously nibbled my bottom one. I freed the lip, and he ran the pad of his thumb over it. A small spark of his special brand of electricity pricked the tender flesh before he moved his hand away. Blue fire blazed in his eyes, but for the first time, I realized, he'd used his gift with no guilt.

"I let go."

"Huh?" What were we talking about again?

A smile touched his lips. One that said he knew exactly why

I was discombobulated. "The scars aren't there anymore because I've forgiven myself. And I no longer believe that this"—he lifted his hand and formed a small blue globe of flickering lightning—"is because I'm cursed. I know I'm forgiven. I don't know what this is all about, but I don't believe it's from Satan."

"What changed your mind?" I asked.

"Love."

I scrunched my eyebrows.

"Love that I don't deserve but am given freely anyway. Truly accepting God's love and forgiveness gave me the strength to forgive myself and simply . . . let go."

"But how did you feel love and forgiveness when you were chained to a wall and tortured in Hell?"

He brushed a clump of hair behind my ear. I really needed to get cleaned up. "I was not forgotten, Audrey. I was not forsaken. Did I suffer? Yes. But it brought me you, and you are worth it. Worth facing whatever Satan tries to throw at me."

I was melting again . . . but the rush of emotion was quickly chased away by the sound of a clock tick, tick, ticking down to the moment I'd be forced to leave this realm—leave this amazing man I'd finally let into my heart.

I just . . . How was I to live with that?

I suppose the answer was that I wasn't. Life was more than just the time we spent living on Earth. The moment I became a slave to that fiery realm, that's the moment I'd truly lose my life.

Until that time came, I would live to the fullest. I didn't want to suffer through an eternity of regrets. The black mark on my back was proof I was here on borrowed time.

I knew exactly what needed to be done.

With a hand placed on his heart, I let my eyes sweep

Logan's face. His strong jawline, the hint of stubble around his mouth, cheeks, and chin, his straight nose and masculine brow that led to his soft and beautiful sun-kissed hair—hair that was currently sticking up all over the place from our tussle.

I sucked in a deep breath, inhaling the woodsy and spicy scent that I would forever associate with Logan, and then finally I brought my gaze back to where they'd begun. Meeting Logan's. I saw a slight question in his eyes.

I smiled, at peace. Laying a hand on his softly prickled cheek, I inhaled in a quiet breath of air.

"Marry me?" I asked.

17

SOUL FUSING

"Hold up a sec here." Kaitlin raised her hand to quiet us. "You mean he asked you to cement your bond and you freaked out so bad you passed out, and then you turned around and asked him to marry you like thirty minutes later?"

Kaitlin, Romona, and I were sitting in Romona's apartment on her plush antique couches with a full tea setting in front of us. I was chewing a cucumber finger sandwich . . . okay three sandwiches. I'd shoved one in my mouth right after the other. Those things were small, and I was hungry.

I lifted a shoulder and nodded, swallowing hard to clear my mouth. "Pretty much."

"And he said yes right away, right?" Kaitlin leaned forward, elbows propped on her knees.

Romona remained suspiciously quiet. That gave me an itchy nervous feeling. My grandmother-slash-best friend was too perceptive for her own good.

I'd opened with the news of Logan and my decision to be permanently bonded because I didn't want to hear about the briefing. I feared the truth. But by some miracle, they hadn't been told about the part I played in Satan's release. They would have brought it up if they knew anything. My knee bounced a nervous cadence as I wondered who knew besides Joe.

Since they hadn't already been told, I was assuming it wasn't going to be common knowledge anytime soon. And in that case, I'd already decided not to tell anyone my time here was limited. However, if anyone could put the pieces together, it would be my grandmother. Or Logan.

I would do whatever I needed to in order to keep that secret from them. I wanted to enjoy our time together while we had it.

"No," I absently answered Kaitlin.

I reached around to itch my back. I tried to ignore it, but when I finally got a shower, I couldn't help but notice the black mark on my skin had grown. The spot had doubled in size, and the veiny black-and-green fingers spreading from it had reached several inches long. I imagined the mark was an hourglass, its growth like dripping sand through a funnel and counting down my time in this realm. The spot remained hidden on my back, but I didn't know how far or to which parts of my body the blackness would spread. A time might come when it could no longer be concealed.

"What?" She huffed and slouched against the couch, arms crossed over her chest and brow pinched. "Are you kidding me? What's wrong with that boy? He's obviously insanely in love with you." Her words snapped me into the present.

Despite believing the same thing, I still blushed. "Well, you know Logan, first he had to explain to me—again—that we wouldn't be married"—I rolled my eyes—"that it would be a bonding ceremony or whatever." I waved a hand through the air. "Same difference, right?"

"Well kinda, except this is for eternity. No divorce and no till-death-do-you-part. But I guess if you don't count those things and the fusing of your souls then, yeah, it's pretty much the same."

I sprayed a mouthful of tea all over our delicious snacks.

"Excuse me? Fusing of souls? Whatever that is, it sounds painful. Can we do this thing without that part?"

Kaitlin and Romona shared a look. Kaitlin's eyebrows lifted, and Romona shrugged.

"What? What don't I know this time? Flipping orientation. Will someone please just hook me up to one of those machines that download all the important information about this realm already so I know what's going on?"

"Calm down, Audrey." Romona rested her fingers on my palm. Concern ripped through my body, and I snatched my hand back. Usually, Romona was all about transferring peaceful emotions my way.

"You can't expect me to calm down when you feel like that."

Romona sighed deeply and pursed her mouth. Her eyes scrutinized me for a moment before she decided to speak. "Audrey, what happened to being too young to go through with this right now? I thought the plan was to wait a few decades before any official ceremonies."

I shrugged and struggled to keep any physical sign of guilt from my body. "YOLO, right?"

"What in the world does that mean?" Romona tilted her head and studied me as if I was an alien species.

Kaitlin snorted a laugh. "As if that applies to this situation."

"I don't get it." Romona's questioning look bounced back and forth between Kaitlin and me.

Kaitlin waved her off. "It's just a saying that kinda means

'seize the day while you're young.' It obviously doesn't apply. Audrey's being weird."

"Hey."

"I call 'em like I seem 'em, girl."

"You're the worst. You know that, right?"

Kaitlin's smile broadened.

"That's cool, I only wanted one bridesmaid anyway." I slung an arm around Romona's shoulders.

"Hey, come on now." The pout Kaitlin put on would have had any guy on his knees in front of her, begging for forgiveness or asking her how they could fulfill her deepest wish.

I just scoffed. "That's what happens when you annoy the bride."

Romona shrugged off my arm. "Audrey, you're not a bride"—her gaze slid pointedly to Kaitlin—"and you know full well she doesn't get bridesmaids, so stop pouting."

"Hey, I don't? Well, that's no fair. What am I supposed to hold over Kaitlin's head to keep her in line for the next few days?"

Romona sputtered and choked on a mouthful of tea.

"Days?" she croaked.

I nodded.

"Days, Audrey?"

Didn't I just nod?

"Yeah, why wait, right? We're already bonded. It's obviously gonna stick. Let's just get this show on the road and all of that."

Romona looked at me as if I'd lost my mind. I turned to Kaitlin for help, but her expression wasn't much different.

"What? Logan was cool with it."

"Of course Logan was cool with it. He's a dude." Kaitlin

snickered.

"Is this about sex?" Romona asked bluntly.

This time, the tea shot out of my mouth and nose. I coughed and hacked and blew my nose until my orifices cleared enough to speak.

"No. Oh my gosh. I can't believe you just asked that. This is not about sex."

Fuchsia. My hair was definitely hot pink right now. No doubt.

Kaitlin slapped her leg as she laughed. "If I were you, it would be. We all know you think Logan's a hot piece of—"

"Say it and I'll break something . . . on your face."

Kaitlin made a zipping motion across her mouth, but her shoulders still shook with unrestrained laughter. Oh man, I couldn't wait until she went through this. I was going to razz her so bad.

A blanket of heavy sadness settled on me when I realized I'd never see that day. I wouldn't be around when she fell in love. That wasn't the only thing I'd miss. I'd also never see my family again. After all the fighting I'd done, in the end, they would end up truly gone to me.

I mentally slapped myself. I couldn't fall apart in front of these two. They'd sniff out my secret like bloodhounds.

I plastered on a fake smile.

"If it's not sex that's rushing this, then what is it, Audrey?" Romona asked seriously. "Because, honestly, something seems off right now. Something's causing you to jump into this. What aren't you telling us?"

Too smart, that one. I needed to get some friends who weren't so sharp.

Oh, right, I wouldn't be making any more friends.

I shoved those thoughts to the back recesses of my mind

where I was trying to bury all depressing feelings.

"You were right before. It's definitely the sex. What can I say? I can't keep my hands off Logan. Might as well make it official and do it the traditional way and all that. Listen, I really gotta go." I stood and inched my way across the room. "Lots of planning and stuff to do. Er, ah, or figuring out what needs to get done. I'm obviously way behind. Sorry I ruined your tea with my snot. Pretty sure I sprayed the whole table."

Romona and Kaitlin both stared at me as I backpedaled toward the exit. Romona's gaze was calculating and Kaitlin's was stunned. No doubt they'd be chatting about me the instant the door clicked shut behind me.

Who could blame them? I was acting supremely weird.

I was saved when my back hit a hard surface.

Thank goodness. I suppressed the urge to shout free-dom!

Turning the handle, I spilled into the hall and slammed the door shut.

Free—and alone—I turned and leaned back against the smooth surface then sank to the floor right on the welcome mat in front of Romona's apartment.

"What exactly does soul fusing entail?"

We were sitting on a white linen couch in Logan's cottage. I'd never been to his home before. In fact, before that morning, I didn't even know he lived in the same redwood forest that bracketed the mountain range as I did. I had assumed he had some small little studio apartment in the city with a bed, bathroom, and punching bag in the corner.

Sneaky boy.

Logan's cottage, which he insisted was a cabin—semantics—was lovely and charming and homey. Not at all the Spartan living abode I'd expected.

We'd been discussing Morgan when I opened my mouth about the soul fusing.

Logan ran a hand through his hair, looking slightly uncomfortable. "Right. Sometimes I forget you didn't go through orientation."

"You and everyone else," I grumbled.

"So, soul fusing, it's really just a fancy way of saying we'll be permanently bonded."

Permanently. There was that word again. My skittishness about the permanence of our bond had bounced back and forth—I was happy about it one moment and fearful the next. We were definitely linked in an irrevocable way, but there was still a choice. When I was sent to the abyss, what kind of existence would I be sentencing Logan to if we went through with the official ceremony? I didn't think it would be anything different until this 'soul fusing' concept came into play. Now I was back to agonizing over whether or not this was a good idea. I definitely needed more intel.

"Does it hurt?"

He chuckled and shook his head. "No. It doesn't hurt. I've heard it's quite enjoyable in fact."

He wiggled his eyebrows.

"Are you seriously trying to make this sound sexual right now?"

"Audrey, I'm a dude about to be officially joined with the woman I love for the rest of eternity. My brain functions in a very limited capacity. Speaking of, did you know we get a year off from hunting after the ceremony?"

"A year? For what?"

He wiggled his eyebrows again.

"You've got to be kidding me. No one can go at it all the time for a year."

"We can give it a go." He wrapped his arms around me, attempting to haul me into his lap.

I pushed him away, grazing his skin as I did. Joy like I'd never felt before shot through me during that brief moment of contact.

In response to his emotions, guilt flooded my system, and I pulled back even farther. I didn't want to taint his mood. I'd become as nervous about the empathy link—the transfer of emotions through skin-to-skin contact in this realm—as Logan had once been. Putting on a good face was one thing, but emotions were almost impossible to control.

"Be serious here."

"Okay, fine." He stopped to study me, and I wondered what he'd felt through our brief touch. Getting a reprieve from the link in the Healing Center had been nice. Since the transfer of emotions would be distracting to the healers, the Center was the one place in our realm the empathy link didn't work. "It's not just for that. It's so we have time to truly and properly connect. It's supposed to be a gift to us so we're not separated for that first year. It's a bonding time for us in all aspects. Emotional and spiritual as well as physical."

"Finally, a straight answer." I chewed on my lower lip.

"What's going on in that beautiful brain right now?" He tapped my head, and I swatted his hand away. This new lighthearted, touchy-feely Logan took some getting used to. I was finally seeing a Logan free of the demons that used to haunt him.

This was who Logan was created to be, and new Logan or old Logan, I loved him. To see him so happy both lifted my spirits and crushed my heart.

How would he be after I was gone? Would going along with this charade of a bonding ultimately break him? Was I pushing him when I should be pulling back?

I chewed on my bottom lip some more. "Logan, why are you okay going through our ceremony so quickly?"

He tilted his head a fraction. "What do you mean?"

"When I told Romona and Kaitlin we were going forward with the ceremony in a few days, they thought something was wrong with me. I'm just wondering why you're so cool with it."

"Audrey." He took my face in his hands. Something he'd gotten in the habit of doing.

I liked it but suspected he was using the move to force my attention when he thought I might try to avoid his gaze. Clever man.

Think happy thoughts.

Happy thoughts that let him feel happy emotions from me. Nothing that let him know my heart was shredded and my soul torn.

Waves of pure joy and love filtered through the empathy link from him to me. I closed my eyes to bask in it a moment. It helped lighten my mood, even if only temporarily. They were beautiful, these feelings he had. Beautiful and infectious.

It should be strange for him to be so comfortable touching me, but I guess after seeing his body broken and knowing I was running out of time—the growing black splotch on my back attesting to that—allowed me to soak up every moment to its fullest.

"Love, open your eyes." He brushed his thumbs over my closed lids before removing his hands.

Love. My insides melted when he called me that. I obeyed.

"I should have claimed you as mine the moment we met,"

he said. My breath caught, and he nodded. "I knew then there was no one in any realm like you. If I hadn't been so consumed with pushing you away, we'd already be together in every way imaginable. So in my mind, we've already lost time. I don't want to waste another moment not being with you."

"That was sorta the perfect thing to say."

His smile was gentle and free from pride. "Only because I'm perfectly made for you."

He kissed my forehead and released me.

Okay, that was cheesy, but still, I couldn't stop my eyes from filling again. This was becoming an incredibly vexing habit of mine. The unimaginable joy we might have had together clashed with my knowledge that it would not be our future, and as a result my eyes continually filled and spilled.

Thank goodness I'd held back the tide until he'd removed his hands. I was walking a tight rope with no safety net. One move that wasn't anticipated, and I ran the risk of my emotions freefalling right into Logan. I'd be completely exposed.

So far, I think Logan thought my tears were kind of cute. Like I was overwhelmed with happy emotions or some girlie junk.

He was clueless.

Maybe when he found out the truth he'd be mad enough that he would get over me quickly. As much as the thought crushed me, it was the best-case scenario.

For the hundredth time, I questioned whether keeping my shame hidden was the right thing to do. If I weren't such a coward, I'd try to find Hugo and ask him for advice. But I was both ashamed to face him and fearful of what he'd say.

Staying away from Hugo, Joe, and the Creator was imperative. I had little doubt that if they found me, they'd be more inclined to chuck me into the fiery pit than help me out.

"I don't like that look." Logan brushed a hand along my cheek, and I flinched.

I hadn't been ready for that touch, and my emotions were untamed. What had he picked up in that brief moment of contact? I tried so hard to keep my thoughts on him when we were together. To keep the darkness at bay ... but I hadn't guarded myself at this particular moment.

Logan's brows furrowed, and his eyes darkened.

We stared at each other.

What was he thinking?

He was probably wondering what *I* was thinking.

He nodded to himself. "All right, you'll tell me when you're ready."

"Huh?"

"Whatever it is that has you feeling like that"—he nodded toward me—"I have faith that you'll tell me eventually."

"You're not going to harass me into talking about it?"

He was quiet for a moment. Thoughtful.

"Audrey, I'm always going to want to know what's going on with you, especially the things that bother and burden your heart, but I realize that I need to earn your trust. Yes, we're bonded and I believe with every fiber of my being that we were created for one another, but there are some things that need to develop over time. So yeah, if you've got some stuff you're going through that you're not ready to trust me with yet, I understand."

I released a breath.

"But, Audrey." He waited until he was sure my gaze was locked with his. "We're in this together now, which means that if you're ever in danger, I need to know."

I tried to swallow, but my throat was dry.

"I'll give you the time and space you need, but I need you to tell me if you're in trouble."

I nodded. What else was there to do? Lies were a slippery downward slope, but since I was already freefalling, I stuck with the program.

Logan clapped his hands once, making me start. "Now, I know just what to do to get you out of this funk. Let's get out of here."

18

ARCHIVES & THINGS

"You're taking me to the training center?" I eyeballed the large building as we walked along the path I traversed most days. I was dressed casually in jeans and a tank, and Logan was definitely not cleared for a workout yet—but I wouldn't put it past him to try for it. "How . . . romantic."

"What?" He glanced at me, his arm slung over my shoulder. "It seemed to me like you needed to work off some extra energy."

I shoved him off. "Oh, shut it already."

He chuckled and rubbed his chest. Pfft, as if that actually hurt. Eye roll.

"Man, you seem extra strong. You taking some performance-enhancing drugs to up your game?" He smiled as he spoke, but ice chilled my veins.

Was I extra strong? Was I developing a new talent? I didn't have my flaming sword anymore. Had I traded my holy weapon for satanic super strength?

"Hey, what's wrong?"

We'd stopped walking, and I was too in my head to care.

Logan faced me. The crease that settled between his eyebrows was the only indication he was worried. He looked very much like the familiar 'all business' Logan I'd known since my first arrival here.

"What just happened? You know I was joking, right? We're not going to the training center."

I shook my head and forced a wooden smile. "Sorry. Just got stuck in my head there for a bit."

He nodded. "I noticed. Are you sure you don't want to talk to me about it?"

That was the problem. Because I did.

I desperately wanted to talk to him about it and have him fix the un-fixable and make it all go away.

But that was a fantasy. This wasn't going away. My fate had been sealed in blood.

I shook my head.

Logan heaved a sigh and continued down the path. This time, he didn't take my hand or put an arm around me.

I didn't blink as we walked through the entrance of a pearlescent, columned building. It appeared to be about five or six stories from the outside. We passed through the revolving doors and . . . were we outside again?

"What is this place?"

Logan's fingers grazed my hand. His happiness mixed with my wonderment. "It's beautiful, right?"

My eyes skated from one place to another. Taking in the dense tree cover, the beautiful flower-lined paths, and . . . wait, was that a purple bunny?

"Yeah, that's one word for it." I didn't realize I'd spoken out loud.

I closed my eyes and sucked in a lungful of sweet scented air. When I opened them again, rainbow light shimmered on the grassy path in front of us. I reached my arm out, and the multicolored light coated my hand and tickled my fingers with warmth.

"I don't understand. Did we just go through a portal?"

"No." With two fingers, Logan tenderly tipped my head and pointed up with his other hand. "We're in a solarium. Can you see the glass?"

I peered through the canopy of leaves above our heads. If I tilted my head just right, light reflected off a spot above us. I would have never known we were in a glass enclosure if Logan hadn't pointed it out.

"Wow . . . just wow." My eyes started to water from not blinking. I fluttered my lashes and glanced at Logan. "So, where are we?"

Logan looked back at me and blinked, unmoving—there was an intensity to the moment I didn't understand. Warmth filled my cheeks and then, like a wave, rolled through my body. There was a spark of blue that ignited from Logan's hand, even as his gaze remained locked on mine.

"What?" Did I have something on my face? Oh gosh, was I drooling or something? I wiped at my mouth. No drool. Phew. Something in my teeth? What was it? "Why are you staring at me like that?"

The blue in Logan's eyes flashed as if backlit, and the next moment the black pupils almost completely swallowed the color. He snaked his arm around my back and pulled me close, cupping my neck with his hand.

I struggled to stop a second full body blush. I had a pretty good idea of what was going through Logan's mind. His emotions overpowered mine.

"You are beautiful beyond words." His lips were a whisper away from mine.

He was the beautiful one.

He leaned even closer so that our lips were just touching. Neither of us moved.

"What color is my hair?"

He blinked once then buried his face in my neck, laughter shaking his body.

"Oops, was that a mood killer?" I asked.

Logan continued to laugh, the sound rich and deep. He placed a loud kiss to the side of my neck before pulling back. At least I still amused him.

"It's whatever color says 'I love Logan.'"

I pushed a hand into my hair and kept it from view. "You know, I don't even want to know."

"Probably not." Only his eyes were laughing at me now.

"Man, I need to find the receipt on this talent so I can return it."

Logan shook his head. "Never. How else would I know how you're feeling?"

"You're joking, right? Because I'm pretty sure I have the worst poker face in the world."

"That's true as well."

Rather than punching him in the gut, I pushed away with narrowed eyes.

"We're in the Archive Building." Logan's eyes still danced with mirth. I couldn't truly be upset with him. "Romona mentioned that you might have identified a new species a while back. I thought we could check to see if the little guys are recorded here."

"Oh. I'd forgotten about that." I slapped a hand to my face. "I really hope someone had already discovered them."

"Why?"

"Did Romona tell you what I named them?"

"No."

"Well, that's why."

With a smile I was still getting used to, Logan took my hand and guided me along the grass-covered path. "Let's go see if your genius is recorded for the rest of eternity."

"Oh, great."

After our quick jaunt through what was nothing short of an enchanted forest, we pushed through another revolving door. This time we emerged into a great library. Shelves upon shelves of books lined the perimeter of an open space reaching six stories into the air.

I'd suddenly stepped into a Disney version of heaven. Should I be looking for Belle?

People with wings strapped to their backs flitted around in front of the books, plucking them from their homes and bringing them down to be read.

No thank you, I was not going there again. Last time I'd tried flying with those contraptions I'd not only crashed into a floating chandelier but also an occupied table. I ended up wearing someone else's meal.

I was shaking my head before Logan could utter a word. "Nope. No way. Absolutely not."

"But you fly so gracefully," he teased.

"Yeah, you mean I crash so splendidly. I'm sure if I even tried that again, Alrik would be around to—"

Reality crashed down on my head. Alrik wouldn't be here to do anything anymore, ever again. He was in Hell, working with Satan.

Logan tactfully ignored my slip. "Aw, all you need is a little practice."

He just meant to tease, but his words pulled up a wash of emotion again. I wouldn't be here long enough to practice anything. All I had were the memories I could make before our time ran out.

Logan misread my face . . . or perhaps my hair color. "Don't worry. This isn't why we're here anyway. We're just passing through."

"It is quite a sight."

We walked down the middle aisle. To our left and right were long wooden tables with a smattering of people seated at them. Large books lay open in front of most of them.

"They're reading the history of their loved ones," Logan told me.

"What?"

I glanced at Logan, and he jerked his chin at the table in front of us where a middle-aged man sat reading a book several times thicker than an encyclopedia. He smiled softly smile even as I spotted the track marks of dried tears on his face. We brushed past his table, and I stole a peek over my shoulder. The man remained hunched over the book.

"These books hold the current stories of every living person on Earth. It's one of the ways people can catch up on their friends' and families' lives."

"This place is huge, but there can't possibly be enough books in this room for every single person in the world."

"The books are also stacked several rows back—as in, several thousand rows. You have to check in with a librarian first"—he pointed at a desk in the corner where a young woman stood in front of a monitor—"and then the book is brought to the forefront and you can go fetch it."

"But books? That seems like a rather impersonal way to find out about someone's life. Wouldn't a recording of some sort be better?"

He shrugged. "Have you ever read a book before? Some people would argue they're the best way to get sucked into a good story."

"Have you ever read someone's history here before?"

A muscle in Logan's jaw jumped—the only indication my question had affected him. I hadn't realized it would be a personal thing to ask.

"Never mind. You don't have to tell me."

He blew out a breath and tipped his head toward me. "No, that's a fair and simple question. Truth is I've been avoiding this place. I probably should have at least checked in on my parents, but I've been too . . . "

Despite not wanting to pry, I waited for Logan to continue. He ran a hand through his hair. "I suppose what I'm trying to say is that I dove into my new existence and did whatever I could to bury my past. With the exception of Kaitlin, this was my fresh start. I took hold of it and didn't look back. But I'm learning that burying my feelings isn't healthy. I need to make a trip here soon—if for no other reason than to honor my parents. They deserve that. Just not today, okay?"

"Yeah, of course."

"But if you have any questions about looking up someone's history, you should check with Kevin."

"Really?"

"Yeah, he visits at least once a week to check up on his family."

I didn't know why, but that surprised me. "Wow, that sounds . . . incredibly hard."

A strange look shadowed Logan's face, one I wasn't familiar

with and gone as quickly as it came. "It's a little different for him. You'll have to ask him yourself, though. It's his story to tell."

My interest was piqued. "What does that mean?"

"Here we are." Logan pushed through a set of ancient-looking doors, cutting off my interrogation in the process.

This guy. Seriously?

I took my eyes off his face and scanned the new area. The room was small, with two unmarked doors and nothing else. I was underwhelmed.

"Ah, yep. Here we are all right." Logan smiled beside me. He pointed to the unmarked door on the right. "That door leads to the Artifacts Room. We're headed through this other door."

Before I could ask him more about the room we weren't entering, he'd opened the door on the left and let me walk in in front of him.

Ahhh . . . another white room.

"Is this a museum?"

Logan's low chuckle echoed off the bleached walls around us. Hallways stretched out forever in front of us and to the left and right. I took several steps to the left and encountered another hallway.

On the white walls of each hallway hung photographs of animals. Most I recognized. A few I didn't. Under each picture was a gold plaque with the name of the animal, dates listed—some with a date range like those seen on a tombstone—and then a person's name. Most of them had "Adam" listed, but a few here and there featured other people's names. It didn't take me long to figure out these were pictures of every species that ever existed, even the ones now extinct, and who first gave a name to them.

"Please tell me we don't have to search this whole place?" I did a slow turn. I couldn't even imagine how long it would take to check each picture.

"Naw, come here." He gestured to an empty spot on the wall with a tilt of his head. "We can look it up."

"Thank goodness. I don't want to waste any more time than I have to."

"You find spending time with me a waste?" The teasing note in his voice betrayed him.

I shot him a side glance. "That's not what I meant, and you know it."

"A couple months ago I might not have."

"Well, quite a bit has changed since then, hasn't it?" I lifted my eyebrows in a challenge to refute me.

"I certainly hope so." He turned to the wall and pressed his palm to it. A screen appeared in front of us, much like the ones at the Healing Center. At this point, things just appearing at a touch didn't surprise me in the least.

"All right, so, tell me what name you chose, and I'll see if it's in the system."

I grimaced and squeezed my eyes shut. "Maybe this wasn't a good idea."

Logan chuckled. "Come on, spit it out already."

"Ah, this is the worst." I covered my eyes with a hand before answering, "Star shooters." When I dropped my hand, I glared at him, daring him to laugh. He ran a hand over his mouth in an obvious attempt to wipe away any evidence of a smirk.

"I think it's cute."

I rolled my eyes.

He moved his fingers over the screen, and after a few moments, nothing came up. "Huh, that's strange. Maybe they'd already been discovered." Logan's eyes remained glued to the monitor, as though searching for something that wasn't actually there. "You sure that was the name you gave them? There wasn't any variation?"

"Yes, of course I remember. I just called them 'star shooter thingies,' and then Romona and I went and had lunch."

Logan shook beside me as he tried to bottle a laugh. His fingers moved over the screen again.

"What? It's not there. That means someone already named them, right?"

"Not exactly," he said. I'd been staring at him, but he directed my attention to the screen with a pointed finger.

"No." I rubbed my eyes and groaned. When I opened them, the picture on the screen hadn't changed. The same cute aquatic creature Romona and I had spotted was captured to perfection.

Its scales shimmered a pretty purple-blue. One tip of the star shape stuck out more than the rest. Two of the appendages opposite the long one were fish-like tales. The image came to life, and the other two points of the star flattened to the creature's body when it swam, allowing it to dart to and fro. It moved like an aquatic hummingbird.

Under the image in big bold letters for all to see was my name, AUDREY LYONS, along with the words STAR SHOOTER THINGIES.

"It's not that bad." Logan laughed behind me. I'd moved forward without realizing it, my nose only inches from the screen.

"Oh, those poor creatures. They sound like a bad frat party shot." I shook my head in shame.

Logan howled with laughter.

I wanted to complain, but I couldn't blame him his

reaction. If the roles were reversed, I never would have let him live the embarrassment down. I deserved a good ribbing for this one.

"Can it be undone?"

Logan shook his head and wiped a tear from his eye. "'Fraid not. Those little guys will now and forevermore be known as"—he cleared his throat—"star shooter"—he cleared it again to get the last word out—"thingies."

I closed my eyes. "Promise me you'll never let me name another species."

He pulled me to his side and tucked me under his arm. My hand naturally came up to rest on his chest, and I looked up into his stormy gaze. He bent his head down and whispered, "Promise."

My heartbeat picked up. What were we talking about again? I nestled into Logan's embrace and sighed contentedly. Since when did a cotton t-shirt feel so good?

"It's nice to see this again." He brushed a hand through my hair and pulled some of it forward. The strands were a pretty lavender shade with only a few wisps of pink through it. "I'd like to believe this color means something good."

My stupid hair . . . but he was probably right. With his lips so close, I had to wonder why we were still talking. My eyes zeroed in on those kissable peppermint lips. With the limited time I had, I wanted as much of him as I could get.

That thought was like being doused with a pitcher of ice water. My body reacted in a visceral way—a chill shot straight up my spine, and my muscles locked. Logan's eyes widened. The hair he held in his hand turned to an icy blue before both our eyes. He dropped the strands and took hold of my face with both hands. My out of control emotions slammed into both of us, and I jerked out of his hold.

"What is it?" I hadn't heard the cold bite to Logan's words since before we bonded. "What just happened?"

"I . . . ah, um . . . I'm not sure what you mean." I stumbled over my words as if I were blindly walking through a field of rocks.

Logan's eyes narrowed. After several heartbeats, he swiped a hand down his face. When he looked at me again, his eyes were filled with sorrow.

He took a step closer to me; I forced myself not to retreat.

"Audrey"—the way he said my name caused my heart to ache—"you can lie to me with these"—he brought his fingers up and ghosted them over my lips—"but that doesn't lie to me"—he pointed at my hair—"and neither does this." He patted his chest. "Don't you feel it?"

I was honestly perplexed at what he meant.

His brow creased in frustration, and he thumped his chest. "In here, don't you feel me like I feel you?"

My eyes widened. He could feel my emotions even when we weren't touching? I still had the Logan-GPS, but I hadn't felt anything from him since we returned to this realm. The last time I'd felt anything of his without the aid of the empathy link was in Hell.

He read my answer on my face. "Well, I can feel you, and it seems an awful lot like you're not only shutting down on me, but you're hiding something. Something big. Something that scares you."

Right now *he* was scaring me. The level of intimacy he was describing felt . . . invasive. At least with the empathy link there was some sort of choice about whether to share emotions, but what he was talking about left me feeling vulnerable in a way I was far from comfortable with.

I took another step back. Logan's face twisted, a shadow of

the agony I'd seen etched on his face when he was chained to that wall in Hell. Except this time, I was the cause of his pain.

"Audrey, please don't." He reached a hand toward me. He *did* know what I was feeling, because I was half a second away from bolting.

A sudden stabbing pain exploded in my chest. I cried out. Was he causing this sensation? Or was I? I pressed a hand to the ache and held the other up, warding him off. He'd almost closed the distance between us without me noticing. His jaw was clenched and his hands opened and closed to fists. The muscles in his forearms bunched up.

"I just." I choked on my words. "Right now I can't."

And then I fled.

19

MEMORIES

The memories that blanketed this pond whispered through my subconscious. I'd passed the glassy waters right outside the Training Center almost every day since arriving in the afterlife. I had confessed my bond with Logan to Romona on the very bench where I was now seated. I stared at the blue-green depths. It looked so perfectly . . . normal. Its rim was speckled with people fishing or kids running in and out of the water along the edge and squealing in delight.

I knew the chilly bite of the water firsthand from when Logan had chucked me into the pond out of frustration. Frustration eventually led to mutual respect, which broke into an awkward limbo after we kissed. Awkwardness became doubt and, somehow in a crazy turn of events, translated into love in the end.

And that's what this was . . . the end. Logan thought this was the beginning, but I knew better. This was the beginning of the end.

Folding my body, I dropped my head into my hands, shielding my eyes from the view if not from the truth. Bear's paw landed on my knee. He'd joined me only minutes after I'd settled myself on the bench. His paw was his way of reminding me he was here to provide comfort. Comfort I wasn't sure I actually deserved.

Logan deserved more than this. He deserved more than me.

A weight dropped into the seat next to me and shook the bench.

I yelped and jolted upright, grabbing the seat to steady myself.

"Heard you've been visiting the archive building." Kevin's smile was so wide I'm pretty sure I could see his molars.

Bear jumped up on the bench on the other side of me and laid his giant head on my lap. I absently ran a hand over his soft, golden fur.

"Kevin. Geez. You know how to make an entrance, huh?" I squeezed my eyes shut and pinched the bridge of my nose. Kevin was an amazing friend. But I wasn't sure I was up to his level of chipper at the moment. Drained and emotional, I wasn't confident in my ability to fake normalcy.

He nodded with a blinding smile still in place. "I saw you over here and thought you looked a little down. Looks like you could use a friend right now."

I shrugged. "I have Bear."

Kevin leaned forward to survey my friend. "Yep. That's part of what tipped me off."

I looked at him. "What do you mean?"

His smiled dimmed and turned into a knowing up-tilt. "You haven't figured out this fluffy guy is pretty tuned in to your emotions yet? He was your Bear long before he was ever Battle Bear. His instincts are to comfort as well as protect. He's over here comforting. I figured that means you need it."

I looked down at Bear. The fur on his forehead scrunched

as he looked up at me. A puddle of drool was already forming on my jeans. A small price to pay for good company.

Bear was my dog, but he was also his own. He came and went like a dog on Earth would never do. And when I took a moment to look back, I realized he was always around at exactly the right times. Just like how he'd found me today.

I looked into those big brown eyes and scratched the spot I knew he loved. *You little genius.* He guffawed out a noise that oddly resembled a laugh before closing his eyes and leaning into the scratch.

"So"—Kevin stretched his long body out; legs straight in front of him with ankles crossed and arms along the back of the bench—"wanna tell me what's up?"

Yes. My secrets were straining to be released.

"Not really," I answered.

"Hmm." Kevin looked at me from the corner of his eye, likely seeing through my façade but too polite to push the matter. "Why don't you tell me what you think of the Archives Building then? That a safe enough topic?"

He wasn't mad. He was simply looking for me to talk. I appreciated that and let out a deep breath. He wasn't going to give me the third degree.

"That place is definitely . . ." I struggled for the right way to explain it. "Otherworldly. But then again, look where we are." I swept a hand in the air to indicate the wonders of this realm.

Kevin nodded. His eyes fixed on the various groups of people in and surrounding the pond. A soft smile touched his lips. "Otherworldly. I suppose it is."

"Logan mentioned you spend time in the Archive Building pretty regularly."

For the first time, Kevin's smile faded. I studied his profile as his face tightened and relaxed again—almost as if I'd said something painful. Had I stuck my foot in my mouth without realizing it? Certainly wouldn't be the first time.

"Yeah." He nodded. "I spend a bit of time in there."

"I'm sorry," I began. I rested a hand on his shoulder. "It's really none of my business. I shouldn't have brought it up."

I hadn't even thought it through. For all I knew, Kevin could have a wife and kids still on Earth he was checking up on. I'd never even asked how old he was when he died. Considering Romona was in her seventies when she passed away, yet now looked to be in her late teens or early twenties, Kevin could have been any age when he passed.

"Naw." He turned his head and shot me a smile. "No worries, Audrey. I like to check up on my family. It's just . . ." He blew out a puff of air and squeezed the back of his neck before looking to the side and appraising me. I wasn't sure what was going on. "How much do you know about my past?"

I chewed on my lower lip, suddenly embarrassed I didn't know much. I was a lame friend. "I'm sorry, Kevin. I really only know that you're in Romona's building because you're waiting for some of your family members to arrive before settling into a permanent residence."

He nodded. "Yeah. Do you have any idea how long I've been here?"

I didn't detect any malice in his questioning, but I also wasn't following his train of thought. "Um, no. Was it rude that I didn't ask?"

Kevin started to laugh.

"What? I never know which questions are taboo here. I don't want to come across as offensive, but I also don't want to seem uninterested."

"Sorry, Audrey. I shouldn't laugh. I just wanted to know how much you knew of my past to know where to start. I've been here for eighteen years, four months, and three days."

"Well." I blinked twice. "That is very specific."

He ducked and bobbed his head at the same time—like that admission embarrassed him.

"So you haven't been aging since you arrived, because that looks about as old as you are now."

"No, I've been aging. In fact, I age every day. Since I arrived in this realm, I age as if it were a regular Earth day."

I widened my eyes as the truth penetrated my self-absorbed thoughts. "But that would mean that . . ."

That what? That Kevin had died as an infant? Died before birth? It meant that he'd died before he'd ever truly had a chance to live. "You grew up here?"

The questions ricocheted around my mind, and I studied his face, looking for answers. It wasn't my business, it truly wasn't. But there was a story here I never knew existed.

"My mother was sixteen when she became pregnant with me. Two years younger than you are right now. She was young and scared and didn't want anyone to know. And so after hiding her pregnancy for three months, she aborted me."

A gasp escaped my mouth at the same time my hands flew up to cover it. Kevin stared at me with sad eyes as I tried to tap down my emotions. I forced my hands to my lap, thumping Bear, and absently twisted my fingers. "Kevin, I—"

His warm hand landed on both of mine, stopping their restless movement. A wistful joy saturated my heart . . . straight from Kevin.

"She was so young, Audrey. And her heart still aches over what she did. I have brothers and sisters now. I have a whole family on Earth that I'm looking forward to meeting in person someday. But in the meantime, I like to check in on them from time to time."

"But aren't you . . . I don't know . . . upset at her? Angry at the life you never got to live?"

He nodded. "Yeah, I could look at it that way. But tell me, what would that really accomplish? Do I wish I'd had a chance to live a long life? Yeah, there are times I think about that. Maybe even a lot. But rather than dwell on what might be perceived as things I was robbed of, I choose to look forward to the day I'm reunited with my family. The day I see my mother, look her in the eyes, and tell her I love her . . . and that I forgive her. She needs to hear that."

Kevin sat back in his seat and turned his attention to the pond. "That's a day I'm really looking forward to. That will be a great day."

A single tear slipped down Kevin's cheek. He let the wetness fall to his chest as a soft smile overtook his face. "I choose love and forgiveness, Audrey, because the same has been given to me."

Kevin left hours ago, yet I was sitting on the same bench. Bear's head lay in my lap as I stroked him. His snore and the large wet spot on my legs said he'd long since fallen asleep.

I didn't want to leave here—this realm. I didn't want to give up all I had and spend eternity in misery. I wanted to be with friends and family, and I wanted to be here to welcome the ones still on Earth when their time came.

But there was nothing to be done. I'd committed an unforgivable offense by freeing Satan, and I couldn't even wrap my brain around the repercussions. Was there a way to count the lives that would be affected? If there was, did I even want to know?

My heartbeat picked up as my Logan-GPS told me he was near.

I couldn't do this alone anymore. He had to know what I'd done. Letting him fuse his soul to someone who was going to leave was just . . . selfish beyond comprehension. What had I been thinking? I had to tell him so we could break the bond. It would be hard, but not yet impossible.

No bonding ceremony for us. It would be cruel. He deserved nothing but the absolute truth.

Fingers wisped through my hair.

"You're sad."

Bear jumped off my lap and trotted off without a backward glance.

"What gave it away?"

Logan moved around the bench to sit next to me. He ran his hand through my hair again and brought it in front of my face. The strands were grey-blue. He let them slip through his fingers and pulled back, leaving what might as well have been a cavern of distance between us.

"I'm sorry for running away."

Logan angled toward me. One leg bent up on the bench so he could fully face me. I mirrored his posture. Our knees brushed against each other when one of us shifted, but besides that we were very . . . separate.

A crease formed between Logan's brows as he studied me.

Ducking my head to avoid his gaze, I chewed on my lip.

"We need to talk," I whispered.

He nodded. "Your place or mine?"

My mouth quirked. "That sounded really cheesy . . . and a little seedy."

With a twinkle in his eye, he did a one-shoulder shrug.

"All right, let's go back to your place," I said. *That way I can kick myself out after I've revealed the truth.*

20

COMING CLEAN

I was pacing. Most likely wearing a hole in Logan's rug. Whatever, he could materialize a new one. The real problem was I couldn't find words, which meant I couldn't stop pacing.

Logan sat on his couch in front of me. But from the look of things, he was just as wound up as I was. He leaned forward with his arms draped across his knees and hands hanging as he watched me walk back and forth. The crease between his eyebrows had returned, but he stayed silent. Whenever I glanced at him, a muscle in his face would jump.

Besides that he was a statue. "Would it help if you sat?"

I jumped at the sound of his voice. "Huh? What?"

The crease deepened. "Do you want to—"

"No, sorry. I heard you." I stopped pacing and pressed the palms of my hands into my eyes until I saw stars.

All my fault. All my fault. All my fault, my mind relentlessly chanted. My secret was a festering wound that wouldn't heal until I cut it out.

And to cut it out, I had to admit to someone it existed.

I had to admit to Logan it existed.

Removing my hands from my eyes, I found Logan's. "It's all my fault."

The words hung in the air between us. I waited for his reaction. And . . . nothing.

"Well?" I prompted.

"Care to give me a little more information than that?" he asked.

I gestured wildly with my hands. "Everything. All of it. Everything everyone's been talking about. Satan's imminent attack. His release. It's all my fault."

"How?" Besides the slight tilt in his head, not a muscle so much as twitched.

Really, that was all he had to say? "Does it matter?"

He straightened, shoulders back and hands gripping the couch cushions. "Yes, of course it does."

"Okay, first let me show you something."

"All right."

I turned away from Logan and lifted the back of my shirt high enough that he was sure to see a good deal of the growing darkness there. A physical representation of my mistake—and the consequence I would pay for it. I squeezed my eyes shut and waited for his outburst. He was going to blow for sure. But the room remained silent for several minutes.

"Love, why are you showing me your back?"

"What?" I turned my neck until I could see him. Logan's stare was blank. "It's right there. It's huge and black and ugly . . . and growing." I lifted my shirt higher so I could see the evidence of my cursed soul myself. Yep, still there.

"Audrey, I don't know what you're talking about. I don't see anything."

He couldn't see the mark? Was I the only one who could?

There was actually a little bit of relief in that. Dropping my shirt, I turned to face him.

I rubbed my forehead. The threat of a headache beat behind my eyes. He couldn't see the darkness. So how was I to make him understand?

"Logan." I looked into those beautiful cobalt eyes. "We can't be together."

He shot to his feet and advanced. I took two hurried steps back.

"What? Why? You need to start explaining all this to me, quickly." His fists clenched at his sides.

I had no fear he'd use them against me, but his reserve of patience had apparently just run out.

"Well, it's . . . complicated." I twisted my hands, mimicking the churning in my gut.

"Uncomplicate it for me." The look in his eyes said *who do I need to destroy?*

My brain . . . blanked. Logan's hands crackled as he struggled to maintain his composure—his frustration leaked out in unseen waves.

I wasn't scared. I was . . . in awe.

"Audrey." One word. A command to start talking.

And so I did. I spilled it all without holding back one gory, ugly detail. The trek through the rings, how I'd somehow slipped into his mind at one point, our party getting sent back to our realm piece by piece until Joe and I were the only ones left. And finally what had happened in the cell he'd been strung up in. How my sword shattered, accidentally stabbing Joe when I went after Alrik, and Satan's release and promise to me.

By the end of my tale, my cheeks were drenched. Logan had taken his seat again on the couch, and I sat facing him on an armchair. The length of the coffee table was all that was between us, but it might as well have been an impenetrable wall for how isolated I felt.

Silence hung in the air.

Then the room exploded.

"No!" Logan roared. He shot to his feet and flung the glass coffee table against the wall. The furniture shattered into a million pieces. Lightning shot from his hand and connected to the window behind my head.

He pointed at something to my left, and a chair exploded. Burned stuffing littered the air around me, assaulting my sense of smell.

He was . . . unhinged.

"Logan." I jumped to my feet, intending to rush to him.

"No." A deadly calm overtook his features as he held his hands up to ward me off. Blue-and-silver lightning crackled around each finger, each knuckle, and halfway up his arm. His breath puffed out as if he'd just run a marathon. With each exhale, his hands sparked.

Throughout his rampage, I'd been more startled than afraid. But now the fear came. The fear that even though I was going to lose him eventually, I'd lost him sooner than I thought.

Was this anger at me? Rage at what I'd done—or at my selfishness in not telling him sooner?

But accusations didn't spit from his mouth. Instead he said, "No one is going to take you from me."

My eyes widened.

He went on. "I don't care what deals you may or may not have made. There isn't a being in existence who will take you from me. You. Are. Mine."

Steel rods pieced my heart.

"Logan." My voice softened, and I took a tentative step forward.

One hand raised higher even though he'd already warded me off. With the couch behind him, he'd have to hurdle over it or blow it up in order to retreat. There was a feral look in Logan's eyes I'd never seen before. My stoic-masked warrior had revealed a chink in his armor.

Me.

"Logan," I said his name again as my fingers grazed his jawline. The empathy link sprang to life between us. A sense of dread and desperation flooded me, like that of a dying man struggling to take just one more breath.

Logan was falling apart, right in front of me.

I pushed aside his feelings as best I could. Buried my own sorrow, guilt, and shame and focused on him. On us. That even though we'd only been given a speck of time together, at least we'd been blessed with that. I gathered all the love in my heart for him, and I poured it into our connection, determined to overwhelm him with positive emotions.

He crushed me to his chest. One of my hands remained gently placed on his face, and the other reached around to bury itself in his hair. Logan's face pressed against my neck. His arms were wrapped around my body in a vice-grip, as if he was determined to never let go. One wrapped completely around my waist, and the other crossed over my back with a hand, securing my shoulder.

Logan must have regained control over his powers because I wasn't getting electrocuted. The longer we stood, the more our emotions aligned. Comfort and love flowed in currents back and forth to each other.

I relaxed in his embrace, unsure of anything but this perfect moment we were experiencing in the middle of our mutual storm.

"Audrey." A whispered prayer into my hair. Logan shuddered.

I adjusted my grip on him, wrapping both my arms securely around his neck, as if I could hold him together by sheer force of will.

Then he was pulling back, and a sound of protest left my throat. My lips only began to form the word no—the actual word was smothered by Logan's kiss. The action was as desperate as he'd been a moment before, but I welcomed the wildness of it. That wildness was truth. There were no more hidden secrets or half-truths between us. And what this kiss might lack in finesse, it made up for in raw emotion.

I felt Logan compose himself through the kiss and empathy link. He was a star that had exploded but was now reversing time and tucking every burning ember and ray of light back into the places they belonged. Our kiss ended softly when he pulled his head back and used both hands to keep mine in place.

Smart man. He knew me well. Without restraint, I would have sought out those delicious lips for another taste.

I had to blink a few times to clear my kiss-fogged mind. Logan's smug smirk told me he knew exactly why I needed those few extra moments to compose myself. I rolled my eyes. Truth was he had a right to be smug, and I wasn't sure my voice wouldn't come out breathy if I tried to talk. An eye roll was the best I could do.

His smile faded, and his features ironed back out to warrior mode. His mouth and brow straight slashes. His eyes focused and intent.

I stared into the familiar face of my old mentor. The mask he had presented to me. The face I'd trained with for those first several months of our relationship.

Logan had slipped into his get-stuff-done mode. I struggled not to smile at his seriousness.

With hands on my shoulders, he guided me to a seated position on the couch. My gaze bounced around the room before focusing on him. Glass lay like splattered blood on the ground. Stuffing from exploded furniture littered the floor, and the skeletal remains of the unfortunate pieces of furniture bent at unnatural angles.

Logan had made a mess.

A giggle slipped out of me. I slapped a hand over my mouth and snapped my widened eyes back to him. *Shoot.* That wasn't supposed to happen.

Logan glanced over the carnage and shrugged. That simple gesture told me all I needed to know. He would destroy the world for me if he had to. What was one living room? Especially one that could be cleaned with a few concentrated minutes of materializing and dematerializing items.

"Audrey, I'll find a loophole."

I was shaking my head without even realizing it.

"I will," he said forcefully. "This isn't the end. There is no conceivable way that this is the end of us. This is the beginning."

My eyes filled with wetness at his words. At the fierceness with which he spoke them. I might have gone to Hell and back to rescue him, but this was a man who was telling me he would spend eternity searching for a way to destroy Hell itself for me.

But that wasn't the existence I wanted for him.

"No, Logan. What possible loopholes could there be? Satan was very specific about what would happen to me. The price of his freedom would be paid by the one who released him. The Creator himself set those terms. Nothing in any of our realms can change that. I stabbed Joe. I'm responsible for Satan's newfound freedom. I'm the reason our realm is in jeopardy. That's a stain too big to be removed from my soul. The time we have now is a gift I don't want to waste. But I won't shackle you to me. That would be the same as condemning you to an eternity of loneliness. Someday there will be someone else—"

"No." He nearly shouted the word, halting my speech. "No," he said again. "I will fight with every bit of my existence to keep you by my side. There will never be someone else. You are it for me. Forever."

I took a deep breath. My heart melted and broke at the same time. My next words would hurt both of us.

"For your sake, I hope you're wrong."

After Logan settled down, he riled himself right back up again when I told him I didn't want to go to Joe, Hugo, or the Creator. We'd had a fairly lengthy disagreement about that. Logan didn't let up until he saw the pure fear in my eyes. When that happened he agreed, for my sake, not to seek Their help. And so as a result, he was on a hunt to find a loophole to my damnation another way.

Logan was a man on a mission. I was pretty sure he wasn't even stopping to sleep. Rather than an idyllic last few days together, I hardly saw him.

I hardly saw anyone.

All my friends were running from one thing to another, or else they were missing in action on some secret defense plan for our realm. And me? I'd just been left adrift.

The original plan had been to train with Romona and

Logan, but then he'd been kidnapped, and now everyone knew Satan was on the loose—no doubt with his gaze fixed on our realm—so all normal activity had been suspended. So that meant no training, and no active assignments for me since I was technically still in training. If anyone should be out there making sure the heavenly realm was protected, it was me. But even as the training center was a flurry of activity, I might as well have been invisible. Satan could literally come for me at any moment, and I was being robbed of my goodbyes. That made me . . . furious.

I didn't regret telling Logan the truth. He deserved to know. But his stubborn refusal to believe I'd doomed myself to an eternity in Hell took him away from me as he . . . Well, I actually wasn't even sure what he was doing every day. He was a mystery.

On the rare occasion I did get to spend some time with him, he'd kiss my forehead and tell me he was going to fix this. Like my unwilling bargain was a broken toy he could glue back together. I didn't know everything, but I knew enough to know that wasn't how these things worked. I'd crossed a line that couldn't be uncrossed.

I wanted this time with him, with my friends, and I was being denied it. Perhaps that's what I deserved. Really, this was just borrowed time anyway.

"Hey, wait up."

I glanced behind me to catch sight of Kaitlin jogging toward me, blonde ponytail bouncing. I slowed my stride so she could easily catch up. With nothing to do, I spent a great deal of time walking aimlessly around the perimeter of our city.

She reached me and wasn't even out of breath. "So, it's off then?"

"Huh?"

"The bonding ceremony . . . You called it off after all?"

Truth was, Logan and I hadn't spoke of the ceremony after I laid the 'my soul is going to spend eternity in Hell for my sins' bomb on him. Yeah, I'd say there would be no soul fusing in the future, but I hadn't told anyone anything one way or another.

"Um, why do you ask? Did someone say something to you?"

Kaitlin cocked her head. The blonde silk of her ponytail disappeared behind her right shoulder. "No. It's just that you said it was happening in a few days, and I haven't heard anything about it. It's been a few days . . . so I figured . . ."

She let the statement hang in the air between us.

"I suppose it's on hold for an indeterminate amount of time."

"What's wrong?" she asked point-blank.

What wasn't wrong? The 'groom' was MIA most of the time on what was most likely some random fool's errand, I expected to get sucked back to Hell at any moment, and the time I wanted to spend with my loved ones was slipping through my fingers like sand because of an impending siege on our realm that I'd unintentionally helped orchestrate when I let Satan free.

"Nothing."

"You know, you and Logan have been acting really strange ever since—"

"Oh, come now, luv—you have so much free time you can speculate over your friends' romantic entanglements? I was under the assumption that dear Audrey and I were the only two hunters in the realm not being run ragged right now."

Saved by the sarcastic bite of Morgan's British humor. I was grateful for that, especially since I knew Kaitlin wouldn't, perhaps couldn't, back down from his taunts.

"Seriously, Morgan, we were having a private conversation here. Is this really any of your concern?" She moved to flip her ponytail over her shoulder only to find the hair was already there. Morgan ruffled Kaitlin's feathers like no one I'd ever met. I'd be willing to bet they had a history of some sort that my fair-haired friend wanted concealed.

Morgan shrugged. "I'm bored out of my mind these days. So why not make this my concern? Not much else to do."

"Are you seriously going to stand here and annoy us simply because you're bored?"

"Annoying you? Who knew?" He grinned. "That gives me extra incentive. Cheers."

Kaitlin's face turned a shade of purple-red I hadn't seen before.

I took a concerned step back and checked her ears for steam.

"You . . ." was all she could get out.

"Are incredibly handsome? Why yes, I already knew that. Thank you for the compliment."

Kaitlin's nose scrunched up as if she smelled something extremely unpleasing.

Morgan pulled his lips back from his teeth as if he'd just witnessed a hideous accident. "Oh, luv, you should never do that thing you're doing right now." He twirled a finger in her face. "It might get stuck that way, and that would be a supreme disappointment to men everywhere."

The look dropped from Kaitlin's face, and she stared at him with a slack jaw. "Do you even think before words come spewing from your mouth?"

"I try very hard not to. Thank you for noticing."

"Ah, I can't. I just can not." Kaitlin turned toward me with pinched features. "I'm headed back to the training center. This whole 'Satan on the loose' thing has us all working double time. Let's talk soon though. I want to make sure you're all right."

"Sure." I nodded. "I'd like that." A half-truth wasn't truly a lie . . . right?

She waved goodbye and disappeared in the direction she'd come from.

"I accept gratitude in the form of verbal or physical affirmation. Whatever you're most comfortable with." Reclined against the back of the park bench, his arms and ankles crossed, he was the picture of male arrogance. I understood why Kaitlin was annoyed.

He opened his arms to me. "So it'll be a hug then?"

I rolled my eyes.

He inclined his head apologetically. "I'm saving these lips for someone else. Nasty business this, no kissing issue. But I suppose we both know there are ways to get around it."

He wiggled his eyebrows at me suggestively. *Ew.*

"Of course," he went on, "I also wouldn't fancy having my handsome mug marred by your beloved." Morgan indicated his face with his hand. He was undeniably handsome—yet he still bore many of the scars from his torture in Hell. He might no longer look like Frankenstein's monster, but several lines still crisscrossed his cheeks and forehead.

If I thought for a moment he was seriously trying to flirt with me, I would have walked away. But as strange as the development was, I was morbidly drawn to Morgan now. I felt a sense of kinship with him, which disturbed me.

I pinched the bridge of my nose. "What exactly am I supposed to be thanking you for?"

"Why, getting rid of Blondie of course, so that you didn't

have to continue lying to her."

"I wasn't—"

"I have a knack for running that particular bird off. It's usually quite vexing, but it came in handy today. It's rather odd that she reacts so strongly to me, don't you think?"

"Probably because she hates your guts."

"Oh, Audrey, you above all should know there's a thin line between love and hate."

I ignored the jab and glanced in the direction where Kaitlin had disappeared. Even if there had been something between them before he sided with evil, he'd have a difficult time wooing that maiden now. She seemed determined to steer clear of him at all costs.

I was confident that, either way, Kaitlin could take care of herself.

"Well, good luck with that." I saluted Morgan and turned to continue my aimless walking.

"I figured someone who only had a few days of freedom left, at best, would be doing more than roaming around by herself."

I stopped so suddenly my feet crossed in front of each other, causing me to wobble. Finding my footing, I straightened and swung to face Morgan.

"What did you say?"

His mouth was in a straight line now, no hint of an amused smirk peeking through.

"Logan's spent the better part of the last two days grilling me for information. I'm sure he hasn't told me the full story, but I'm bright enough to fill in the blanks. Especially since I got a look at you shortly after your return."

The bottom of my stomach dropped out. "What do you know?"

"You see, the problem with deals with the Devil, luv," he said, ignoring my question completely. "You can never get out of them without paying a price. It seems to me that you may have bargained away all of your chips. Very unwise."

"I didn't bargain anything. I was tricked."

"Well, yes, they don't refer to him as 'the Great Deceiver' for no reason. Perhaps it makes you understand how Eve first fell prey to his schemes? And Adam followed right along. Tell me, have you ever given their story much thought?"

"Adam and Eve?"

"I've often wondered if it was the serpent who deceived Adam as well, or if Adam purposely damned himself to stay by Eve's side. Maybe he couldn't stand to be parted from her."

I blinked at Morgan. Was he saying what I thought he was? That Logan would willingly follow me into eternal damnation?

A sad smile touched his lips. Morgan pushed off from the bench and shoved his hands in his pockets, his shoulders hunched up near his ears for a moment. His pose screamed of hidden vulnerability.

Then his shoulders dropped, and his usual swagger returned.

"Well, it's been lovely talking with you, but I have a feisty blonde to nettle. Perhaps if I get good enough at it, they'll find something for me to do."

He set off but stopped after a few steps, turning his head to look back at me. "For what it's worth, Audrey, I hope you're able to take in as much beauty and enjoyment as you can. Take it from one who knows. However bad you're imagining your impending servitude might be, it will undoubtedly be worse. And I'm sorry for that."

His long strides ate up the distance quickly, and soon he, too, was out of sight. I stood there, staring at nothing. His words about Adam and Eve—and Logan—echoed in my ears. For the first time since returning from Hell, I was terrified for someone other than myself.

21

DESPERATE TIMES

Morgan's cryptic talk about Adam and Eve didn't just disturb me, it terrified me. Only minutes after finishing the conversation with him, I abandoned my wandering and bolted for Logan's cottage. I was prepared to camp out on his couch if I had to, until he returned and gave me answers about what he'd been up to.

And what was I going to do next? The black mark on my back had grown to almost a foot in diameter. I couldn't shake the feeling that when it got to a certain size, or reached a particular part of my body, that would be the end. I just didn't know the size or its destination.

Was my only move to protect Logan going to the Creator? I wasn't willing to do that for myself, but to make sure Logan stayed safe—in *this* realm and not the one buried deep within the Earth—I would risk getting hurled to Hell. If Logan was looking to take my place in Hell, I had to talk some sense into him. If not, he'd force my hand and I'd have to go to the Creator. Hopefully it wouldn't come to that.

My feet itched to pace, but I forced myself to remain rooted to the cushion beneath me. A half-hour after I'd planted myself in his living room, I felt Logan's presence nearby. Finally the hinges on his cottage door announced his arrival.

Evening had come, and I hadn't turned on any of his lights. I was sitting in the shadows like a stalker, waiting to be acknowledged.

Logan slammed the front door after he entered then punched a fist into the wall, leaving a rounded hole. He pressed both hands to the flat wood, and his shoulders and head sagged.

Did he not know I was here? He could feel me through our bond just as well as I could him.

I held my breath as I waited for his next move. He stood like a statue, so stuck in his thoughts that my presence must not be registering. Was he even breathing?

The cottage remained quiet until I heard something dripping, the sound similar to a leaky faucet. But this was Heaven, and things here didn't leak. Which meant . . .

Logan's hand was dripping blood onto the marble tile.

I sprang into action.

Logan startled and spun when my hand connected with his shoulder. He really hadn't realized I was here. I took a step back when I saw the wild look in his eyes. His hair was a disheveled mess, and not in a stylish way. In the sticking-up-at-weird-spots-since-he'd-run-his-hands-through-it-and-grabbed-it-out-of-frustration-a-few-too-many-times way.

"What happened? What's going on?"

For a few beats, the only sound coming from him was the continued dripping of blood from the cuts on his hand.

"Can you seriously ask me that?" he snapped.

I took another step back.

"Are you mad at me?" My voice was small.

"At you? No." He ran his fingers through his hair again, leaving streaks of red in his hand's wake. Regret crossed his expression, and he said, "What am I doing?" His arms shot forward, and before I realized his intent, I was smooshed against his chest—face first into his t-shirt, squeezed so tight I could hardly breathe.

Definitely more uncomfortable than endearing. I pushed back a little to get a breath of air.

"I'm so sorry," Logan went on. "I'm just not going to lose you."

His grip tightened, and my heart sank . . . because he *was* going to lose me.

I cleared my throat. "Hey, why don't we take care of that hand of yours? Then maybe we can sit down and have a talk?" I pushed gently against his chest again, and this time he let me go and let me lead him over to the kitchen sink where I washed the blood off.

As I held his hand over the sink, the red swirling down the drain wasn't what sent my heart pounding—the fact that hardly anything filtered through from the empathy link was what freaked me out. Logan looked over my shoulder at nothing while I worked. The worst hadn't even happened yet, and the man I loved was already turning into a shell of himself.

I secured the bandage around Logan's hand. He could get it fixed easily at the Healing Center in the morning; tonight we had more pressing matters. I led him back to the couch, took his face in both hands, and forced his attention. Still, all that came through the empathy link was a numbing void. What was happening?

"Talk to me," I demanded. Finally a pinprick of emotion leaked though. Fear. But he locked it up quickly and gently returned my hands to my lap, pulling his away. He clearly didn't want to be touched right now.

Okay, I could respect that. I didn't like it, but I could respect it. Sometimes emotions were so overwhelming that the thought of sharing them with someone else added to the burden. I wished he'd let me bear some of his pain, but that wasn't natural for Logan, and perhaps we just weren't there yet in our relationship.

Pain twinged in my chest as I realized we'd never have time to "get there."

"Really, Audrey, it's nothing. You know I'm just trying to find a way for us to stay together. I'm sure I'll figure something—"

"Don't lie to me, Logan." My voice was level, but his eyes widened. "And perhaps more importantly, don't lie to yourself."

"But, Audrey—"

I shook my head. "How much more time are you going to waste?"

He opened his mouth to answer, but I wouldn't let him proceed.

"I know you talked to Morgan about me. You can talk to whomever you want, you can search through the ancient texts, try to bribe angels, or whatever it is you do every day, but the facts aren't going to change. A price has to be paid for what's been done."

Logan shot to his feet. "Then I'll pay it instead."

I stood as well and craned my neck to look into his eyes. That was exactly what I was afraid of. "No. You stop whatever you're doing right now. I'm begging you. Begging you to stop and just be with me, here, now, while we can. This is my mistake. This is my price to pay."

"You wouldn't have even been in Hell if not for me. If I

hadn't kissed you, you could have stayed safely in this realm. That would have been better."

I sucked in a lungful of air, suddenly angry. "There are so many things wrong with that, I don't even know where to start." A tendril of hair turned red. I batted it out of my way. "First, do you believe if we weren't bonded I would have left you in Hell to rot? Second, Satan was using *you* to get to *me* the whole time, so I was the reason you were down there to begin with. Third, you're not the one who literally stabbed the Son of God. I get that lucky title all to myself, and fourth . . . fourth . . . if you're saying you regret kissing me in the first place, I will hate you forever."

I poked his chest on the last weak point of my argument. I'd backed Logan up to the wall without even realizing it. He was breathing hard, jaw grinding. But I was breathing harder. For me, anger was probably a little too quick to mingle with fear.

But I wasn't the only one who was angry. "First," he bit out and took a step forward, forcing me to take one back, "if you think there is anything short of eternal damnation that would make me regret bonding us, then I obviously haven't done a good enough job of expressing my feelings for you— something I will fix the minute we're done with this ridiculous argument."

My thoughts ran away from me before I could beat them into submission, and my entire body flushed. But Logan wasn't done.

"Second, bonded or not, I would rather you left me in that den of horrors for a lifetime than watch you not only get taken from me but also spend an eternity with a similar fate.

"Third, I will find a way out of this. Even if you've already given up, I will *never* give up on you. And fourth"—He backed me up until I bumped into the couch, lost my balance, and sat

down. Leaning in he put his hands on either side of my head—
"we both know there is no scenario in which you would hate
me forever."

A cocky grin appeared on his mouth that I both wanted to
slap off and smother with a kiss. Vexing. He narrowed his eyes
at me, practically daring me to do either.

"Well—"

I wasn't sure what my rebuttal was going to be, but it didn't
matter because Logan crushed his lips to mine before I could
get another word out. Whatever was going to escape my
mouth was swallowed by his, and like every other time we'd
come together like this, rational thought flitted right out of my
brain.

He had skills. Mad-crazy, mind-boggling kissing skills. So
good, in fact, I had no idea whose emotions belonged to whom
as his mouth pressed against mine time and time again. Anger,
fear, love, devotion, and desire all swirled into a tornado of
feelings that were impossible to segregate. But who had time
for sorting out feelings when they were kissing the love of their
life? Certainly not me.

Logan pulled back, and like always, I mindlessly protested
and leaned forward. He chuckled at my response. This was
getting embarrassing.

When the fog cleared from my brain, we were both staring
into each other's clear eyes. He uttered one word before diving
in for a second helping.

"Mine."

It branded my heart and my soul. I knew that whatever lay
ahead, we were going to face it together.

I opened my eyes and then slammed them closed again against the brightness streaming through Logan's large front window. I went to rub my face, but my arms were trapped.

Huh?

I looked down. A tanned, toned forearm was not only draped across my waist, but pinning my left arm in place. My other arm was somewhere above eye level. Whatever pillowed my head radiated heat and was oddly lumpy. My right hand was also really warm. I craned my neck to see the traitorous hand clasping Logan's.

Shoot!

How did I end up curled into him on his couch? I remembered a kiss, and that was about it. Did I pass out from lack of oxygen? It would have been worth it.

Whatever the reason, this was still an embarrassing situation. What if I drooled in my sleep? What if the weight of my head had caused his arm to go numb and he was too polite to shove me off? Why hadn't he woke me up and sent me home?

I mentally slapped myself. *Focus!* I needed to figure out how was I going to discreetly get off this couch. I shimmied my way toward the edge, ready to slide off the make-shift bed, when Logan made a sleepy sound and used the arm around my waist to haul me more firmly against him.

Ahh. Double shoot!

I tried to shimmy away again only to be hauled back a second time. But this time, a bolt of amusement shot through the empathy link.

I gritted my teeth and swatted at his hands. His arm was definitely higher now than the first time he'd pulled me back. Boys. My body shook with the rumble of Logan's laughter. I pried his heavy arm away and rolled off the couch . . . straight onto the ground with a resounding thump. Logan's chuckles turned into full-blown laughs.

I rubbed my hip.

"You're awful. You know that, right?" I called up to him.

His head appeared right above mine, and I yelped.

"We both know you don't believe that."

"You know nothing," I snipped back.

"I know enough." He wiggled his eyebrows.

I put my hand on his face and pushed.

"Pig," I said under my breath as I got to my feet and headed to the bathroom. I needed a toothbrush, STAT.

His laughs followed me down the hall, and although I was mildly annoyed, hearing him happy brought a secret smile to my face.

The grin stayed in place until I closed the bathroom door and turned to look at myself in the mirror . . . then screamed.

There was a thud down the hall, and then seconds later the bathroom door burst open. Logan was fully alert, all traces of humor washed away.

"What are you doing?" I yelled. "I could have been peeing in here."

His brow furrowed. "You screamed."

"Yeah, 'cause of this." I pointed a finger at my head.

Logan's features relaxed, and his eyes twinkled. He swept a hand down his face until he reached his mouth and covered it.

"Are you laughing at me?"

He shook his head, hand still over his mouth.

I pointed at the door. "Out."

He nodded once and left. As soon as the door clicked shut, I heard his bellows of laughter.

"I can hear you," I shouted.

"I know," he yelled back.

Shaking my head, I turned to the mirror. My hair looked like a birdie had made a nest in it, left, and then a rat had decided he wanted to give it a go. And the colors closely resembled Rainbow Brite's magical horse's mane.

I rubbed my eyes then pinched my nose.

"I think you're adorable," Logan yelled from somewhere in the house. Less to make me feel better and more to annoy me.

Jerk. This mess I called hair was at least eighty percent his fault. If he hadn't run his hands through it so many times yesterday evening, it wouldn't be this crazy.

My cheeks warmed at the thought, and I watched all the red lighten to magenta.

Maybe I wasn't as mad about that part as I was telling myself.

I shut my eyes and materialized a brush. Time to get to work. This nest wasn't going to fix itself. Over an hour later, I emerged from Logan's bathroom. I'd taken the opportunity to shower and change into fresh clothes as well as brush my teeth and fix my hair. The look on Logan's face when I sat down at the kitchen counter was worth the extra effort. I may have applied a little makeup as well. But he didn't need to know that.

He paused from making us breakfast. "Wow, you look amazing."

I cocked my head. "You mean I didn't look amazing when I woke up this morning?"

"Oh, you looked amazing all right. Just a different type of amazing."

I stuck my tongue out at him.

He winked. "You do realize that is in no way a turn-off to me."

When he turned back to the stove, I turned my hair brown again.

"Should we talk about last night?"

His shoulders tensed for a moment before he forced them to relax. "Talk, or reenact?"

Stupid hair, stay brown.

"Logan, you know what I mean. Talk about the big stuff we brought up before all the, you know, other stuff happened."

Brown, brown, brown.

Logan scooped something out of the pan in front of him and set the fluffy concoctions on two plates. He turned and put them down on the island then walked around it to take a seat next to me.

I looked down and smiled. He'd made me an omelet.

"Is this the only thing you know how to cook?" I asked.

He smiled back. "No, but I was feeling a little nostalgic today."

"Nostalgic about hiding out in a bunker in my dad's tool shed?"

"Something like that." His smile widened. "Eat up."

I dug my fork into the fluffy eggs already remembering how delicious they'd been last time.

"Audrey."

I stopped with my utensil mid-air, my mouth already half open. Logan reached over and steered the food home. He continued when I started to chew.

"I've considered what you said last night, and I see your point. I've been running myself like crazy these past few days. I've been a man obsessed, but I haven't considered what you need from me right now. So as long as you can accept that, I'm not giving up hope; I want to spend more time together. With or without this blood price hanging over our heads."

I went to interrupt him, but he silenced me with a tilted head and raised eyebrows, then continued. "It is *our* heads, not yours. We're in this together. But regardless of anything else going on, we should be together now."

I nodded my agreement.

"Great." He smiled broadly and then shoveled his omelet into his mouth, finishing his meal before I'd even gotten through half of mine. "Okay, so I gotta head out for a bit."

I started choking on my bite of egg. Logan slapped my back until the chunk was dislodged.

"What?" I croaked. "You just said we were going to spend time together until . . . well until we can't anymore."

"Yep. You're absolutely right." He stood and walked around the island to set his plate in the sink.

I watched him with wide eyes. He came back around and quickly kissed my forehead, the touch too brief to pick up much from the empathy link. I had a feeling that was the point.

"I'll be back soon. I promise. I need to handle a couple of things, and then the day is ours."

With that, he walked around the corner and out of view. He was really leaving me. What was happening?

The front door opened. I heard some muted shuffling, and then Logan yelled back to me, "Audrey, you have a guest to keep you company until I get back," and then the front door closed.

This was surreal.

A soft pitter-patter of footsteps echoed off Logan's wood floor before Bear appeared. I shoved a huge bite of omelet in my mouth and jumped off the stool.

"Hey, buddy. It's good to see you."

He sat on his haunches, and I knelt on the floor in front of him while he raised one of his overgrown paws and put it on my shoulder. I hugged my old friend. His chin came down on my opposite shoulder, and his furry arm kept me anchored to his warm body. I smiled into his fur, soaking in the comfort only Bear could give. He was a good boy. I was going to miss him.

It wasn't long before wetness coated my cheeks. As if he knew the reason for my sadness, he adjusted his chin so that I was more securely pressed against his warmth.

I'm not sure how long we sat like that, but when I finally pulled away, Bear rewarded me with a giant lick up the side of my face.

Gross. I could have done without that.

As if sensing my thoughts, he licked the other side before I could stop him.

"Thanks for cleaning off those tears, buddy."

His tongue lolled out in a doggy smile. Grabbing my unfinished plate off the counter, I set the food on the ground for him to enjoy. While he was happily munching away, I went and washed my face off. So much for the makeup I'd put on this morning. Logan had hardly even stayed around to appreciate the effort.

I stared at my reflection in the mirror.

"What's going on?" I asked myself.

Giving my head one good shake, I exited the bathroom in search of Bear. He was on the living room floor, wiggling around on his back, mouth open and tongue hanging out the side.

With a grin, I dropped to my knees to wrestle with the beast. He weighed as much as I did, so we were evenly matched. I laid my arms on the ground and put my tush in the air, moving it back and forth to mimic Bear's wagging tail.

"Whatcha got, old friend?" I playfully taunted.

He jumped from side to side before assuming the same position as me. Each of us waiting for the other to make the first move.

The front door opened and then slammed shut. I craned my neck to see Logan leaning casually against the entrance, a wicked smile on his face and his head tilted to the side. And he wasn't looking at my face.

"Hey there." I plopped down and turned so I was facing him. "Stop staring at—"

"Your lovely smile?"

"Haha."

"Please don't stop on my account. I was enjoying the show."

"When did you become such a guy?"

His eyebrows shot up, and faster than I was able to track, he was on me, pressing me back into the plush rug. I was shocked, but I can't say I minded. Bear jumped around us, barking in intervals, happy to be playing a new game.

"Audrey, my love." Logan's voice was quiet, but its timbre had deepened. "What could I have possibly done to lull you into the false belief that I am anything other than one hundred percent red-blooded male?"

"Not this for starters." Were my words a little breathy? If so, I'm sure the temporary lung hiccup was just because I wasn't able to get in enough oxygen. Not because anything he said was affecting me.

Liar.

Logan chuckled and pulled me to my feet, his amusement obvious through the empathy link.

Tease, I mentally shot at him.

Logan's eyes widened, and he took a step back. "Did you just call me a tease?"

I slapped a hand over my mouth. "Did I say that out loud?"

"No. No you didn't."

We both blinked at each other.

"Then how did you know that?"

"I heard it. Here." He tapped his head.

"Is that normal?"

"I don't think so."

"You try it," I said.

"Well, what did you do?"

"I don't know. I literally just thought the word at you."

He shrugged. "Worth a try I guess."

A moment later, his voice echoed in my head. I was prepared to hear something, but I still stumbled back and landed on my backside.

"Did you just say I was hot stuff?" My face mirrored Logan's, wide eyed and open mouthed.

"You really heard that?"

I nodded.

"Well that's . . . pretty cool. Let me try it again." He closed his eyes, and several loud thumps of my heart sounded before I heard him again.

"Logan, stop sending me secret messages about my body parts."

He bent at the waist and started to belly laugh. "Sorry, you're just too easy to fluster sometimes."

"You're awful, and I hate you."

"You said that last night too."

"Yeah, well maybe today I mean it."

He leaned back against the wall and shot me a smug look. "Not likely."

Why does he have to be so smokin' hot when he's being conceited?

Logan's smile widened. "I heard that too."

"Would you get out of my brain? This"—I frantically moved my hands around my head like a hyped-up rave dancer—"is off limits."

Logan pushed off the wall and extended a hand to help me up. His smug exterior hid a layer of worry and concern I didn't think he wanted me to pick up because he released me as soon as I was on my feet.

"I will do my best," he promised. "But it would probably help if you tried not to focus on how gorgeous I am. You know I'm more than just a pretty face. You're going to give me a complex that you only want me for my body."

I almost swallowed my tongue, but instead, a wad of spit went down the wrong pipe. I doubled over in a coughing fit.

Logan rubbed my back until the hacking subsided and then bent to look at me. A few latent coughs were still coming out every few seconds.

"I'm sorry, Audrey. I just really like knowing I can get under that shell of yours. That was immature. Do you forgive me?"

I might have believed he was sincere if he hadn't been grinning wildly.

I glared at him.

"Come on." He extended his hand. Now that everything was out in the open, I was no longer as apprehensive about the empathy link. "Let's go make some new memories together."

I grasped the hand he offered and straightened. "I'd like that very much."

22

MAKE BELIEVE

The next days were some of the happiest and darkest of my existence. There was no more talk of a bonding ceremony, for which I was glad. I couldn't stomach the thought of Logan not moving on with his existence after I was gone, just as much as I couldn't stand to think of him with anyone else. But I loved him enough to want the best for him and chose to think not of some possible future love but instead of his having a future. Something I'd lost the moment I released Satan from his chains.

Logan made good on his word to spend time with me, but he would mysteriously leave for short periods of time and not tell me what he was up to. He never left longer than an hour, but his disappearances made me suspicious just the same. Whenever I started to grow morose, he did whatever he could to lighten my mood. And for my part, I tried to make these last few days happy for him as well. I put on a good face, but I knew there was truly no fooling him. We weren't just contending with emotions now. Worried or fearful thoughts would filter to him unknowingly, and he was always quick to reassure me that things would be all right.

But our bond went both ways. When he thought I wasn't paying attention, I'd catch glimpses of his worried thoughts as well. He wondered what an existence without me would be like and was always plotting ways to change my fate but managed to keep the details concealed from me.

I asked him to abandon his search, for I felt deep in my heart the efforts were hopeless. The darkness marring my back had finally reached its tendrils around my body. The grotesque veins that slithered around my waist and over my shoulder pointed toward the same place . . . my heart. I now felt as if that was the end game. Once the dark thread reached my heart, my time would be up.

But I deserved whatever dark punishment awaited me. Isn't that what the black mark was telling me? I begged him just to enjoy the time we had left. He said all the right things, but those fragments of thoughts still leaked to me.

Other than his odd disappearances, we spent all our time together. Our friends were extremely busy with the mess I'd made with Satan, yet they still didn't know the hand I'd played in those events. For whatever reason, Joe must have held back those details, and for that I was extremely grateful.

Logan and I managed one meal with our hunter buddies at Celestial Heights. The dinner was bittersweet. Logan held my hand almost the whole time, and we shared both joyful and sorrow-filled emotions.

Always in the back of my mind was the thought I should approach the Creator, Hugo, or Joe. The idea floated around my consciousness night and day. Distracting myself during the day was easier, but at night I had horrible nightmares of Hell. I'd wake up in a panic, desperate for comfort, but stopped myself from seeking it from the true source of peace, knowing I wasn't deserving. How could I go to the Creator? I'd betrayed

Him.

Each nightmare was a penance I bore. A penance Logan bore when my screaming woke him up. He'd moved me into a spare bedroom at his house and would come running moments after I'd sit up, often drenched in sweat. But I refused to be consoled. I knew that whatever hurt me, hurt him as well. But I reasoned that each tortuous moment I endured would gain me a little more time in this paradise. There wasn't much logic to those thoughts, but without seeking guidance from the Creator of all, logic was elusive to me at best.

The last few nights, Logan had ended up sleeping on the hardwood floor beside me with only a blanket and pillow for comfort. Perhaps I was being cruel, but we were already too connected. Ceremony or not, our bond slid into place more firmly every day—even every hour—we were together. I was determined to keep some of him intact for the moment I was ripped from his life. Sharing a bed, even if all we did was sleep, was an intimacy I couldn't engage in.

Two weeks had passed since we returned to our realm. Fourteen days of a different kind of living hell. And then Logan announced at breakfast that he'd arranged some girl time for me.

"I just think it's important you spend some time with your friends and not just me right now."

I tried not to read into that too much. I chose to take him at face value rather than believe he didn't want me around.

"Yeah, okay." I speared a sausage link and brought it to my mouth.

"Audrey?" Logan waited until I met his gaze. "If you think I can't tell you're getting worse by the day, you're wrong."

I blinked at him before speaking. "What do you expect me to say to that? I'm trying."

His smile was gentle. "Yes, love, I know you are. And so am I. But it's selfish for me to keep you all to myself. You have so many other people here who love and care for you."

"If that's what you want, then all right." I shrugged. I didn't have much fight left in me.

Logan's concerned gaze bored into me. I felt it through our bond. He sensed I was emotionally slipping away from him.

"You'll have a good time today," he said in an upbeat tone. "You'll see."

I snapped my head up and looked at him. "A whole day?"

A day was practically an eternity for us now.

"Trust me . . . please?"

A knock sounded at the front door. He jumped out of his seat and jogged out of the kitchen.

"So, this is where you've been hiding her away," came the slightly peeved voice of my best friend and grandmother. Romona entered the room on high alert, as if looking for a defect in Logan's home. Her reaction struck me as rather funny. "How many rooms did you say this place has again?"

Way to not so subtly ask where I sleep at night.

"There are three, *Grandma*. Logan set me up in the guest room on the second floor." I didn't tell her he'd been sleeping in there too.

She smiled sweetly at me then turned back around the way she came. Kaitlin dodged her on the way into the kitchen.

"What's she doing?" I asked.

Kaitlin's smile was large. "I have an idea."

Logan entered the kitchen, shaking his head. "She just ran upstairs."

"Why?" This was weird.

"Logan!" Romona yelled from somewhere above. "Why is there bedding on my granddaughter's floor?"

I covered my face with one hand.

"Romona's trying to make sure your virtue is still intact. Like I couldn't have taken that whenever—"

"Not another word." I pointed at him.

Footsteps pounded the stairs as Romona came jogging down.

"Logan—" she began.

"Audrey's been having nightmares. I've slept on the floor a night or two so I'm there to wake her up if they get bad."

"Oh." Her brow furrowed for a moment as if trying to come up with something to condemn him for.

I was both mortified and amused. Especially when Romona seemed bent on giving Logan a tongue lashing regardless.

"So"—I clapped my hands once to break the awkward tension—"what are we up to today ladies?"

Kaitlin rubbed her palms together. "Oh, we have big plans for you today, Audrey."

I pointed a finger at her. "No. Whatever it is you have planned, cancel it right now. I want nothing to do with whatever plans are attached to that look. None whatsoever."

"Too late. Everything has already been set in motion, and your jailer over there"—she jerked her thumb over her shoulder at Logan—"has already given his stamp of approval. You have zero choice in the matter."

"Jailer?"

"Yep, total hostage keeper."

"That's hardly fair," I argued. "You all have been extremely busy, w-with"—I stumbled over my words—"with all the bad stuff going on."

"Today is different," Romona inserted. "We have it blocked off especially for you. Doctor's orders."

"What doctor?"

"It's just a phrase. Come on." She tugged my sleeve. "Let's go do some girl stuff."

I reluctantly slipped off my stool and followed the girls to the front door.

"I'll see you later?" I asked Logan.

He laid a palm on my cheek. Love poured into me through the empathy link.

You couldn't keep me away, he said directly to my mind.

With a soft kiss, he gave me a gentle nudge out the door with the command to 'just relax' right as Romona and Kaitlin linked arms with me and dragged me away from him and what had become my haven over the last few days.

I craned my neck to see him standing in the doorway, watching us walk from view. Something turned in my chest, and I had an ominous thought that I might never see him again.

Believing I existed on borrowed time, every moment felt as if it could be my last. If I had the courage, I would have prayed for more time. But when I dug deep to try, I found that well empty.

23

GIRL'S DAY

"What exactly is happening right now?" I lifted my eyebrows at Kaitlin—she was less than trustworthy—before turning to Romona for answers.

She was misty eyed with a soft smile on her face. The look did absolutely nothing to put my mind at ease.

The tent in front of me was a deep burgundy made of thick material. Velvet maybe? Kaitlin lifted the flap and pulled me through, Romona right on my heels. When the drape closed, we were in our own personal bubble. Just us and the eight— wait, no, ten—strangers standing around at different stations within the tent. What was this, a salon?

"Why are we at a spa . . . in a tent?" I looked around at the reclined seating area, complete with greenery and a bubbling water feature, and the pedicure chair with little fish swimming around in the footbath.

Ahh, no thank you.

Several seats were positioned in front of a mirror with large exposed light bulbs, and a massage chair waited in one of the corners. Curtains concealed two partitioned areas.

An ornate purple chandelier hung from the middle of the tent, and white twinkle lights ringed the sides, giving everything a soft glow. Next to each station stood several women with broad smiles on their faces.

I didn't get it. The space was quite magical and beautiful, but . . . huh?

"Not exactly a spa day," Romona started, "but it's probably best if you think of it that way."

Kaitlin clapped her hands. "You ready for some pampering? Because I know I am."

"Are you really going to keep me in the dark about all this?"

"Yes," they said in unison and then exchanged a look.

I considered being mad at them, but I couldn't do it. Honestly, getting pampered was my favorite guilty pleasure, and I *had* wanted to spend some more time with Kaitlin and Romona before . . . the stabbing sensation was back in my chest. I shoved the pain aside and reminded myself to live for the moment. I didn't have any other guarantees.

I needed to find a way to say goodbye to these two women. Kaitlin would be difficult . . . but Romona, she wasn't just my best friend; she was family. Leaving Romona was going to break me almost as much as parting from Logan.

I closed my eyes and shook my head, willing the tears to recede. A gentle hand grasped my shoulder.

"Audrey," Romona asked, "are you all right?"

I shook my head. They deserved more than I was giving. Maybe I should have come clean to all my friends like I did with Logan.

I just didn't know how.

Whenever I tried to pray and ask for guidance, I simply couldn't. I felt too . . . unclean to present myself to the Creator and ask for help. I was on my own.

"No," I answered honestly, "but this looks like a lot of fun. Where do we start?" I gave Romona a watery smile to reassure her. She pulled me into a hug and patted my back.

"We're all here for you, you know that, right?" she whispered in my ear. That was a strange thing to say.

I pulled back.

"Of course." I searched her eyes for answers to questions I didn't know to ask.

"All right, peeps," Kaitlin interrupted, "let the beautification begin."

"No! Five hundred percent absolutely not! This is not happening." I dug in my heels. I had just learned what was behind curtain number one and wanted nothing to do with it. "Kaitlin, stop pushing me forward, or so help me, I will throat punch you so hard you won't be able to talk for a month."

She shoved me forward, her shoulder against my back. My feet slipped over the plush carpet without my having to lift them. Darn this beautiful rug and its strangely slippery qualities.

"Stop being a baby, Audrey, and put your big girl panties on. Or rather, take them off so the aesthetician can wax down there as well." She snickered.

"Kaitlin, don't be crude," Romona snapped from somewhere behind her. "Audrey, it's just your legs and underarms."

I tried to turn, but Kaitlin did some weird mixed martial arts movement on me, and the next thing I knew, I was lying flat on my back across the semi-reclined table with the wind knocked out of me.

"I . . . will . . . kill . . . you," I huffed out.

"Oh silly Audrey." Kaitlin just laughed at me. "I'm already dead."

I tilted my head and caught Romona watching wide-eyed from behind Kaitlin.

"Traitor." I croaked out.

She held up her hands. "This was all Kaitlin's idea. I had nothing to do with this part."

"Guilty by association," I shot at her.

"Oh chill out, Audrey. I promise, you'll thank us later. Body grooming is very important." With that, Kaitlin spun on a heel and hightailed it out, pulling Romona with her.

I would kill them both.

"So." A woman with a kind smile and arms as thick as some of the bulky male hunters appeared above my head, holding a tongue depressor covered in what I could only guess was scalding hot wax. "Where should we begin?"

Double dead . . . both of them.

What must have been a million hours later, I limped out from behind the curtain, looking for my 'friends' with the intent to inflict some serious pain. Hair had been pulled, plucked, and ripped from various areas of my body. That was the first and last time I'd ever go through that. Friends don't force other friends into painful hair removal.

When I finally spotted Kaitlin and Romona, I stopped in my tracks. They were wrapped in silk robes, looking positively radiant. We'd all had relaxing facials, which gave our skin a lovely dewy look, but while I'd been tortured, they must have gone through a couple more of the stations because they both wore expertly applied makeup and sported Hollywood hairstyles. Romona's latte-tinted skin glowed even brighter, and her makeup accentuated all her best features without overwhelming her face. Her dark hair was pulled back into a low bun of loose braids that gleamed beneath the chandelier and twinkle lights.

Kaitlin's makeup was on the heavier side, with its smoky colors making her blue eyes pop like crazy. Her face was flawless and sun-kissed like the beach girl she'd always be. Her hair was swept into a side-do, and it looked like the stylist actually made flower designs out of her blonde locks. She did a little spin for me. The braid of interlocked blonde flowers wrapped around her head and flowed over her shoulder. I'd never seen anything quite as exquisite.

"You both look . . . amazing." I blinked a few times. This couldn't just be a girl's day. "Are we going to a pop-up-prom or something?"

The corners of Romona's lips curled in a secretive smile.

Kaitlin gave me a toothy Cheshire cat grin. "Getting warmer," she said. "Now it's your turn."

I practically jumped into the seat offered me. Yes please! I'd spent way too much of my afterlife in workout clothes or body armor. I was more than ready to pretty it up.

The makeup artist, a petite redhead, gave me a sweet smile and then turned me away from the mirror so I couldn't see her work. I found myself facing my friends again.

"Hey now, what gives?"

"You trust us, right?" Kaitlin asked.

I shook my head. "No, absolutely not. Would you like me to remind you what I just went through?"

She shrugged. "Either way, your reveal is going to be a surprise. Just sit back and think happy Logan-filled thoughts."

I made a mocking noise deep in my throat. I loved her, but she was a pain sometimes.

"Don't worry. You're going to look lovely." Romona took my hand, and waves of calm comfort filtered through the empathy link. Underneath that was a bubble of excitement I rarely picked up from her. Whatever the end game was, she was looking forward to it. I might not trust Kaitlin not to put me in clown makeup for the fun of it, but I trusted Romona.

I nodded once. "Okay, ladies," I said to everyone still in the tent with us, "do your worst." I closed my eyes before snapping my lids back open. "No, I didn't mean that. I meant do your best. Your absolute best."

There was a chorus of light laughs around me.

24

THE REVEAL

I held my breath as the stylist did her work. The anticipation was killing me.

"You're really not going to let me look?"

"No way, no how," Kaitlin answered.

"You look beyond beautiful." Romona's eyes once again misted over. "Trust me, just a few more minutes and we'll let you take a look at the finished product. You're going to want to see this all at once."

I blew out an annoyed breath of air. My makeup was done, and my hair was mostly ready, but these two bullies were sticking to their word and wouldn't let me see what had been done. All I knew was that my hair was half up and half down, and that was it. I tried to touch my head once to get a feel of what was going on back there, and Romona slapped my hand away. My own grandmother!

Romona took both my shoulders in her hands and looked me in the eyes, her face a mixture of pride and something else. "Okay, now for this next part, you're going to have to keep your eyes closed while we dress you."

"Oh, come on. Don't you think you're taking this a little too far? I get it's all fun and games to treat me like makeover Barbie for the afternoon, but really, you want me to let a stranger dress me?"

Her smile was radiant. "No strangers. This will be Kaitlin and me. Just this final step and then no more surprises. I promise."

"Do I have to change my underwear?"

Kaitlin burst out laughing behind me.

"What?" I twisted to look at her over my shoulder. "It's a legit question. At least let me have that privacy."

I turned my attention back to Romona, who pressed her lips together and then finally spoke. "That's not unreasonable. Kaitlin, will you please go grab her undergarments and we'll all turn around while she changes into them?"

They were taking whatever was going on way too seriously.

Kaitlin slipped behind mystery curtain number two and came back out holding some very tiny panties and what could only be described as a modern torture device parading as delicate silk and white lace lingerie.

I checked behind me. All the women who were still in the tent with us were currently facing away, and Kaitlin was holding the garments out to me with a grin.

"What?" I looked at Romona for help, but her face was peacefully blank. "This is a joke, right?"

"No-*pe*." Kaitlin answered.

With my thumb and one finger, I picked up what I'd thought were supposed to be underwear from Kaitlin and held them in front of my face.

"This is missing a butt."

Kaitlin burst out laughing.

"Go find me one with a butt, and I'll consider putting it

on."

"Audrey, all the cool kids are wearing them these days."

"Oh shut it, you." I narrowed my eyes. "Like you'd wear these."

She lifted a perfectly plucked eyebrow at me.

"Oh, I'm definitely wearing something similar. Care to see?" She turned and started lifting the back of her robe.

"Stop," I yelled and yanked her robe back in place. "I definitely do not want to see that."

"I'm just messing with you. You're right. I wouldn't be caught dead in one of those, but they aren't really for you anyway. Just think of—"

"No, she's right," Romona cut in. "If she's uncomfortable with what she's wearing, she's going to be distracted from . . . you know, the important stuff."

She eyed Kaitlin, who huffed and said, "Oh fine," under her breath.

With a twirl of her hand, she materialized a bit more substance to the panties I held. They no longer resembled dental floss but covered all the important bits—even if they were still made of silk and lace and had some see-through parts. I would take this win . . . however small it was.

"Thank you," I said rather magnanimously. "Now I'll just slip back here to put these on." I started toward the curtained-off area, and both Romona and Kaitlin sprang for me, yelling no at the same time.

"Whoa there," I said and froze in place.

"You can put them on out here," Romona said, recovering from her momentary panic. "Your . . . outfit is back there, and we don't want to ruin the surprise. We won't even look. Although if you need help with the corset top, let me know."

"You mean the torture device? Yeah, sure." I rolled my eyes.

This was getting ridiculous.

After Romona and Kaitlin turned to give me privacy, I slipped out of my clothes and pulled on the underwear before giving the corset-like top piece a valiant effort. In the end, I did need their help getting into it. There was a whole bunch of lace-up hooks in the back I couldn't reach. But at least I was mostly covered when they helped me, even if I was now having trouble breathing.

After that they somehow talked me into closing my eyes as I went behind the curtain with them. I followed all their instructions to lift my leg, bend my arm, suck in my stomach and whatever else they threw at me. Getting me into this contraption of a dress must have taken them at least half an hour. When I tried to touch any of the material, I got my hands slapped again. They were dress ninjas who knew every time I tried to figure anything out.

At the end of the dressing session, the only thing I knew was that I now wore something long and strapless . . . and heavy. They could have just stuffed me into a cupcake-shaped gown for all I knew. But if they thought I was going to take one step out of this tent without getting a look at myself, they were in for a rude awakening.

"Okay,"—Romona held my left hand—"just a few more steps. Then I want you to lift your foot. You're going to be stepping onto a short pedestal."

A pedestal? "We are still in the tent though, right?"

"Absolutely." That was from Romona, so I believed her.

As Romona guided me, Kaitlin was somewhere behind me, lifting up my dress to make walking easier. She better not be showing my rear end to a tent full of people.

"Okay, now one small step up."

I followed their directions. Kaitlin asked me to lift one foot up at a time, and some tall yet still comfortable shoes were slipped on my feet as Romona steadied me.

Excited and nervous energy bounced off both girls. I didn't feel malice or even humor through their empathy links, so that relaxed me a bit. If this was some elaborate joke, Kaitlin would have been throwing off some major vibes by now.

"It's just perfect, isn't it?" Kaitlin swooned.

"She's more lovely than I ever imagined," Romona answered.

"Okay, people, are you done making me your dress-up doll yet? Am I allowed to open my eyes?"

"Yes," breathed Romona, almost too quietly to hear. "Open your eyes."

Finally.

I let out a lungful of air and opened my eyes. I blinked a second before I realized I was actually looking at myself. The tent had been transformed while I got dressed, and most of the stations had been cleared, and in front of the pedestal I stood on were three floor-to-ceiling mirror panels. They were tilted in just the right way for me to see myself from several angles.

I gasped, not sure what to look at first. My dress was white. I stuck on that for a moment. The gown was the most beautiful one I'd ever seen. It hugged my chest and torso to perfection and then flowed in soft layers to the floor, allowing just the end of my shoes to poke out.

But it also showcased the ugly black-and-green veins that snaked over my shoulder. Thank goodness they were invisible to everyone but me—my own personal reminder. I forced my attention back on the dress.

The part that hugged my body was an intricate interlacing of several different materials—lace and silk and a tulle-like covering I didn't quite recognize.

I touched it with my fingers. So soft.

"It's called orneza," Romona said. "It's a material not yet invented on Earth. It's a little like tulle, but it floats a bit more when you walk." She indicated the semi-full skirt that was made up entirely of layers of the magical substance.

"It's . . . white," I replied dumbly.

She smiled and nodded.

"What do you think of the rest?" She indicated my hair and makeup. I hadn't even looked at my face yet.

Too shocked by the wedding dress they'd put me in.

What exactly was going on here?

My eyes lifted to the mirror once again, and my breath caught. They'd turned me into a fairy princess. Minus the pointy ears and iridescent wings. My skin glowed. I turned my head each way and realized they'd applied a thin layer of shimmery powder. I pivoted so I could appreciate the unblemished side of my body.

The deep chocolate of my eyes was accentuated by shades of gold, brown, and pink. My lashes looked impossibly long and dark. A brush of color made it look like a faint blush kissed my cheeks at all times. And my skin was like fine porcelain.

I lifted my gaze to the top of my head where a delicate band of twisted metals sat. Intricate braids weaved in, out, and around the band, giving it a peek-a-boo look as well as making it appear the band and my hair together created a delicate diadem atop my head. The rest of my hair flowed in loose waves nearly to my waist—a silky, smooth river. Each loose curl brought out the natural highlights in my hair.

Had my hair grown that long without my realizing it? I'd spent so much time with it up during training, and I'd been so distracted these last few weeks, the locks must have grown without me taking note.

I was . . . overwhelmed. I'd never felt so beautiful. I'd never been so beautiful. Heavenly makeovers were magical.

But this dress. What was happening couldn't actually be happening . . . could it?

I turned to ask them, only to find that my dress had a train that was several feet long. Romona and Kaitlin had both changed into dresses of their own. Both were the same light shade of lavender, flattering to each of them, but differing styles. Romona's was cap-sleeved and flared at the waist to end right above her knees. Kaitlin's was one-shouldered and flowed to the same spot without the flare. But the material and shade were exactly the same.

They looked an awful lot like bridesmaid dresses.

"You tell me right now: What's going on?" But didn't I already know?

Romona stepped forward. "All of this was Logan's plan."

Kaitlin cleared her throat loudly.

Romona rolled her eyes. "Okay, it was Logan's idea, but he didn't plan out all the details. You're having your bonding ceremony today, Audrey."

"But why am I dressed like a bride? You told me this wasn't a wedding? And that I don't get bridesmaids. And how did you all pull this off? And when? And . . . what?"

Do not hyperventilate.

I took a shaky step off the short pedestal and finished with a choked-up, "And I can't." I caught a glimpse of my shoes, which were just as gorgeous as the rest of my transformation. Light lavender to match the girls' dresses with a decorative crystal broach that sent a rainbow of colors everywhere when it caught the light. "You don't understand. This can't happen. Logan knows why. He knows."

I wasn't making sense to them, but how could I? They didn't know what was hanging over my head.

Romona took hold of my upper arms. She gave me a light shake and forced my attention. When I looked up, she was crying, ruining her perfect makeup.

"Audrey, stop. Do you love Logan?" Her voice was strong regardless of the tears pouring down her cheeks.

"Wh—well, yes. Of course I do."

"Would you travel to Hell and back again, literally, to save him?"

"Yes, absolutely. I mean, I already did. Why are you asking me this?"

"Then that's all that matters. You both love each other and have each other's backs, no matter what."

"But, Romona, you don't fully understand. There are things—"

"Yes. I do understand. I understand everything."

I was struck speechless. She couldn't possibly know. I shook my head . . . but then I noticed her emotions leaking through the empathy link. A great sorrow lay in her heart. One she must have been covering up all day. Her devastation matched mine.

She knew.

"How?"

"Logan told all of us."

I gasped, my head snapping in Kaitlin's direction. Tears tracked down her face as well.

"How long have you known?" I asked.

Romona pressed her lips together. "Not as long as we should have. You should have told me yourself."

I opened my mouth to say something but stopped when I came up short. She was right. "But I understand why you didn't," she continued. "The point is we love you. All of us. We're going to fight this together. But today is your day. Yours and Logan's. And if you think for one moment that man wouldn't storm the gates of Hell or any other realm to be with you, then perhaps you don't deserve him to begin with."

I sucked in a breath. Conflicted. Bonding with Logan for eternity when all we had was maybe today was selfish, wasn't it? The ugly mark and its tendrils didn't let me forget I was running short on time. But bonding with me was his decision as much as mine.

"I don't know what to do."

"You do what you know is right." Romona squeezed my arms to keep me in the present. "And the right person is out there right now, waiting for you to walk down the aisle and promise your forever to him."

I gulped and glanced at Kaitlin. She was one of Logan's oldest friends. We were close, but I knew deep down she'd always have his best interests in mind. She nodded at me once. "You need to go out there and make an honest man out of that guy."

"Hey now, we haven't done a single thing that would imply we haven't been completely honorable these last . . ."

I stopped when I realized she was laughing at me.

Rolling my eyes I took a deep breath and looked at myself in the ginormous mirrors. But really I was trying to look inside. What was the right thing to do? Did I want to complete the bond with Logan? Absolutely. What held me back was the desire to do right by him. I was looking out for his own good.

I knew who I really needed to talk to about this. But I hadn't approached Him since returning from Hell. Too worried He'd turn away from me. Too afraid He'd send me back to Hell immediately. But this decision couldn't be made without consulting Him. I had to know I wouldn't be hurting Logan even more than I already had. I had to know that I wouldn't be putting his eternity in jeopardy.

I turned to my friends. "Okay, at the very least you two need to go get yourselves cleaned up. You're both hot messes right now." I gestured at their faces. "Like I'd let any bridesmaids of mine walk down the aisle looking like that."

Kaitlin let out a short burst of laughter, and Romona smiled.

"Like I'd go out in public with running mascara," Kaitlin scoffed. "It's like you don't know me at all."

"Thattagirl." Romona gave my arms one final squeeze before heading to the opposite corner of the tent where a makeup station was still set up. How did I miss that before? I guess they'd planned for a possible makeup malfunction before the ceremony. I'd bet they thought they'd be fixing me instead of them.

I stepped back up on the pedestal, but instead of looking at myself, I bowed my head. It was time.

25

CEREMONY

Kaitlin and Romona chattered happily across the tent. I tuned them out. My hands shook, so I squeezed them into fists. I needed a moment to collect myself. A moment to gather all the courage I had and focus it on one singular goal. I wanted to shadow box to pump myself up, but considering the circumstances and my amazing but gigantic gown, that didn't seem practical.

Okay, Audrey, you can do this.

But that wasn't actually the truth. The truth was that I couldn't do this. I couldn't do anything apart from the Creator. Apart from Hugo's wisdom and Joe's guidance. I'd been running myself ragged for the last two weeks trying to exist without them. Ashamed of my own mistakes but unwilling to do what needed to be done because of fear.

"Father," I whispered. And waited.

And nothing happened.

I cracked an eyelid. I was still in the tent. I didn't realize until then that I'd expected to be transported somewhere else like the first time I spoke with the Creator in the afterlife. But I was in exactly the same spot. Was it because He hadn't heard me? Or didn't want to listen?

I closed my eyes and continued, "Father, I'm not sure if you can hear me or not. In fact, I'm not sure I want you to hear me, which I feel really bad about, but I need to confess something. And I need to ask for your forgiveness . . . and I need to ask for your advice." I paused for a heartbeat. "If not for myself, for Logan, who I know you love."

I sucked in a cleansing breath and then released it slowly. "I've been hiding from You. But I guess You already know that. I've been . . . scared to come to You because I'm ashamed, and I'm afraid You'll cast me out." There, I'd gotten the first part out. "I made a terrible mistake, and it's all my fault Satan was released. Then I lied to everyone I care about . . . about the whole thing. I've been plagued with guilt. And I know that what I've done is too big to really ask for forgiveness. But You deserve to know, straight from my mouth, how sorry I am. For all of it, but especially for hiding from You . . . and of course, for freeing Satan . . . That was really bad."

I hung my head even lower. This wasn't making me feel any better. If anything, my gut tightened. Emotions I hadn't even realized were there were coming to the surface.

"But I guess I wanted You to know how sorry I am for all of it, and I want to ask for direction. Is it all right to go forward with this when it will only mean heartbreak for Logan?"

I waited. And waited. And waited.

And I never heard an answer.

My friends finished their makeup, and I never received an

answer from the Creator. At least not one I could interpret. My heartfelt pleas were met with silence.

When I told them, my friends, who now knew all the horrible details, told me this was okay and that I could move forward. And of course, I wanted to complete the bond with Logan. So I did what I could to pump myself up.

Bring the soul-fusing on. Wait, I still didn't really know what that was.

I supposed I was so far away from the Creator that He couldn't be bothered to listen to me anymore, even if I petitioned for Logan and not myself. My heart was heavy, but for Romona and Kaitlin, I put on a brave face.

"Okay, someone, please explain to me why I look like a bride and you both are dressed as bridesmaids. I've been told repeatedly that this isn't a wedding. So what gives?"

"Ah, well, yes, that was Logan again," Romona explained. "He put a lot of thought into this, and he wanted it to be special for you. So we threw some of the less important details of soul-fusing out the window and replaced them with things you are familiar with."

My heart melted. That man. There wasn't anyone better.

"And that," Romona interrupted my thoughts, "that look right there is why I'm okay with all of this."

Her words sobered me. I stood up a bit straighter.

"We all know nothing is certain right now, Audrey." Kaitlin picked up the conversation. "Logan has been working like a madman to try to figure out how to change your fate. Maybe he'll be able to . . ." She visibly sobered, pulling her shoulders back and boring her eyes into mine. "And maybe he won't. But you have the most determined person I know in your corner, so if anyone can figure out how to get you out of this mess, it's him."

"Great pep talk," I said dryly.

"Oh, and make sure you give him at least one really awesome night to remember."

"Kaitlin!" I shrieked.

"Too easy, girl." She jerked her chin up. "You might want to change that back before we head out of this tent. Because the minute we do, it's show time."

Of course my hair had gone wacky.

"So, who all is out there?"

"Oh, like half this part of the realm."

"What? You're kidding, right?"

"Nope. I took a peek already. They've all been sitting out there for the last half hour, waiting for you to pull yourself together. It's not every day you see a wedding-slash-bonding ceremony up here."

"Oh my gosh! Why didn't you tell me?" I stopped my impending rant. "Wait, why can't I hear anything? You're messing with me, aren't you?"

Her eyes widened, and she pointed to herself. "Who, me? I'd never do that."

"Romona?"

A slight grimace flitted across Romona's face. "Kaitlin's only exaggerating a bit. There is quite a crowd. And you can't hear anything because we've had a sound barrier around the tent since the moment we walked in. They've been setting up out there all day."

"You can put sound barriers up?"

She started to answer, and I waved her off.

"Sorry, never mind. That's not important. Tell me everything I need to know. Then let's do this thing."

A bouquet of exotic purple, blue, and fuchsia flowers was shoved into my sweaty hands. The colorful blooms stood out against the whiteness of my dress. Romona and Kaitlin held smaller versions of my bouquet and were lined up in front of me. Kaitlin bounced on her six-inch heels in excitement and turned to give me the thumbs up. Romona smiled at me serenely.

"I'm so very glad to be able to be part of this, Audrey. I know your parents—" Her words caught, and she cleared her throat. "Your parents would be so proud of you right now."

"Oh yeah, I'm sure. Getting hitched at eighteen and on the brink of being dragged into Hell for eternity. I'm sure they'd be thrilled."

Romona frowned. "Nothing is certain yet, Audrey. Nothing. You enjoy this day, and put your trust where it always should have been. I understand how you must have been shaken from what happened. But you forgot one very important detail along the way."

I cocked my head at her.

"The Creator is bigger than any mess you can make. Hold on to that with everything you have."

"But I betrayed Him," I argued.

"You aren't the first one," she said sadly before facing forward.

The drape had been opened, and Kaitlin was just about to step out of the tent. Soft harp music floated through the gap. I snorted. If Logan had arranged for that, he didn't know as much about me as he thought.

I craned my neck to the left, but I couldn't see much

beyond Romona and Kaitlin—only the beginning of a gold aisle runner covered in light pink-and-gold-tipped rose petals.

Pretty.

The fabric drape swished closed behind Kaitlin, and it was eerily silent again.

Romona turned and squeezed my forearm. "You got this," she said before turning back around and marching her way toward the same spot Kaitlin had just vacated. After several beats, she winked at me over her shoulder and slipped out of the tent as well. Leaving me completely alone. Something I didn't want to be at the moment.

I was doing the right thing here, wasn't I? Was I being selfish? And oh my gosh, I didn't even have anyone to walk me down the aisle. That was messed up. *I shouldn't be making this walk alone.* I dropped my hand, still clenching my flowers in a death grip, and brought the other up to my face.

I was alone.

Something nudged my backside, and I yelped. Bear trotted around me and sat at my right side. Watching me expectantly, he tilted his head as if to ask what the holdup was.

"You're right. Alone or not, the man I love is waiting for me down that aisle. I think I've let him wait long enough, don't you?"

Bear answered with a thump of his tail, and his tongue rolled out of his mouth. I'd take that as an agreement.

"Let's go, buddy," I said.

Bear walked with me to the tent exit. The moment I opened the flap, he took off without a backward glance.

Wait, what?

I'd thought he was going to walk with me. The furry booger trotted down what I now saw was a very long aisle with his head held high, soaking in all the excited murmurs sent his way.

"There goes not doing this alone," I said under my breath.

I took my first step out of the tent, and a sea of bodies got to their feet, obstructing my view of the end of the aisle, where my groom—er, future bonded-for-eternity mate—waited for me. If I could just see Logan, everything would be all right. But I couldn't, and I was alone.

So I froze.

My ears buzzed, so I couldn't even hear the music playing. Was I on the verge of a panic attack? Oh no, not now.

A soft touch to my elbow drew my attention to my left. I looked over to find the Creator, clothed in brilliant light, standing by my side.

He once told me He had many different faces, but He looked exactly as I remembered. Dressed in a linen robe with a gold sash, tall by anyone's standards, and radiating strength and compassion from an ageless face full of grace and mercy. Beauty personified.

"May I?" He asked, indicating my arm.

I stared open mouthed at the being I'd betrayed. The one I loved. I nodded.

The Father slipped his arm through mine and led me down the petal-strewn path. My eyes didn't leave His face or the radiance that emanated from it as we walked down the aisle. At some point we stopped, but my eyes remained glued on Him.

"Audrey," He said to me in a gentle voice, "you've never been alone. And you'll never be forgotten. You are my daughter, purchased with the blood of my Son. You'll understand soon enough."

A soft gasp escaped my lips. His smile reached his eyes, crinkling the corners.

"I've been looking forward to this moment. It's time to look up, princess. Your groom is waiting."

How had I forgotten where I was? I hadn't even searched for Logan.

Snapping my eyes up, I met his gaze. He was standing in front of me with his hand extended. And as I lost myself in a cobalt-blue ocean, the hand at my elbow melted away, and I knew the Creator was no longer visible.

I wasn't even sure if He'd appeared to anyone but me—but a phantom kiss was pressed on my cheek before the evidence of His physical presence fully dissipated.

I took Logan's outstretched hand, and he pulled me forward. I finally snapped out of my daze to take everything in. We were standing under a portico of purple wisteria. Checking behind me, I spotted Romona standing back a ways with Kaitlin next to her. Bear had plopped himself in front of Logan and was sprawled on the ground.

Was the furry mutt asleep?

Behind Logan stood . . .

I gasped and took several steps back. Logan moved forward with me and captured me around the waist, halting my retreat. He deftly plucked the flowers from my hands and handed them to someone behind me.

Standing up directly behind Logan was Joe. Not in hunters' garb, or in faded jeans and a smudged white t-shirt, but in a stylish black tux.

"Shh." Logan had bent to whisper in my ear. "This is how it was always meant to be."

Joe gave me a reassuring nod. Kevin stood next to him with a broad grin, and behind him was Morgan.

This was getting more bizarre by the moment.

I locked eyes with Logan. "This is a weird dream, isn't it?"

He grinned and then pinched my backside . . . hard.

I yelped.

"Not a dream, love. At least not the type you're talking

about."

"That was cheesy . . . and it hurt." I resisted the urge to rub the sore spot. I was still aware we had an audience.

"Are you ready yet? I've been waiting a lifetime for this moment, and I don't want to wait a second longer."

Any remaining doubts I might have had fled. "I may not fully understand what's happening, or what all this means for our future, but I'm one hundred percent ready to commit all that I am to you forever."

"Then let's do this."

At my nod, he pulled back to a proper distance. "Don't freak out again, okay?"

I rolled my eyes at his warning. What else could they throw at me today?

"Thank you all for attending this sacred ceremony." That voice was familiar.

I looked beyond Logan and thought I might faint.

Hugo is officiating our ceremony?

I cast my stricken gaze at Logan. He smiled and squeezed my hands. His hair was as wild as usual but just the way I liked it. He was clean-shaven and filling out an elegant black tux and tie in a way that should be sinful. What had been distracting me? Oh right . . . the Holy Trinity showing up at our ceremony.

I glanced at Hugo, and he winked at me before going on. I made the mistake of looking at Logan again, and I was a goner.

The shock of everything had finally subsided, and he was all I saw. Hugo was talking, but rather than hearing words, I only felt love. It poured in waves from Logan and overwhelmed my senses.

This was it. This was my one perfect day of existence.

And with that thought, my world exploded.

26

NEW WORLD

Sulfuric smoke stung my eyes, and the world was eerily silent. Wait, no, I was deaf.

I was sprawled on my side with bits of the wisteria arbor littered over my once pristine white dress. The skirt was now ripped in several places, and I was covered in grass stains and dirt smudges.

I blinked several times, but my vision was still a thick cloud of smoke. Human-like shapes darted in and out of view.

Logan, where was he?

I sat up and shook my head. *Whoa, bad idea.* I pressed both hands against my skull to make sure my brain stayed put. For a moment, it had felt like it was going to fall out.

My hearing was slowly returning. Screams echoed in the mist, and then shouted commands filtered through until I could hear the clash of battle. My name might have been shouted as well, but in the chaos, I couldn't tell.

I shoved myself to my legs, shaky at first but steady after a few steps. The clouds of smoke or mist or whatever blinded me to what was really happening. I swatted at it, but the substance didn't dissipate.

A familiar roar followed by a blast of fire about thirty feet to my left froze my steps and chilled my heart.

The dragon.

Satan was here.

It was happening.

Something . . . I needed something to fight with. Preferably something long, pointy, and very sharp.

I turned in a circle, like an idiot. I needed to materialize a weapon, fast.

Oh gosh, where's Logan?

Something soared over my head and hit the ground to my right, hard. I heard the crunch of bones and a groan.

I sprinted toward where I thought the person had landed and found Kaitlin lying twisted on the grass. She wore full body armor, her beautiful dress long gone. I thought she was unconscious until she managed to flip herself over, eyes tightly closed, cradling her wrist to her chest.

I hovered above her.

"That. Sucked."

"Kaitlin, oh my gosh. What can I do?"

Her eyes snapped open. "Audrey?" She gasped. "You need to get out of here, immediately. He'll come for you."

There was a spooked look on Kaitlin's face I'd never seen before. Her eyes were open so wide I could see the whites all around her sky-blue irises. She tried to shove herself to a sitting position but cried out and wrapped her uninjured arm around her middle. A few ribs must have been broken as well. She sucked in a few pain-filled breaths and then shot me another frantic look. "Audrey, run."

Panic really started to sink in at her command. I wasn't going to leave my friend here at the site of my bonding ceremony turned battleground, but her words made me want to do just that.

I dropped to my knees. "No, I'm not leaving you. Tell me exactly what's going on. Do you still have your sword on you? Materializing things under pressure isn't really my thing."

She shook her head. "No. It flew out of my hand when that red dragon backhanded me. But here." She closed her eyes, and a moment later a short sword appeared on the ground next to me.

"Thanks. Now what else is out there? I can't see anything through this smoke."

"It's just that giant dragon."

I sat back on my heels and blinked at her. "Just the dragon?"

"Isn't that enough? He's huge."

"You know that's Satan, right?"

"Yeah, I kinda assumed so."

But why was he alone? Why hadn't he stormed our realm with a legion of demons as well?

"What's going through that head of yours?" she asked.

I waved her off. "Nothing. I'm just surprised he came alone."

She snorted. "Yeah, I wouldn't mind a run-in with Alrik. I have a giant bone to pick with him."

Not knowing how to respond, I took my ruined dress in my hands and started to rip strips of fabric from the skirt to bind up her wounds.

Shouts and roars from the battle had increased, but the screams had ceased. The civilians must have escaped while the hunters went up against the evil being that had no place in our home.

Guilt hammered my chest, and my heart was split on what

to do. I should have been helping them. I should have been the only one bearing this pain. But leaving Kaitlin's battered body wasn't an option.

I helped her to a sitting position and started to wrap her injured arm to her ribs. I knew the fabric was only a temporary bandage, but it would have to do. Thank goodness my skirt had so many layers. She grunted and gritted her teeth during the process but didn't cry out in pain.

"Have you seen Logan?" I asked.

She shook her head.

Do not panic.

A shadowy figure appeared as I was putting the final wrapping on Kaitlin's wrist and broken ribs. I snapped my gaze up, and he solidified.

"You"—Morgan pointed at me—"go. I've got her."

"Me? Go where?"

Morgan was wearing traditional hunter armor, which threw me for a moment. I'd only ever seen him in his bulkier demon-scaled battle gear.

"Go anywhere," he snarled at me. "Just get out of here. Whatever else he's after right now, he's sure to be after you too."

In a fluid motion, he bent and picked up Kaitlin.

"Put me down, you overgrown gorilla," Kaitlin spat.

"Overgrown gorilla? Hmm, I like it. Thanks."

"It wasn't meant as a compliment."

He winked at her. "I'll take it just the same, luv."

He stalked off with Kaitlin still grumbling insults at him. He glanced over his shoulder at me before being swallowed by the smoke. "Get far away from here, Audrey. This isn't your fight."

When they were gone, I was left alone with an unseen battle

raging around me. This one was most definitely my fight.

I picked up the sword Kaitlin had materialized for me and strode straight toward the threat.

27

THE CHASE

Stalking through the smoke, I caught my breath at the sight that unveiled itself before my eyes. The red-scaled dragon—Satan in beast form—was twice the size of his previous incarnation. I wasn't sure if he was more powerful without his chains or if he'd always been able to manifest into any size he wanted.

Red-hot burning lava shot out of his unhinged, snake-like mouth toward a group of hunters who banded their shields together as a barrier. I swallowed a cry until the fire cleared and I saw the hunters were unscathed. Breathing a sigh of relief, I tightened my grip on the sword.

Show time.

"Hey you! Big ugly! Yo, slime bucket!" I gritted my teeth. Seriously, that was all I could come up with? But my insults did garner his attention. "You want me? Here I am!"

The scaled monster twisted his neck in my direction. Slitted pupils dilated and then returned to straight lines. What might have been a chuckle bounced around the dragon's chest.

"And there she issss," he hissed. "The one who made all

thisss desstruction posssssible."

"You don't belong here," I yelled.

Satan turned his massive body toward me, using his tail to bat away the hunters he'd been trying to barbeque—mowing them over like he'd swept his hand across a chessboard and scattered all the pieces. I winced but couldn't spare them a glance. Hunters were made of tough stock; they'd bounce back.

Satan lowered his oversized head to my level, his snout almost touching the ground, and I stared into the face of pure evil.

"I belong wherever I want, little lamb. A large part of that isss due to you." His scorching breath washed over me and blew my hair back over my shoulders.

I hid a shudder.

"I'll sssee you in a bit. I have to grab sssomething before we leave." Leathery wings pumped, and he lifted off the ground.

Wait, what?

"Don't look so forlorn. I'll be back for you. Promissse." His forked tongue drew out the last word.

His wings continued to flap as he hovered in the air a moment longer, clearing out the area of mist and smoke. Then he shot into the sky and headed toward the marbled city.

No.

There were people in that city. Non-hunter people that wouldn't know how to defend themselves let alone fight off the beast.

I did a speedy assessment of the area now that the smoke had cleared. Remnants of our ceremony lay like carnage across a battlefield. Broken chairs were everywhere. The gold aisle runner I'd walked down was shredded to ribbons and scattered like ash. I still couldn't find Logan. The only people present were armor-clad hunters ... and me, in my torn, dirty dress, gripping a short sword with stringy clumps of red-white-and-brown-streaked hair hanging in my face.

I glanced back at the sky to watch Satan fly toward the city. His form grew smaller by the moment. I sprinted in his direction but skidded to a halt when a mass of golden fur cut me off.

Battle Bear stood in front of me on his hind legs, razor-sharp claws out and fanged teeth bared. He wasn't going to let me pass. I tensed to fight my way past him. Unreasonable animal.

He growled at me once before dropping to all fours and presenting me with his side, crouching on the ground to give me access to his back. *Huh?*

He turned his head as if waiting on me.

"Was that growl because you were mad I left you behind when we went to rescue Logan?"

He huffed and actually nodded at me, and my eyes widened.

"Am I forgiven then?"

He stuck his tongue out at me. *Double huh.* It slowly dawned on me that he understood everything I said.

"You are a lot smarter than I've been giving you credit for, aren't you?"

Another nod. Well then, I wasn't about to turn down the free ride. I fisted some of Bear's fur and pulled myself to sit astride him. I grasped his pelt with both hands, anticipating the bumpy ride to come.

Bear pushed up, readying for our sprint when my name was yelled.

I twisted to look, and Logan was running toward me. He was safe. The knot in my chest loosened a notch.

"Audrey, no. You'll be taken," he yelled. "The bond, it

wasn't completed."

And thank goodness for that. Logan and I had run out of time. I didn't have to look at the veins wrapped around my body to know that. He wouldn't be shackled to me for the rest of eternity. He'd be free to love someone else. It stabbed my heart to even think that, but leaving was the right thing.

Logan would never allow me to get in the middle of the battle I had every intention of fighting. Water threatened to fill my eyes, but I stomped the sentiment down. This could very well be the last time I saw his face—the face I loved so much, currently twisted in anguish as if he already knew I wouldn't heed his warning.

He knew me pretty well after all.

When he was only feet away, I spurred Bear on.

"I love you," I shouted and faced forward. I left a broken man in my wake. My last image of Logan was of him falling to his knees—anguish etched on every part of his face.

Some signal must have gone out to the citizens of the city to take cover, because the streets were empty—not a soul in sight as we barreled past the pristine white buildings.

Thank goodness.

Like the last time I'd ridden Bear in search of Satan, my friend seemed to know exactly where he was going.

The trip was short. Bear was headed full steam for a building I recognized. The Archives Building. The closer we got, the faster Bear's pace became.

"Whoa there, buddy. I think you may want to slow down a bit."

He half turned his head and snorted at me. O-kay then.

I looked up—we were headed straight for the entrance. As in straight for the glass revolving doors.

"Bear," I cried and hunched over, flattening my body as much as I could to his side with my face buried in his fur. There was no stopping him now. He was going to go straight through the entrance without stopping—straight through several sheets of glass.

I screamed as we hit the first wall of glass and hung on until the jarring noises stopped, along with the jolting ride.

I looked up. We were in the solarium, covered in shards of glass, yet both amazingly free of injury. I slid off Bear's back and landed on legs of jelly. I leaned against him until I was able to stand without help.

After I gained my bearings, I marched in front of him and grabbed the fur of his cheeks in my fists. "What were you thinking? We could have stopped outside and entered like normal, non-insane beings."

He snuffed as though he were laughing. I backed up a step, and he shook his body like he was shaking off water. I covered my face as glass flew off in all directions like droplets of liquid.

I pointed a finger at him. "You know, you can be a real pain sometimes."

Another maybe Bear chuckle.

I sighed. "But yes, I still love you."

Something shattered in a different part of the building, and I jumped at the noise.

Apparently we'd found the dragon. I looked down at my ruined outfit. This wouldn't do.

Closing my eyes, I concentrated to change my disaster dress into body armor. I waited until the change was complete to open my eyes and then just stared down at myself. I'd managed to materialize all my armor, including a baldric to hold my sword on my back for comfort and ease of use, but the armor was all white.

What the what?

Whatever, close enough.

I set off on the same path Logan had taken me down only a week before. The loud thumping behind me said I wasn't alone. "Bear," I shot over my shoulder, "you stay here. It's too dangerous for you."

He growled and then head-butted my back, sending me stumbling several steps forward before I righted myself.

"Was that really necessary?" I asked

He issued another growl.

"Ugh, fine. You can come."

We crept forward along the tree-lined path—well, I crept, Bear lumbered. I didn't spy a single creature and hoped they'd found hiding places.

We passed through a second set of doors, which Bear barely fit through, and entered the library. Completely vacant, the room was eerily quiet.

Quickly moving through the center aisle, we reached the end of the room, and I grasped the handle that led to the next part of the building.

The dragon wasn't here—but a roar from somewhere beyond the room shook the walls in the library. Books rained down from all six stories of shelves, creating a tidal wave of sound when they smacked the floor. I surveyed the wreckage of the once pristine room with my heart in my throat. Those books were priceless. They contained the histories of all the living humans on Earth. And now piles of records lay in scattered heaps on the chairs, desks, and floor of the grand room. Something about that was very wrong.

This whole situation was wrong. Those fallen books represented the consequences of my actions. They represented lives that would be disrupted, broken and ruined by my moment of anger. The burden of my transgressions weighed me down.

Another ear-piercing roar made the earth tremble beneath my feet. Maybe I couldn't right my wrong, but I could do everything in my power to stop further damage. My soul might have already been damned, but if I was going to spend the rest of my existence in Hell, I was bringing that dragon back down with me.

I blew out a lungful of air and pushed through the door in front of me.

28

ARTIFACTS ROOM

Bear shrank to his normal dog size to fit through the doorway this time. Just as I remembered from my visit with Logan, we entered a small room with two doors. The one on the left led to the room full of beautiful pictures. The other door led to what Logan had called the Artifacts Room. That was the one place I hadn't been before, and the place I expected Satan to be. Although why, I had no idea.

"Bear, you're staying here."

He huffed at me and took a few steps forward. I curled my hands in his fur and forced him to stop.

"Seriously, I mean it. You are not to go in there. He'll rip you to shreds."

Bear let out a low growl, and the hair on his back stood on end.

"Don't even think about pulling an attitude with me. Stay." I pointed a finger at him.

He let out another low growl but plopped his butt on the smooth floor. I pressed my lips together. He could be as mad at me as he wanted, but I wanted him safe.

I placed a quick kiss on Bear's head before sprinting to the door. Glass shattered on the other side and I sped up, stretching for the knob . . . and then slammed right into the smooth surface.

Ouch.

The stupid thing was locked.

Rubbing a hand under my nose, my glove came back bloodied. Great, I'd probably just broken my face.

I stepped back and put my body weight into a few solid kicks. The door didn't so much as groan, but I did.

I turned to look at Bear, who was sitting with what looked suspiciously like a smile on his furry face.

"A little help?"

He cocked his head at me.

"Seriously?"

He got up and trotted over to me. More glass smashed behind the unopened door. A vicious roar shook the building. This wasn't the time for games. Whatever Satan was doing in there, I was running out of time to deal with him before more hunters showed up. I didn't want anyone else getting hurt because of me. Logan was most definitely searching for me and could appear at any time. He had to be flipping out, knowing my intention was to face Satan alone.

I rolled my eyes. "Bear, will you please help me get past this door?"

He inclined his head, and then before my eyes, my sweet, goofy, lazy dog transformed. He let out a bark that turned into a thunderous growl as his teeth elongated and his head expanded. His ears shortened, but everything else grew in length and girth. After a few blinks, Bear was no longer just Bear. He was now Battle Bear.

I patted his oversized belly. "We gotta get you some armor,

buddy. You'd look good in it."

Bear shoved me to the side with his massive head. Once I was out of the way, he backed up several steps before ramming the door and the wall around it. He tore at the barrier with his razor claws and sharp teeth. When he backed up, the door wasn't just open; there was a full-on hole in the wall three times larger than the previous entrance had been

"You are truly frightening. Okay, thanks. Now stay here."

I ran through the opening, followed by the sound of claws clicking against the floor. Why did I think he'd obey?

After several steps, brightness blinded me.

What the what?

I threw a hand up to shield my eyes and skidded to a halt. Bear rammed into my back, sending me sprawling.

That did not tickle.

I struggled to my feet and shot a scolding look over my shoulder. Bear was up on two legs, towering over me ... He shrugged.

How did he know how to do that? Whatever, not important.

With momentary blindness abated, I tilted my head up and saw ... the sky? Most of the ceiling in this part of the building had been ripped clean off, and light shone straight in. The museum-like open room where I stood might once have been beautiful but was currently in a state of complete disarray. Debris from the hole in the roof littered the area, along with smashed display cases. Glass, wood, chunks of marble, sheet rock ... pieces of the room were everywhere. Interspersed in the mess were books, artwork, ancient weaponry, weird contraptions I didn't recognize—all the things that must have held some sort of value. If the Creator was all-powerful, why was He allowing this destruction?

Another angry roar sounded to my left, shaking the room and forcing my attention. Satan. He was over there somewhere, still in his gigantic dragon form.

I had no idea what he was looking for. I only knew my mission now was to keep it from him. But what could Satan possibly want? What could be so important to have gone through all this trouble to obtain?

I glanced back at Battle Bear and motioned for him to drop to all fours. At least that way he was a little less conspicuous. The Artifacts Room was just one large room the size of a small warehouse. The only places to hide were behind the artifacts or cases holding them.

The element of surprise was the only thing I had going for me. This was a flimsy plan—scratch that, this wasn't a plan at all. I'd followed the monster to this place with the blind determination to stop him, but what could I really do against him? I didn't have a magic sword anymore. I was just me. And there was no way I was going to be enough.

Crouching down, I peered around a fallen bookshelf. A giant membranous wing snapped out from the far side of the room and tossed what looked to be a wooden trebuchet against the wall. Satan was about a hundred feet away. My gosh, that ancient weapon had to weigh a ton, and he'd flung it out of the way as if it were no more than a tin can.

I sat down with my back against the bookshelf and buried my face in my hands. All I had to go up against him with was a burning desire to right my wrong and protect my loved ones. I was going to fail.

But I steeled my resolve. I would give whatever I could. It would never be enough, but it was all I had.

I bowed my head in a silent prayer of thanks to the Creator for what I'd been given and asked for His forgiveness of my part in releasing this abomination.

When I lifted my gaze, I was ready. Ready for the fight I was sure to lose. Ready to do whatever I could—even if I only managed to weaken the beast for my fellow hunters. Ready to face the embodiment of pure evil. And most of all, ready to face my end.

.

29

FACE OFF

What I wasn't ready for was a fight with my overgrown bear-dog. I'd commanded him to stay put. The big, stupid, lovable, terrifying butthead would not stop tailing me as I tried to creep closer to where Satan was searching in the back of the Artifact Room.

"For the last time, you overgrown ball of fur, will you please stay put?"

Bear growled low and shook his head at me. At this point, I liked him better when he didn't understand English. He had been way more obedient on Earth.

Grabbing the fur on the sides of his giant head, I looked into his big chocolate eyes. "Listen, buddy, you know I love you. And I know you are one fierce fighter. But right now, you are too big to be following me around. That crazy unhinged dragon over there is gonna discover us any minute if you keep trying to follow me. And now that you're here, you're too vulnerable to shrink back to regular Bear size. So I need you to just stay put, okay?"

He blinked at me twice. What did that mean?

"When the other hunters arrive, you can join the fight, okay?"

Another blink. Geez, was this how Logan felt when he was trying to keep me from danger? Because if so, it explained his general grouchy attitude those first few months of training.

"Listen, boy, you are so important to me, and I can't stand the thought of you getting hurt. That dragon over there could seriously injure you. So I need you to obey me and wait for the rest of the hunters to arrive . . . please." I wasn't above begging at this point.

His furry head dipped and dropped to my shoulder. The move was so like what he used to do when he'd give me hugs on Earth. I felt a prickle behind my eyes. I was going to miss him so much, but he was letting me go. I breathed a sigh of relief. When he lifted his head, there was a strange shininess to his eyes. Almost human-like.

He nudged me with his giant snout. I had to go, and I couldn't tell him everything would be all right and that I'd see him soon, because I didn't know how the next few minutes would play out. So I placed a gentle kiss on his furry nose and whispered my love to him before scurrying over to an overturned bookcase I could hide behind.

Pushing Bear out of my thoughts, I refocused my attention on my enemy with one goal in mind: Keep him from obtaining whatever artifact he was looking for, at any cost.

Sneaking up on Satan was surprisingly easy. Avoiding the flying debris was the hard part. He thrashed through display after display of artifacts in his dragon form, tearing apart everything in his path, and then flinging it out of his way. He was making so much noise and so hyper focused on his task that I didn't have to worry much about being super stealthy. I reached an overturned display case not fifteen feet from him in a matter of minutes.

My heart beat so hard I heard the rush of blood pumping through my veins. My arms were shaking, so I grasped my borrowed sword with two hands. This was going to be like going up against a giant with a steel toothpick, but it was what I had to work with.

Audrey, please stop.

Logan.

His desperate plea echoed in my head as if he was very far away, but the desperation in the tone still shook me to my core. The look on his face as I'd raced off with Bear would forever haunt me. Running from Logan wasn't the farewell that I imagined, but knowing Logan, he would have forcefully removed me from this fight. Hearing his voice in my head right now was like a dagger twisting in my already bleeding heart.

Logan, I love you, I whispered back to him, putting as much concentration as I could into the words and hoping he received them.

His thoughts again: *Love, please. Just wait. We're almost there.* Even if his words hadn't been dripping with desperation, I would have still picked up on his fear through the bond.

I can't. This is my fight.

Before he could answer, I threw up mental shields I didn't even know existed. I couldn't afford to be distracted right now.

I stood to my full height and stepped right behind the creature from my nightmares. Every fiber of my being screamed at me to run the other direction, but instead, I bent over to pick up a heavy chunk of white marble. I hurled it at the scarlet dragon with all the strength I had.

The hunk landed with a thud and slid harmlessly off his scaly back. But the rock did its job of garnering his attention. He whipped around to face me, all teeth and talons and a mouth full of fire.

The stupidity of my plan practically smacked me in the face. I still had a lot to learn in the art of war, but right now my primary goal was to distract him long enough for greater forces to arrive—and if possible inflict some injury that made it easier for other hunters to take him down.

If this red-scaled dragon and I were both going to be thrown back to the pit today, I wanted to make sure he returned to his fiery domain empty handed.

The dragon's mouth opened, and a strange hiss-like laugh echoed off the walls. He folded his wings in front of him and slowly transformed, wings turning into a swirl of black mist and smoke, his figure shrinking and distorting until what had once stood stories high in front of me now only towered above me at the height of an angel. The blackness snapped back and folded behind him, revealing the face of the false angel.

"Oh, little weakling. Finally dressed like the helpless sheep you truly are."

I glanced down at my white body armor and steeled my expression. Who cared what color I wore?

"Throwing pebbles at a giant has only worked one time in history, and you, my stupid sheep, are no blessed shepherd boy. You're a damned soul who turned against her maker, and whose time has officially just run out."

My blood ran cold at his words, but I didn't flinch. Distraction was the name of the game right now. And if he wanted to hear himself speak, well that was fine with me if it kept him from searching for whatever he was trying to find.

"Why do you hide behind that fake mask? Are you really so ugly you can't stand to show anyone your true form?" I asked. My weapon of choice . . . kindergarten insults.

He raised an eyebrow. "In a rush to see my true form, are you?"

I shrugged, probably looking a little odd with my sword at the ready. "Just seems silly to keep up a façade. It seems rather . . . weak to me. Why constantly pretend to be something you're not?" I only half-thought through my speech—I was word vomiting to keep his attention. A trickle of sweat slid down the side of my face. "Unless you're wearing the costume to relive the glory days or something. Hoping to get back into the God-club, are you?"

He cocked his head in that creepy birdlike manner and then let out a roar of laughter. "Are you trying to bait me into a fight? Or simply trying to distract me from my task? You really think I'm that stupid?"

"More like hoping you were that stupid."

A slow smile spread over Satan's false face. Something about the way it bunched the flesh seemed very off. "I'd be happy to show you my true form. You'll be spending enough time with me that you may as well get used to it."

I thought I was prepared for what was to come, but I so wasn't.

The flesh on Satan's face started to fall off in bloody chunks. With that creepy smile still in place, holes stretched to reveal the blackened flesh of the demon beneath. His body grew in size, which caused his angelic . . . casing . . . to stretch and burst apart like an overstuffed sausage.

Spikes jutted out from his elbow joints, and the end of each finger turned into a razor-sharp claw. He snapped his hands open and closed several times, and sparks flew from the points of contact.

His wings, which were creepy enough as shadow and mist, solidified into flesh-toned patchwork, as if he'd sewn them together using strips of human's skin. My stomach rebelled, and I fought to control my nausea.

His knees cracked backward, and an extra joint appeared near where his shins used to be. As his hair fell, multiple pointed barbs punched through his skull, turning his head into a weapon. Each pointed barb oozed onyx-colored liquid.

His face was most disturbing of all. He still had pits for eyes, but a red dot had appeared in their depths. There were only a few pieces of flesh still dripping off his face, but everything underneath was charred and scaly, like every other demon I'd seen. His nose was now completely gone, and in its place were two slits, very reptilian in nature. His cheekbones were cut sharply and over exaggerated, and his smile was downright horrifying. His lips of flesh were still in place, but the lower portion of his face was now pushed out like an animal's jaws. And behind that stretched, fleshy smile were rows of jagged, triangular teeth.

His chuckle, deeper than before, bounced around in my ears, creating a stabbing sensation. I gritted my teeth to keep from squeezing my head between my hands. I got the impression he had purposefully slowed down this change so I could take in each horrifying moment, a fear tactic that was extremely effective.

Despite myself, the tip of the sword I held trembled.

"You have every reason to fear me. I am the lion that prowls in the night, seeking to devour you. I am the death everyone fears. I am destruction, despair, and the desperation that claws at your chest. I am power." The floor shook on his last word, as if the power he claimed was manifesting in the very room where we stood.

"You are not the most powerful being in the world." Dread locked in my chest, but I fought him with truth.

"From this moment on, I'm the most powerful being in your world."

I didn't even register the hit until my back slammed against the hard surface, creating an Audrey-sized dent in the marble wall. Small pebbles and fine chalk dust rained down on me as I slid to the ground.

My chest throbbed—presumably at the point of impact. The assault had happened so fast I didn't see a thing. I rubbed the sore spot and struggled to my feet. I was searching for my weapon when I was lifted off the ground by my throat and slammed back into the wall. Gasping for air, I scratched at the hand that held me in place.

Satan's grotesque face filled my vision. The slits that were his nose expanded and contracted, and sulfur breath washed over my face. I choked on the stench as I struggled for air. Bile bubbled in my stomach, screaming to be released.

The skin on my throat where the vile creature held me burned as if his hand leaked acid. Sharp claws bit into the back of my neck, and blood trickled down my spine from the split flesh.

One strong squeeze and he could easily separate my head from the rest of my body.

I kicked and thrashed, but the efforts were no more effective than a fish flailing at the end of a hook.

Black ooze from the barbs on Satan's head dripped down his face and onto the ground. I couldn't see where they landed, but I heard a sizzle below after each drop.

He leaned in, and his stretched lips of flesh and rows of

pointed teeth filled my waning vision. "That's right. Squirm like the worm you are. It amuses me."

He punctuated his words with a squeeze to my neck; the burning and bloodletting intensified. My airway was completely restricted. I couldn't even gasp for air.

My limbs became heavy and my movements sluggish. My mind screamed to continue to fight, but my body wouldn't comply.

The vise around my neck released, and as I fell as if in slow motion, I watched the monster's arm whip around and strike a blur of golden fur, sending it smashing to the other side of the enormous room.

"No!" I tried to scream as Bear's body lay motionless on the ground, but all that escaped was a weak wheezing noise.

Red blood dripped off the foot long spike that protruded from Satan's right arm-like appendage.

Bear wasn't moving, but Satan didn't give my friend a second glance as he refocused, pinning his red glare on me.

"You don't know it, but you've already failed." He reached into the folds of his stretched and torn garment and pulled out an object I was wholly unfamiliar with. The gold orb he held was semi-translucent with a green mist-like substance swirling lazily in its depths. "I already have what I came here to get." His eyes narrowed as he looked down at me, lying on my back on the floor. "But it's time I stopped toying with my dinner and took it home to devour. I'm looking forward to painting that armor a lovely shade of red."

30

THE END

I'd failed. Failed on a scale so epic I couldn't even wrap my brain around it. There would be no more cherished moments; there would be no more goodbyes. This was it. And in the end, I had done nothing except provide Satan with a bit of sport for his own twisted enjoyment.

Even in the face of hopelessness, something inside screamed at me to fight, to never give in. I crab-walked backward and then turned to stumble away from the monster who claimed ownership of my fate.

He followed. I broke into a sloppy run, throwing glances over my shoulder as he steadily shadowed me. I'd already born witness to his otherworldly speed, so I knew he was allowing this pathetic attempt to flee—no doubt another amusement.

Tripping over debris, I fell face first onto the unforgiving floor—bruising a good portion of my face—but scrambled to keep moving, even if that meant on my hands and knees. I imagined Satan got some sick enjoyment out of watching me scurry along the ground like the disgusting bug he already perceived me to be.

My anger reached a boiling point, and as I attempted to stand, my hand brushed over a familiar object.

The pommel of a sword. It could have been mine, or it might have been one of the artifacts from this room, but I wrapped my hand around the hilt. Historic relic or not, I didn't care. I was going to use it against my enemy. Causing even one drop of his blackened blood to shed would be a victory at this point. I didn't have much left to hope for. But that voice inside urged me to keep fighting.

I went to stand, but what felt like a cinder block landed on my sword hand, crushing the delicate bones and trapping me on the ground. I cried out—soundlessly. Something in my vocal cords must have been damaged when Satan squeezed my throat.

A black hoof—three times the size of any Earthly beast's—pinned my hand in place and twisted to ratchet up the pain and damage. Spears of agony shot through my hand and up into my arm then radiated throughout my chest and the rest of my extremities. I wanted to pass out, but I couldn't. Acid burned up my esophagus, gathering at the back of my throat. I tipped my head upward and silently screamed the name of my God.

In a flash of blue light, Satan flew off me. I watched, half-detached because of my pain, as he was blown into a set of bookshelves. Struggling to a sitting position, I cradled my broken hand to my chest, not looking at my mangled limb for fear the damage would be more than my mind could handle.

The blast had originated to my right, but I kept my eyes fixed on my tormentor as he roared and shoved himself to his cloven feet. Chucking the remains of the shelves he'd crashed into behind him, his rage stirred the atoms in the air and affronted me from every angle.

Warmth radiated from behind me, but I didn't dare take my eyes off the monster.

"This one is not yours."

Joe.

Satan opened his mouth, but instead of letting out a bellow, he loosed a stream of fire that shot straight for me. I ducked in a pathetic attempt to protect myself, but the scorching fire never reached me.

I lowered my arm to find a shield of crackling blue electricity blocking the flames from touching me. Twisting to my left, I found Logan standing with his arms stretched out in my direction, a bolt of his familiar blue lightning coursing from his palms to the electric field hovering in front of me.

A hand landed on my shoulder, and healing warmth rushed through my body, knitting together the broken flesh and bones that Satan had mangled. I flexed my hand against my chest without pain. Joe gave my shoulder one more squeeze and took a step back, eyes fixed on Satan.

"This one is mine. You cannot have her."

"No!" Satan bellowed. Black spittle shot from his mouth. "The chain's curse was set by your very word. A price has to be paid."

"I'll pay it instead," Logan said.

What? No!

Logan's words were spoken with conviction. He strode forward with confidence and determination, his eyes capturing my gaze.

My heart jackhammered in my chest.

What are you doing? I sent the message to Logan without speaking.

Loving you, he sent back.

Rather than melt at his misguided romantic gesture, I

crossed over the freaked-out threshold. His intent was there in his eyes. He would do this. He would try to trade places with me without my permission.

No.

I jumped to my feet and ran at the monster who masqueraded as an angel. Satan's mouth twisted, and a sound emerged that may have been a laugh. I didn't know what my end game was here, but I had to reach Satan before he had the chance to take Logan away.

I sprinted toward my horrific future.

Audrey, Joe's voice whispered in my mind, *trust that you are mine and follow me.*

I froze, as did the world around me.

The snapping of a single set of fingers echoed off the walls, and I was free. I pitched to the side to keep from running into the immobile Satan-statue in front of me and then took three steps before I regained my balanced.

Turning in a slow circle, I saw everything suspended in time, including the spittle flying off Satan's chin. I poked at hovering goo expecting it to be hard, but it stuck to my gloved fingers like slime.

Nasty.

Logan was mid-step about twenty feet away, immobile as well. I was about to rush to him when a voice cracked the silence.

"How is it that after everything, you still doubt Me?"

I spun to find the Creator, Hugo, and Joe standing in the middle of the room.

I gasped for words. "Whoa, yeah, of course you did this. It's the whole control of time and space thing you've got going on, right?"

The Creator's face wasn't harsh, but it wasn't soft either.

Lightning flashed in His eyes when I spoke. Someone was a little peeved at me. I'd thought that whole walk down the aisle thing meant things were smoothed over between us, but obviously not.

Hugo gave me a small shake of the head that let me know I was treading on thin ice right now.

I winced. The weight of my shame forced my gaze down.

"Sorry," I whispered.

"I asked you a question, child." The Creator's voice boomed in my mind as well as throughout the room. Only a fraction of His power released, and before I knew it, I was on my knees.

"What . . . what do you mean?" I squeaked out.

A warm hand lifted my chin, and I looked into Joe's pain-filled eyes. "You know Satan is the Father of Lies, dear one. Yet you've existed these past weeks in fear rather than seeking my face. I've been waiting for you to come to me, yet you haven't."

I sat back on my knees and hung my head once again. When I looked back up, it was into the denim-washed eyes of my former trainer, Hugo.

He enclosed me in a hug and whispered in my ear, "Tell me why you didn't come to me."

He rubbed my back, soothing my fears.

"Because . . ." This was an ugly truth to reveal. "I thought you would send me to Hell for what I did, and so I hid from you."

He set me back, and it was now the face of my Creator staring at me. "Hell can never have you, dear one. You are Mine, now and forever. You were bought with My Son's blood long ago, and nothing can take you from My hand."

Several beats passed as I pieced together the meaning of His words.

"You will not be spending an eternity in Hell, dear one."

Was this a dream?

"My blood covers all your transgressions, great and small." Joe was now standing behind the Creator and next to Hugo. One of each of their hands rested on the Creator.

Tears welled in my eyes; the floodgates had opened and relief washed through my body.

"But what about this mess? I mean, he's free"—I pointed at Satan's still form behind me—"and he has . . . whatever artifact he was looking for." It hit me suddenly that Satan was stuck in suspended animation. "Wait, we can just take it back now."

Springing up, I went to search his shredded garment for the round contraption he'd showed me before but was stopped when Hugo appeared in front of me. "What?"

He shook his head and herded me away from the fallen angel.

"I have a plan and a purpose for everything." The Creator nodded toward Satan. "Even this."

"You planned to have Satan released from Hell so he could break into our realm and steal something?" This made no sense.

"The plan for the end times was set in motion a very long time ago, yet no one knows the date or the time but Me. This is but another way the Deceiver continues to unknowingly play his role. The device he sought will transfer his power to another, as it has been written and foreordained. The device was created for that very purpose, and now it will find its home with him until the day is right for him to use it. The day of My choosing."

I took a step back, shocked. "But . . . then you just . . ." Where to even begin? I hardly even knew what I wanted to say. "Are we all just chess pieces to You?"

I slapped a hand over my mouth and squeezed my eyes shut

at my outburst. Surely I was due for a bolt of lightning right about now.

When I finally cracked one of my eyelids open, Joe was standing alone. The look on his face was not one of anger or condemnation but sadness.

"Audrey, is that really how you think I see you?"

I opened my mouth to reply, but the words caught in my throat. I didn't think he felt that way, but if I was interpreting what he said correctly, that meant I had been used to free Satan on purpose. I'd suffered so much because of what I'd done. Logan had suffered. This didn't make sense.

"You would not have suffered at all had you sought me out, but you chose to turn away from me."

But Logan—

Joe cut off my train of thought and answered my question before I could even ask it. "Did Logan not come away from his ordeal a stronger person? Free from the chains that he'd shackled himself to for so long?"

I opened my mouth to protest, but I couldn't. He was right. Logan did return from Hell a healed man, and had I sought out Joe, I wouldn't have feared an eternity of torment.

"My deepest desire is for you to know me better. I petition my Father on your behalf daily. My love for you is immeasurable. And all I ask is for you to trust in me. To let me help you with your burdens. My heart is full of love for you, not malice. It is not my desire to lose a single human being, and you have and will always have a part in that plan."

Sadness filled my heart, for I realized my transgression against Joe had not been the mistake I'd made in Hell—as awful as plunging the blade into him had been, doing so had been unintentional. No, my true offense had been when I tried to hide from him rather than run to him for forgiveness.

"You were forgiven before you even thought to ask." He spoke softly to me, knowing my mind without me having to verbalize the words. "That mark you bore, it was intended to send you running to me, not away. It was never a representation of your curse, but your refusal to seek my face, to seek forgiveness."

I'd completely forgotten about the black stain on my skin.

"Just like the physical scars that don't heal properly represent your internal struggle, your refusal to turn to me was like a poison in your veins, spreading every day. You no longer bear that mark."

My eyes began to fill with the heaviness of that news. I had jumped to the exact wrong conclusion. Logan had been right all along. The answer was always to seek the Son; nothing good would ever come from hiding. I wanted to say something, to thank him for this act of forgiveness, but words failed me.

He smiled and nodded. Walking forward, he placed a hand on my shoulder. "Audrey, the Father knows all things. His ways are not your own. The path you are on may look dark, but you must hold tight to the truth that He is good and works all things for good."

"I won't forget again."

His eyebrows rose.

"All right, I'll *try* not to forget again. Better?"

He smiled. "How about we put the beast back in his cage . . . together?"

"We can do that?"

"Yes." He pressed a sword into my hand and stepped back. "You've always had the power of my Spirit inside you. Let's see you set it ablaze."

As seeds of doubt took root in my soul, Joe's smile fell.

"I . . . can do that?" I questioned.

"With faith the size of a mustard seed, you can do that and so much more."

"So I should just, like, tell it to flame? Is there a manual?"

The corners of Joe's mouth ticked up, but he quickly pinched his lips together to cover the action. "What do you think is the source of your power?"

"Faith?"

"So use that now, and tell the flame to appear."

I closed my eyes. *I can do this. I can do this. I can do this,* I chanted.

Hugo's words boomed in my mind. *You can only do this through my power.*

Right, not my power but the Spirit's power in me. With renewed vigor, I imagined the flames as they used to be, burning bright blue with intense holy fire. Licking only the blade. Hungry for enemy blood.

When I cracked one eyelid open, the sword was blazing. Exactly how I'd imagined it to be.

Joe's face was lit by the flicker. He smiled broadly as he lifted his hand and pierced it on the tip of the weapon.

"Whoa, what are you doing?" I swung the sword out of his reach, but trickles of blood rolled down from the end of the blade.

"My blood was used to break Satan's chains, and along with the sword of the Spirit"—he nodded at the weapon I held—"my blood will form new ones."

"Oh my gosh, give a girl a heads up next time." I pressed a palm to my overexerted heart.

"Audrey, I'm fine. Look." Joe shoved his hand in front of my face, and there was no gash. Only a round scar marred the center of his palm. "Would you like a heads up on what we're about to do?"

"Yes, please." I smiled broadly and bounced on the balls of my feet, more than a little ready to watch Joe kick Satan's butt.

He chuckled. "Then let me tell you."

In a blink, the world around us was set back in motion. I stood shoulder to shoulder with Joe, rather than a hair's breadth away from Satan where I'd been when time stood still. I grasped the sword of the Spirit in my hand, and the blade flamed with holy fire.

"I said," Joe began, "that you cannot have her. She's been purchased with my blood. The price was paid long before the deed was done. But you"—Joe pointed a finger at Satan, authority ringing from the Son's voice—"no longer belong here."

I flicked my gaze to the side to see Logan staring at Joe and me in awe. A small army of hunters surrounded us, but they all held their positions, waiting for orders from Joe.

Satan let out a rage-filled bellow and charged us. Joe turned to me and, with a nod, sped right back at him.

The two collided with a force that sent a wave of power crashing into everyone. Some of my fellow hunters stumbled and fell from the quakes.

I stood strong with my feet planted despite the blast and waited for my moment.

31

DEFEAT

The battle raged: Joe versus our ancient enemy. But after only a few short minutes, it was obvious Joe was toying with Satan. Anyone could see it. There wasn't a scratch on Joe, yet Satan's black blood was splattered and smeared all over the floor where they fought.

And now I knew the truth. Joe wasn't just more powerful than Satan in this realm; Joe was more powerful in any realm. And despite all of Satan's well-laid plans, he had unknowingly been following the Creator's script all along. The mighty red dragon was a puppet in this game, and his strings were about to be reattached.

Joe released a blast of power from his hands, and Satan flew back into the wall.

Well, that was a cool trick.

"Audrey." Logan was at my side. He squeezed my shoulder to get my attention. "What's happening?"

My gaze remained glued to the conflict in front of me as I waited with my blood-tipped blade for Joe's signal. I replied to Logan without turning his way, "Something amazing."

"Are you hurt? Are you okay?" No doubt the blood smeared on my white body armor from my previous injuries hadn't gone unnoticed.

The unveiled anxiety in Logan's voice forced my attention. His other hand was fisted, surrounded by a crackling ball of blue electricity. His face looked carved from granite except for the muscle that twitched in his jaw. His full lips were tight, and his blue eyes blazed.

I covered the gloved hand on my shoulder with mine and matched the intensity in his eyes. I didn't have time to explain everything that had happened, but he needed some small assurance. We'd have time—all the time in the world—to catch up later.

And with that thought, I smiled—a full, heartfelt smile. No longer was my eternity uncertain. I would spend it with the man I loved. I was certain of it.

"Everything is fine. Everything's going to work out." I squeezed his hand. "I promise."

He nodded once to let me know he believed me, even if he didn't fully understand. I snapped my focus back to the main event, putting aside my celebratory mood for later.

Joe stood with his foot on Satan's chest. Satan hissed and spat at Joe and squirmed on the ground like an overturned bug.

"Gotta go, babe," I said with a wink. "That's my cue."

"Wait, what?" Logan yelled after me as I ran forward with the sword at the ready. The power of the Spirit flowed through my limbs and into the blade.

As I reached the pair, Joe lifted his foot. Satan sprang up and extended his jaws. His roar of anger was cut off by the sword I shoved into his gut. The injury wouldn't kill him, but the holy blood mixed with the power of the Spirit and Creator would do its job.

Satan's jaw opened for a different reason this time. His strangled words of disbelief were followed by his frantic attempts to pull the blade from his body.

Taking several steps back, I watched his frenzied movements as he registered the horror of what was about to happen.

"This can't be done!" he yelled. His voice pierced my eardrums like razors, but I refused to do so much as flinch.

"It has been done. It's time for you to leave and for me to make repairs to my kingdom." Joe turned his back on Satan as if he were no more than a passing nuisance rather than the Prince of Darkness.

I watched in morbid fascination as a chain appeared from the entry point of the sword. The binding twisted and grew, snaking itself around the now thrashing beast and constricting his movements until finally a shackle appeared and clamped onto the lower part of his leg, right above the hoof that had crushed my hand not so long ago.

The bellow that followed shattered all the remaining glass in the room. I was forced to cover my ears this time, as did my fellow hunters.

"Enough!" Joe commanded, his voice booming above the noise and echoing across the room. Then all was quiet.

Something pushed against my leg, and I saw Bear, back to his regular size. I took a brief second to be thankful he was okay, laid a hand on his unusually stoic muzzle, and gave it a scratch.

"It's finished." Joe's voice carried in the silence.

A crack appeared in the floor beneath Satan. The chain that bound him grew and slithered into the ground.

Satan renewed his struggles in silent defiance, for the Son

had restricted his speech. The chain pulled taut and brought the beast down, dragging him across the floor in front of me.

I stared at him. The thing that once haunted my nightmares but whom I now understood had no hold over me.

The red glow in the pits of Satan's eyes latched on to me. The hatred emanating from him was palpable, creating an itchy, restless feeling across my skin.

I wanted him gone.

The fissure in the ground opened wide enough to fit his horrid body. I turned away. It was done. I didn't need to see the end.

Before I took my first step, a thud on my back brought me to my knees.

I blinked down to see a black spike protruding from my chest. Reaching a hand back, I felt the thick barb lodged in my back.

The object that had impaled me dragged me back several feet before being pulled from my body with a sucking sound. Freed, I lay on my side, unable to move, but numb to pain.

When Bear's frantic barking assaulted my ears, spears of agony sliced across my chest. Something warm and sticky soaked my cheek. The flow of red spread across the white marble floor, and warmth drained from my body. Fluid pooled underneath where I lay.

Logan was running to me, the color draining from his face. Sound snapped back into its rightful place when he reached me, gently arranging me so he could press his hands on the holes on my back and chest.

"Audrey, it's going to be all right," he was saying to me. "Joe's still here; he'll fix you right up."

"Wh—" I wanted to ask what happened, but my strength was fleeing as quickly as the blood gushed from my wounds.

"Satan managed a partial transformation before he was sucked back to Hell. He struck you with his spiked tail. But it's going to be all right."

He'd already said that, but his voice shook this time. The slickness of my blood made his dark armor shine.

I couldn't die since I was already dead, but I was bleeding out so fast. Something didn't seem right.

Logan looked in the other direction.

"Please," he pleaded with someone.

"On her back," Joe commanded. He slipped a hand beneath me, and I felt the entry wound knit together. The thought that I'd been struck exactly where my mark had first appeared drifted lazily through my mind and then blew away.

The wound on my chest still bled freely. Joe held my head in his hands as Logan moved both hands to cover the hole on my front. "It's time for you to go too, dear one."

Wait, what?

"Your journey here has ended for the time. It needs to be picked back up where it left off."

I tried to shake my head or ask for an explanation, but my body was numbing, and I was incapable of speech.

Joe leaned over and kissed my forehead. *Trust in me.* The words whispered through my mind.

"What's happening?" Logan all but shouted the words I wanted to scream.

Joe said something to Logan. My hearing was dimming by the second, so I only saw Joe's lips move. When they stopped, Logan gazed down at me with fear-filled eyes.

Dread pooled in my stomach and curdled.

Vaguely aware of other hands on me, I looked down the length of my body, and the faces of my friends swam in and out of my blinking vision. Romona held vigil at my other side.

Kaitlin and Kevin knelt on either side of my legs, and Bear was on his belly with his head rested on one of my ankles.

I couldn't feel him. I couldn't feel anything.

Tears flowed freely down Romona's and Kaitlin's cheeks. I caught a quick glance of Morgan's somber face behind Kaitlin before I focused on Kevin's red-rimmed eyes. And Logan . . .

With hands still pressed to my chest that I could no longer feel, he was red faced and yelling at Joe, who stayed stationary at my head, keeping me steady.

I could no longer hear nor feel my body. In that there was some mercy, for the pool of my blood had grown past the circle of my friends. I vaguely wondered how much blood one person had in their body to spill. If I could grimace at my gruesome thoughts, I would have. But I was paralyzed except for the movement of my eyes.

My vision blinked out for more than a second, and when it returned, I looked into Logan's face.

The world had changed. I was no longer in the Artifact Room but instead somewhere in the foothills of the mountain range I loved so much.

Feeling and hearing had returned but not movement. Soft grass pillowed my body, and Logan no longer held his hands to my chest to staunch a crimson flow.

My friends and Joe stood off to the side.

A soft summer breeze kissed my cheeks, and I felt no pain, but I saw it reflected back at me in Logan's eyes.

He bent down and pressed a gentle kiss to my lips, and pulling back slightly, he whispered, "I love you."

I smiled up at him. Of course, I already knew that. My eyes grew heavy, and I was helpless to keep them open. As they closed for the last time, I was able to whisper back, "Always and forever."

32

REALMS

Beep . . . beep . . . beep . . . beep . . . the sound went on at a steady cadence of about a beep per second. It was both familiar and offensive. The rooms of the Healing Center were usually peaceful. This incessant beeping was downright annoying.

I tried to peel open my eyes, which were dry and filled with crusty goop, and only managed to open my lids a sliver. Florescent lights blinded me, and I pressed my eyes shut once again.

Florescent lights? What?

Had the Healing Center gone back to the dark ages?

Lights off, I thought, but nothing happened. The same unpleasant brightness remained, and I squeezed my lids even tighter.

I expanded my senses. My body ached. I needed to do some serious stretches, but when I tried to move, to bring my hand up to cover my eyes, nothing happened.

The beeping noise increased its pace.

Forcing my eyes open, I looked around without moving my

head. I was lying in a scratchy and uncomfortable bed, covered only by a thin white blanket that had seen many washes. Several machines were stationed around me, one of which I recognized as the source of the beeping. Its screen showed a peak every time a beep sounded, and I recognized it as a heart rate machine. Next to it stood a pole that held several bags of liquid.

The beeping grew faster.

My mouth was dry. I went to lick my lips. They were chapped and peeling.

A whiteboard hung on the wall in front of me. Unfamiliar names were written on it, along with times of the day. A TV was suspended from a mount near the ceiling, and a muted soap opera was playing.

My breathing increased, and the beeping grew frantic.

What was happening? Where was I?

A stout woman dressed in mint-green hospital scrubs walked into the room, mumbling about faulty equipment. She went straight to the heart monitor and turned it off without even glancing at me.

Was I invisible? Somehow transported and trapped in an Earthly hospital?

Nothing about this made sense.

I tried to talk to the lady, but my voice failed me. Instead of coherent words, a weak wheezing noise emerged. If the woman could hear me, she was too focused on checking the various machines around her to notice. She checked each one, talking to herself about this or that, medical jargon that made zero sense.

Had that heart monitor still been on, it would have been flipping out right now, because my heartbeat was so fast and strong I could feel it thumping in my chest. One beat swallowing up the next.

I made another attempt to grab the woman's attention, not caring what noise came out of my mouth. I just needed to let her know I was here.

The only thing I knew was that I was in some sort of medical facility that wasn't the Healing Center. That meant I was either in a medical ward in another and more primitive section of the realm, or I was somehow trapped on Earth. If the latter was true, this woman couldn't see me. The living couldn't see the dead.

There was a crash at the end of my bed—the sound of someone tripping. My gaze snapped to the source.

My mother stood shock still. And she was looking straight at me.

The fist pressed to her mouth shook, and the tears that filled her eyes spilled down her cheeks.

I blinked back the wetness that filled my parched eyes.

She could see me. Something was very wrong . . . or very right.

"Oh, Mrs. Lyons." The woman in the mint-green scrubs hustled to my mom's side. "Is everything all right? I know it's hard to see your baby like this. Let me help you clean up this mess. Take a seat. I'm sure your husband can get some more food."

My mom didn't look away from me, not for a moment, her body a living statue where she stood. When the lady tried to usher her into a seat, Mom finally moved. Her hand snapped down and grabbed the woman's wrist.

"Linda, she's awake."

The woman, Linda, gasped and finally looked at me. Her mouth opened and closed several times without making a noise, until she uttered, "Thank the Lord." She jerked her gaze back to my mother.

"I'll find a doctor." Linda ran from the room.

"Baby." Mom sobbed and stumbled to the edge of my bed. She gingerly sat on the side of the mattress, in one of the few places free of tubes and wires. Grasping my hand, she offered a brilliant smile as tears flowed from her eyes. "Can you hear me, sweetheart?"

I tried to squeeze her hand but didn't have any strength. Tears leaked from my eyes and spilled down the sides of my face.

"You were in an accident, baby. You were asleep for a very long time. We didn't know if . . . That doesn't matter now. You're back with us, and everything is going to be okay. I promise, it's all going to be better now."

My mom's face was so full of hope and joy. But my mind was a mix of disbelief and horror.

I had no idea how this was possible. I was truly back on Earth. Back in the body I thought I'd lost so long ago. Somehow I'd been given a second chance at life . . . and it was cracking my soul in two. For as unbelievable and miraculous as this was, this meant that I had unknowingly . . . unwillingly . . . left my other half in the heavenly realm.

And there was only one way I was ever going to be able to return.

Being alive was torture. My body hurt everywhere, and it didn't feel like my body anymore. I'd been lying sedate for almost a full year, so my muscles had atrophied. Weakened and shrunk from disuse—now that I wanted to use them again—they rebelled.

I'd apparently spent most of that time at some fancy center for coma patients thousands of miles from my hometown. The financial strain I'd seen my parents suffering when I took part in the battle at their house made a lot more sense now. They hadn't been given any guarantees, and the longer I remained in a coma, the lower my chances of ever waking up had grown, but my brain activity had stumped the doctors. According to their machines, my mind was functioning in a way they hadn't expected, and so my family had trudged on with the hope that some day I'd wake up—and that 'some day' had finally come.

A physical therapist came in twice a day to move my body for me while I basically just watched her and tried not to cry when she twisted one of my limbs in a way it didn't want to go.

A week after I woke up, I was finally able to move some parts of my body on my own, and I no longer felt quite so claustrophobic in my skin. I was told that next week I'd be taken to the in-house rehabilitation center twice a day for my physical and occupational therapy.

I wanted to explain everything to my family. Where I'd truly been all this time, but I was unable to communicate properly. My muscles weren't the only parts of my body that had turned against me; my vocal cords and part of my mind had followed suit.

I could barely get a word out, both because my voice had been unused so long and also because parts of my brain were scrambled. At least, that was what my doctor said, but in a more sensitive way. Even though I could think relatively clearly—yeah, I suffered little glitches now and then when I'd temporarily forget a name with a face and things like that—I was told I was going to have to re-learn how to speak and read and write.

All of that news blew . . . big time. It meant I was stuck lying in this bed, feeling like a geriatric patient rather than the healthy eighteen-year-old I should have been, struggling out a word here and there, unable to explain what had happened to me.

I saved my tears for the dead of night when I knew the only people who might see them were the nurses. My family was beyond overjoyed to have me back. My parents had both been visiting me the day I 'miraculously awoke,' and so they made plans to stay with me for a few weeks and then switch off and on until I could go home. I had video calls with my sisters and brother that basically consisted of them talking at me while I just attempted to smile.

Everything was hard. Everything hurt. And I was a conflicted mess of emotions. Thankful to have my life returned, bitter to have lost the new existence I was building. I didn't know whether to be angry at the Creator for sending me back or grateful.

My heart—my poor, shriveled, beat-up heart—hurt, big time.

Even thinking Logan's name brought a fresh onslaught of tears to my eyes. Picking one existence over the other would have been a near-impossible choice. But I hadn't been given that choice.

Was I relieved about that? Or angry? I didn't know.

My opinion changed hourly. I'd spend time with my parents, listen to their stories from the last year—how much they had missed me and how happy they were to have me back—and think that despite the pain of leaving all I had built in the afterlife, being back on Earth was the right thing. But then in the dead of night I'd lie awake wondering what my friends, what Romona and Bear, were doing and how they were going on without me.

And I'd ache.

Then him.

I would have given up the world to be with him. How could I for one second think this Earthly life was preferable to an eternity with the other half of my heart?

The cycle went on and on, around and around, back and forth.

Did he know where I was, what had happened to me? Did he visit me when I wasn't aware? Now that I had a living future . . . what should I do with my second chance at life? But what kind of life could I have without him? I would wait for him, but would he do the same?

What my family had gone through was a nightmare . . . one they were finally waking up from. Did I feel the same or not?

And I prayed. I prayed long and hard, beseeching the Creator for answers. But I didn't receive any. It felt as if my lifeline to Him had been cut off, and all I was left with was my knowledge of Him.

And therein lay my choice.

Would I choose to believe what I knew to be true, that the Creator, my God, was a good God who wanted good things for me, or would I rely on how I felt in the moment?

Abandoned, betrayed, and broken.

I knew all of that to be untrue. I knew He was with me, even now in this bed, day and night. I knew my God wouldn't leave my side.

The day on the mountain He'd showed me the many times He'd carried me through life's trials. But this was so much bigger than those incidences. And the desire to give in to my feelings, rather than grasp the truth with both hands like a lifeline and hold tight, was strong.

I knew now that even if I did let go and rail at Him, He wouldn't leave me. But that didn't mean I felt any better.

"Honey, are you crying?"

Shoot.

I attempted to lift a wobbly hand to my face but didn't have the strength.

My dad turned in the chair he occupied near my bed and pulled a tissue from a box. He quickly dabbed under my eyes and soaked up the moisture that had unwillingly collected.

"There you go." His lips were smiling, but the emotion didn't reach his eyes. He knew I was in pain; he just didn't understand the extent of it. "Audrey, I promise things will get better. You're growing stronger every day. We'll be out of this place and back home in no time. You'll get back to your old life, I promise."

I tried to give him a reassuring smile, but I'm pretty sure the expression was crooked at best. I nodded slowly to indicate I understood. Getting out even a word took an exhausting amount of effort, and I didn't feel up to it. A great deal of my mental strength went toward not thinking about a few key things and trying to live in the moment again. Pretending I wasn't this broken shell of a person.

If I kept this up, I might never talk again. But I didn't know how to process and move through the pain of what I'd lost to keep on living. I didn't even know if I wanted to process it, because it meant I'd have to move on, and I wasn't ready for that.

For the very first time, I could appreciate not having had my memories immediately returned when I arrived in the afterlife.

This was beyond overwhelming.

"Baby," my dad went on, oblivious of the true cause of my

inner turmoil, "I know life seems impossibly hard right now, but you're a fighter. You. Are. A. Fighter." The fierceness in my father's eyes told me he truly believed that. That he desperately wanted me to believe that as well.

The prickle behind my eyes warned of more tears to come. I blinked them away. My parents needed strength from me right now.

"My sweet Audrey, you *will* fight your way back to us." My dad gripped my hand tightly. "And you will go on to have a beautiful life. Full of laughter and joy and someday a love and family of your own."

There was no holding back the tide of tears after those words. They welled up and spilled over onto my face unfettered. For what my dad didn't know, couldn't know because I couldn't yet express it myself, was that I would never have a love in this life because I'd already given away my heart, and I refused to take it back. Part of myself belonged to someone I most likely wouldn't see again for many years—for a lifetime.

So this life, this future, he spoke of, would never be a reality.

Yes, I'd go on. I'd live my life. And not only for my family, but for myself and for the Creator who gave it to me. I'd even live it for the people I knew who had moved on to their eternal existence, for life was truly a precious blessing. But I would never have love and a family. For there was one thing I'd resolved.

My heart belonged now and forever to Logan, and I wasn't ever going to be whole again until the day I found myself back in his arms.

33

TRAINING

"**J**ust one more step. That's great. Now just one more, and I promise that will be it. That one was so good I'm sure you can do another."

"Hate . . . you," I pushed out through clenched teeth as my pathetic muscles shook with fatigue. Sweat dripped down my face and soaked the back of my t-shirt as I forced one foot in front of the other again . . . and then again.

Lying jerk-face.

"Yeah, I know. You say that every time." He chuckled. "I'm over it. You're not my grumpiest patient by far."

"Something . . . else . . . I can work on," I puffed out. A chunk of wet hair fell in my face. They'd shaved my head after the accident, and the shortened grown out length was always getting in the way.

Jared just laughed at me again.

You won't be laughing when I throat-punch you with one of these crazy cane contraptions.

But I'd never do that. Jared was my regular physical therapist at the hospital, and even though there were times I truly hated him, the truth of the matter was he was just here to help me. We'd been working together for almost a month now, and according to him I was making 'amazing improvements.'

Pfft.

Being able to feed myself and walk a few incredibly slow laps around what I called the "baby loop"—imagine a track and field circle for toddlers—didn't feel super amazing to me. The grueling work left me sore every day. I felt like I was training for the Olympics rather than simply getting back to a normal range of motion.

Jared was a cheerful taskmaster. He was quick to smile, and I'd yet been able to get under his skin in an irritating way. He basically ignored my sour moods, pretending I was talking pleasantly with him instead.

He was one of the younger therapists, probably in his mid-twenties. He had a mop of sandy-brown hair and hazel eyes with slight laugh lines running from the corners. His broad smile always reminded me of Kevin, which used to rub me the wrong way because I didn't like to be reminded of my friends from the afterlife, but I'd gotten used to it over time.

He was certainly attractive, but I only noticed it in a detached way. Like I would notice the attractiveness of a stranger, not someone I spent time with on a daily basis. I wondered more than once if they'd assigned me the young 'hot' trainer, thinking it would be more motivating for me. It probably would have made a difference to the girl I'd once been, but it didn't matter in the least to the warrior I'd become.

Throwing insults aside, I was determined to move on with my life. And in order to do so, I had to push myself to the limits. In the past month, I'd regained my ability to read almost completely. My writing was a bit sloppy, and that tied my mental and physical therapy together. Speech was the most frustrating. All the words were in my head, but I struggled to get them out. The doctors and therapist were very optimistic that it would come along as well and were quick to remind me how far I'd come in what they considered a short period of time, but my inability to communicate normally was still super frustrating.

In the days when I could hardly communicate at all, I'd decided not to tell my family about what had happened to me while my body wasted away without my knowledge. I debated it, but I couldn't find a reason to unload that burden on them. At best, they'd believe I dreamed it all up. At worst, they'd think I had more severe mental issues than had already been identified.

And in a weird way, keeping the secret meant I could keep all of it. I didn't want someone to tell me I had to give it up.

I would move on with my life because there had to be a reason I hadn't died when I was struck by that car—some purpose the Creator had for me here on Earth in a living body—but I'd always carry those loved ones with me. I didn't want to talk to someone who would try to force them from my thoughts in a futile attempt to make me forget and live a "happier, healthier life." If the Creator had wanted me to forget, then I would have woken up without any memories of my year as a demon hunter or the relationships I had built during that time.

There was a reason for the remembering.

So instead of telling anyone about the afterlife, I spent time silently beseeching the Creator, Hugo, and Joe for wisdom, guidance, and a break from the soul-wrenching pain of loss I hid from all others. I knew they were with me and were the help I needed. It took supernatural effort to keep from being angry at my situation. Every day, I had to intentionally choose to believe there was a plan and purpose in all of this.

Some days were harder than others.

"All right, I think that's good for today, Audrey. Up high for the amazing work."

Jared held his hand so high that under normal circumstances I would have had to jump to reach it. I rolled my eyes and halfheartedly swiped at him with my high-tech crutch. He deftly stepped out of the way. "Close enough."

I wrinkled my nose and stuck my tongue out at him. He had hints of Kaitlin in his personality too. I mentally slapped myself. I wasn't ever going to let go of my friends, but I had to stop constantly comparing people to them.

Jared was just Jared. He was his own person, just as each of my friends in the heavenly realm were their own person and could never be replaced.

"Oh, maybe I shouldn't have taken you out of the running for the grumpiest patient after all."

I flopped into my wheelchair and shook my head. "Sorry, am I a . . ." *No, that wasn't right.* "I am in"—*there we go*—"a"—*get the word out, Audrey*—"ju-junky mood today."

I sighed. Having to concentrate so much on something that used to be so easy was wearisome.

Jared's smile didn't quite reach his eyes. Like most people around me—lots of brave faces hiding their pity for me. Maybe someone else would be annoyed by their insincerity, but frankly, I'd rather have their poorly veiled pity than anything more forthcoming. If they wanted to believe I was buying what they were selling, that was fine with me.

In truth, I was doing a lot of play-acting myself. My parents now switched weeks flying back and forth from the hospital to stay with me, and for their sakes I made an effort to look happy. I wasn't fooling them any more than they were fooling me. It was a charade we all played that I was happy to keep up.

Things would change, I told myself over and over again. Life wouldn't always be this hard; it wouldn't always hurt this much.

But a little voice in the back of my mind mocked me and told me that I was fooling myself if I thought I could go on without him. When that voice popped up, I locked it away into the far recesses of my mind—for my sanity.

I was barely paying attention as Jared wheeled me back to my room.

"You know, soon you'll be able to start taking short walks on your own in-between our sessions."

I barked out a laugh. Awesome. More pain for more of the day.

"Cool, right?" He purposefully ignored my mocking response. "Okay, here we are. Temporary home sweet home."

"Yay," I weakly replied.

He stopped before he wheeled me into the room. I looked up at him with a question in my eyes, and he came around the front of my chair. He crouched down until he was level with me, his gaze intense and his lips pressed into a hard line.

A serious look from Jared? Uh-oh, these were few and far between. Someone was channeling a little Shannon right now.

Oh, shoot. I did it again. I batted thoughts of the prickly angel away.

"You're a fighter, Audrey. You'll get through this and be stronger because of it."

I wanted to laugh in his face, but that word popped up again—fighter—it got me every time. These people didn't know that I had been a hunter. They didn't know how appropriate the term was.

Who knew that battling with fists and weapons would be

one of the easier ways to fight?

"You want me to do . . . wh-what?" It had taken a few months, but I was finally able to get a full sentence out. Yeah, I usually had a break and often a stutter, but I finally felt like I could communicate with people again.

Jared bounced up and down like an excited puppy. "We're gonna go for a jog . . . on the 'big kids' track."

He pointed his thumb behind him. I didn't have to look, but I did anyway. In the west wing of the hospital was a full gym. It had all the bells and whistles: not only a full-sized running track, but also a climbing wall and a bunch of fancy machines. The gym sat in the very center of the wing. All the rooms on this side of the hospital looked down on it, reminding me of a hotel atrium. Maybe the architect of this place had thought the view would be inspiring for the patients, but in reality it just made anyone using it feel like they were on display.

I shook my head. "Noo. Definitely not ready for that."

He nodded, a maniacal smile on his face. "Oh, yeah, you are."

"I ju-just got com-fortable slow walking. I only d-ditched my wheelchair las-st week. What makes you th-think I'm ready for that?" I pointed out the windows that looked down to what patients called the coliseum.

It didn't just feel like people were on display down there—that they were being judged—it was a fact. Sometimes when patients got bored, they'd sit on the sixth floor and watch the action. Cringing whenever someone wiped out . . . which always happened. I should know. I'd spent enough time as one of those quiet observers.

One truly delightful ten-year-old always tried to take bets on how long it would take for someone to bite it. I ignored him because I found that to be extremely disrespectful, but I never said anything because he was just a little kid. He was missing an eye from an accident, and his head was shaved bald with a bunch of stitches visible on his patched eye side. I felt bad for him, but I also thought he was a little punk.

Kids . . . shudder . . . at least I wasn't lamenting the loss of never having to have them. The booger eaters here drove me a little batty. But the circumstances that landed them here made me entirely depressed, so I basically ignored them when I could.

"This is happening, Audrey. Embrace it. Seize the day. Run free and all that."

"What?"

Jared was weird.

"Come on." He grabbed my hand and all but hauled me to the elevator that brought us to the ground floor.

I reluctantly followed him out when we arrived because I didn't want to be dragged again.

Upon stepping into the training space, I was immediately both intimidated and swamped with nostalgia. The hospital's atrium-like rehab training area in no way looked like the training gyms I'd spent so many hours in with both Hugo and . . . him, but something about the atmosphere brought back a wave of familiarity. And with it a swell of emotions, both good and bad.

Jared led me around the large open space, pointing out different areas and activities and letting me know when he thought I may be ready for each. He was completely oblivious to my near emotional overload.

"All right, now that tour time is over, let's talk about the training plan for the day."

Jared turned to me, and his expression instantly dropped. "Audrey, I'm so sorry. We can just have this be a tour today and start tomorrow if you need time to work up to this. I know sometimes I push you a little hard, but it's because I always know you'll rise to the challenge."

"Huh? What?" I didn't understand his one-eighty degree change. He did a quick search around and then took off, pulling a fresh hand towel from a rack.

"Here." He handed me the white piece of cloth and shifted on his feet, looking extremely uncomfortable.

I looked up at him with knitted brows. Why had he given this to me?

"It's for . . . you know, your face."

My face?

I reached up and touched a hand to my cheek to find it wet. The other cheek was also covered. I'd been crying without even knowing. Since when was that a thing I did?

I quickly scrubbed my face with the abrasive towel, wiping away the evidence of my weakness.

Geez, who cried like that without even realizing it had happened? I was turning into a total spaz.

"All right, so we'll just go back upstairs and do some similar exercises to yesterday's and—"

"No," I interrupted his nervous jabber. I knew a lot of patients leaked out tears during physical therapy. The sessions were often extremely painful. I could only assume he was acting so weird because tears weren't something he'd ever seen from *me* before. Sure, witty comebacks and playground insults, but never tears.

"Let's do . . . th-this. You were right. I c-an handle it."

Jared placed a brotherly hand on my shoulder. "Really, Audrey, we can start tomorrow."

I shook my head. "It's really okay. I-I would like to . . . move forward."

Jared pressed his lips together and searched my face. After several beats, he gave a sharp nod. "All right then. Step up to the starting line. I'm expecting four laps from you today."

I swallowed a groan. I should have taken the out. This was gonna suck.

34

REVELATIONS

Telling Jared yes was a mistake—a big, fat, huge mistake.

I leaned heavily on the railings as I limped back to my room. I was taking a detour through a part of the hospital I rarely traveled simply because I knew there would be railings for me to use. I'd refused to be wheeled back out of sheer stubbornness. A decision I regretted at the moment.

I hadn't even made it four laps. After two and a half speed-walked laps, I was on the verge of collapsing. Jared called it quits with his usual cheerfulness, telling me how great I'd done even though I knew I was a failure.

One step in front of the other.

Keeping my head bent, I focused entirely on my forward momentum. I was like the Little Engine That Could. *I think I can. I think I can. I think I can.*

There was a break in the railing in front of a patient's door. Sucking in a fortifying breath of air, I took several slow shuffle steps until I reached the other side. I happened to glance up and see the patient's name scrolled across the plate next to the door.

For some reason, I found the name sobering. This was the section of the hospital that housed the more critical and long-term coma patients. The ones who weren't expected to ever wake.

In some ways, this wing was more like a nursing home than a hospital. Each patient had their own room. They were usually decorated by family and friends, even though the patient most likely would never appreciate their efforts. People visited on a regular basis but hardly ever spent the night. Sometimes patients' families would bring in their own furniture to place around the room. Things that made them comfortable and probably humanized their loved ones.

L. London was printed on the removable sign.

I stopped and just stared at the name. *A. Lyons* could just have easily been affixed to that spot, or any of the rooms along this hall.

A shiver ran down my spine. As much as I ached for the afterlife, how would I have felt if I'd known my body was withering away in this realm? My family in limbo, hoping for a day that might never come. They'd lived like that for almost a year, and I'd had no idea.

I was about to move on when the sound of waves tickled my ears. The door to the patient's room was open a few inches, and soothing notes were coming from within.

I knew better. I knew I shouldn't. But the ocean had a hold on my heart.

So I gently pushed the door open wider and poked my head through. With a sense of awe, I stepped inside, closing the door behind me without rational thought. Someone had transformed this room into an ocean paradise. The rhythmic lull of the surf was only part of the illusion. A mural of blended blues completely overtook the wall to the right. It looked like I was standing in the curl of a wave right on the cusp of breaking. It was breathtaking.

Several large glass jars filled with shells and sea glass sat on the windowsill. In front of the open window was a wind chime made of rope and shells gently tinkling in the breeze.

Other than the hospital bed, the furniture in the room was a stylish mix of whites and creams. It reminded me of colorful shades of sand. I glanced past the pictures on a small bookshelf, somehow feeling like it would be an invasion of privacy to look too closely—but who was I kidding? I'd already invaded this family's privacy when I walked in the room. My gaze landed on a large surfboard that was mounted to the wall above the patient's head.

That's odd.

The board wasn't shiny and new but rather faded in places and on the brink of overuse. A pain twisted inside my chest.

The ocean was *our* place, but knowing this patient had loved his sport as well hit a little too close to home.

I finally let myself look at the form lying in bed—almost unrecognizable as a human being under the machines keeping him or her alive. Ignoring all the machines that littered the room had been easy at first—with the beautiful harmony someone had taken great care to transform this space—but they jumped out in stark contrast when I stared at the patient. They beeped and wheezed, keeping the person before me alive.

Out of a strange sense of curiosity, I took a step forward. I could now tell the patient was a male. Tubes came out of him everywhere, running out from under his blankets. His head was shaved, and sensors were attached to different points on his skull, most likely monitoring brain function that wasn't even there ... but I didn't know enough about these severe cases to do more than guess.

His hair might have been light brown, but the cut was shorn so close to his scalp I could only go by the color of his eyebrows. His eyelids were taped shut, which I found a little disturbing. A flexible plastic tube ran from his mouth. His features were hollow and gaunt. Guessing his age would have been a shot in the dark. I didn't see evidence of wrinkles, which would suggest he was incredibly old, yet his body had that withered look that one often associates with the elderly.

Then again, I thought, *so did mine before I started physical therapy.*

His shoulder bones stuck out under his hospital gown—evidence that he'd once had a large build. His right hand peeked out from his thin blanket. He had long, thin fingers that, like the rest of him, were most likely leaner than normal due to whatever time he'd spent here.

I didn't know what made me scrutinize this poor soul so closely. Perhaps because I sympathized with him? Perhaps because I felt like he could easily be me?

His chest rose and fell to the cadence of the machine that was breathing for him. I was transfixed by that motion, and I honestly didn't know how long I stood there, just watching him breathe.

"Excuse me, what are you doing in my son's room?"

I startled and jumped away from the bed. Something on the shelf behind me fell over. I had been so busy with my creeper behavior that I'd missed someone entering the room.

"Oh, g-gosh. I'm sorry." My mind short-circuited on me, and I just stood there like a complete idiot, looking at a well-dressed lady. She was probably around my mother's age, but with blonde hair pulled back in a stylish twist. Her heels clicked on the floor as she walked farther into the room . . . her son's room that I had totally trespassed into.

A small frown pulled the corners of her lips down, and her brows pinched in a way that made me believe she was deciding between confusion and anger. I really hoped for the former.

But then she stepped closer, and I saw her eyes.

I took a step back. For a minute, I couldn't breathe.

She had his eyes. His exact same eyes.

She said something, but I missed it, transfixed by her cobalt-blue gaze.

Lots of people had blue eyes, I reminded myself, trying to shake off the unnerving recognition. She tilted her head, waiting for an answer to a question I hadn't even heard.

"I . . . I'm sorry. Wh-what?"

"I asked if you know a patient here."

"Oh. No. I am a pa-tient. I'm st-ill in re-hab." That one took a while to spit out. I pointed at my mouth and let out a quiet, self-deprecating laugh. "See?"

Her features softened at that, as if my hardships excused my bad behavior. Hey, I would take whatever I could get. I wasn't allowed in her son's room.

"I'll j-ust go now." I went to make a speedy exit, but then I remembered I'd knocked something over on the shelf. I quickly turned to straighten what looked to be a picture frame before retreating, but I stopped once I had repositioned it.

There were several people in the shot. Teenagers. And in the middle, with his arm draped over a beautiful blonde, was a younger version of Logan.

My vision blurred for a moment before snapping back to normal. I clutched the shelf of the bookcase to stay upright, my knuckles turning white with the grip.

"Do you know him, my son . . . Logan?" The woman was right next to me, pointing to his image.

I gaped and floundered for more than a few seconds. How

was this possible? He was dead. I knew he was.

But so was I—and here I was.

Reality slammed into me—hard.

I stumbled back a step, and the woman—Logan's mother—took a hold of my elbow to steady me.

"Are you all right, dear? Do you need to take a seat?"

A distant part of my mind wondered why she was being so nice to me. She had walked in to find a stranger lurking around her son's hospital room. She should be shooing me away, but she was treating me with kindness instead. Maybe because of my condition?

She steered me toward the loveseat opposite his bed, the one facing his feet.

"I . . . ah." My hands were shaking and my breathing erratic. I had to get this under control.

I glanced up into her deep-blue eyes and almost lost it again.

This was Logan's mother. Sitting right next to me. And that meant the gaunt figure lying on the bed was . . . it was Logan.

He was here, with me . . . yet he wasn't here. I knew that better than anyone.

Did he know he wasn't actually dead, or was he just as much in the dark about it as I was? A memory tickled my mind, of when we were in the Archives Building and I asked if he'd checked up on his loved ones. *"I've been avoiding this place. I probably should have at least checked in on my parents, but I'd been too . . ."* If Logan had checked on his parents even once, he would have figured out where they spent their time—but by his own admission, he hadn't. So there was a chance he had no idea, just like I hadn't known.

His mother stared at me with her brow furrowed. "Maybe I should get some help?"

She went to stand, but I grabbed her wrist. She looked back at me with surprise splashed across her face. I had to say something.

"Uh . . . please no. I'm-I'm s-o sorry." I swallowed to wet my dry throat. "Your—ur son, Lo-gan. He ta-ught me how to . . . surf. Di-didn't know h-e was here."

"Oh, I see." She sat back down on the sandy-colored loveseat. "That must have been a while ago. He's been here for almost four years now."

A tear leaked out of my eye. "I'm . . . so sorry."

"Oh dear, please don't say that. It looks like you've had your own struggles. Logan will come back to us . . . someday."

She patted my hand, but I heard the hopelessness that betrayed her words. He wouldn't be in this wing of the hospital if they thought he was going to come back to them. This wasn't where they housed the patients they expected would wake up.

But I had, so why couldn't Logan?

That wasn't a realistic expectation, I told myself.

But miracles happened every day.

Two sides of my mind warred. I was on overload.

How could he be here? How was it we were both in the same place? Was it because he was going to come back to me, or was it so I could find closure to move on with my life?

I didn't know, but I wasn't going to figure it out in this short visit. My world had just been blown apart . . . again. I needed some time.

"Wo-uld you mi-mind telling me wh-at happened?"

"Oh." The color drained from her face. I shouldn't have asked.

"Never mind. That was insensitive." I was able to get it all out at once.

She patted my hand and gave me a weak smile, her eyes

filling up with water. "No, it's all right. It's supposed to be good for his father and me to talk about this. Can I ask your name, dear?"

"My name is Audrey." Another full sentence.

"Well, Audrey, I'm Mrs. London. But you can call me by my first name, Celeste."

35

HOPE

I was scaring my mom, I know I was, but it couldn't be helped. After our brief talk, I'd asked Mrs. London—Celeste—if it would be okay if I visited Logan again. She'd smiled and said that would be nice and promised to add me to the list of allowed visitors. I'd then asked for a nurse to take me back to my room—more from mental exhaustion than physical.

I'd hardly said two words since.

My mother wasn't dumb. She knew something was up, and in true Mom-fashion, she was trying to shove food down my throat to make whatever was bothering me better. I'd only been able to eat a few bites of the feast she'd bought at a local eatery. After months of complaining about hospital cuisine, I should have been shoveling the food in my mouth, but now eating was like trying to swallow ash. Anything that made it down just soured in my stomach.

I finally pushed the food away, claiming to have a headache and needing sleep, which only worried my mom even more. I faintly heard her in the background trying to track down my doctor and checking up on my physical therapy sessions. I knew I should be putting her mind at ease, but I needed some time.

Logan's mom had told the story of a car crash. He'd been in the backseat of a car that had rolled off the highway and then several hundred feet down a steep embankment.

Logan had been rushed into surgery for several broken and shattered bones, but though he had healed from those injuries, he'd never woken up. He'd sustained a major head injury during the accident.

Three others had been in the same car. The driver, one of Logan's childhood friends, was now a quadriplegic. The front passenger had escaped with only minor injuries, which was a miracle considering the damage to the car.

And the fourth passenger had lost her life. The fourth passenger had been Kaitlin, the girl whom Logan had his arm around in the picture where I first recognized him.

Kaitlin was in fact dead, not in a state of limbo like Logan and me. Or had been in. Or rather, that he was still in, and I no longer was.

My head ached with the desire to make sense of it all. How was it Logan and I had been in the afterlife even as our bodies remained anchored to Earth?

I spent the late afternoon and into the evening replaying all I could remember about the heavenly realm. When I'd first arrived, Joe had never confirmed that I had died. I came to that conclusion myself. Now I found myself wondering about my memories—questioning them. How much of it had been real? Any of it? Some of it had to be, how else would I have known Logan and Kaitlin at all?

And there were little details that made sense now. Like why the zombie trees had reached for me . . . they'd recognized the

Earthly life still in me where the rest had none. The revelation was small, but being able to make sense of anything right now was a comfort.

But what did this mean for Logan? Was this the real reason why the two of us seemed to have extraordinary supernatural powers? Him with his electric lightning and me with the flaming sword. Had we been singled out because we were living in the land of the dead?

I put two hands to my head and pressed against the raging headache. I might never know the answer to these questions. Most of all, I wanted to know if Logan knew now, or if he'd known then, that he was lying prone in a hospital bed.

My instincts said he didn't know. But I couldn't just ask him. Our ability to communicate was completely gone.

I knew nothing.

A ball of anger swirled in my gut. I contained the churning emotion to that space, but I wasn't sure how long I would be able to ward it off. Why was none of this explained? Why was I left in the dark? If the Creator was good and cared for me, why was He putting me through this second heartbreak?

Logan was in one way so close to me, but in another, he was just as far as he'd been since I'd woken up back on Earth.

After several minutes of talking, Celeste had finally confessed that the doctors hadn't given any hope of Logan waking, but she didn't believe that to be true.

I knew miracles could happen, but I also knew that just because the Creator had the power to wield them didn't mean he was going to.

In this case, I didn't even know what to hope for.

But I knew that I'd visit Logan again. Or the shell that used to be him. I knew he wasn't really inside there anymore . . . but maybe, one day, he would be again.

"I made four laps around the track today. And I stink pretty bad right now, but it's not like you haven't seen me look worse." Three weeks had passed, and his condition had stayed the same.

I held Logan's warm but listless hand in mine and prayed he'd show some sign of recognition. If I could command his soul to his body by sheer will alone, he'd already be back with me.

"No throwing up so far though, so I guess I have it easier here than . . . the other place."

My speech had drastically improved over the last several weeks. I spent at least two hours a day visiting and talking to Logan. Some days Celeste would be there and I'd talk to her instead. I was pretty sure my one-sided conversations with her son would freak her out. There was a part of me that believed I could talk him awake.

So far I'd been proven wrong, but I was willing to spend the rest of my life trying if that's what it took.

"But there's no one here taking bets on whether or not I'm going to toss my breakfast, so it doesn't quite feel the same . . . well, except this one kid, but he really annoys me. There's a makeshift viewing gallery on the sixth floor, and you know how I hate to make a fool of myself in front of others, so that pushes me more than Jared probably realizes. If I tell you how handsome Jared is, will it make you jealous enough to wake up?" I imagined pressure on my hand that wasn't there. "Yeah, I didn't think so, but it was worth a try. How about I tell you a little about my plans?"

Unbeknownst to my parents, I'd already started to scheme ways I could stay in the area. I knew they expected me to go home with them next month. The current plan was to keep up some of my therapy at home and also finish high school. I was a year behind, but I was a good student and only needed a few classes to actually graduate. We'd already worked out an agreement with my old school that I would take those few classes at home and then officially graduate after the first semester. The school was bending over backward to help me out, and I appreciated it, I did, but things had changed.

Whether he was conscious or not, there was no way I was leaving Logan's side. Not when I'd found him again.

So I'd been working on an alternative plan my parents didn't know about. One that they absolutely weren't going to like, but considering I was legally an adult, they couldn't do anything to stop me.

The only thing I hadn't worked out was money. I was going to need it if I was going to stay on the West Coast instead of flying back to the Midwest with my family. I still wanted to graduate high school and then eventually go to college, but if I was going to stay in the area, I needed to find a place to live. And apartments required rent. I was going to have to find a job and work.

I could do it, I knew I could. Living out here would be hard, but I would make it work. I was determined. I would live on my own, finish high school, apply to nearby colleges, and spend all my spare time with Logan.

This was going to happen.

If he ever opened his eyes, I was going to be one of the first faces he saw. And if he didn't, I would still be here to grow old with him.

I knew he would be willing to make the same sacrifices for

me . . . even though I wouldn't want him to. I'd want him to live out a long and happy life. He'd probably want the same for me, but if that was the case, he was going to have to open those beautiful blue eyes and tell me himself. Otherwise, I was going to be sitting by his side for a long time to come.

"So basically, if you don't want me getting butt sores from sitting in this chair so long, you're going to have to come back to me." I sighed and shifted in the chair, running a hand through my shortened locks.

Watching Logan lie motionless was only marginally easier than when I first learned whose room I'd trespassed into. Now that I knew the figure was him, I saw the Logan I knew through the gaunt features of the person in front of me. His appearance was vastly different than my memory, but if I looked hard enough, I could find him.

"Audrey, it's so nice to see you again."

I looked up to see Celeste stroll elegantly into the room. She sat on the couch to my left.

"Oh, I'm so sorry, Celeste. Here, you can switch with me." I moved to stand, but she waved me off.

"Don't be silly. We both know he'd rather have a pretty girl holding his hand than his mother."

We both chuckled as I resettled in my seat. We chit-chatted for a while as I worked up the courage to ask the question that had been scratching at the back of my mind. I should have just let go of my curiosity, but it nagged at me.

When we hit a natural break in our conversation, I took a deep breath and went with it.

"Celeste, I know this isn't my place to ask, but . . ." *Oh, I should really just leave this be.*

I chewed my lip in indecision.

"It's all right, sweetie." She turned her head to the side.

"What do you want to ask?"

I bunched my eyebrows and released my lip. "I was just wondering if Mr. London ever visited. I know I'm not here all the time, so maybe I just keep missing him, but . . ." I took a breath; all of that came out really quickly. "I was just wondering, I guess."

Logan had mentioned that his parents were together, but perhaps something had changed since his accident. It so wasn't my business, but the absence of his father nagged at me.

"Oh." She sat back against the couch, her body sagging in on itself. Her face fell, and she suddenly looked extremely tired.

"I'm so sorry. I shouldn't have asked. It's none of my business." But I still wanted to know. I looked down at where I gently clasped Logan's hand, embarrassed that I'd brought up what was obviously a touchy subject. Now my mind was going wild with possibilities.

"No, it's all right, Audrey. Logan's father . . ." I glanced up.

She was visibly trying to compose herself.

Oh my gosh, they were divorced now. That must be it. This was so awkward. I should have just done some internet research instead.

She took a deep breath before continuing, "Logan's father and I don't agree on Logan's care."

I snapped my head up to watch her more closely. That was not where I'd thought this conversation was going.

"He doesn't think that Logan should be cared for in this way, so he refuses to visit." Celeste's eyes started to tear.

I became lightheaded as the blood drained from my face.

Logan's father didn't want his son on life support. Logan's father wanted his son to die. His mother kept him alive, hoping that he'd come around someday despite what the doctors said.

"You have to understand," she went on quickly. "Richard, Logan's father, loved—loves Logan very much. But seeing him like this is just too much for him. And we just have vastly different opinions on Logan's treatment. It's just too hard for him to visit because whenever he does and he sees Logan, the way he is now, it just . . ." She let the sentence drop.

"He wants to let him die," I quietly mumbled.

"He doesn't see it that way. He thinks Logan is already gone." She sounded incredibly weary. As if this were an argument they'd had often. The beat-down tone in her voice scared me. They couldn't do it. I'd lose him all over again. I couldn't survive that.

"No"—the strength and volume of my voice startled her— "you can't let him do that. You can't. You have to fight for him. He can wake up. I know it."

Celeste's eyes opened wide. I knew the conviction in my voice did not match the story of a girl who had just gotten a few surfing lessons from her son and now visited out of a sense of kinship. But I couldn't stop the words tumbling from my lips.

"You have to keep him alive. Look at me. I woke up. He can too."

She blinked at me. "I know, dear. I believe that too. Despite what everyone says, miracles happen every day. But I do have to wonder . . ." That pause scared me. "What if keeping him like this is the wrong thing to do? What if he's suffering?"

"He's not." I was quick to answer.

Her brow furrowed and then smoothed out again. A small, albeit sad, smile graced her lovely face. Logan had definitely picked up some of her features, just in a more masculine form. "It's all right Audrey. I understand." She understood nothing. "But not everyone is as fortunate as you. Don't worry yourself about it. You have a bright future ahead of you."

Don't worry about it? Now it would be the only thing I *did* worry about.

Should I try to explain to her what had happened to me while I was in a coma? What had happened to Logan? Would she even believe me?

Probably not. Who would believe such a story?

I squeezed Logan's hand and closed my eyes, silently pleading with the Creator not to take him from me a second time.

36

CHANGING PLANS

"Audrey, this makes no sense." My dad's eyebrows bunched together in concern and confusion. He paced back and forth on the linoleum floor of my small room. I sat patiently in a chair by the window, waiting for him to calm down. My mother stood on the side of my bed, wringing her hands as she watched my father.

I'd royally botched breaking the news that I had no plans to leave the area. Or maybe there was no good way to drop that bomb? They knew I'd been regularly visiting one of the other patients, but they thought I was just doing so out of a sense of kindness. An assumption I didn't bother to correct them about.

How was I supposed to explain that I knew a patient who had lived on the other side of the country from us and spent the last four years in a coma?

They'd never believe me.

Now they just thought I'd developed a weird—and unhealthy—obsession. I can't say I blamed them. They didn't have all the information, so my actions did seem rash and nonsensical.

"I'm so sorry. I know this doesn't make any sense to you guys. But I need . . ." I struggled to find the right words. What could I possibly say to make them understand?

"Audrey"—my mom rounded the bed and took my hand—"we're so close to getting you back again. Your father and I are both here to bring you home. Sweetie, you still have therapy to undergo, classes. We have everything set up for you at home. Not to mention the fact that we want you back with us. We almost lost you once." Her eyes filled with tears. "This feels like we're losing you a second time."

Her response broke my heart. "Oh, Mom, you'll never lose me. I'll always be your daughter. This is just . . . It's just something I have to do. I promise I've thought it through. I'm still going to keep up with classes and physical therapy, but I need to stay here. I know it doesn't make sense to you. I get it, I really do."

An idea came to me. I wasn't sure if it would make a difference, but maybe it would help a little. "What if you come with me to visit Logan today? You've not met him yet."

"What do you think that will accomplish?" my father asked.

I turned to look at him, chewing my bottom lip. "Don't you want to meet him?"

"Audrey, we wouldn't really be meeting him. We'd be—"

"Honey"—my mother squeezed my hand and shot my father a wide-eyed look—"I think that would be a good idea. Let's meet this boy you're willing to turn your life upside-down for."

I sucked in a huge breath of air. "Yeah, let's do this."

It was visiting hours, but that didn't explain why Logan's room was packed full of medical professionals. A wall of them hovered around his body, and several others were milling around the room with their heads down, writing on charts or tablets. What was happening? My heart jumped in my chest.

Is he finally—

"Audrey." My thoughts were cut off by Celeste's surprised voice. Her eyes were red rimmed, but she was clearly trying to keep her composure. "I didn't think you'd visit until later today."

"Um." A million questions ran through my head. "I wanted my parents to meet Logan. I hope that's okay." I glanced around the room again. People were talking in hushed voices, and I couldn't pick up any of the conversations. "What's . . . what's going on?"

Celeste wrung her hands, and her gaze darted left and right. "Maybe it would be better if you came back later today. Then we can talk."

"Is Logan okay? Why are all these people here?"

"I can tell you about that—"

"Is this the young lady you spoke to me about?" A man dressed in a grey business suit laid a hand on Celeste's lower back. He had brown hair that was sprinkled with salt-and-pepper patches around his ears. Logan's mother was already a tall woman, but this man towered over her by several inches, even in her signature heels. She looked up at him with worried eyes and then nodded. His expression was stern but not uncaring.

"Yes, Richard, this is Audrey. She's been visiting Logan for the last few months. He gave her surfing lessons . . . before the accident."

Logan's father? What was he doing here?

"What?" I heard my dad ask behind me.

Oh, shoot. He knew I'd never been to this side of the country before. I hadn't lied to anyone, but I certainly hadn't thought this meeting through very well.

I took a closer look at Logan's father and started to see bits of his son in him. The slant of their eyebrows were the same. His eyes were green rather than Logan's blue, but the shape was similar. They had broad shoulders and a tapered waist as well as that impressive height. He looked to be in his late forties, but he obviously still took care of himself. I had a wave of longing to know what Logan would look like at his father's age. Healthy, whole, and living life together with me.

Logan's dad stepped forward and extended his hand to me. I clasped it and received a firm handshake. There was an upturn to the corners of his mouth, but so slight, I wouldn't call it a true smile.

"Audrey, I'm Richard, Logan's father."

I nodded.

"Thank you for taking the time to visit my son. That was very kind of you."

"You're welcome?"

"And these are your parents?"

I nodded mutely and stared while our parents introduced themselves. I never would have expected this was the way they'd all meet, but the introductions needed to be made one way or another. Might as well get the formalities out of the way since I was going to be a fixture in Logan's life moving forward.

"Celeste tells me Audrey will be leaving to go home shortly." The words snapped me out of my reflective daze.

"Well, that's what we were hoping for, but Audrey seems to

have made some plans of her own."

Four heads swiveled in my direction. The urge to start backing away slowly was strong, but I held my ground. The scrutiny of four sets of eyes on me was no joke.

"Could someone please tell me what's going on in here?" I asked, again. "Is Logan okay? Has there been a change? Is he waking up?" There was no way to hide the hopeful note in my voice, but one look at his mother said I had gone down the wrong rabbit hole. Her eyes started to fill, and she brought a tissue to the corners to keep the tears from spilling over.

Panic welled inside my gut, churning at a fevered pace and making it feel like I was going to vomit my lunch all over the floor.

"He's not getting better." It wasn't a question. "He's getting worse? How could he get any worse?"

I looked back and forth between his parents. Celeste's eyes continued to well with tears. Richard's face was a stoic mask— so reminiscent of Logan's go-to when he hid his feelings.

My heart pinched as Logan's parents shared a look, seemingly communicating without words. My gaze ping-ponged between the two of them until finally Richard stepped away from his wife and faced me.

"I know Celeste wanted to tell you this herself later today, but I think considering the circumstances, now is probably the best time. As you know, my son is brain dead."

I flinched at the matter-of-fact way he used the perfectly acceptable medical term.

I hated those words. Celeste and I never used them to describe Logan.

"I'm sure you know that means that although we can keep his body alive, he's not really with us anymore."

I had a very bad feeling about where this conversation was

going.

"You don't really know—"

"We do. We do know that's what it means."

I was too shocked at being railroaded to continue.

Richard went on, "We have two choices here. We can continue to keep up this charade of him returning to us someday, or we can bring some good to this awful situation, which will also bring some closure to his mother and myself."

I shook my head. Celeste wouldn't let this happen. She wouldn't let Logan's father take him off life support.

I looked to her for confirmation that what her husband was saying was just a review of what they considered to be the situation, not a decision that had already been made. But tears were free flowing down her cheeks now. No amount of tissues could hold the tide back.

They had decided.

"No. No you can't seriously be thinking of doing this."

"It's what's—"

Celeste laid a hand on her husband's arm, silencing him with her touch and a soft look in his direction. He nodded and took a step back.

"Audrey, you have to understand this wasn't an easy decision to make. But Logan can help a lot of people."

No, what? Logan already did help a lot of people. I'd been by his side as he defended humanity. He was owed the chance to return to us . . . to return to me.

"Help a lot of people?" My voice came out high pitched and shrill. I was half numb and half hysterical.

She nodded.

"We've decided to take him off life support and donate his organs to people who need them. This way his death won't be in vain." Her eyes begged me to understand.

I stood shell-shocked for several moments. They were going to let him die. I didn't think or care about anything else they said. My chance to live a life with Logan in it was slipping through my fingers.

I'd made a terrible mistake by not telling Celeste the whole truth. If she just knew that Logan was out there and could possibly wake up like I did, she wouldn't be allowing this. She wouldn't be giving up.

I had to make her understand. I had to make them all understand.

"No." My whole body vibrated with pent-up anger and fear. "No, you can't do this." My voice rose over the low din of voices conversing around us. "You don't understand what you're doing!"

The room became eerily quiet except for the noise from the machines as I garnered the attention of everyone present—people who were here to either oversee the process of taking Logan off life support or to harvest his organs afterward.

Logan's parents gawked at me with wide eyes. I didn't even spare my parents a glance but rather beseeched the ones who were moving this process forward.

"You don't understand because I haven't told you the full story."

Logan's father snapped out of the shock caused by my outburst first. His tone wasn't cruel, but it was unyielding. "I'm truly sorry, dear. I understand you've formed some sort of . . . mild attachment to my son, but that doesn't give you any right—"

"Attachment?" I let out a hysterical laugh. I'd formed more than just a mild attachment to Logan.

"Look"—his voice hardened to steel—"this is obviously not a healthy attachment. A few surfing lessons and spending some time with my son while he is completely unresponsive doesn't give you any right to tell his mother and I what's best for him or our family."

How could I explain this without sounding completely insane? My mind scrambled to come up with a plausible way of making them understand . . . without getting myself committed. I was truly worried someone would force a psychiatric assessment on me. The last thing I needed was to see another therapist. But that was a small price to pay if anything I said could sway their minds.

"Listen, I know Logan better than what you think. I know he can still wake up. He can come back to us, just like I did."

"Sweetheart"—my mother stepped up and put her hand on my arm—"your situation was very different than this young man's. You can't say things like that. It's not fair to his loved ones. It's not—"

"I'm one of his loved ones," I practically yelled in my mom's face and pounded a fist to my chest.

She blinked and took a step back. My father wrapped his arm around her shoulder. Their faces were twin masks of shock and concern. I couldn't hold back the tide anymore. Everyone was against me, and no one was fighting for Logan. I'd fight for him until my last breath.

"Out!" I yelled to all the medical professionals in the room. "Everybody, out! This whole thing has been canceled." I pushed my way past Logan's parents and started shoving doctors away from Logan's body. There were plenty of gasps around the room, but I ignored them all.

Keeping Logan safe was my top priority. I'd fought through Hell and back for him; I wasn't going to lose him now.

Nobody left the room. They all just stared at me. I'd taken a position at Logan's head and growled at anyone who tried to touch him.

"Tell them to leave!" I shouted at his parents.

Fresh tears poured down his mother's face, and a look of stubborn resolve came over his father's.

I didn't like that. His expression was too similar to the look Logan got when he was determined to get his way.

Now I knew where that stubborn streak came from.

"We most certainly will not." Richard looked at my parents. "Go control your daughter. She's not welcome here anymore."

"Hey"—my dad stepped forward—"my daughter has been through an incredibly trying ordeal over the last year. Let's all take a beat for a moment."

Yeah, way to go, Dad.

"Your daughter's been through an ordeal?" Richard barked a humorless laugh. "You get to leave here in a few days with your child. You get to go and resume a perfectly normal life. We've been living in a nightmare that started four years ago that we can't wake up from. Whatever infatuation your daughter has with our son"—Celeste reached for her husband, probably to stop his words, but he pulled away from her grasp and glanced at her—"yes Celeste, it is most certainly an infatuation. From what you've told me, I'd say this girl is borderline obsessed with Logan."

I sucked in a painful breath of air and reminded myself they didn't know how well I knew Logan—but that barb still hurt.

And Richard wasn't finished with his rant. "My son has been lying here, day after day, with no hope of waking up. To come in here and question our decision, one that was unimaginably hard to come to, is insensitive at best. I want you all out of here, for good. If you cared at all for us, if you cared at all for Logan, you'd leave us to grieve in peace."

My dad nodded. "I apologize, Mr. London. You're right.

We were all out of line. Regardless of what Audrey's been through, this is a family matter."

Wait, what? No. I tensed, ready to fight anyone who tried to make me move.

"Audrey, come on. It's time to leave." Dad held his hand out toward me from across the room.

My breathing picked up as I eyed all four parents.

I didn't have a magical sword to protect my loved one in this situation. I couldn't physically fight my way to a victory. All I had was a story no one was likely to believe.

The shell chimes in the corner of the room started to softly move back and forth, even though the window wasn't open. The sounds reminded me that I didn't just have a story. I had the God of the universe listening, the Holy Spirit living inside me, and the Savior of mankind protecting me.

I took a deep breath to steady myself. Time to lay it all out on the table. Time to trust that I wasn't the one in control.

I'd fight for Logan in the only way I could—by trusting his future to the One who created it.

37

MY STORY

"Wait, please." I held a hand out as if the gesture alone could stop the momentum of what had already been set in motion. "There's something I need to tell you all. I haven't been completely forthright about how I know Logan."

My gaze swept the room. Everyone was staring at me. From my parents, to the doctors, nurses, medical technicians, and finally Logan's parents. That was where my focus landed. That was who I needed to convince I wasn't lying. I'd deal with the fallout from my parents after.

Richard's face was still hard. His arm was wrapped possessively around his wife's waist. His lips pressed together in a tight line as if it took effort not to talk. His brow was pulled low over eyes that blazed.

I wasn't too proud to admit I was intimidated.

Celeste was a hot mess, and I realized the arm around her waist might be there to help her remain standing. Her eyes were bloodshot from crying. Tear tracks ran down her face, and her normally perfectly coiffed hair was in disarray—the bun was half out and off-centered. She held her hands to her chest, and her shoulders were slumped as if she was protecting herself.

With a stabbing pain, I realized she was protecting herself from me.

This was not how I wanted to explain my experience in the afterlife. Under duress with at least twenty people staring at me.

But I was out of choices. I took in a fortifying breath and started my tale.

"When I got hit by that car, I thought I had died. And not because I realized the severity of my injuries on the road; I knew something monumental had happened because when I closed my eyes here on Earth, I opened them again in a whole different world. And in that place—that whole different world—I met and I fell in love with your son."

Miraculously, they listened—maybe because I didn't give them an option. I talked and talked and talked some more.

I went back to the beginning and explained how disoriented I'd been when I first woke up in a different realm, without my memories. I retold my first meeting with Logan and how contentious our relationship as mentor and mentee had been. And then how things had slowly changed. I left out a lot of private details because—awkward—who wants to talk about their first kiss with someone to their parents? But I revealed most of what had happened to me, especially the parts relating to Logan, in the months my body had been lying in a coma in this very building.

I poured my heart and my soul out in a desperate hope that something I said would give them a reason to hold on, at least a little bit longer, to the possibility that their son could come back to us.

And then when I was finished with my tale, I waited.

My cheeks were wet with the tears I'd spilled.

This whole time my attention had been on Logan's parents, but now I took a moment to survey the room. The medical staff gaped at me. My parents appeared shell shocked. Their hands intertwined, eyes wide, and silent. And finally I took a good look at Logan's parents—not just to tell my story but to gauge their reaction. I'd confessed the truth as if I were on trial, and they were the judges.

Richard's face hadn't softened, but the anger that had brewed there seemed to have morphed into confusion. Celeste brought a shaky hand up to cover her mouth. Fresh tears dripped down her cheeks.

"You really saw our baby?" she asked, her voice trembling and muffled by the hand she held in front of her face.

I nodded. "Yes, I truly did. He is . . . amazing, and . . . I love him. I know if there is any way he can come back to us, he'll move heaven and earth to do so."

Celeste turned into her husband's chest and sobbed.

"Oh, sweetheart." My father lifted his arm and offered his hand. There was a suspicious shine to his eyes. His silent invitation was clear, and I was too raw to turn it down. I rushed into his embrace. He squeezed me tightly while my mom rubbed her hand up and down my back.

They knew the truth, and they weren't rejecting me.

"Please, leave now." Richard's voice was cold and commanding.

I jerked my head up in response.

"Wh-what?"

He was still holding his crying wife in his arms, but his face was unmistakably hostile.

"You've said your piece. I think it's clear your delusions go deeper than any of us expected. Now I want you to leave us alone. You've done enough damage." He said the last part with a pointed look at Celeste.

"No. I told you the truth. I *do* know your son. He can come back—"

"Stop!"

I took a step back at the sharpness in his tone. Even Celeste went rigid in his arms. "I will protect what's left of my family." His focus transferred over my head. "I think your daughter needs some serious help, but that's up for you to decide. For right now, you need to remove her from this room."

It hadn't worked.

Despite everything I'd told them, they were going to go forward with it. They thought I was delusional. Or that I'd made it all up. Or . . . it didn't matter really what they thought, except they didn't believe me. They didn't believe I'd met their son. They didn't believe that my love for him was real. They didn't believe he would ever come back to us.

My body felt like a giant ice cube.

How could it have come to this? How was it even possible that I'd found him, alive, on Earth, only to lose him again? It was . . . too cruel to be true.

I vaguely registered my father coming to my defense and my mother soothing his temper. He gently clasped my arm and tried to pull me toward the door. I took an obedient step in his direction before what was happening really and truly sunk in.

Logan.

They were going to let him die, and I was just going to walk out that door and let them?

No way, no how.

I ripped my arm from my father's grasp, hearing my mother gasp in surprise.

"You can't do this," I yelled, and tried to push my way past people to reach Logan again. But this time, arms caught me—restraining me from going any farther.

"No, let go." I fought against people I didn't even know or see. I didn't bother to take in their appearance, as my gaze was fixed on Logan's prone form.

It didn't end like this. It couldn't.

I maneuvered out of one person's grasp, just to be caught by another. Frustration churned deep in my gut. My muscles retained the memory of their training, but I was so weak, all of my defensive techniques were useless. It was like trying to restrain a bunny.

"No." Tears streamed down my face. "Don't do this," I begged. Begged.

I heard voices behind me, but the entirety of my conscious focus was on Logan.

"Audrey, please stop fighting." My mom's pleading voice broke through my hurt-filled haze.

I spotted her to my right. She wrung her hands, and tears fell from her eyes as well.

"Baby, please. Just let it go. We need to leave the Londons to make this decision. This isn't your fight."

Isn't my fight?

I amped up my struggles.

This was the most important fight of my life. If the situation were reversed, Logan wouldn't have let me go. He would have stood guard over me night and day if he had to. He would give anything to make sure I was protected.

And I was going to fail him.

Premature grief crushed my lungs.

"You have to stop, Audrey," my mother pleaded, but I wasn't paying attention to her anymore. I'd defeated countless creatures of darkness. I'd gone up against Satan himself. I couldn't let a couple medical technicians take me down.

I could kick one in the shins and duck under his grip. From there I'd have a straight shot to run—something sharp bit into my backside. I yelled out in pain.

Did someone just stab me?

I twisted my head to see a giant syringe depressed all the way and sticking out of my right butt cheek.

What?

Someone in a white lab coat quickly removed the ridiculously long needle from my backside.

I tried to renew my struggle, but my vision suddenly blurred around the edges.

No!

I'd been drugged.

I fought like a rabid beast to reach Logan, but my movements were becoming uncoordinated and sloppy, until they turned sluggish and my vision winked in and out.

"Please," I think I pleaded out loud, but it may have been in my head. I no longer knew.

The last thing that went through my mind before I succumbed to whatever drug they just pumped into my system was *I failed you. I'm so sorry.*

And then all was quiet.

My skull was stuffed with bricks and cotton. A strange combination, but one that made it impossible to lift my head because of the weight. The world seemed strangely muted.

I groaned at the uncomfortable sensation and tried to lift an arm to my head, but something prevented me from moving. I blinked several times to bring the room into focus. It blurred for a while before my eyesight cooperated.

"Oh, honey, she's waking up."

Okay, so my mom was somewhere around here.

With a great deal of effort, I turned my head to see her sitting by my bed. My dad walked from the window to join her. Both of them wore grave looks. Pinched brows, pressed together lips, their skin leeched of color.

"What happened?" I croaked out. "Why can't I move?" My legs were straight, and although I could bend my knee slightly, something was preventing full mobility—and it wasn't the bricks and cotton.

Was I restrained?

"Oh, Audrey." My mom's hand covered her mouth as her eyes filled with tears.

I looked to my dad for an explanation.

"Sweetie, how much do you remember?"

I blinked up at him. The cotton made it hard to understand his question. "Remember?"

"Baby, you were hysterical. The hospital staff had to sedate you. You're being restrained at the moment to make sure you won't hurt yourself. Someone is going to be in later to evaluate you."

"Evaluate what?" I asked

Several heartbeats passed before he answered. "Your mental state. We think all of this has been harder on you than we realized. We, your mother and I, believe getting you home as quickly as possible is the best course of action."

I wanted to shake my head, but the heaviness prevented the movement. I squeezed my eyes shut. I knew I should be more alarmed by what my father was saying and the fact that I was strapped to my bed like a criminal, but the fog hadn't fully cleared. There was a reason I didn't want to leave, but I needed to dig for it, because I couldn't remember why I cared.

I attempted to lift my hand again, wanting to press it to my eyes, but was stopped by the soft restraint.

"Can you . . ." I swallowed. My throat was beyond dry. "Take these off of me?"

I opened my eyes to see my parents share a look.

"Audrey, why don't you go back to sleep and let the drugs wear off a little? We'll get a doctor to come in and assess you so we can get these removed. We think that, considering the circumstances, we should play by the rules right now."

What circumstances?

My mind tried to push past the fog, but the effort left me exhausted. My rapid blinking wasn't doing much to keep me awake, so I succumbed to sleep once again.

I woke up some time later to soft voices. The heaviness no longer weighed me down, but my memory was a bit hazy.

My parents were talking to my primary doctor off in the corner of my room, their voices too low for me to overhear.

"Excuse me," I asked to get their attention. "May I have some water?"

"Oh, sweetheart." My mom broke off from the small group and rushed to my side. She grabbed something from a table and brought it into view. It was a cup with a straw. She propped a few pillows up behind my head so I could drink.

The liquid coated my scratchy throat in a soothing balm. My throat was raw and painful as if I'd been screaming for a long period of time.

I nodded my thanks to her.

She stood, and the doctor took her place by my side. "Audrey, I'd like to remove these restraints, but I need your word before I do that you won't try to get out of bed."

Restraints?

I glanced down my body to see my wrists and ankles secured to the bed with some kind of padded handcuffs. I had a vague recollection of waking up like this before, but I couldn't push past the block in my memory to remember why.

"Okay, I'll stay here."

He smiled warmly and unlocked all the cuffs then helped me into a seated position.

My body was sore all over, but I didn't know why. I hadn't woken up this weak in months.

"I've been talking with your parents, and we all agree that the best thing for you physically and emotionally is to return home with them. Your physical therapy has progressed to a point where you can continue with outpatient treatment." He paused for a moment, and I knew there was something important about that pause. "And you can also seek treatment for your emotional trauma in your home state as well. We want to make sure you're on board with this plan."

Wait, I was remembering important things now. I wasn't planning on going home with my parents. I wanted to stay here. Stay here and be with . . . Logan. That was it. Had I not talked to them about my plans yet? I thought I had.

I glanced at my parents standing near the foot of my bed. "But I wanted to stay in this area. I thought"—yes, I'd definitely had this conversation with them already—"we already had this talk."

There was silence in the room as the three adults traded looks.

"Audrey," my father finally began, "I'm so sorry, sweetie, but there's nothing left for you here."

"But there is, Dad. I already told you I wanted to stay near

Logan. I was—"

I gasped, remembering the trip to Logan's room to introduce him to my parents when they pushed back about me staying.

I'd wanted them to understand, at least in part, why I had made the decision.

I remembered Logan's parents being there along with all the medical personnel. And I remembered my desperate fight to reach him at the end when my confession fell on deaf ears.

I brought a shaky hand to my mouth.

My vision swam.

"Tell me he's not gone. Tell me they didn't go through with it while I slept. Tell me you didn't let them do this to me." The last few words ended on a sob.

My mom rushed around the other side of the bed to pull me in her arms. I didn't want to be comforted at the moment. I wanted information. I wanted someone to tell me everything was all right and that what I thought had happened had not.

My father's face twisted in regret.

"I'm so sorry, baby girl, but there's nothing left for you here," he repeated.

Burying my face in my mom's shoulder, I let out body-racking sobs.

I didn't try to hide my anguish like I had when I first woke up and realized all I'd lost. There was no use. I was completely undone, and the weight of losing Logan was compounded by the weight of all the other losses I'd repressed.

I cried for Logan. And I cried for Romona and Kaitlin and Kevin and Bear. I might have even cried a little for Jonathon. But most of all, I cried for myself.

And the silent cry I lifted to the Lord was only this: *Why?*

38

HOME

I wasn't even allowed to go to his funeral. My parents said the Londons had asked that I stay away and not contact them. I wondered how much of that "request" was Richard and how much was Celeste. I thought I'd formed something of a friendship with Logan's mom in the time we'd spent together at her son's bedside, but I suppose thinking that I was delusional and had made up a relationship with her son was reason enough for her to want to keep some distance.

Yet another name to add to the list of people I'd lost, but in this case she was also my last Earthly connection to Logan.

His mother had been telling me stories of his childhood as we sat vigil, and I loved hearing about them. I'd cherished every scrap I was given, and I mourned every tale that would now remain untold.

I lay on my side and stared at the blank white wall. It wasn't the fresh bright white I'd become used to in the afterlife, but the dull white that came with time. I hated both colors equally.

Squeezing my eyes shut, I remembered the beautiful mural painted on the wall in Logan's room. The swirls of blue and aqua that were reminiscent of the ocean and the color of his eyes.

I think he would have loved to see that painting.

By now a fresh coat of white paint was probably drying on the wall as the staff readied the room for the next patient.

"Audrey, sweetheart, everything is ready. It's time to go." My mom laid a gentle hand on my back.

I'd hardly said anything in the few days since "the event." I didn't realize how much pain and loss I hadn't processed when I woke up back on Earth until I lost Logan for the second time.

I'd created a house of cards that came crashing down that day.

The real work of rebuilding my life was just beginning. And even I knew I wasn't handling it well.

I'd briefly been forced into talking to one of the hospital's grief counselors, but I only answered the questions I absolutely had to, and I stonewalled everything else. I refused to talk about my time in the afterlife anymore, having already poured my heart out and been rejected.

My own parents now looked at me strangely, but they hadn't forced any more treatment on me. When my doctor thought I was asleep, he'd recommended I seek counseling for my "issues" when we returned home.

My parents hadn't brought the subject up to me yet. Perhaps they'd let me settle in at home first? Maybe they'd bring it up on the long plane ride home? I wasn't sure, but I knew that it was only a matter of time. They did think I was delusional. What parent wouldn't want their child to seek help in that situation?

"Audrey." My mom ran her hand up and down my back. Something she used to do when I was little and she was waking me up from a nap. "You have to wake up. We need to get going so we can catch our plane."

Nodding, I rolled over and slipped out of bed. I pulled a pair of my favorite boots on over my jeans. I'd dressed for the cooler mid-western weather this time of year rather than the sunny temperate California weather I'd unknowingly become accustomed to. I grabbed an oversized purse and walked to the door without a word. I'd forgone any long goodbyes with my trainers and doctors, not wanting to have to fake a levity I didn't feel.

I walked down the hall to the elevators that would lead to the main floor exit with my head down, listening to my mom's quiet steps behind me.

My parents had handled me with kid gloves the last several days. I wasn't trying to punish them, but I couldn't help feeling betrayed.

They hadn't believed me.

I knew that my story seemed implausible, but I still wanted them to back me up. But when I'd laid all my chips on the table, they'd let me be drugged and taken from the man I loved.

I tried not to be angry with them, I truly did, but I was.

I'd forgiven them for their betrayal in my mind, but my heart still hurt.

One minute, one hour, one day at a time. Baby steps. I could only hope that one day I'd wake up and time would pass at a normal pace.

I pushed at the revolving doors and within a few steps was standing in the sun. It warmed my head, neck, and shoulders as I sat in the car my father had rented that would take us to the airport.

I never looked up. It didn't seem fair that the sun could shine so brightly when on the inside I lived in a land of eternal rain and darkness.

A stack of papers dropped in front of me with a loud smack, shocking me out of my daydream. I yelped and put a hand to my chest, then swatted at James, who was already jumping out of hitting range.

"You're a punk." I loved the kid hardcore, and I had a new respect for him after what I'd witnessed when Satan's legion had attacked our house, but my little brother could still be an annoying jerk.

"I don't know, sis. You think you can keep up with all this work? At this rate, maybe I'll graduate before you will."

Rolling my eyes at him, I ignored the rib just like he ignored my comment.

Once a week, he collected a stack of assignments for me from my teachers at school so that I could graduate at the end of the semester. The arrangement was unconventional, but it would work. I was taking some additional advanced courses to get ahead in college. Also, the extra work kept my mind off of . . . things.

Staying busy helped me get through each day. And as much as I feigned annoyance, seeing James so alive and vibrant pulled me out of my shell.

My little brother had grown since I last saw him. Even though he was several years younger, he was now almost a half-foot taller than me, and if I had to guess from the way he was starting to fill out and his outgoing personality, getting to be popular with the ladies—but he still had a great head on his shoulders. I was proud of him . . . not that I planned on telling him that anytime soon. The last thing the boy needed was an ego boost.

He plopped down in the chair next to me. "So," he began, "you planning on going to the Homecoming dance next week?"

I laughed out loud. "Um, yeah, no. Not in a million years."

"Aw, come on. It's what all the cool kids are doing these days." James's cheesy pout was way overdone, and he knew it.

I shoved him lightly.

"You're weird, you know that?"

"Yep. Proud of it," he quipped.

"Yeah, I can tell. So, which lucky lady are you escorting this year?"

He tapped a finger on his lips as if considering. "So many choices. Maybe I'll keep my options open and go stag."

"Maybe I'll go after all . . . as a chaperone."

His face puckered as if he sucked on a lemon. "Way not cool, sis. I can't be seen consorting with the enemy. I've got a rep to uphold."

I shook my head. I knew James didn't care about any of that. This was just his way of trying to get a smile on my face . . . and his antics were working.

"I didn't realize it was so hard to convince people you're a dork. It's super obvious to me."

"Ouch, that really hurt."

"I'm sure it did."

James tilted his head and considered me for a moment. The scrutiny made me uncomfortable. "You know," he finally began, "there will probably be a lot of your old friends home that weekend. Why don't you see if one of them wants to go with you?"

"You're actually serious."

He shrugged. "Who doesn't want to relive the high school glory years?"

Most people, I thought.

"Who knows, it may be fun for you, even if for a laugh."

Oh gosh, he was serious.

"Which parent put you up to this?" I'd been home several months, and although I'd been doing better—I only cried myself to sleep most nights now—I wasn't the same Audrey my family was used to. They'd brought up counseling and I'd refused, but I knew they were worried about me. We also never talked about everything I'd confessed to Logan's family and half the hospital that day. I wasn't sure if they were just hoping it had been an isolated moment of insanity or if they were worried that bringing it up would break me. They handled me like I was made of china these days.

If they only knew. I'd been to Hell and back. I was made from tougher stuff than that.

But at the same time, I recognized the dark edges of depression that threatened to crush me every day. I just wasn't ready to admit it to anyone besides myself.

"Neither," James went on. "This was 100 percent my brilliant idea."

"Well, in that case . . . the answer is still no."

"I guess I should take down that Instagram pic of your face announcing that you're looking for a hot date then."

My breath caught. "You wouldn't."

Oh, but he would. That's why I was suddenly very nervous.

"Wouldn't I?" He jumped out of his seat and started to run for the stairs, yelling as he went, "If I take it down fast enough, I guess you'll never know either way."

"You're a brat," I screamed at him.

"I know," he yelled back.

I was too old to be fighting with my brother like we were five-year-olds. I grabbed my phone off the table and opened my Instagram app. That brat had like 4,000 followers. I was going to kill him if he had really plastered a pic of me on there.

I tapped my finger on the side of the phone while I waited for the app to open and then quickly went to his page. I didn't see any pictures of me, and I didn't really want to know if he'd just deleted me a moment before I jumped. Not many things humiliated me these days, but that would probably do it.

But ... he was right. For the first time since I'd arrived home, a lot of my old friends and former classmates probably would be in town. Most had left home this past fall to go to college, but homecoming was a big deal in my town and often attracted a good number of alumni to watch the game.

I'd hardly talked to anyone from my old life since waking up in the hospital out west. At first it was because my motor skills didn't really allow me to communicate well, and then after a while, I kind of lost interest. I had a few girlfriends I still kept up with to some extent, but the effort was halfhearted on all sides.

People had moved on while I lay in a bed on the other side of the country. They'd finished their senior year of high school, graduated, and prepared to go to college. And I was stuck in a weird time bubble. Moving forward was like trying to walk while being immersed in a mud pit all the way up to my neck.

Slow and messy. There was progression, but every step was hard earned.

I had to carve out a new normal. I was just a little stuck on how to do that.

How was it that moving on in the afterlife had somehow been easier than moving on with my real life? It didn't make sense.

The eternal existence I had expected to experience was still there. I could still have it someday. Logan would wait for me— I told myself that daily. But now life, this life, stretched out in front of me like a purgatory I had to get through rather than cherish.

My thinking was all messed up, I knew it was, but I didn't know how to snap out of it. Probably at least in part because I didn't want to.

39

DREAMS

Dreams are funny things. While asleep, somehow your brain can convince you that riding a giant banana like a broomstick over your house is perfectly normal, but when you wake up, your mind knows that it's not normal and that your super weird experience wasn't rooted in any type of reality.

Everything makes sense until you wake up.

This wasn't one of those dreams. This was altogether different.

When I opened my eyes, I knew three things to be true: I was in my room, I was conscious, and I was still asleep.

My dream self sat up and looked around. Everything was the same in my dream as in reality—no flying bananas.

When my gaze moved back to my bed, I was startled by a figure sitting at the foot. He was just like I remembered, and letting off a faint brightness that allowed me to see every one of his facial features.

My heart instantly lifted. I'd missed him.

"Joe?" I tentatively asked.

He smiled at me, the laugh lines at the corners of his eyes crinkling, but sadness still sat in the depth of his gaze.

"Why have you missed me, Audrey? I never left you."

I sucked in a breath. In the months since I'd awakened, I'd cried out to him numerous times, but the comfort I'd felt in his presence while in his realm was absent.

"It felt like you had," I admitted.

"But that's not what you know to be true. You know I promised never to leave or abandon you. With everything you have experienced, why have you doubted that? Why have you doubted me? Why have you doubted my goodness?"

Joe cut straight to the heart of the matter, because even before I lost Logan for the second time, I'd been riddled with doubts. I'd just stuffed them down deep.

"I don't know. This life . . . It's just so hard."

"I never promised it would be easy, only that I'd be with you every step."

"I know, but when I can't feel you . . ." I let the statement hang in the air between us. I wasn't sure what to say.

"Did my Spirit not teach you to push past what you feel to hold on to the truth instead?"

I hung my head. "Yes."

His finger touched my chin and brought my gaze back to his. "Then choose to believe. I know your heart is heavy. Let me carry your burdens for you."

"But you've already done so much for me."

"And you believe I've also taken much from you." It wasn't a question. He knew my heart better than I did.

I chewed on my lip.

"I don't know how to go forward. I don't know if I want to." Big fat dream-tears slid down my face.

Joe pulled me into his arms. I curled up in his lap like a

small child and let the sadness and loss wash over me.

"But you must, my precious one. You have a plan and a purpose here, and it's not to hide yourself away from the world but to be a light unto it."

Why? Why did you take him?

I never would have spoken the words out loud, but they echoed in my head on a repeat loop I was unable to stop. And of course, he heard my silent question.

"I work all things together for good."

"This doesn't feel good to me. I miss him so much my heart aches every minute of every day. I miss them all. It's too much."

"I know it's too much. That's why you must share your burden with me. The answer is so simple, Audrey. Simply let go and trust that I am good. Blessed are those who do not see yet still believe."

I sobbed harder. And he rubbed my back like my mother used to.

"You are to run the race before you with endurance but never alone."

I lifted my tear-stained face and looked into his ageless eyes. "Will you let him know I love him and that I'm waiting for him?"

"He already knows." Joe wiped the wetness from my face. "It's time for you to live the life you've been given. And remember that your sadness is my sadness, your pain is my pain. You have not and will never be forgotten. Your prize is waiting for you at the end of this leg of your journey."

I sucked in a cleansing breath of air. Joe set me back down on the bed and coaxed me to lie down. He leaned over me and pressed a kiss to my forehead. From the point of contact, warmth radiated throughout my whole body. I closed my eyes to hang onto the feeling. When I opened them again, I was awake and Joe was no longer sitting on my bed, but I knew I wasn't alone.

The semester ended, and I graduated with honors. I wish I could say that I cared, but I didn't really—except for the fact that it gave me broader options in terms of universities.

I spent the winter months applying to an array of colleges, but I secretly had my eye on one in particular.

After my dream visit with Joe, I put real effort into changing the way I was living my life. Things didn't change overnight, but months later, my slow progress could be seen.

My relationship with my parents had improved. I focused on their love for me and not what I perceived as a betrayal. I reached out to a few of my closer friends and made an effort to stay in touch. I found that I missed exerting myself physically, so I started taking a few martial arts classes—much to my parents' surprise. I even started seeing a counselor. That was tricky, because there was only so much I could talk to her about, but it still helped.

I wasn't okay with Logan's parents' decision, but she helped me see the good in it, especially the lives that were most likely saved or improved because of the sacrifice made.

When I took a step back, I realized Logan would have wanted exactly what his parents had decided rather than to just waste away in a bed for the rest of his life. If it wasn't for the nagging what if questions that haunted me, I might even have been able to get over it.

I couldn't completely let go. What if he had woken up

someday? But at least now I was trying to get past it.

My parents had heavily hinted that I should get out and start dating. My answer to them was always the same. I'd smile and tell them maybe, but I knew in my gut that wasn't for me. I'd already given my heart away, and I wasn't interested in getting it back.

My heart was exactly where it belonged.

There was an existence after this life, and so one day I'd receive my happily ever after. I'd just have to be patient and wait for it.

But that didn't mean there still wasn't a tremendous amount of life to experience in the meantime. I didn't think the pangs of longing every time I thought of Logan would ever go away, but I was learning to live with them, and to live a full life rather than the half one I had settled for when I woke up.

The conversation I wasn't sure would ever happen came up the day I announced to my parents where I would be going to college. They sat and listened while I outlined my detailed plan—because I hadn't chosen an in-state school to save money. No, I'd picked an expensive private school on the other side of the country. But I'd been smart about it. I'd received several scholarships and grants, and I'd planned out the rest in financial aid to make it almost as affordable as if I'd stayed closer to home.

I also insisted that my parents use the money they'd originally saved up for my education to help pay off my medical bills. I hadn't forgotten what I overheard in our kitchen when I was a hunter—what it had been like for them to struggle under the financial burden of my care.

They were shocked into silence by my announcement until I got to that last part about how I wanted them to use my college savings. At that point they launched into their own argument: that money had been set aside for my schooling for a long time. I argued back that I'd figured out a way I wouldn't need it so they could get back in a better situation—if not for me, then for James.

A few months back, they'd nearly lost the house. They had tried to downplay the situation, but I knew they needed the money. In the end, my carefully explained financial plan was what finally convinced them.

"Audrey"—my mom's cautionary use of my name had me sitting up a little straighter—"are you sure it's a healthy decision for you to go to a school in California?"

And that began the conversation I had been waiting for.

"Yes," my dad chimed in, taking my mom's hand in a show of support, "we're obviously a little caught off guard by this choice, but it's clear you've put a responsible amount of thought into it. You're nineteen now, so your mother and I won't try to stop you from moving on with your life in whatever direction you choose to go. But can we have an open conversation about this?"

I pressed my lips together and put a cap on the irritation that threatened to bubble up from my gut. I'd already had this discussion in my head a thousand times, and I knew where my parents were coming from. If I was in their shoes, I'd bring it up too.

Taking a moment to compose myself, I glanced back and forth between them. My parents. The two people who loved me most in this world.

A genuine and gentle smile settled on my face and calmed my emotions. I silently sent up a word of thanks for the extra measure of patience.

"I understand your concerns. I really do. I can give you a long list of reasons why this is a great place for me to get a degree. And if I did, that would probably put your mind at ease. But I know what you're really worried about is my underlying motive for going to a school in that location."

I paused. This next part was going to be hard for my parents, but I wasn't going to lie to them. "I could go to a number of different universities that would be a great fit for me, but I did choose this one because of Logan, and I know that's not what you want to hear. And before you ask, no, I don't plan on seeking out the Londons. I want to respect their decision to be left alone. And I do realize you think that I'm hanging on to a strange delusion that I invented, and I understand why you'd think that. The story I told that day does sound impossible, but it doesn't matter if you believe me or not. Everything I said happened."

"But, Audrey," my father interjected, "we told you about so many of those events while you were in your coma. About the shooter at your school, about your Grandfather's stroke. Do you not think there's a possibility that maybe your mind just created that world you spoke of while you were asleep?"

Okay, we were going there.

"No, Dad. I know you don't believe me, but even if my mind invented some fantastical dream world when I was out based on the stories you and Mom told me, it still doesn't account for Logan. It's okay that you don't believe me. If our situations were reversed, I might not believe me either, but that's really not the point. I'm not moving out there to obsess over him but rather because I really do enjoy California. I think I can be happy there for four years. I like the sun and the beach. And things that remind me of him . . . help."

Mom's eyes were a little dewy. "Honey, real or not, how can you ever move on completely if you don't let go of him?"

That was a valid point.

"I have faith that it will work out, Mom. I don't need it, because I'm an adult, but I'd like your blessing on this decision. And I realize you're going to need a measure of faith in me to do so."

I waited while my parents exchanged worried looks. After what felt like forever, my mom gave my dad a small nod. He huffed and ran a hand through his hair before leaning forward and kissing her cheek. There were a few whispered words between them, and I waited patiently for their response.

"All right, Audrey, your mother and I may never truly understand what happened to you during those months we lost you, but if this is what you want to do, we'll stand behind you."

I let the hot breath of air I'd been holding leak from my lungs. "Thank you."

"Audrey, no matter what, we're always behind you."

40

BEGINNINGS

Salty wind slapped me in the face and sent my hair flying in all directions. I was letting it grow out, and it fell just below my shoulders. Thank goodness, I was finally able to get it into a proper ponytail—but today I'd let it free. I would pay for that decision with a bundle of knots later, but at the moment, I didn't care.

I closed my eyes to soak in the day. Tipping my head back, I absorbed the warmth of the sun. The gritty sand softly exfoliated the skin between my wiggling toes. The repetitive beating of the surf against the beach matched the tempo of my heartbeat.

I was more at home here than anywhere else. This had been a good decision.

I'd started summer courses at a college in Malibu, California. I'd already taken a semester off, so what was the point of waiting until the fall to start? My dad had flown in with me to help me get settled. I met and moved in with my bubbly new roommate, Ashlynn. I already knew things were going to be interesting with that one. She had a thirst for life and a carefree demeanor that was contagious. Classes had started mid-week, and it took me a few more days to get oriented. But the song of the ocean had called to me the whole time, and now I was finally here.

A full week passed before I could break away and soak it all in.

The sun hung heavily toward the sea, telling me it was late in the afternoon. I didn't care. That meant if I stayed out long enough, I could catch the sunset. I loved sunsets.

I laid out a towel and sank down onto it, forgetting my textbook for the time being and just lazily enjoying all the free vitamin D. Eventually I fell asleep to the lull of the lapping waves.

The chilling air woke me slowly, and I lifted my arms above my head and cat-stretched on my towel. I froze mid-stretch with the overwhelming feeling of a presence hovering near me.

Oh gosh, I hope it's not a creeper checking me out in my bikini.

With my eyes still closed, I brought my arms down to my side and cracked my eyelids open. I was right ... there was someone seated at the foot of my towel, just off to the right. Thankfully he wasn't watching me. Instead he was staring at the ocean in front of us.

The sun was sitting right on the horizon, making it difficult to make out any of his features. Through squinted eyes, I could really only make out that this was a guy in board shorts, knees pulled up and arms draped over them. I couldn't even guess at his age.

I quietly slid my arms behind me so I rested on my forearms, giving me a better view. I tilted my head. He wasn't quite as close to my towel as I'd thought, but this was a big beach. He definitely didn't need to be sitting here.

His behavior was kind of unnerving.

How in the world was I supposed to tell this stranger that he was invading my personal bubble?

I almost laughed to myself. Who was I kidding? This was me. I was the queen of blunt. I was going to say it exactly like that. But I wanted a moment to study this weirdo before I shooed him away.

He didn't have any tan lines on his back, but his skin was a little too white for him to be a local. I'd quickly learned to pick out the people who lived in the area from the tourists based on level of tan alone. I, for instance, stuck out like a sore thumb, even with my somewhat naturally darker skin tone due to my heritage. There wasn't the telltale evidence of natural coloring across my cheeks and nose yet, or a tan line circling my neck from my suit strings. That actually reminded me that I should probably reapply my sunscreen.

Premature aging . . . no thank you.

I sat up and extended my hand toward my bottle of sunblock but stopped mid-reach.

His hair.

There was probably only an inch of growth on his head, but the color. Even though the halo the sunset cast on him . . . I knew that color.

My breath caught in my throat.

There was no way. Lots of guys had light hair in the beachy areas of Southern California. It had to be just a coincidence.

I forced a normal cadence to my breathing. Inhale, then exhale. Then repeat.

I could control my breaths, but I couldn't control my rapidly beating heart.

This dude needed to turn around so I could see he wasn't Logan and stop freaking out.

I was going to have to get used to this, I told myself. The sun bleached out people's hair fairly easy, and with all the surfers in this area, there were going to be people who looked like him. I needed to learn to desensitize myself.

Time to rip off the bandage.

"Yo, dude, you want to find somewhere else on the beach to plop it? You're blocking my sun." Leaning forward, I waved my hand in front of me in a shooing motion. A motion that froze the moment the guy twisted around.

My arms suspended awkwardly in the air as I took in his familiar face.

Eyes as blue as the ocean on a sunny day, brows several shades darker than the hair on his head, straight nose, strong jaw, and lips I could still remember the peppermint taste of.

And just as I was drinking in the sight of him, he was doing the same to me—his gaze searching every feature of my face before colliding with mine. And when it did, I swear a field of electricity pulled us together.

"You're awake." His deep voice was the final piece.

It was really him.

I was up on my knees, reaching for him, and I didn't even remember moving. Reality clicked in right before my fingers touched him, and I snatched my hand back.

"Oh my gosh. I can see the dead." *Wait, that doesn't make sense.* I shook my head once, my mouth spilling words as soon as I thought them. "No, *I* must be dead."

How could I bask in the miracle that was seeing Logan again when I couldn't remember how I'd died?

My breathing changed to short bursts in and out. I was going into some type of shock.

"Oh no, not this time," Logan said before he shifted his body to press his weight into me, causing us both to tumble to the towel. "Just look at me and breathe, Audrey."

The warmth of his body in contrast to the chill of the closing day caused goosebumps to break out all over my skin. Taking my face between his hands, he forced my attention.

My breathing picked up a notch.

"Not helping," I puffed out.

A smile broke free on his face. "Then we'll do things the fun way. Less talking, more kissing."

His mouth covered mine before I even had a chance to process his words.

His lips were as soft as I remembered, and they moved over mine with skill. He gave my bottom lip a teasing nip to ensure he had my full attention.

It worked.

The next moment, I didn't care that I was dead or how it had happened, but only that we were back together again.

My hands snaked up his arms and buried themselves in his hair—shorter than I remembered, but just as soft.

Who cared what realm we were in as long as we had each other?

I was lost in the feel of him . . . until water slapped me in the face and along the side of my body, and a familiar voice yelled, "Get a room, you two!"

Ashlynn?

Logan pulled away, and I tilted my head back to see an upside-down view of my new roommate.

"You can see us?" I asked.

She shot me a funny look. "The whole beach can see you two, you goofball."

Huh?

"Are you dead too?"

"You have an odd sense of humor, you know that?" She

tilted her head. "I see you found her after all."

"Yep, thanks for the help," Logan said. "She was asleep when I came by, so I waited until she woke up."

"Well, that was chivalrous of you. I probably would have poured water on her," she said with a twinkle in her eye.

"Isn't that pretty much what you just did?" Logan asked with a brow hiked up.

She smirked. "Hey, Audrey, I'll see you back at the dorm later, yeah? You won't get lost, right?"

I shook my head, still watching her from my horizontal position as she jogged away.

What was going on? She could see us. I could see him. They'd met.

My head was about to explode.

The only way I could be with Logan was if I were dead. Unless he wasn't dead.

But he'd died.

Hadn't he?

"What's happening right now?" I whispered to Logan. His face hovered just above mine, and half his body pressed me into the sand.

His eyes swept my face. "I'll never get tired of looking at you," he whispered back. "You're not dead, Audrey. I'm not dead either. We're both here, on Earth, now. Alive. Together."

Moisture gathered in my eyes and spilled over. "But how? I was there. I tried to fight for you, but no one believed me. Your parents . . ." my voice gave out. That horrible, awful day. The worst of my life. And that included the day I got hit by a car.

That day I'd fought for him in every way I could, and I'd lost.

He murmured words of encouragement and sympathy over and over again. "It's all right; I'm truly here."

Finally he sat up, pulled me to him, and guided my head to his chest. He buried his face in my hair and kept talking to me until my tears were spent, and even though I still didn't know how this was possible, I was just happy that he was real.

This was real. It was happening.

I pushed back against him, and he let me go. I finally took an objective look at him.

He was clearly Logan. I recognized everything about him. But he wasn't the Logan I'd seen lying in that bed . . . and neither was he exactly the Logan I'd first met.

His shorter hair was only one of the changes about him. He wasn't emaciated like he'd been at the hospital, but neither was his build as large as it'd been before. His skin was several shades lighter than I was used to, his face a little thinner.

They were all slight changes, but each one told a story.

"Please, tell me what happened. How are you here?" I touched his face to reassure myself, and he captured my hand and held it to his cheek, closing his eyes to soak something indiscernible in.

When he opened them again, I noticed they were the one thing about him that had not changed a single bit. His cobalt eyes, and the look in them when he gazed at me was exactly how I remembered.

"I'm here because of you. I'm here because you helped save me."

"Your dad said I was delusional. They kicked me out of your room, out of their lives. I wasn't even allowed to go to your funeral. Um . . . er . . . I guess there wasn't a funeral."

"Yeah"—he scratched his head and ducked it—"you certainly made an impression on my parents that day." He chuckled softly.

"This's not funny. I was led to believe you'd died. They

were going to take you off life support. What happened?" I all but yelled the last part at him.

He held his hands up in front of himself to pacify me.

"Don't try that with me, mister. Start talking."

"Okay, all right." He took my hands, and any levity in his voice completely disappeared. "It's just a long story. And if I'm going to explain properly, I have to start at the beginning."

I nodded for him to continue.

"So, after the battle with Satan, you just disappeared. As in, your body literally vanished from the pool of blood you'd been lying in. As you can imagine, I didn't handle that well."

I could imagine. In fact, I imagined that even more things in that Artifacts Room got broken real fast. I kept my thoughts to myself as he continued.

"At first I thought you'd been transported to Hell, but that's when the Son explained to us that you were still alive. None of us knew, Audrey. We had no idea that you weren't actually dead."

"Ha, you're one to talk."

"Yeah, I'll get to that in a moment." He squeezed my hand and flashed a quick grin before continuing. "I calmed down marginally when I found out what had happened to you, but if you were alive, that meant we were separated. At the same time, I couldn't begrudge you a life on Earth. I *wanted* you to live. I wanted to be happy you were alive. But I wanted to be with you too, and if we were in separate realms, that wasn't going to happen for a long time. You can't imagine how hard that time was on me."

"You're kidding, right?" I lifted my eyebrows.

He nodded slowly. "You're right. If anyone can imagine how I felt, it's you. As much as I wanted to be content with you having a full life on Earth, the thought of you having it without me gutted me. I didn't last long before I started sneaking trips down to see you."

"You visited me when I was recovering? You were there?"

He nodded. "Some of the time."

"Hold up, you broke the rules to see me?"

He quirked an eyebrow at me. "Someday you'll realize the depths of what I would do to be with you."

My insides melted, and my cheeks warmed. He brushed his thumb over one of them before speaking again.

"Whenever I could sneak away, I'd come and visit you. I'd talk to you, but you couldn't see or hear me. Being there but not able to interact with you was its own form of torture. I watched you struggle to recover . . . but I watched you slowly move on as well."

I was shaking my head before he even completed the sentence. "That's not what was happening. I just stuffed all my emotions down. I wasn't dealing with anything during that time. Were you ever with me when I visited you? If so, that had to be super weird for you."

He took a deep breath. "I didn't know I was in a coma either, Audrey. I didn't know until the day you found me. When we walked into that room, I didn't even recognize myself in that bed. It wasn't until I started looking around and seeing familiar objects that the pieces started to fit together. And then of course when my mom walked in, I knew right away."

He chuckled, but how he found any of this funny, I didn't know. "I was so surprised I actually knocked over a picture when she walked in." Oh, so that was him, not me.

"I went straight back to the realm when you left my room and demanded I be put back in my body. I'll bet you can imagine how well that went over."

"Well, seeing as I spent weeks by your side without you waking up, I'm gonna guess not well."

"Right. When I was denied my demands, I went a little"—he held up his thumb and pointer finger about a millimeter apart—"ballistic for a while. I was there, you were there, we could actually be together again in the same realm, but for some reason I wasn't allowed back."

"Is that . . . normal? Does what happened to us happen to everyone in a coma?"

He shook his head. "No, we were the exception. That's why no one would have even thought to guess it. Audrey, it's also why we had powers others didn't. It's because part of us was still alive, and in the spiritual realm, that made us extra powerful."

"I just . . . I can't wrap my brain around all this information. I have a million questions, but I don't know if I can process it all right now."

"Okay, that makes sense. You tell me what you want to know." He leaned back on his arms and pressed his lips together, his gaze steadily holding mine.

"I guess I want to know how you're alive. Your parents were going to take you off life support. Did they? How long have you been awake?"

Looking him up and down, something occurred to me. He might be leaner than the Logan I knew in the afterlife, but he was a far cry from the one I'd spent time with in the hospital. To work his way back this far after four years in a coma, he must have been awake for months.

Months where someone could have told me, but they didn't.

I jumped up. My legs were shaky. "How long, Logan? How long have you been awake while you left me to mourn your death?"

A frown marred his handsome face, but he didn't make a move toward me. "Audrey, you may not like this."

"How long, Logan?"

He sighed and ran a hand down his face and back up into his short hair before meeting my gaze. "Seven months."

I gasped. Not long after I'd left the hospital. He'd been awake almost since the time I went home. And he was just now making himself known.

I took an unsteady step backward.

"Audrey, please let me explain."

But I didn't. Instead, I turned and ran.

41

BETTER TOGETHER

I forgot about the chill of the evening as I bolted from Logan. His voice was swallowed by the sound of the waves crashing, but he was no doubt giving chase. The ocean wind sent my hair flying into my face. Only after several minutes of sprinting did it occur to me that I hadn't been caught.

He'd let me go. Or maybe something else had happened.

I whipped around, sweat dripping down my face, but I couldn't see much in the failing light. The sun had descended below the horizon, and only the leftover brightness lit the beach.

I turned in a circle and realized I had no idea where I was. There were no people around. A chill of fear skated up my spine.

I'd run from Logan, but in the back of my mind I'd assumed he would catch me. He always had before.

Darting my gaze left and right, I jogged back the way I'd come. I was still upset beyond reason that he'd been awake for so long without me knowing, but I'd been foolish to not let him explain. I also was incredibly stupid for having run so far.

Nothing looked familiar. I swiveled my head back and forth as an irrational fear of being attacked overtook me. I was on the verge of hysterics when I slammed into a hard chest.

We both went down in a tangle of limbs.

"Don't do that ever again." There was a strong note of desperation in his voice. "Please, promise me you won't do that again."

I pushed hair out of my face and stared down at Logan. Something to his left caught my eye, and I turned my head to see a plain silver cane lying discarded on the sand.

Logan had come after me; he'd just been unable to catch up with me.

"We don't run from each other anymore, Audrey. Even when things get hard." My attention snapped back to him, and I took in what he was saying. "Aren't you tired of always running? I know I am."

He was so right. We'd run from each other for too long. We should have always been walking together.

"Yeah, I am."

I clumsily shimmied off him and stood, watching as Logan glanced around before spotting the cane. He snuck a peek at me before grasping it and struggling to his feet.

"As you can see, I'm not quite the same man I was before." The lighting was so dim I might have misread it, but I caught something akin to shame in his eyes before he diverted his gaze.

"Will you let me explain this time?"

I nodded, and we started a slow trek back.

A brisk pace was difficult for Logan, so I slowed my steps. I wasn't sure if this was a regular thing for him or if my crashing into him exacerbated whatever physical limitations he was already dealing with.

"I watched you during those weeks at my bedside. I saw you make the decision to stay there and keep vigil over that shell of mine, and I knew you'd do it for the rest of your life . . . and I didn't want that for you. I would be ruining your life. I didn't want to realize that at first, but it became clear to me eventually. So I went to the Creator . . . and asked him to end my mortal life."

My gasp was stolen by the wind, and Logan plowed on. "Of course, He was aware of the trips I'd made to see you. I knew He would be, it's not like anything escapes His notice, but at the time I was making them, I honestly didn't care. But He allowed them just the same."

I tried to catch Logan's eye as we walked, but he remained focused on some unseen point in the distance. His jaw was clenched, and a muscle twitched on his cheek.

Was the walk that painful for him? Perhaps he was angry at me? Or was rehashing these events just difficult?

If the latter, I would have spared him from the pain if possible, but I needed to know. There was no way we could move forward without an explanation of how this was even possible. Especially now that he'd dropped the bomb on me of asking to die.

My insides churned at the thought. Why would he do that? What had happened to his promise to be with me, no matter what? I needed to know it all.

"What happened next?" I asked when the silence stretched and I was no longer sure Logan would continue.

"You were there. You saw what happened next."

"You mean . . . that day?"

He glossed over his conversation with the Creator. I almost pressed for details, but I realized that was Logan's story. I'd hear it someday when he was ready—or not at all. But I didn't have a right to force it out of him, no matter how badly I wanted to.

"Yeah, that day." He stopped walking and turned to me, grasping my upper arms gently but firmly. "Audrey, you were fierce that day. I know that will always be a horrible memory for you. And the way you were treated"—he looked over my shoulder before recapturing my gaze—"it took three hunters to keep me from throwing those people off you."

My eyes widened. It had never occurred to me that there might have been an unseen audience.

"You . . . fought?"

He cupped my cheek. "The first moment someone laid a hand on you, I couldn't stay complacent anymore. I fought for you. But you . . . you not only fought for me, you fought for us."

"You were right there in front of me, even if I couldn't reach you. From the first moment I realized it, I had hope. I thought it had to be for a reason."

I stepped forward and reached for him. The gusting wind had turned into an early evening breeze, balmy but cooling. His skin was chilled until the heat from my hands warmed him.

"I had hope . . . until the moment I was told you were gone."

Pain lanced through my heart at the memory of the crushing agony I'd felt all those months ago and a little bit every day since. My pain-filled emotions must have reflected on my face because Logan pulled me toward him with both arms.

"I'm so sorry. Everything I did . . . everything I've done . . . I thought every decision was to protect you. But so many of those choices just added to your suffering. I'm not perfect,

Audrey."

I huffed a weak laugh with my face buried in his chest.

Turning to lay a cheek on him, I asked, "What happened next?"

He leaned forward and nuzzled the hair hanging over my neck, inhaling my scent.

After that sprint, I was a little worried I was veering on the ripe side, even though the sweat had already dried from my body.

"They changed their minds."

"Your parents?"

"Yeah. I mean they still thought you were completely insane."

I pressed a fist into his gut, and he let out a lighthearted laugh.

"Don't worry, that was more my dad than my mom; she thinks you're great."

"Even now?"

"Especially now." He pushed my hair behind my ear and pressed a kiss to my neck.

"Are you trying to distract me?" If so, it was kind of working.

"You're the distraction, love." He placed another kiss to the spot and then picked me up and set me away from him.

I might have pouted a little.

"Don't give me that look. Do you want to hear the rest or not?"

I nodded.

"Then let's get back to your stuff."

I started walking and realized he wasn't following. I turned to see him slowly bending and then remembered his cane. Rushing back, I picked it up and offered it to him.

"This is part of the story, I take it?"

He nodded, and we continued back. This time in silence.

Not long after, we seated ourselves back at my towel. I slipped a sundress over my bathing suit, which made the slight chill in the air the perfect temperature. Logan had—to my disappointment—brought a t-shirt, which he shrugged on before carefully lowering down next to me.

While he did, I examined his legs. One looked slightly thinner than the other, but I probably wouldn't have noticed if I wasn't trying to find the reason for his slight limp.

I turned my body so I could watch his face but made sure part of my leg was pressed against him. I needed the physical reminder that he was here to keep me grounded. Part of my brain still screamed that this was just a cruel trick or a dream I was going to wake up from.

"So, your parents changed their minds?" I prodded him to continue.

"Yes and no. They were pretty shook up from everything you said that day, even though they didn't believe you. My dad went into protective mode and did everything he could to make sure you wouldn't be allowed near me anymore." He picked up and squeezed my hand. "That's why your parents never knew the truth. They weren't given any additional information and had no reason to believe my parents had altered their course of action.

"With the stress of that day, my mom convinced my dad to let a few days pass before they went through with taking me off life support. She was never all about it anyway, but she had resigned herself to the course of action.

"I went back to being a hunter, resigned that I'd wait a lifetime to be with you. What I didn't know was that a few days turned into a few weeks, and then a month, and then two. And my father was visiting me again."

He looked at me with such vulnerability in his eyes. "Did you know that beside the day you saw him, he hadn't been to visit me since the first year I was in the hospital?"

I shook my head. "I knew he didn't come regularly like your mother, but she didn't give me those specifics. I'm sorry, Logan."

He smiled at me. "You have nothing to be sorry for."

"I'm sorry for any pain that comes your way. And learning that your dad hadn't been to see you in years had to hurt."

"He had his reasons, and he's apologized for it."

I sensed there was a story there, but I'd leave that for another time. We still had so much to catch up on.

"I had just returned from a hunt when the Savior came to see me."

"You talked with Joe? He came to me too, in a dream. He told me to have faith and move forward. That's what I've been trying to do ever since."

"You've been doing a great job. At times, maybe a little too good." He chuckled, but his eyes darkened for a moment. "Yes, we talked. My existence had started to become . . . a dark place. He pulled me back and set me on the right path. And he told me I would be returning. I was . . . shocked. I didn't even know there was still a 'me' to return to . . . again. I got over the initial shock quickly and wanted to rush back right away, but instead I was told to wait. Which gave me time to give a proper goodbye to people."

I instantly wanted to know how everyone was doing, but I

pushed the desire aside. We'd have time to catch up on that later.

"I didn't start to have doubts until I woke up, captive in my own body. And that, ultimately, is what kept me from you until now."

"I don't understand."

Logan's lips flat-lined. His features were only discernible by moonlight now. He faced the ocean rather than me.

"You'll understand part of it. When I woke up, I had to relearn everything. I wasn't able to speak a word until two weeks had passed. I could hardly even stay awake. I wasn't able to move my body because of my deteriorated muscles. I was a shell of the man you knew, and because my case was so unusual, the doctors couldn't make any promises. I might have progressed to a certain point and then just stopped."

"Do you mean to tell me you let me go months"—I threw up a hand to stop Logan from interrupting—"months without knowing you were alive because . . . you were . . . embarrassed?" An angry mound of hot lava churned in my gut as I spoke, demanding to be spewed. "Days and weeks and months of depression. Of anger at the Creator, of questioning everything I thought to be true."

"And that's the part you won't understand. I was only part of a man, and I didn't want you to be shackled to that any more than I wanted you to be tied to the empty shell you'd been ready to throw your life away for."

"You had no right—"

His eyes flashed. "I did. I did have a right to make that decision. There was a point they weren't even sure I'd ever be able to go to the bathroom on my own. Do you know how that made me feel?"

I lunged and grabbed Logan's face, forcing him to look me

in the eyes. He could easily have pulled away but didn't.

"You listen here. Believing I would care about any of that—any of it—is beyond insulting. Had you lain in that bed for the rest of your days, awake, I would still have been happy to spend my life with you. Since when did you start to believe I cared for you, that I loved you, for how much you could bench press? It was you, it will always be you, in whatever shape I can have you. It's you I will love."

I jerked out of my rant when something wet dropped on my left hand. I glanced up at the cloudless night, thinking it had started to rain, only to look back and realize that a tear had slid from Logan's eye and down his cheek.

I'd never seen Logan cry before.

"I don't deserve you," he whispered.

"That's not true." I leaned forward and kissed the wetness from his cheek, sliding my hands to rest on his shoulders. "It's not about what we deserve. Frankly, what we both deserve is a million times worse than what we've been given. It's that we're better together than apart . . . at least when we're on the same side."

The corner of his lips quirked at that.

"We're better together, Logan. Don't let your pride get in the way of that."

He brought a hand up and rubbed his face. "I almost did," he confessed. "Even coming to you like this"—he swept a hand out to indicate his body—"was hard for me."

"Were you scared I'd reject you?"

"I was scared of a lot of things."

"If our situations were reversed, would you have hesitated a moment to be with me?"

"No, never. Even if I had to take care of you for the rest of our lives, I would have been happy to do so."

"Then you shouldn't have deprived me of that same joy."

Logan hung his head, but he brought his hand up to draw me closer. "You're right. My pride kept me away from you. Will you forgive me?"

"Always."

Our foreheads rested against each other, and we breathed the same air.

"What do we do now?" I asked.

"Whatever we want," Logan answered with a smile. "We have a lifetime to figure it out. You game?"

"Yeah, let's do this thing."

The lips that brushed mine were soft and tender and tasted of peppermint. I knew this beautiful moment—the one I'd given up believing we'd be able to share in this lifetime—was as close to perfect as anything in this world could be.

And I silently lifted my thanks.

EPILOGUE
KAITLIN

I lifted my face to the sun and took in the perfect California day: a slight breeze in the air, tinged with salty brine; clear blue skies; and a temperature that was warm but not yet on the verge of crossing over to hot.

"Everything seems to be in order." Romona scanned the crowd of people rather than perimeter around them. But who could blame her? This was her family, and today was the day she'd watch her granddaughter wed.

The huntress's words were even and professional, but not even the amazing Romona could contain the shining excitement in her eyes.

Her face radiated joy.

"You know, I still think we would all fit in better if we were wearing formal attire. All this black makes it look like we're going to a funeral." I nudged Romona playfully with my hip.

"We're not supposed to be blending in. You know that. We're supposed to be sending a message that this event is not to be interrupted."

I faked annoyance and crossed my arms. "But I look so

much better in strapless gowns."

"I would disagree with that," a smooth accented voice spoke behind me. My spine straightened as a zing of awareness ran down it. I shook it off with real annoyance as he went on. "This look has always had a certain . . . appeal to me."

"Do you really have to be here?" I asked Morgan without turning to address him.

He stepped up next to me, refusing to be ignored. "Probably not. I don't think there's ever been a more fortified wedding in all of history. Bloody He—"

"Watch it," I warned. I purposely kept my gaze fixed on anything but the handsome Brit to my right.

I gave myself an internal shake. Not handsome. Evil is not handsome. Ugly. He's very ugly.

Romona huffed on the other side of me. She didn't tolerate Morgan's presence much better than I did.

"Feel free to leave anytime," she added.

"And miss my best mate's big day. Never." The mocking tone to Morgan's voice covered whatever his true feelings were. That had always been the issue with Morgan, even before his betrayal and redemption I never trusted what came out of his mouth. There were layers to him that concealed his true self, and I didn't have a desire to peel them back.

Liar, a whispered voice mocked in the back of my mind.

"I'm going to do a perimeter check." I fled the tension-filled moment, quickly moving to the outskirts of our protective border.

Morgan wasn't wrong. Perhaps we'd gone a little overboard with the security today, but besides this being a highly anticipated event for us all, I knew there was one supremely evil being gunning for the stars of today's show.

The consensus was it was better to be safe than sorry. So

several dozen hunters as well as a handful of angels were stationed at various points around the grounds of the beautiful garden where our friends would recite their vows.

After making sure everyone was where they were supposed to be, I stopped to take in the moment.

The ceremony was to be held in the private gardens of the Hillstead Mansion, which was situated on a cliff high above the churning sea. The reception would take place in the mansion afterward.

The garden was in full bloom, mixing the sweet scents of the flowers with the salty sea below. Red roses, blue iris, and pink azaleas created a secret garden experience that was breathtaking.

Rows of white chairs were set up in an open space in the wooden gazebo. Wisteria vines wrapped around the structure, and delicate bunches of purple blooms hung down like clumps of grapes from the rafters.

The event was going to be lovely—although bittersweet. My heart warmed at being able to share this moment with my dear friend, even though he didn't know I was here, but a prick of sadness welled inside.

I'd never have a day like this. I didn't get a second chance.

A soft melody started from the string quartet, announcing the ceremony was about to start and that people should take their seats.

As if signaled as well, a chorus of shrieks rent the air. I jerked my gaze up to watch the spot of darkness in the faraway sky grow into a churning cloud.

We should have brought more reinforcements.

PLEASE WRITE A REVIEW

Thank you for reading *Dominion*! If you loved this book, please write review on Amazon and/or Goodreads. I'd like to know what you think, and so will many others.

Reviews are the lifeblood of authors and help others decide to purchase a book. If you like this series, and want to see more from me, please leave a review. Thank you!

Please review this book:
http://review.DominionBook.com

JOIN THE FAN CLUB

www.facebook.com/groups/juliehall

Join the fan club - we're a crazy fun bunch! We love reading, puppies, and Red Bull. Okay, the Red Bull is all me.

If you love my books, get involved and get exclusive sneak peeks before anyone else. Sometimes I even give out free puppies (#jokingnotjoking). You'll get to know other passionate fans just like you, and you'll get to know me better too! It'll be fun!

Join the Fan Club (it's free)!
www.facebook.com/groups/juliehall

See you in there!
~ Julie

ACKNOWLEDGEMENTS

I almost can't believe the books that have been cycling through my head for the last several years are finally all out. It has been a crazy rollercoaster ride of ups and downs and there's no one who has experienced all the highs and lows with me more closely than my amazing husband. He is my technical wizard, my graphic making genius, my fearless formatter, my rock steady supporter, and the biggest driving force behind getting this series to publication. He clocked in hundred of hours of behind the scenes work to help get *Dominion* and the rest of the *Life After* books into your—the readers—hands. That level of support is almost unheard of in the book writing community, so my first and biggest thanks has to go to my husband, Lucas, for never giving up on me even when I was ready to give up on myself.

The next person I have to acknowledge is my fearless assistant, Amanda. And yes, I do mean fearless. This feisty little ball of energy takes on whatever I toss her way, even if the idea is half-baked at best. She's not only a busy worker bee, but the best cheerleader a girl could ask for and a cherished friend. She's survived all my releases, freak out moments, breakdowns, self-doubt, happy and mad moments and everything in between . . . even rolled with the punches when I made her eat disgusting food live on the internet because I thought it would be funny. And it was hilarious! Amanda not only helps spread the word about my books, but helps keep my world running on a schedule, and keeps me from falling into author despair on a regular basis. If anyone ever doubts that God puts special people in our lives for a reason, just come to me and I'll tell you the full "Julie and Amanda" story and you won't be a doubter anymore.

To my Beta Readers, you know who you are. Whether you're an "alpha beta," "beta beta," or "beta" reader, you have been with me through some really rough spots, both in life and throughout the development of this series. Why anyone would voluntarily be a beta reader, I honestly have no idea. You really pulled through for me and gave me that extra bit of encouragement that I needed to push through to the end.

My Super Secret Readers' Squad, you are the best group out there. I really believe that. You not only lift me up, you help me make these stories better, help spread the word, and most importantly you put up with my 3am Facebook posts to our group and don't hate me for it. Big fat sloppy kisses for just that last point alone! Please don't ever leave me!

The readers in "Julie's Warriors," how can I thank you for being so awesome? Stupid question . . . more giveaways, right? You guys are so interactive you make promotions fun. Keep doing what you are doing. I'm in that group on a daily basis and love learning more about each of you!

All my group admins and influencers who go the extra mile to promote my books, I couldn't do this without you. You are the best and I'm humbled you'd take time out of your busy lives to tell people about *Dominion* and the other books in this series.

A great big thanks to all the authors who have helped me

along the way. There is a whole batch of amazing authors who have endorsed the series, given me helpful hints, pointed me towards resources, and most importantly guidance on how to create the best books possible. You amaze me every day and I've appreciated your help and encouragement more than you'll ever know.

And finally, thanks to you, my reader. If you're reading this page, chances are you've read through the entire series. These books were written with you in mind every step of the way. My hope is that they've kept you engaged, entertained, and perhaps even on the edge of your seat a time or two.

I'd love to hear your thoughts on the series. Please feel free to reach out to me at **Julie@JulieHallAuthor.com**.

ABOUT THE AUTHOR

www.JulieHallAuthor.com

My name is Julie Hall and I'm a USA TODAY bestselling, multiple award-winning author. I read and write young adult paranormal / fantasy novels, love doodle dogs and drink Red Bull, but not necessarily in that order.

My daughter says my super power is sleeping all day and writing all night… and well, she wouldn't be wrong.

I believe novels are best enjoyed in community. As such, I want to hear from you! Please connect with me as I regularly give out sneak peeks, deleted scenes, prizes, and other freebies to my friends and newsletter subscribers.

CONNECT WITH JULIE

Visit my website:

www.JulieHallAuthor.com

Get my other books:

www.amazon.com/author/julieghall

Join the Fan Club:

www.facebook.com/groups/juliehall

Get exclusive updates by email:

www.JulieHallAuthor.com/newsletter

Follow me on:

Amazon: www.amazon.com/author/julieghall

Facebook: www.facebook.com/JulieHallAuthor

BookBub: www.JulieHallAuthor.com/bookbub

Goodreads: www.goodreads.com/JulieHallAuthor

Instagram: www.instagram.com/JulieGHall

Twitter: www.twitter.com/JulieGHall

CPSIA information can be obtained
at www.ICGtesting.com
Printed in the USA
LVHW091534240920
666906LV00011B/563